Blackwood Milk Farm

Book 4

A Mist Valley Slice of Life Adventure

Eden Redd

D1526981

Blackwood Milk Farm: A Mist Valley Slice of Life Adventure

© copyright 2023 Eden Redd

All Rights Reserved

Join my mailing list and receive updates on new titles!

Editor

Lucid Dream Editing

A special thank you to **TJ Zuendt!**

Your eye for details is deeply appreciated!

Blackwood Milk Farm Book 4 is part of the Blackwood Series.

Enjoy the stories!

Table of Contents

Blackwood Milk Farm

Book 4

Chapter 1

A Deal in the Dark

The night air was warm. The sky was illuminated by distant stars as a deep peace flowed over the Blackwood Estate. Inky shadows clung to the farmhouse as a small breeze washed over the area.

Beyond the front gate of the estate, the primal forest stood like an ancient guardian. Leaves fluttered in the breeze as crickets played their nightly symphony. Birds slept on high branches, waiting for dawn's early light.

The symphony of crickets abruptly stopped, as a sound of a breaking twig touched the air. Across the road from the main gate of the Blackwood Estate, a bush shuddered. Starlight reflected from a pair of slitted eyes. They stared out, looking at the dark farm with deep caution.

Another pair of slitted eyes appeared beside the cloaked figure. The two figures remained crouched beside a pair of bushes. No words were spoken as they stared and listened. They knew they were far enough from the house to not be heard, but they also knew that they had to be careful.

After a long moment of silence, the pair nodded to each other. They moved on all fours, emerging from the shadows and bushes. They walked on all fours across the dirt road. When they approached the front gate, they both looked up to see the bell hanging on a rod, perfectly still despite the small breeze.

The first figure was thankful to the gods of darkness and stealth. They knew the bell was heavy enough to not ring to the breeze. Only a true visitor could ring it loud enough to be heard from anyone inside the farm home.

The pair turned their gazes to the left. They saw the covered patio, and stones circling the sitting pond. Beyond them, a workshop stood dark. To the left, and further in the distance, a barn and winery stabbed into the starry night sky.

The pair of cloaked figures took a moment to mentally admire the new additions to the farm. With a heavy heart, they returned to the task at hand. One lifted a scaled hand and touched the top of the fence. Silently, they climbed over, making sure they stayed low.

The second cloaked figure did the same, climbing over and down onto the property. They turned their hooded heads from left to right, surveying the estate. They looked at the windows to the farmhouse again, thankful there were no lights on.

A scaled hand reached into a hip satchel. Their hand remained in it as they looked around with sharp senses.

The second cloaked figure sniffed at the air. Something didn't feel right. The air felt off, a thin scent on the breeze. It was one she never noticed before during other visits to the farm.

The first cloaked figure pulled out a thick roll of rolled-up parchments. He took one step toward the front porch to the Blackwood home, eager to finish their task. Their partner behind them reached out and touched their shoulder, stopping them in their tracks. The first one glanced back with concern in their slitted eyes.

A sharp whistle broke the silence, and an arrow stabbed into the ground, an inch away from the first figure's scaled, clawed foot.

The pair froze in fear as another cloaked figure stepped out of the inky shadows along the side of the house. They held a bow in hand, with an arrow nocked. Steely eyes stared at the two cloaked figures as they aimed at them.

Terror struck at the cloaked pair. The first one launched back and crashed into their partner. Both hit the ground and scrambled to get back up. The roll of parchments hit the ground as the pair turned to flee.

Another arrow shot through the air and struck the ground before the pair could reach the fence. They stopped in their tracks, fear coloring their eyes. The arrow shot was so accurate, it had passed between the fleeing pair without ever touching them.

"Stay where you are, or my next two shots will find each of your backs," came an annoyed voice from behind them.

The two figures fell to their knees, and put their scaled hands into the air.

"Please Lord Blackwood, spare us!" the first one pleaded.

"We meant no harm!" the second one added with fear in her voice.

Asher stepped into the starlight, bow and arrow aimed at the slythans on their knees. He eyed them as they remained still, only their hands trembling.

"I didn't take it too seriously with Lady Windswell spying on my home, but after recent events, I couldn't allow it to continue," Asher said with subdued confidence.

The pair of slythans remained silent with wide eyes staring forward.

"Out with it. Why are you both here in the middle of night?" Asher said before glancing at the roll of parchments on the ground between him and the slythans. "Come to plaster more posters on my front door like before?"

The pair stayed quiet, fear constricting their throats.

Asher rolled his eyes. "Stand up and turn around. I want to see the shadows that visit my home from night to night."

The pair on their knees didn't move.

"If you don't do as I say, I will dump both of your bodies on the mayor's front door," Asher threatened.

Scaled hands shook a little more. Hesitation washed away as the pair slowly stood up, turned around, and faced the Lord of Blackwood.

Asher's eyes had adjusted to the dark night many hours earlier. Even in the starlight, he could make out their reptilian features. Scales flowed from their short snouts. Their scales gleamed with tiny, iridescent colors. Their wide eyes were slitted, much like a cat, or a dragon. Their cloaks covered most of their bodies, except their hands and feet. Asher had seen many slythans before, knowing their scale colors ranged from a deep green, to a rusty red. He couldn't see their short tails, but he knew every slythan had one.

For a brief moment, he wondered if one of the two slythans was responsible for leaving a note on his porch about the truth of Lady Windswell's intentions.

Knowledge and experience poured into his mind's eye as he looked upon the pair of slythans. Their race, much like several similar races, were descended from dragons. That thought burned like acid on his thoughts. A memory flashed, and Asher had to push it away. If he dwelled on it, he would have carried through with his threat.

The two slythans bowed their heads in shame.

"Please, forgive us, Lord Blackwood. We were only..." the first one stopped when the female elbowed him.

"You fool! She'll have us whipped for sure!" she admonished her cohort.

Asher's eyes narrowed. "Fear of your lady is enough to stare at death as he stands before you? Fear does not breed loyalty."

The slythans glanced at each other, before facing forward, and lowering their heads again.

"We meant no harm," the female said, gathering her courage. "We were instructed to put many parchments on your door. They are to the Summer Dusk Banquet on the Windswell estate. It takes place every year, in Lord and Lady Windswell's courtyard. It is to celebrate the end of summer, and greet autumn."

"Why not simply leave a letter?" Asher asked with suspicious eyes.

The pair glanced at each other before looking at Asher again.

"As it was told to us, there will be no mistake with the invite. You, and all who dwell on your estate, as well as the entire town, are invited. Our mistress will not take no as an answer. Nor will she accept an excuse of ignorance to her banquet."

Asher eyed the pair. He admired their bravery, but disliked the mayor's tactics to get her way.

"Tell me, is it usually you both who spy on my estate?"

The slythans looked down, and gave a single, small nod each.

An idea bloomed in Asher's mind.

"How much does she pay you?" Asher asked.

The pair hesitated to speak.

Asher looked at the lizard people with a serious gleam in his eyes. He then lowered his bow, and eased the tension on the bowstring. He didn't put it away, only kept it pointed down as to show his small willingness to bargain.

"I can pay you more, to keep this incident between us. Leave the parchments, and tell your mistress that the deed was done. But if you want to earn a little more, both of you can work for me, in secret."

The slythans stared at the man with wide eyes, unsure what they just heard.

Asher continued with devious cunning, "Since I arrived here, my home has been spied upon, by the former mayor, and now the current one. I've let it go on long enough.

"I propose, you work for me. If you agree, I can give you a monthly pouch of gold, of say, twenty coins apiece?"

"It would take us a year to earn that much," the male slythan blurted out.

Asher gave a confident nod. "Then the price sounds correct. We can keep this just between us. Once a month, on your midnight visits, come to my door and you will be paid. If this bargain is spoken to anyone else, especially your mistress, I will feign ignorance and the payments will cease.

"As part of this bargain, I will want you to tell me what your mistress has planned, or designs she may have for the town. If you feed me lies, and I found out, I'm sure your mistress will have strong words for you as punishment. I am a man of honor, and I will honor this bargain."

"If the mistress finds out we are spying for you, she will have us killed," the female said with an edge of panic.

Asher could feel the fear coming off the pair. He could tell they were interested, but hesitant. He couldn't let this opportunity slip by.

"If you are discovered, or about to be discovered, my estate will be a safe haven. Come here, and you will be under my protection. From that point, we can plan your future, either on my farm, or safely leaving Mist Valley to start a new life."

"On your honor?" the male slythan asked with hope in his small eyes.

"On my honor," Asher said with truthful confidence.

The former ranger put the arrow back in its quiver. He then put the bow over his head and let it hang across his chest. His hand reached into his belt pouch. He pulled out a small sack purse, and tossed it to the slythans.

The male caught it with both hands. He opened the top as his cohort moved to his side. The pair looked down at gleaming gold coins.

"There should be a little over fifty in there. Take the extra as proof of my word, and my commitment to our bargain."

The slythan held the pouch to his chest and gave a deep nod and bow to Asher. His partner did the same.

"We will honor the agreement. When we speak next, we will tell you anything we find, or hear."

Asher bowed slightly to them.

"No names. It will aid in our secret pact," Asher told them as he stood up.

The slythans nodded again, before turning and walking to the fence.

Asher watched them climb over the fence, and slink back into the shadows and bushes. Before long, they were gone, like they were never there in the first place.

A small weariness sank into Asher's shoulders. He turned and walked the short distance to the porch stairs. He climbed them onto the porch, and to the front door.

Asher's mind drifted a little as he let himself into the house and closed the door behind him, locking it. Small memories of spending the last week hiding in different spots, and waiting for the spies to appear had finally taken its toll. Including his farm responsibilities, and being with the ones he loved, exhaustion began to seep into his spirit, and he wanted nothing more than to sleep an entire day away.

The house was quiet, save for the small creaks along the floor as he made his way to the stairs. He climbed them, one foot after the other. When he reached the second floor, he walked down the long corridor.

A light under one of the doors alerted him, and he listened. The sounds of soft conversation drifted on the air. Megeth, and her two lich apprentices, were still up. The trio were night owls, often sleeping off the day, and staying up most of the night. Aside from Lynette sneaking into his bed a few times, they stayed to themselves, discussing arcane knowledge that Asher was not privy to, not that he wanted to know. Lichs and their kind were mysterious and constantly scheming. Megeth was a lich of honor, and a friend to his uncle, so there was a mutual respect, but what happened beyond the farm was none of his business. Not that he wanted to know.

The quiet discussion carried on as Asher walked past the door to Megeth's room. Lynette and Tianna had a separate room, but tended to spend most of their time with their mistress.

Asher thought about the many women under his roof. As much as he wanted to dwell on all of them, weary muscles said otherwise.

He reached his bedchamber door, opened it, and stepped in.

The chamber was dark, with the exception of starlight filtering in from the window. Elven dressers, and a cabinet stood next to Asher's dresser and desk. Elara's furniture took up many of the empty walls of the large bedchamber. Fully moved in, she made herself at home, bringing a moment of distilled happiness to the young lord. When he turned his attention to the bed, his happiness grew a little more.

A naked body lay on the large bed, the blankets bunched up next to her. Asher smiled as he saw Elara on her side, fast asleep. The room was warm, as it had been most nights during mid-summer. There was little to no need for blankets.

Asher lifted his bow over his head, and then pulled up his quiver strap next. He placed them down next to a small table by the door. He then took hold of his clothes and began to undress.

A thought needled him as he dropped pieces of clothing on the floor. It burned at his memory, reptilian kobolds attacking him and his new friends. How they fought for their lives in some fortress over ten years ago. When the last of his clothes were on the floor, next to his boots, he made his way to the bed.

Elara's eyes fluttered awake the moment Asher crawled onto the bed. She stirred as he crawled closer.

"Anything tonight?" she asked with a weak whisper.

"Yeah, but we can talk about it tomorrow morning," Asher said as he plopped onto the bed next to the beautiful naked elf.

Elara's arm and leg lashed against him, the elf pulling herself close to him and snuggling to his side. Asher turned on his side to face her, and she snuggled even closer.

"Aren't you hot?" Asher whispered.

"Yes, I am. But it's hot in here too," she said with a small smile and closed eyes.

Asher couldn't fight his smile. He held the elf close, feeling her heat and flesh against his. Despite his tired exhaustion, a part of him began to fill with blood, and slowly rise.

Elara snuggled to his neck, lost to his musk, when she felt something getting harder against her.

"Someone's not tired," she said with a low, amused tone.

Asher chuckled. "I am very tired. At least, most of me."

Elara gave a small nod. "Lay on your back. Maybe a quick one to help you sleep."

"You don't have to do that," Asher smiled lovingly.

"I know. I want too," the elf yawned as she clumsily slid over him and collapsed on his chest.

"Just... stick it in," she yawned.

Asher kept his grin as he took hold of her firm ass. He was ready to maneuver the light elf, when she hissed out a relaxed exhale. He looked at her, and even in the dark, he could see she was fast asleep again.

The young man held the voluptuous elf to him. The night sank into his mind, body, and spirit. After a time, he fell into dreams, his last thought was how he was going to protect the ones he loved against the scheming mayor of Star Fall.

Chapter 2

Planning Dreams

Heat curled along Asher's senses. A familiar face looked at him with a warm smile. His spirit floated as the oppressive heat wrapped around him. The darkness turned into light, the face fading away. Eyelids slowly opened to the morning sun.

Asher squinted as shafts of sunlight touched his unprepared eyes. He growled as he turned away from the window. He blinked, trying to relieve his gaze from the lingering flash orbs in his eyes. As it cleared away, he saw a pair of oval, emerald green eyes staring at him. They watched him with a dreamy gleam. A small, loving smile filled her lips. Blonde hair flowed over her neck.

"Morning," Elara whispered with a loving tone.

Asher blinked again, the flash orbs gone, but the oppressive heat remained.

"Morning," he said gruffly.

Elara reached across the small distance, touching his chin, and running her finger along his strong jaw.

"It was too hot and bright on my side of the bed. So, I moved over here."

Asher gave a lazy nod.

"I apologize about last night. I wanted to, but the warmth of the room, and as tired as I was, I couldn't keep my eyes open."

Asher smiled at the beautiful elf. "I understand, and don't worry. I was exhausted too. It was nice to get a full night's sleep, and I always love when we're close."

Elara's eyes squinted a little in amused happiness.

Asher let out a low sigh. "It's still so hot in here."

Elara nodded. "I didn't think Mist Valley would ever be this hot and humid. I thought the mountains surrounding the valley would keep it cool. The morning mist was barely visible before it vanished with the morning light."

Asher nodded as his gaze drifted down to Elara's naked body. He let his eyes linger, never tiring of her beauty. Her womanly curves and voluptuous shape spoke arcane knowledge to him, and he would study her for as long as he drew breath. She was perfect for him, and his heart swelled at that thought.

Elara looked at Asher as he looked at her body. She was on her side, and comfortable, despite the oppressive heat in the bedchamber. A squirming sensation filled her senses, enjoying Asher's rugged handsome features, and strong body. All she wanted to do was cuddle and hold him close. Love dripped from her soul as small memories washed on the shores of her mind, her lover coming to rescue her just a few weeks ago.

A tingling touched Elara's nipples, waking her from the rosy inner thoughts. Her hand moved to her breast, and touched a nipple. When she felt moisture, she smiled. Asher was looking at her leaking breasts, with love and fascination. When she felt his cock stiffen and touch her thigh, she grinned.

"I suppose I'm not the only one who needs to be milked this morning."

Asher shifted his gaze to meet her eyes. The couple simply stared at each other before laughing. It echoed through the bedchamber as the pair giggled and chuckled like two kids sharing a funny moment.

"I just wish it wasn't so hot," Asher said as he put his hand on her hip.

Elara flopped on her back, her nipples leaking rivulets of pale milk. "It's unbearably hot. I don't even want to touch myself. I wish we had a frost crystal."

Asher lifted his head and leaned the side of it on his hand. With his other hand, he ran his finger along the under-curve of her breast, up to her nipple, and circled it.

"I don't know if they have them in any of the shops in town," Asher said.

Elara closed her eyes and let out a long exhale, enjoying her lover's light touch.

"Nyn could create one," the elf mentioned.

Asher's ear perked up. "She can? It's been hot for a week. Why hasn't she made one or more for the house?"

The mature elf opened her eyes and looked at Asher. A sad, dark gleam filled her oval eyes.

"She's still punishing herself for what happened with Sontar Spellweaver."

A memory caressed Asher's thoughts from a few weeks before. How Elara and Nyn made their way back to Elara's province to ensure her life was settled. Elara didn't want to go back, but knew she had to or the elves she worked with would worry, or grow suspicious. For a mature elf to live a life beyond the elven cities was unheard of. Her former boss found out she had returned and kidnapped her.

Asher's gaze darkened as he remembered how Nyn came back, bloody, and bruised, after trying to defend Elara from Sontar. She escaped, and made it back to the farm. She alerted Asher and he went back to get Elara. What followed was a harrowing rescue and escape, Sontar and his followers trying everything they could to keep Elara in the province.

"She shouldn't be so hard on herself," Asher said with an understanding tone.

"Yes, she shouldn't be," Elara sighed. "Every time I tell her it wasn't her fault, she behaves like I didn't say anything. You've seen how withdrawn she has become. She doesn't eat with us anymore, taking her meals in her room."

The elf sat up and leaned on one hand. "I don't know what to do. She always had a strong spirit, one I always admired. She helped me understand, the guilt I felt with my desires was merely in my own mind, and nothing I should be ashamed of. When Sontar's followers used their magic against us, she put up a brave fight, but I saw the haunted look in her eyes as she escaped."

Elara looked down. "I think she was ready to fight to the death, but changed her mind at the last moment. I don't blame her. After everything that has happened to all of us in the last five months, I'm not ready for any of this to end."

Asher touched Elara's hand, giving it a reassuring squeeze. "Maybe she will come around, with time."

The mature elf looked down on her young lover with understanding eyes. "I'm not sure you know how long elves can dwell on what they consider personal failures. Her honor is broken. Her oath of keeping me safe was shattered. She never led an adventurer's life. She doesn't know what it means to fail and learn from it, because she's never failed at anything before."

Asher listened intently, drinking in every word.

Elara continued, "You know, Nyn and I lived simple, uncomplicated lives in the empire. We were lost in written, sensual adventures. The very act of me stepping into a portal, to find a mysterious milk farm, was one of the most exciting adventures in my life. Meeting you and how we live is an adventure on a grander scale for Nyn and I."

"I never considered farm life as adventurous," Asher grinned.

Elara let out a laugh as she grabbed her breast. She gave it a squeeze, squirting milk in Asher's face. The sudden splash of milk surprised and stunned the young man, to the point he couldn't react. A second later, he laughed from deep in his soul.

Elara let go of her breast and giggled.

"This farm life is just the kind of adventure I always wanted. I think Nyn wants it too. I want to help her, but since she feels she failed me, I may not be the person who can help her at this time."

"I can talk to her. See if she needs another ear to talk to," Asher offered.

"That may be for the best," she said as milk leaked from her heavy breasts, and onto the bed.

Asher glanced down at the many wet spots.

"Changing the bedsheets is turning into a full-time chore on its own," he quipped.

Elara giggled. "Yes, but oh so worth it."

Asher saw the playful look in her eyes. Their love and connection glowed brightly, the pair never wanting to leave each other's side. It was enough for the couple to bask in it for a moment.

Elara perked up. "Oh, you didn't tell me about what transpired last night. I'm eager to know the details!"

Asher parted his lips to tell her what happened, when the small sound of a door opening stopped him.

The bedchamber door opened a crack, an eye staring in.

Asher and Elara turned their gazes to the door, just as it burst open. A green blur reached the foot of the bed, bent their knees, and jumped.

Time slowed as Asher and Elara looked up at the floating goblin with a wide, excited smile and crazy eyes. Blyss soared over them, her long, dark green hair flowing around her head like fine seaweed. She wore a long black shirt that Asher recognized as one of his. Time returned to normal, and the short goblin crashed on the bed between her master and mistress.

"Master!" Blyss shouted with glee before pouncing on him and nibbling his neck.

"Help! I'm being attacked by a horny goblin!" Asher laughed as he held her close.

"Oh no!" Elara laughed as Blyss's hips began to hump Asher's hip.

The goblin nibbled and humped her master like a wild animal. Having a hold on her, he twisted his body and forced the goblin onto her beck, between him and Elara.

Blyss licked her lips as she looked up at her master with wanton eyes.

"Is it time for morning prayer, master priest?" Blyss asked with the innocence of a succubus in heat.

Asher grinned, knowing they were still acting out the monastery and priest play. For the young man, the play had turned into a much deeper experience than he ever thought possible. His initial trepidations faded away as he embraced the role, playing it to the hilt, as it were. He had grown accustomed to it, and even enjoyed it, taking care of his flock with lurid prayers, and sensual punishments.

"Oh! I forgot, I still must earn my next rank," Elara smiled.

Asher remembered how each disciple had to earn their ranks in the play. They were broken down to three ranks, lost soul, novice, and acolyte. Blyss and Amber had already earned the acolyte status. Megeth, Lynnette, and Tianna were still novices by choice. Asher remembered how they wanted to take their time earning their final rank. Paasha was still a lost soul. Nyn, and a few of the other new residents, hadn't partaken in the play.

Asher smiled brightly at the trapped goblin and Elara.

"If we can cool down the house, I'm sure we can spend a little extra time earning your faith and penance," Asher grinned.

"I don't mind sweating as we pray," Blyss said with a mischievous smile.

"We know," Asher and Elara said at the same time, and laughed.

The former ranger let go of the beautiful goblin and sat up. He stretched his arms into the air before letting them drop down to his sides.

"I still have a lot to do this morning. I must water the grape vines and inspect the winery again. I want to make sure everything is ready for when we start brewing wine."

Blyss sat up. "Paasha is making a meal to break our fast. After that, she and I can water the vines."

"We all can help," Elara said warmly. "Then afterwards, we can spend some time in the sitting pond."

24

"My swimming is getting better," Blyss added, proudly.

"All sounds like a great start to the day. I'll make my inspection and then come back to help water the crops."

Asher looked at Elara with endearing eyes. "Want to inspect the winery with me?"

"I want to, I really do, but my breasts are sore. If I don't relieve the pressure, I won't be able to concentrate.

"You go ahead. I know it won't take long. Then you can come back."

Blyss moved closer to Elara. "I can help, beautiful mistress," she said with a bright smile.

"Thank you, my sweet," Elara smiled.

For a moment, Asher looked at the elf and goblin with a dreamy gaze. Never in his life would he have thought his life would become such a thing of beauty. He wanted nothing more than to stay and aid them with morning milking, but he knew the day could get away from them rather quickly. There was much to attend to, and the longer he took, the less time he would have to spend with the women he loved.

The young man slid out of bed and onto his feet. He moved to his dresser, opening a drawer, and pulling out a new shirt and leggings. He began to dress as Blyss moved to the foot of the bed, reached down, and pulled a small trunk from underneath. Elara stared at Asher with loving eyes as Blyss pulled out two specially made jars with corks on top.

When Asher finished getting dressed, he took a long, loving look at the elf and goblin. Elara held one breast in her hand, with a jar pressed to it. She squeezed it, and a thin stream of milk squirted into the jar. Right next to her, Blyss held a jar to Elara, her green hand squeezed the elf's other large breast, with milk squirting into the jar. Relief filled Elara's eyes as creamy milk spilled into each jar.

Asher felt the urge to stay. His chores and duties won his attention, and he sighed his urge's defeat. He stepped over to the elf and goblin, giving them each a kiss on the head. He then turned, and headed for the bedchamber door, wanting to end his chores as quickly as he could, so he could enjoy the rest of the day with everyone he loved.

Chapter 3

Summer's Kiss

Asher felt a bead of sweat slide down his right temple. The farmhouse was hot, almost too hot. He wiped away the sweat as he reached the bottom of the stairs and made his way toward the kitchen. His plan was to get some food and eat it on the way to the winery. A hope gleamed that the outside air wasn't as hot and humid as inside the house.

The smell of eggs filled his nose before he walked into the kitchen.

When he entered, he quickly noticed Paasha standing on a small stool, over the metal oven with a pan of frying scrambled eggs. The mature goblin was wearing a simple, black dress. The hem was down to her ankles. Her black hair with the white lock was tied back into a ponytail.

Asher's gaze slid to the kitchen table. On it were several used, empty plates. Stray pieces of egg and bits of bacon were left behind. Two full plates of eggs and bacon remained in the middle of the table. Beside the plates and food, Amber sat in subdued misery.

The faun sat back in her chair, with a nearly empty plate of food beside her. Sweat dripped from her hairline, neck, and even her chest. She was wearing a short, green dress, but the fabric was so thin, sweat had seeped into her top, and under her breasts. She fanned herself with her hand, trying to get an ounce of coolness on her pink, glowing skin. Even her furry thighs had wet, matted fur.

When she looked at Asher, it wasn't her usual bright eyes and smile. The faun was dwelling in misery, and looked like she wanted to rip off her own skin.

"Amber?" Asher asked with concerned eyes.

"It's... too... hot," she struggled to say.

Paasha turned around on the stool and bowed. "Morning master. I cook. I feed everyone," the goblin said in broken common.

Asher's gaze shifted between the goblin and faun. Where Amber looked like she was turning into a melted candle, Paasha seemed unaffected by the humid heat. Cooking over a hot stove, he didn't see a drop of sweat on the motherly goblin. The contrast was amusing and concerning at the same time for the former ranger.

Asher centered his gaze on the sweating faun. "I'm going to inspect the winery again. I think it might be cooler there. Want to join..." Asher didn't get a chance to finish.

"Yes!" Amber said as she stood up on her hooved feet and rushed towards the kitchen side door.

Asher glanced at Paasha.

"I make plate for you. It be waiting here," she said with a small nod.

"I'll be back soon. Thank you, Paasha," Asher said as he made for the door, following the flustered faun.

Paasha watched the door open, and the pair leave. Her heart lifted in her chest with joy as she turned back to cooking, humming a goblin tune.

Outside, Asher balked at the searing heat. The shadow of the farmhouse still stabbed out from the rising sun to the east of the home, but it didn't do anything to alleviate the oppressive heat.

The faun stared out with deflated shoulders.

"I hate this!" Amber shouted to the clear blue sky.

Amber was usually excited, knowledgeable, and open minded. Much to Asher's surprise, this was a side of her he never witnessed before. The heat was baking away her usual calm and helpful demeanor, and now, a miserable creature stood, cursing the summer heat.

"Amber, maybe a dip in the pond will help," Asher mentioned.

Amber turned her horned head to Asher. She had a faraway look, like she wandered the desert for a hundred years. For a tiny moment, she looked lost, or unsure what she heard. When it clicked, she simply nodded.

The faun grabbed at her soaked green dress and pulled it over her head. Naked to the world, she threw it to the ground and stormed off toward the sitting pond. The faun cursed under her breath as she moved with hurried hooves toward the pond and patio in the short distance.

Asher scratched at the back of his head. The heat was getting to everyone. He knew, if he didn't come up with a solution soon, the frustration would only grow.

I have to find Nyn and see if we can make this frost crystal Elara mentioned, or there might be a mutiny.

Asher chuckled to himself when a small movement to his right touched the corner of his gaze. He turned his head to see a blonde goblin in a thin blue dress, sitting in the shade of the house. Not far from her, Fern was on her side, breathing heavily.

The blonde goblin sat, staring at nothing. She didn't blink as she was perfectly still. Keefa had only been on the farm a few weeks. She talked very little, and had even less interaction with Asher.

A memory played of a clan of goblins coming to his estate, demanding Blyss come back to them. Blyss had run from the clan, and their clan leader wanted her back. He forced Paasha, Nuha, and Keefa onto their knees, shouting that if Blyss didn't return, their necks would be sliced open because of her betrayal. The three goblins helped her escape in the first place, and were willing to sacrifice their lives to help Blyss. It was enough for Asher and Blyss to fight the clan, with a little help from the lich, Megeth. Afterwards, it was only natural, and the right thing to do, to allow them to become part of the farm and family.

But after a few weeks, only Paasha made herself at home. Nuha, and Keefa, stayed to themselves. Blyss didn't seem bothered, as far as Asher could tell. Despite everything that happened, Asher wasn't sure what to expect, so he carried on, giving everyone enough space to adjust to this new life.

"Keefa, are you okay?" Asher asked the blonde goblin.

For a breath, she didn't move. Her eyes slowly blinked, like she was waking from a trance. She turned and looked up at Asher with golden yellow eyes.

"I okay," the goblin stated.

Fern lazily moved a hooved foot, but didn't get up.

Asher stood, watching the goblin as she looked at him with a blank gaze.

"I'm going to inspect the winery. Would you like to join me? It might be a little cooler."

Keefa slowly blinked, before she stood up. She didn't bother to brush off the dirt patches on her yellow dress.

"I will go with you, clan father," Keefa said and bowed her head.

Asher gave the goblin an uncomfortable smile. He still hadn't gotten used to the title of clan father. There was a small ritual, where Paasha accepted Asher as their clan father, and she would be clan mother. It was a goblin tradition, Blyss, Keefa, and Nuha gave their blessing. Blyss was present during the intimate ritual, but not Keefa and Nuha. Afterwards, the goblins were very eager to help, but seemed shy around Asher from time to time. He didn't think much of it at first, and spent a lot of time focusing on daily duties. With the heat, and little work other than tending to simple farm chores, he figured now would be the time for all of them to get to know each other a little better.

"Let's go take a look," Asher smiled as he turned and started walking.

Fern stayed where she was, laying in the shade. She looked at Asher as she breathed slowly.

Man, and goblin made their way past the workshop and toward the winery.

The sun glowed hot with merciless power. Sweat continued to bead along Asher's brow as he walked. The grass was turning yellow from the days of bright heat. Everything in the valley was drying up, and for a moment, Asher dreamed of autumn.

When Asher glanced at the blonde goblin walking beside him, he noticed that she too was not sweating.

"In bad weather, we goblins can control our bodies to heat, or cool," Keefa said, as if she read his mind.

Asher nodded. "I thought I knew a lot about the different races, but this is a new one for me."

Keefa nodded, before she turned her head and looked at the tall, yellow grass. Asher followed the goblin's gaze, seeing something moving on all fours through the grass. At first, he wasn't sure what he was seeing. As his eyes focused, the sight slipped into focus as he saw a goblin with short hair, leaping through the grass like a cat pouncing.

"HA!" Nuha shouted as she lifted her green hands with a squirming snake.

Asher watched as the goblin took hold of the snake's head and body. She instantly broke its neck and let out a gleeful shout.

"Nuha loves snakes, and snake soup," Keefa said like it was the most normal thing in the world to say.

The goblin turned her attention to Asher and Keefa. She lifted the snake and smiled in triumph.

"We eat well! I killed three snakes!" Nuha grinned.

The thought of hot soup only made Asher feel hotter. It had now become imperative he talked to Nyn, or they would all die of heat sickness.

"That's great, but please, don't kill all the snakes. They help keep the rat population down," Asher shouted to the goblin with a wave of his hand.

Nuha gave a strong nod. She then glanced to the side and leapt into the tall grass again, on the hunt.

Asher and Keefa continued walking toward the winery in the small distance. The young lord couldn't contain his excitement. His pulse increased as he looked upon the building that was going to change their lives.

A stone base surrounded the house-like structure. It was sturdy, and blended well with the standing wood walls, and triangular roof. It didn't have any windows along the ground level, so as to help control the internal temperature of the building.

Asher spent many weeks researching the wine-making process. When the winery was built, Dina and her artisans used the latest information they could find on creating the best kind of winery.

The man and goblin reached the sturdy, well-made door, and opened it.

The moment they stepped inside, cool air flowed over them. It soothed his heated body as they stepped in and closed the door behind them. With a quick glance around, he drank in the insides of the larger chamber.

The floor was made of stone-tiles. Not only did they look good, as it was told to the young lord, the stone tiles acted like a heat-sink to keep the chamber at a consistent temperature. He glanced over to a large fireplace. It was designed to keep the winery warm during the winter months, so any brewing batches didn't freeze.

The slanted ceiling had a pair of glass windows installed. With a pull of a lever, the windows could be opened to let fresh air in, or bad air out.

Asher's gaze shifted to a pair of metal vats in the center of the main chamber. One was a small vat, while the other one was much larger. Each of them had metal tubes reaching up from either side of the vats to a pair of slightly raised platforms. Each platform had a wood tub. There, the grapes would be placed and crushed. The juice would filter through the bottom of the tubs and down the tubes to the vats.

Asher remembered what he learned about each vat. One was smaller for smaller batches, while the larger one could handle much larger batches. They were separate, so two different wines could ferment.

Asher stepped closer to the large metal vat. He opened a porthole and looked inside. The vat was empty, but the young lord pictured it filled with fermenting wine. A chimney stabbed up from each vat. He remembered how a special air-lock was placed within the metal pipes, to allow the fermenting process to continue, and let gas escape. After fifteen to twenty days, the wine would be ready to be poured into casks, and stored away. Asher smiled as he closed the porthole and locked it shut.

He glanced at the raised platforms again, seeing the built-in empty crates, pulley system, and ramps for moving grapes onto it.

The cool winery air soothed his heated nerves to the point where he began to relax. He turned his attention to Keefa, wanting to speak a little of the process, when he noticed the goblin looking away, dejected.

"Keefa?" he asked with concern.

The goblin turned her ovals eyes to him, the sadness remaining.

"Have I... angered you?" the goblin asked with a soft tone.

Asher lifted an eyebrow. "Angered me? No, I'm not angered about anything at the moment, except for the heat. Why would you say such a thing?"

Keefa looked away. "You haven't claimed me and Nuha. It be our way. Clan Father must take us to ensure clan is strong."

Realization dawned on Asher as he stood before the blonde goblin. He remembered he was supposed to lead them, for they pledged their loyalty to him. He never dove deeper into the meaning behind it, busy with chores and farm duties.

Asher reached out and touched her chin. He gently moved her face to look up to him. Keefa looked up with bright, oval yellow eyes, unsure of what was happening.

"I must apologize. I was giving you both time to get used to the farm. I didn't want to rush anything, for I wasn't sure how you felt about being here."

Keefa kept her gaze on him, drinking in her clan father's handsome features.

"Rush? clan father, you can take what you will. I am yours," she said warmly.

"Keefa, I may be your Clan Father, but everyone here is free."

The shy goblin looked down. "I... not used to this. I'm happy to share my body with you. I'm ready to suck your cock."

Asher fought off the urge to smile and chuckle. He saw the lurid innocence the goblin displayed, much like Blyss and Paasha. He quickly summarized that goblins were truly free with everything about themselves and their clan. There was no shame, or hesitation. They lived everyday like it was their last. It reminded Asher of the powerful, but short lives, goblins often led in the wild.

But they were not in the wild anymore, and Asher knew there would be adjustments for all of them living on the farm.

"Keefa, you know we are all free here. If you want something, you can take it."

Inner demonic whispers chided the young lord, speaking to his own needs as well.

"As I'm sure, if I want something, I can take it," Asher said with a small smile.

Keefa's eyes widened a little, and her own small smile bloomed. "Clan Father, I live to be with you, and our clan."

A bond took root in the moment. The young lord gently cupped the goblin's chin, tilting her face up. He bent down, pressing his lips to hers. Keefa's eyes widened before they half-closed. They pair enjoyed the simple kiss in the cool winery

Asher nodded. "We can talk more later, if that's okay?"

"Yes," Keefa said with a strong nod and pinkish green cheeks.

Asher's heart warmed at Keefa's sudden upbeat attitude. He turned and made for the basement door, the goblin close behind.

The door opened and the pair made their way down. Asher touched a crystal embedded in the stone wall. Small mystical torchlights glowed to life along the stone staircase. The air was much cooler as they made their way down to the basement floor.

Lights lit up the large, wide basement cellar. Shelves with curved indents lined the walls. Stone archways ran along sections of the cellar, adding support to the structure above.

Asher admired the incredible work. The cellar was built to have a consistent temperature as the wine aged, and kept it from spoiling.

He turned his attention to a pair of spigots sticking out of a cobblestone wall. Asher approached them and looked them over. He knew they were connected to the vats upstairs. When it was time, they could line up casks at this location, and pour the new wine into each one.

Not far from the spigots were a few work tables and two cabinets nearby. It was the work area for bottling and corking wine bottles.

Asher glanced at the shelves again, seeing shelves with smaller grooves for individual bottles of wine. He daydreamed of when the winery was operational. He knew the grapes would not be ready until autumn, but he found it difficult to wait.

"Maybe I can start a smaller batch soon, to test it out," the young lord muttered to himself.

"Clan Father?" Keefa asked.

Asher shook his head and smiled. "It's okay. Just thinking out loud."

He then changed the subject, "I'm cool enough now. Let's head back up and to the farmhouse. I still have some things to do, and I don't want the day to get away from us."

"Yes, clan father," Keefa smiled.

The pair made their way back up the stairs and into the winery. They stepped out the front door, Asher closing it behind them.

Heat blasted his senses as he stepped back out into the sun. He lifted his hand and placed it over his eyes to block out some of the morning brilliance. He looked at the sitting pond and patio beside it. Amber was still in the pond, swimming around. She had a look of relief in her eyes as she swam on her back in slow, lazy circles. When Asher looked at the covered patio, he saw Nyn sitting in a chair, a black book in her hands.

"Keefa, let's visit the pond," Asher said as he looked at the dark-blue haired elf with concerned eyes.

Chapter 4

Metal and Frost

The sun burned brightly in the clear, blue sky. Asher and Keefa walked side by side until they reached the pond and patio.

Despite the respite from the cool winery air, Asher was already heating up again in the sunlight. When he looked upon Amber, swimming naked in the pond, he had the urge to take off his clothes and join her, but his attention was pulled to the elf sitting in a thin, light blue dress, under the protective shade of the patio.

Nyn didn't look up from the black book in her hands. She looked down with dark eyes, Asher guessed either lost in an erotic tale, or trying to ignore the outside world. Remembering what Elara told him, he guessed she was trying to shy away from everyone.

"The water is wonderful," Amber said as she swam around in circles.

Asher nodded, but didn't take his gaze off Nyn. "Keefa, would you give me a moment?"

"Yes," the goblin said as she sat down on the pond's edge and dipped her bare feet into the cool pond waters.

Asher walked over to the patio, and stepped under the slanted roof. Relief flowed over him, happy to not be directly in the sun's wrath. He walked over to a seat across from Nyn, and sat down.

Nyn didn't lift her gaze from the book as she spoke, "I know why you're here."

Asher smiled. "How did you know I was going to ask about frost crystals and cooling the house?"

Nyn lifted her icy blue gaze to meet his. After a small moment, her gaze melted into faint sadness, and she looked away.

"We can talk, or we can just sit here. I'm okay with either," Asher said with an understanding tone.

Nyn lifted her gaze and looked at Asher with worried eyes.

"I don't want to leave," she whispered.

Asher kept his expression steady, and filled with understanding. "No one is asking, or telling you to leave."

Nyn looked away and put the book down on her lap. "I failed Elara. I failed you."

Asher looked upon the sad elf. Moments of experience flashed across his mind, showing times where he tried to console friends and guildmates, when one of theirs passed on, or was killed during quests. The entire guild would come together to mourn, but the period of mourning was different for everyone. Some guild members could not forgive themselves, questioning every action they took, and still couldn't save a friend. Even for Asher, there were many periods where it took a long time to understand, failure didn't mean your life was over.

It was a lesson to learn for next time. But there were other guild members who could never let it go, and left the guild from their guilt.

Asher resisted the urge to try and explain with words. The haunted look in her eyes was enough to tell him that her guilt was stronger than her reasoning. He decided to try a different tactic.

He looked upon the beautiful elf, seeing her sweat soaking into her simple, thin blue dress. Much like Amber, the heat was getting to all of them, except the goblins.

"Nyn, when you're ready, we can discuss anything you want, but right now, I need your assistance. The heat is getting to everyone, and we should do something about it. Elara told me you know how to create a frost crystal. I can use your help with this."

Nyn slowly blinked as she looked at him.

"What do we need to make a frost crystal and cool down our home?"

Nyn's heart quickened at the words "our home." Despite everything she just said, Asher still considered her as part of this home, this family. The guilt receded a hair, but it continued to chain up her heart.

"Frost crystals are easy to create, but require a rune stand to hold them. The stand is only a few pieces of thin metal, with three runes etched into them. They must be crafted together to hold the crystal, but I don't know how to smith metal," she said with a low voice.

Asher smiled. "I've learned my way around a blacksmith's forge. If we start now, we can have it ready by this evening," he said as he held out his hand to her.

Nyn looked at his outstretched hand. Her heart twisted in her chest, new emotions spilling into her. Her hand trembled before she curled her fingers into her palm.

Asher kept his hand out to her.

The elf sighed. She stood up, but didn't take his hand. She held her book in one hand at her side.

Asher lowered his hand to his side. He didn't take it personally. He knew she was working it out. All he had to do was be there for her, and let her speak when she was ready.

"It's going to be hot, but we will have to work with the forge in the workshop. If this works, we'll be cool for the rest of the summer."

The young lord turned and walked toward the workshop. Nyn followed.

Amber and Keefa watched silently as Asher and Nyn made their way to the workshop. The pair then turned their gazes to each other as dragonflies floated in the air above them.

The workshop sliding door opened. Asher stepped in, and it was just as stifling as it was outside. He quickly moved to the door on the other side, unlocked it, and slid it open. A small breeze flowed in, giving a tiny relief, but Asher knew, working the forge was going to be much hotter.

He turned to the dour, beautiful elf. "I'll get the forge started. While I'm doing that, there is some parchment over there on the shelf. Can you draw out the runes needed for the metal stand?"

Nyn gave a small nod before stepping over to the shelf. She picked up a small roll of parchments and a small case with ink and quill. She set them on a work table and readied everything.

Asher moved to the forge. He began gathering coal and wood. He planned out what he had to do. His knowledge was amateur at best, but considering he, and everyone else, didn't want another hot night, he was going to work to make this happen.

When he looked at Nyn as she began scribbling on the parchment, his heart beat with a loving flame, happy they were spending time together, and hopefully, working out her guilt.

"Let's get started," Asher whispered to himself as he dumped wood and coal into the cold forge.

***

The sun hung low in the sky. The heat of the day remained as light dimmed across the tops of trees, and the mountain peaks across the valley.

In the workshop, sweat poured off Asher's brow. Using metal tongs, he bent the last piece of the molten hot metal into place. The metal glowed as two pieces connected, and began to fuse.

Asher let out a tired sigh, the heat making him dizzy. He dunked the metal stand in the water barrel beside him, enjoying a small respite from the glowing heat.

Nyn was close by, sweat gleaming off her body, and soaked into her dress. Her pointed ears were a little wilted, as bags filled the skin under her eyes.

The pair had spent hours working in the workshop. Asher hammered at metal as Nyn drew designs on parchment. Sparks flew as metal clangs sang. During their time in the workshop, food and water was brought in routinely by Blyss and Paasha. The goblins often checked on them as they worked, but quickly left to not disturb them.

Asher's shoulders and arms burned with acidic fire. He mentally chided himself to work a little more with the forge, so he would be better accustomed to this kind of work. He was no stranger to hard labor, but working a forge during summer was a whole new experience.

The young lord pulled up the metal stand with the tongs and gave them the once over.

The stand was a simple design. It had three, curved metal legs and a thin metal ring along the top. Asher noted that the ring was wide enough to put his head in it. He smiled at the thought, but wasn't going to take the chance to do that, not wishing to burn his head or hair.

"It will suffice," Nyn said as she compared the physical stand to what she drew on a piece of parchment. "The runes will need to be added next, to slow the mystical degradation. Frost crystals only remain for a few hours before they melt away. The runes on the stand will slow the process, allowing the crystal to remain for close to a month," she explained.

Asher nodded as he moved to a work table and put the stand down. He placed the tongs down next to it on the table, before moving to a shelf and picking up a small wood box. He brought it over to the table and set it down. Nyn moved to his side as he opened it.

Inside the simple box were etching tools. A small row of engraving pens lined one side, next to a row of small hammers. Asher had been wanting to try his new tools for weeks, and now, he was ready. He picked up an etching pen and small hammer. He turned to the metal stand. Nyn had already placed her parchment down with three rune symbols drawn on them.

"Once the runes are etched into the metal, we have to bring the stand inside and place it down. Then, I can start casting the spell to create a frost crystal," Nyn explained.

Asher nodded. He glanced at the parchment, and then looked at the circular metal band. He took a breath, and began working.

Part of Asher's mind began to wander as he started tapping a small hammer against one flat end of the pen tool. Hours had slipped by, but a few moments glowed his mind's eye. He would occasionally glance at Nyn, and he could see she was deep in thought. There were a few times where she parted her lips, as if to say something to him, but quickly closed them and looked away. He could feel she wanted to talk, but could not bring herself to speak more than was necessary.

"The winery looks amazing. I cannot wait until we begin our first batch," Asher said as he tapped away at the tool.

Nyn simply nodded, and looked away.

"I think I told you before, my mother loved wine. It is part of the reason why I wanted to have my own winery. I remember red was her favorite."

"I know what you're doing," Nyn said with a small exhale.

"What am I doing?" Asher said as he looked down at his work.

"You're trying to ease me into talking about my failure," Nyn said with dark eyes.

Asher stopped tapping and looked at the beautiful, sad elf. "You don't have to speak about anything you don't wish to say, but I do want to make it clear, this is your home, and we are your family."

"Will we be family after I leave and never return?" Nyn said with a sharp edge.

Asher nodded. "Yes, but we both know the truth."

Nyn looked at Asher, and her heart quickened again.

"I said I would stay here for a few months. I should return to my province. Elara has exiled herself from her home, but I never made such an oath."

Asher stopped what he was doing. He put down the tools and stood tall. He faced the beautiful elf, a sternness in his eyes.

"I felt our oaths and bonds. Not just your bond with Elara, but the bond you have with Blyss, Amber, and me as well. This life we have together, is beyond simple exploration, and we both know it."

Nyn's lip quivered and she looked away with hard eyes. "You don't know what you speak," she said darkly.

"Don't insult both of our intelligences. You think I don't know what it means to live with guilt. I lost friends, and lovers. I live with guilt, but I don't let it shatter my life."

Asher stepped closer to Nyn. She looked up at him with an icy gaze, but as he stood before her, her cold demeanor began to melt.

Asher's stern expression smoothed into a warm smile and knowing eyes.

"We don't expect you to simply push away the guilt. I want to only give you some perspective. No one died. We all were hurt, but we made it through. We are all here, healthy, and happy. The guilt you feel may be eating away at you, but know this, my feelings have never changed for you. Neither has Elara's feelings."

Wetness touched Nyn's eyes. She looked down as her heart sagged in her chest.

"I never failed at anything before. I led a life of being an upstanding citizen for the empire. I excelled at everything I have ever done. I had a perfect life, until I failed my friends," she looked into Asher's eyes, "my lovers."

Asher took her hand into his, and held it to his chest. "I thought we had a perfect life here."

Nyn's eyes widened.

Asher kissed the back of her hand. He then lowered their hands, but he never let go, their fingers entwined with each other.

"Elara and I don't forgive you, because there is nothing to forgive. You fought well, but even the best of us can be overwhelmed. You don't have to carry it like a chain around your neck. Let us love you, and be there for you."

Nyn didn't blink as Asher's words stabbed deep into her heart.

"You snared my heart. I fear... you may break it," Nyn said with a defeated whisper.

"You snared my heart. I fear, there is not enough time in the world to explore our bond," Asher said with a soothing tone.

Nyn's eyes trembled at the weight of his words.

"You mean every word," she stated.

Asher nodded. "Every word. You can leave if you wish, but we both know, that's not what either of us want."

"I'm afraid I will never return to my home, not because I can't, but because I don't want to. This life... was a fantasy, a dream. I never thought it could become this real."

"If it will make you feel any better, neither did I," Asher smiled.

Time stood still between them. A small smile stabbed into Nyn's cheeks. Her shoulder trembled, as she half-laughed, half-cried. Asher couldn't resist anymore, his arms embracing her and holding her close.

"We belong to each other, and that is a bond that will never break," Asher whispered into her pointed ear.

Nyn held him around the waist as his strong arms held her close. She looked away with a small, wicked smile.

"I haven't allowed myself to be my true self around you," she whispered.

"I can only speak for myself, I felt that you were holding back," Asher whispered back.

Despite the oppressive heat, the couple didn't want to break their embrace. A door opened between them, and deeper parts of themselves began to spill out.

"Asher," Nyn said with a sultry whisper, "If I stay, it means my former life will die. We will be slaves to each other."

"I long accepted that, before you even said the words," Asher said as he pulled his head back and kissed her forehead.

Nyn's eyes trembled at his display of pure affection. The touch of his lips on her forehead set her soul on fire. The hard walls she built around her heart cracked, and began to fall apart. A new, brighter flame surged along her soul, and she made no attempt to put it out.

Asher pulled away and gave the beautiful elf a smarmy smile. "It's getting hot in here. Let's finish the work, so we can bring it to everyone in the house and finally cool off."

Nyn nodded, her icy blue eyes melting at Asher's relaxed, confident demeanor.

Asher picked up his etching tools and began working on the metal ring of the stand. Nyn moved closer to his side, looking over his craftsmanship, but stealing loving glances as he concentrated.

An hour later, the sun had fully set. Asher stepped back with Nyn. The pair looked at the finished metal stand and ring.

"I think we did a good job," Asher said as he looked it over.

"It is good work. We may need a few more of these stands for the house, but for now, this will work for the bedroom," Nyn added.

Asher nodded as he put his tools away. After everything was secured, he reached over and picked up the metal stand. He glanced at the carved runes along the metal ring. They nearly matched what Nyn designed. He felt he could have done a better job, but considering the heat and work involved, it wasn't bad for a first attempt.

Nyn's facial expression was blank, but her eyes shined bright as she looked at Asher.

The pair moved to the workshop doors, closing, and locking them in turn. Once outside, the humid heat was like a heavy fog sitting on their spirits. There was no relief as the pair sweated, their clothes soaked in it.

Man, and elf, made their way to the farmhouse, eager to prepare the frost crystal and mystical stand, when the kitchen door opened and a cloaked figure stepped out.

Asher smiled as he saw it was Tianna, one of Megeth's apprentices. She wore a simple, one piece as she walked along, the hooded cloak parted down the middle. Asher couldn't help but wonder if she was boiling alive within the cloak covering her head and shoulders.

Tianna, Asher, and Nyn stopped about ten feet from the house, the trio facing each other.

"Greetings, Lord Blackwood," Tianna said softly and with a small bow.

"Greetings Tianna. How can I help you this evening?" Asher asked.

"Mistress Faydra sent me to inform you, there will be no worship and punishment tonight. She and Lynette are in the prayer chamber, basking in the Mother's holy presence. She wanted to send her apologies, and me, to ease the change in plans."

Asher wished he could say he was surprised, but it seemed most days and nights, very little surprised him anymore. Megeth had spent every other night, enjoying the play of priest and disciple. Since she was one of the undead, she wanted to enjoy the feeling of life running through her from the elixir. During their sessions, she had professed several times how alive she felt as Asher spent the time blessing her cracked soul, and body. She also needed time to savor their experiences together. But for Asher, it was relief, because he desperately wanted to spend time with his lovers, and friends.

"Thank you for telling me," Asher smiled before he caught the meaning of her words. "Tianna, you don't have to please me."

Tianna looked down with her normal, sad, and shy expression. "I want to. I know I don't say much, but I want to be here to ease your demonic urges, and my own."

Asher simply smiled, knowing anything he said would fall on deaf ears.

"Let's get inside and see if we can start the evening on the cooler side," Asher smiled.

Chapter 5

Needful Bonds

Asher, Nyn, and Tianna stepped into the kitchen, the side door closing behind them. He glanced over to the hallway arch, and the common room just beyond. Elara and Amber sat on opposite sides of the couch. The elf and faun fanned themselves as the humid heat pressed down on them. Elara was wearing a thin, nearly see-through, short white dress. Amber was in her emerald green dress. Even from a small distance, Asher could make out the sweat seeping into their thin clothes.

The young lord walked into the common room, with the metal stand in hand. Tianna and Nyn followed.

Elara and Amber turned their gazes to the trio, their eyes falling to the stand in Asher's hand.

"Is it complete?" Elara and Amber said as they stood up in unison.

"Almost," Asher said as he was distracted by Elara's erect nipples under the thin fabric of her dress.

"I need a little time to begin the ritual," Nyn added as she stepped to his side.

Elara looked at her friend, and immediately saw a change. Her often-reserved friend glowed with a new light in her eyes. Hope swirled in Elara's heart, hoping the time she spent with Asher helped her understand she never failed them.

Asher woke up from his momentary distraction. "Where are the goblins?"

"They went to bed already. Blyss told me they use a lot of energy to cool or heat their bodies during extreme weather. They were sleepy the moment the sun went down," Amber explained while she fanned herself for dear life.

"Nuha mentioned something about making snake soup soon. I honestly wasn't sure what she was talking about, and thought better to not ask," Elara smiled.

The voluptuous mature elf shifted her gaze to Tianna. "Are you taking him away from us for the evening?"

Tianna bowed her head. "No, mistress. I was sent to please him for the evening."

Elara gave Asher a wicked glance. "If we can get the bedchamber cool enough, there may be more than one of us being pleased tonight."

Asher's inner demons licked their lips. Elara's own demons matched his, the couple enjoying the lewd bond they shared.

"Please, I need cool air," Amber pleaded.

Several different urgencies filled the young lord. The thick heat was enough to keep everyone at arm's length for the last two weeks. The summer slowed down the intimacy to a degree, and if this didn't work, it was going to be a miserable few more weeks.

Asher's fingers tightened around the metal stand as he turned and made for the stairs. Four women followed in his wake.

The group made their way up the stairs and down the long corridor. When they reached the master bedchamber, the door opened and they spilled inside. Asher moved to his desk and set down the stand beside it. He pushed it a little so it was close to the wall, and out of sight to anyone coming in.

"I will need some time to perform the ritual," Nyn said before turning her gaze to Elara. "If we both share our mana, it will be completed much sooner."

Elara's heart squirmed as her true friend was returning to her.

"I would be honored to share our mana," Elara said with a happy smile.

Asher looked at the two elves, and his own spirit glowed happily.

Amber let out a frustrated sigh. She moved to Asher and looked up into his eyes, a madness filling her gaze.

"A cold bath, so we won't be in their way," the faun said.

Asher looked down upon himself, seeing that he was covered in grime, and smelled like metal and smoke.

"A cold bath might be in order," he said.

The young lord barely finished his words as Amber took his hand and pulled him with her. She led the charge for the private washroom.

Tianna watched the man and faun enter the washroom. As the door closed, she glided toward it like her feet weren't touching the ground.

Inside the washroom, Amber moved with heated urgency. She rushed to the large, metal tub and touched a blue crystal. From the faucet, water poured out and splashed into the tub. She then turned to Asher and leaned her furry rear against the edge of the tub, enjoying the small coolness against her.

Asher looked at her with concerned eyes. "You haven't really fared well with the humid heat, have you?"

Amber shook her antler-horned head. "I haven't, and for that, I must apologize. I haven't laid with you in the mornings, letting you suck on me because being close to you makes me hotter. I've missed us being together, dreaming of autumn and winter."

A sultry gleam filled her tortured eyes. "I have been lax on my duties of becoming a true disciple of yours. I want to earn my title of acolyte, like Blyss. She is dedicated, and I am envious of her ability to cool down in such evil heat."

Asher watched as the faun was beating herself up. A small concern filled him, wondering if the heat was bringing out their true selves under duress. The truth revealed itself that they worried he would not desire them, even if they didn't feel like sharing sensual moments.

To the young lord, even he felt the heat pressing down on his own desires a little. It had become a shared feeling they all experienced, and he knew he had to help show them that they were all as important to him as when they first met.

The sound of splashing water echoed in the tiled chamber. Amber looked away, sweat dripping down along her temples and neck. She was uncomfortable as she waited patiently for the tub to fill with cold water. When a shadow touched her, she looked up to see Asher's loving gaze upon her.

"I miss you," Asher said with loving eyes.

Amber's heart cracked in her chest. "I always miss you. It is why I have been so miserable. I miss your touch. I miss your lips and mouth, sucking on my nipples in the mornings. I miss when you push me down and force your cock into me. I miss moaning your name," she confessed.

Asher reached down and took hold of her green dress. Amber didn't fight him, raising her arms as he pulled it up. When it cleared her hands, he tossed it aside, and looked down on the naked faun.

Amber made no attempt to cover herself. She enjoyed her lord's eyes on her, drinking in her naked beauty.

Asher let his gaze slide along her now tanned flesh. Long reddish-brown hair spilled down over her shoulders. Firm breasts hung, unassisted. Pink nipples stood erect as her breasts began to swell a little more. Her stomach was smooth as her hips flared out a little. Light brown fur ran from her waist, down her hips and along her deer-like legs. Hooves rested on the stone floor. Her furry thighs were parted with her pink slit exposed to her lord and master.

"I ache for you," Amber confessed.

Asher nodded as his hand moved to her slit. Amber's eyes weakened as Asher's finger touched her. A charge ran though her, surrendering to his touch as his finger moved and massaged her. The moment he touched her clit, she let out a soft exhale.

Asher put his hand on her shoulder, and shoved her back.

Amber's eyes widened to the size of saucers as she fell back, splashing into the cold water, hooves up.

The young lord couldn't hide his laughter as Amber splashed around in the cold water. Her horned head burst from the sloshing water and gasped for air. She looked up at Asher as he laughed and pulled his shirt over his head.

The sudden chilly blast of cold water instantly soothed the faun's frayed nerves. She calmed down as the heat was pulled from her body. Water continued to flow into the tub as she hugged herself from the initial shock.

Asher slipped off his leggings. He chuckled to himself as his manhood hung low, but was getting thicker by the moment. He lifted a leg and stepped into the tub of cold water. When he lifted his other leg, Amber's hands shot up, grabbed his arm, and she pulled with all her might. Asher lost his balance and fell into the shockingly cold water and between the faun's arms and legs.

Amber leaned back with her own mischievous grin, the Lord of Blackwood caught in her grasp.

Asher was much bigger than the faun, but he couldn't deny the sultry power she had when the mood struck.

"You're so dirty," Amber smiled.

The faun's smile turned into a look of pleasant surprise as something thick and hard prodded her valley entrance.

"And I think you need to be taught a lesson in retribution," Asher said as he moved his hips, the tip of his cock sinking into her.

Amber's eyes cooled as heat glowed from deep within. Despite the cold water, it wasn't cold enough to put out her own desires. She moaned her approval as Asher teased her with his cock-head. The tip of the spear gently pushed and pulled at her.

A cloaked shadow slipped into the washroom, and closed the door behind them. Tianna looked at the couple already in the tub. Amber glanced at the cloaked woman for a moment, before moaning to Asher driving himself a little deeper into her tight, sacred world.

Tianna stared at them for a breath, before she shrugged the cloak and hood off her shoulders. It pooled on the stone-tile floor. She sauntered closer to the tub, making her way around to the soap and sponge on a small rack beside it. She pulled out a small stool from under it, and sat down. Her dark purple hair was tied back as she looked down on the engaged couple. She took the soap into her hand, plunged it into the water, before pulling it out and rubbing it on Asher's back.

The young lord felt Tianna's touch and the soap. He relaxed as he stabbed his manhood into the moaning faun.

"Fuck me," Amber begged as water and soap sloshed around during their deep embrace.

***

Nyn and Elara sat on the hardwood floor, their hands over the metal stand, and fingers weaving mystical energies.

In the middle of the metal ring, a small shard of frosty energy glowed to life. It glowed a pale blue as the elves poured their mana into it.

The sound of muffled splashing and laughter filtered into the bedchamber as the pair of elves focused.

Nyn whispered arcane words, pulling together the mystical energies from the elemental sphere. She spoke the ancient elven words of water and ice. Elara repeated the words. Mana bloomed a little brighter between them. The mystical strands entwined, filling the shard with their power.

Nyn felt Elara's energies coiled into hers. The simple ritual took a turn, Nyn concentrating on the spell, but her heart yearning for more. The often cool and in control elf faltered. The spell blazed brighter. She re-spoke the words, taking control of the spell and forcing her mana into the shard.

The glowing blue shard grew bigger. It floated within the runed metal ring. When Nyn spoke the final command phrase, the spell cemented into place.

Nyn and Elara sat back as misty cool air began to flow off the shard. The heat in the bedchamber began to lessen, chilly tendrils spreading out.

Relief flowed into the two elves, but not from the frost crystal. Elara looked at Nyn, and Nyn looked at Elara.

"You're not leaving," Elara said with a small, happy smile.

Nyn looked at her dearest friend. "How could I? This farm, and the people who reside here, have become special to me. I... didn't want to believe it. But our lover convinced me."

Nyn slowly blinked as she looked at her friend. "You convinced me."

Elara sat up, enjoying the cool air filling the chamber. She reached over and curled her hand around Nyn's hand.

"We have been friends a long time. I know we shared correspondence and many discussions over wine about the secret lives we craved.

"When I sent you a letter, detailing what I discovered and experienced with Blackwood, I wasn't sure you would join me on this adventure. My heart filled with joy when you arrived."

Nyn's cool demeanor cracked with a knowing smile. "How could I resist, after everything we discussed, and experienced together? Our friendship showed me life was not simply taking dictation and serving the empire. I dreamed of being free, and we shared a love of stories and experiences."

Elara's eyes took on gleam as memories slipped into her thoughts.

"I still remember how we were so passionately discussing black books over wine. How the moment took us, and we wanted to share our bodies in my home."

Nyn eyed her friend with a hazy gaze. "It is one of my happiest memories. In that moment, I felt alive, sharing my soul with a kindred spirit."

Elara gave a single, slow nod. "And now, I can never see myself returning to our old lives. I have fallen for our growing family. I have fallen for Asher. He has broken me in a way I wish to never be mended."

Nyn looked down. "He is special. You both are special to me. That is why it pained me to not protect you. It burned me that I could not aid in your rescue. For the love I have for you both, I wasn't strong enough."

"You are very strong," Elara said with dreamy confidence. "Always know this, your soul matches my own, and our dear Asher's soul. I know you hold back, fearing he will take advantage of your trust. I know it takes a long time to earn your complete trust, but deep down, you know you can trust Asher.

"I have allowed myself to be completely free with him. I know you will be too, once you truly let him in."

Nyn looked down. "I fear my enthusiasm may break his spirit. I fear he may turn me away when I have truly given in."

"You know, as well as I do, that will not happen. He is a beautiful enigma in a world of pain and loss. The empire has grown rigid, but out here, we can be as free as we wish. Asher is young, but he carries an old soul. He is perfect for us, and I know, I'm not the only one who has felt it."

The air grew cooler as the two friends lingered in their honesty. Elara squeezed her friend's hand as she slowly stood up. Nyn followed suit, standing up with her friend, and not wanting to let go of her hand.

"I'm sorry," Nyn said, implying she failed her dearest friend.

Elara stepped closer to her with endearing, half-closed eyes. "I'm sorry you have endured this pain. But I am happy you won't have to endure it much longer."

Elara leaned toward her friend and kissed her on the lips. Nyn's eyes half-closed as their lips touched and tongues danced. The cool air and mood struck the elves. Bodies pressed together and the oppressive heat of the summer vanished, and was replaced with welcomed body heat.

When they parted their lips, hands remained on each other's hips. Chests touched as they looked into each other's eyes.

"I need you to help me love Asher and our family. He needs us to love him freely. It is the dream we spoke of many times," Elara said.

Nyn felt the shift in her heart. The self-imposed barriers began to fade away. Her heart warmed at the thought of being completely free with her lovers, especially Asher and Elara.

Muffled moans flowed from the closed washroom door. The two elves looked over as heat coiled along their nerves.

"Amber has been remiss without him," Elara said before she turned her gaze to Nyn. "But that doesn't mean we can't have our own fun until they're finished."

Nyn's eyes took on a sultry gleam as Elara pulled her friend onto the comfortable bed.

***

Water splashed out of the tub as Asher drove his soul into the faun. Amber's eyes rolled into her head, orgasms shattering her senses to shards. The young ranger looked down on her with satisfied eyes as she was lost to tidal waves of bliss.

Tianna remained close, watching the engaged couple. Her thighs rubbed against each other, wetness soaking into her simple one-piece outfit. She barely blinked, seeing the virile pair unleashing a needed storm upon each other.

Milk leaked from the faun's erect nipples. It clouded the water as she gasped for air, pinned against the end of the tub. Her body shuddered with each new flash of orgasmic bliss. She didn't remember the last time she felt so many. Her body needed his, and she reveled in the moment as he drove his meaty cock into her thin valley.

Asher grunted as his own urges cracked his spirit in half. Spurts of intimate affection painted her inner world, before flooding it.

The young lord's hips slowed, as the faun squeezed him. Amber had enough presence of mind to milk her lord, taking every drop of his soul.

Asher looked down on her for a moment, before lowering his lips to hers for a kiss. Clarity struck him as their tongues danced and played. Amber was still hungry, pulling her tongue back and gently biting his lower lip. Asher stayed close, moving his hips slightly.

When the moment dimmed, Asher pulled out. Amber's hand and arm fell into the water. She grabbed his thick shaft and stroked him. Her eyes slid back into place and looked at Asher with insatiable eyes.

"Please... again," Amber begged, not wanting to let go of him.

Asher slightly hovered over her as she stroked his cock underwater.

"We have all night, but I must attend to my lovers," Asher said with dreamy amusement.

"Please, I need you all the time. I can't live without you fucking me. I need your seed to survive," Amber whined as she squeezed and stroked his still hard manhood.

Asher moved a hand along the faun's side. Fingers moved up, past the waterline, and touched her swollen breast. He gave it a squeeze, a small rivulet of milk squirting a few inches into the cloudy water. Amber moaned to his touch, moving her hips, and trying to pull his cock to her slit.

"If you're good, I'll come on your tits," Asher said like it was the most natural thing in the world to say.

Amber's eyes lit up as she smiled. "It would be my honor to have Lord Blackwood coming on my tits."

Asher grinned as he pulled away, his cock slipping from the faun's grasp. Amber pouted as she remained in the tub. Her hands rubbed along her now cool skin, enjoying the afterglow of the watery tryst.

The young lord stepped out of the tub and stood up to his full height. Tianna moved to him with a towel. Asher lifted a hand to take it, but Tianna ignored him, using the towel to dry him.

"Thank you, Tianna, but you don't have to be so attentive," Asher mentioned as she ran the towel along one arm.

"I live to serve," the lich apprentice said as she then began drying his chest.

"That is not what we do here. You're our guest."

Tianna spoke as she dried him off, "Lord Blackwood, I always knew my place in Valoria. As much as I desire power, no matter how much I acquire, I will always serve. I serve my mistress. I serve my sister. I serve you.

"When I enter lichdom, there will still be others among the dead more powerful than I. It is something I have come to terms with, and enjoy."

Tianna lowered herself to her knees and used the towel to dry Asher's hanging manhood. She was delicate, and thorough, ensuring it was completely dry. She then looked up with blank, purple eyes.

"I like you as our master priest. I also like you as just a man with powerful urges. With time, I may even love you as much as I love my mistress, but that will have to be for a time in the future," Tianna said before licking the tip of his cock into her mouth.

Warmth flowed along the young man's cock as lips moved along the shaft. He could feel her tongue snaking along it, rubbing it just the right way. For Asher, he enjoyed it, but his mind began to wander to a pair of elves just in the other room.

Amber rested her arms on the edge of the metal tub. Her chin rested on her arms, seeing a sideways view of Asher standing and Tianna on her knees, his cock half buried in her mouth.

"Not many people can understand our private world. We are different, celebrating our intimacy and bonds. Some would say we are a cult, but we know, this is our life," Amber mused as she watched with interested eyes.

Lips moved along the meaty shaft as Asher drank in their words.

I feel I have been hesitant to accept this new life. Why? What am I afraid of?

Asher let the thought linger as Tianna deep-throated his member, her lips touching the hilt. When he pictured Elara, a new feeling overcame him.

I'm not afraid. I never was. For the first time in my life, I could have everything. I have to stop being a fool, and embrace this life.

Confidence surged throughout his body and spirit. The inner demons sang their approval.

Asher put his hand on the top of Tianna's head. He kept her to task, she lovingly sucking on his cock. The moment stabbed deep into him, and by pure will, thought, and desire, his cock thickened.

Tianna tasted a drop of come, and she licked at his throbbing head. She moaned with her mouth full. Her moans vibrated in her throat as spurts of molten seed struck it. She sucked it down, rewarded with a few more spurts. She slowed down, drinking his come and sucking on his thick shaft. She milked his manhood of every drop, before sliding her lips off his cock.

"You taste... divine," Tianna said with faraway eyes.

Asher let go of her head and looked at Amber.

"Tianna, help dry Amber. When you're both ready, come to bed, so we can continue the conversation," Asher commanded.

"Yes, my lord," Tianna said as she stood up onto her feet once again.

Amber watched with heated eyes as her lord, lover, and friend, left the washroom without a second glance at her. She squirmed, knowing he wanted her to follow him. She was about to get out when Tianna wrapped a towel around the back of her neck.

"The lord wants you cleaned and dry," Tianna said with soul piercing eyes before she leaned in and kissed the surprised faun.

Asher stepped out of the washroom and into the bedchamber. Cool air touched his naked skin, relief further sinking into his body. The humid heat curse was broken, the frost shard floating in its stand.

A moan to his left drew his gaze to the large bed. A smile bloomed across his features as Elara was on her back with her thighs parted. Nyn's head was buried between them. Elara's hand was on her friend's head, keeping her to task as wet sounds rose from their union.

"Taste my love for you," Elara seethed with heavenly bliss.

Nyn's eyes were close, snuggling between tender thighs and licking as Elara's engorged clit.

Asher walked to the edge of the bed and simply watched the beautiful mature elves. His cock was half-hard, but grew harder by the moment. He drank in their intimacy, seeing Elara's expression soften as tendrils of pleasure crawled up her entire body.

The blonde elf glanced over to Asher. Her eyes fluttered as Nyn licked her clit just the right way. The lurid licking continued to play as her hips moved and ground against Nyn's mouth and tongue.

"My love, show her how much she means to us," Elara whispered with closed eyes.

Asher moved around the bed and moved to the foot of it. He climbed on, seeing Nyn on her stomach. His cock grew harder, seeing her unguarded elfhood. He crawled closer until he was over her. He took hold of his cock and pressed the head to her dripping slit. Nyn moaned into Elara's valley. She whimpered as Asher's cock slowly invaded her.

73

"She has been so attentive to my needs. I thought it would only be fair to show her how much we adore her, love her," Elara said with a sultry tone.

"We do adore her," Asher said as he moved his hips slowly, wet inches sliding in and out of the prone elf.

Nyn's nerves tightened as pleasure vibrated along her soul. Not seeing, but only feeling her human lover, caused her to moan louder. She moved her hips up, giving him a better angle to plunge his staff into her. When his hips touched her plump ass, she let out a silent whimper.

Asher looked up to Elara looking at him. She licked her lips, enjoying the view of her lover fucking her best friend.

"I think... she's beginning to accept... this life," Elara said with a heavy breath.

Asher nodded as he increased the tempo, his hips striking Nyn's ass hard.

"I think, we all are," Asher said with such genuine understanding and love, it glowed.

Elara's senses caught the moment, heat filling her cheeks. Her breasts swelled as milk leaked from them. It struck her in such an intimate way, it shattered what little control she had. She threw her head back as her eyes widened. A pressure pressed on every nerve. The universe opened its arms, welcoming her to it. When she metaphorically reached for it, nerves tightened to the breaking point, before they shattered into millions of pieces.

The mature elf let out the deepest moan of her life. Strings of inner explosions rolled over her blasted nerves. Her toes curled as her eyes slid into her head. Through the dozens of euphoric orgasms, she still felt Nyn's mouth and tongue loving her. The velvet cloud deepened, not just because of her friend truly becoming herself, but also for her true lover, accepting and embracing what she knew they all felt all along.

Elara trembled and shuddered. Honey squirted into Nyn's mouth as she licked Elara's clit and drank her love. Body heat and cool air swirled to create a perfect moment of intimate happiness.

Asher's body moved with purpose. Seeing Elara and feeling Nyn overpowered his reason. He moved like a rutting beast, his urges becoming his religion. Through the haze of burning desire, and demanding urges, the young lord moved past them as he put his lips to Nyn's pointed ear.

"You are important to me, to us. Never forget it as I fuck you. Every time I take you, know that you are part of this family. Know that every time you orgasm, it's because you have many who treasure you beyond gold and gems. You are worthy of our love, just as we are worthy of you."

Nyn heard the words as her body betrayed her. Her soul opened to Asher's heat and truth. His love pushed into her with such a powerful need, she could only bend her spirit to him. Something deep within unlocked, and she let go, falling upwards to the divine light.

The elf lifted her mouth from her friend's dripping slit. Honey and love dripped off her cheeks, mouth, and chin. She leaned into his powerful thrusts, each one breaking her down, piece by loving piece. When his tempo increased, and his cock thickened within her tight inner world, the match was lit and suns exploded along her soul.

Nyn let out a soul-shattering moan as she shuddered hard. Asher's hand tightened on her hip, and he fucked her through her tidal waves of orgasms. Time lost all meaning, the elf staring at her friend from between her legs, her eyes fluttering as she was lost to her own orgasms. She felt Asher's youthful urges punishing her as she bounced from each hard thrust. It overwhelmed her, unable to tell where she was in the universe, only that she was drowning in it.

"You... have my heart," Nyn managed through the storm before she collapsed and passed out.

Asher grunted just as Nyn collapsed. His cock thickened and spurted. He pulled out and spurted a few more times, painting her back and ass with his loving lust. A groan fell from his lips, squeezing his cock with a death-grip, milking his come onto the beautiful elf under him.

The dreamy haze remained for a time, before it slowly began to clear. Asher blinked as he looked down on the elves before him. Elara was breathing hard with closed eyes. Nyn was the same under him, lost to spirals of paradise.

The young lord rose up to his knees, still stroking his cock to the beautiful elves. The hunger had abated, but after a few moments, it clawed its way back. Soreness was quickly washed away as blood once again filled his cock.

When Asher's gaze fell upon Elara's full, leaking breasts, he licked his lips. He moved over Nyn and to Elara's side. He closed his lips on her leaking nipple, and began to suck.

Milk and mana spilled down his throat. It further revitalized him, but it was tender affection between them that truly fueled him. He put his arm across her stomach, and held her hip. He kept her close, sucking on her precious milk.

The washroom door opened, Amber and Tianna stepping out. Amber let out a sigh of relief as cool air touched her damp skin and fur. The faun looked down on the tangled bodies of Asher, Elara, and Nyn. Heat crawled up her neck as she climbed onto bed, behind Asher. The faun reached around and took hold of his wet member, stroking it slowly as he drank from Elara's tit.

Tianna looked down on the four of them. The lich apprentice stared with unblinking eyes, seeing beyond normal sight. She saw the bonds between the four of them glow brighter, deeper. Knowledge cascaded over her mind, knowing there was no way, magically or otherwise, to create such a deep bond. It was nearly supernatural as she felt a tingling within. Wetness surged into her one-piece between her thighs. She took hold of her outfit, pulling the straps down over her shoulders and snaking her hips out of it. The piece of clothing fell to the floor, the woman stepping out of it, one leg at a time.

Tianna crawled onto the bed. She moved close to Amber. While the faun was stroking her master, Tianna moved her hand around the faun's furry hip and made her way down to her slit. Fingers explored her pink folds, until they grazed her clit.

Amber whimpered as Tianna ran a finger around her clit, before gently massaging it.

"Serve him well, as I pleasure you," Tianna whispered to the faun.

Amber's eyes half-closed, feeling her lord's throbbing cock in her hand as Tianna massaged her yearning clit.

Elara's eyes fluttered as she returned to her body. A tingling touched her right nipple. The muddy pleasure slowed her senses, feeling lips and tongue on her before Asher came into focus. Tender body heat glowed as she gave her lover a loving, sultry smile.

Asher licked and sucked on her swollen breast. Every drop was nirvana. Feeling Amber gently stroke him only added to the moment. A fever took root, pushing Asher's needs to the surface again. He let go of the elf's nipple and looked at her with dreamy eyes.

"I felt it, all of it," Elara whispered.

"As did I," Asher said with a low, loving tone.

The couple stared into each other's eyes, knowing they'd reached a deeper point between them that could no longer be denied. It was beyond simple love, chains anchoring their souls to each other.

From between Elara's parted legs, Nyn stirred. The mature elf lifted her head, dazed eyes staring at Asher and Elara. A small, genuine smile formed, like a weight was taken off her soul. She was up on her knees with her hands touching the bed and holding up her upper body.

Asher and Elara looked at the dazed elf. Elara slid away from Asher and beckoned with her hand. Asher did the same. Nyn crawled between them, turned, and fell onto her back. The man and elf moved closer, their hands on her, sliding along her smooth skin. Asher squeezed one of her leaking breasts, while Elara slid her fingers and hands down her warm, inner thigh. Amber continued to stroke Asher, the head of his cock touching Nyn's other thigh.

Nyn basked in their touch and body heat. She writhed as a mix of wetness and come dripped from her slit.

"Lord Blackwood, I believe this one will need extra care," Elara said with a wicked smirk.

"I believe she does. What should I do with her, Lady Blackwood?"

Elara squirmed at the title, running a finger along Nyn's clit. The dark blue-haired elf let out her own sultry gasp.

"Anything that will show her how important she is to us," Elara said with a loving whisper.

Nyn gasped as Asher licked at her leaking nipple. Her lips parted as she felt Asher close his mouth over her nipple and began to suck. Pleasure flooded her as Elara closed her lips around Nyn's other nipple. The tingling pleasure only grew as Asher and Elara had their hands between her thighs, the pair rubbing her clit.

Intimate sensations blasted her nerves to glass as she was trapped between them. She let out a heated gasp, bodies close and mouths sucking on her nipples. Her soul slipped down their throats as her moans grew louder.

For Elara, feeling and tasting her friend swirled along her senses. Love glowed as she knew her friend would stay by her side. The three of them would love each other in such a way, bordered upon dreams and fantasy.

For Asher, his heart glowed so brightly along his spirit, his feelings would never dim for the two, mature elves. Their trio had reached such heights of intimacy, there was no way to return unchanged from it. The horizon glowed with more sensual adventures, and deeper connections. It was enough to shatter his willpower as he drank her milk.

Amber stroked her lord, feeling his cock thicken in her hand. She let out her own moan, feeling the ecstasy from everyone on the bed. She let out a low moan, feeling herself closer to climax as Asher's cock readied to spurt his love.

The moment struck, and the faun moaned loudly as thick ropes of come spurted from Asher's cock and onto the fingers massaging Nyn's clit and down her inner thigh.

Nyn let out a euphoric moan as she closed her eyes. A tear formed and slipped down as pleasure rolled through her entire body.

Tianna stared as she felt the faun orgasm to her touch. Something shifted in her own soul, and she basked in it.

***

The bedroom was dark, except for small shafts of starlight penetrating the window and touching the floor with a celestial glow.

Blyss was on her side on her bed. Across from her, Paasha was on her side, looking at the beautiful goblin. The pair were each wearing one of Asher's long shirts, as they listened to moans from the master bedchamber.

Blyss's heart yearned to join them, but she held back. The clan mother wished to speak, and speak they must.

"Our clan must be stronger," Paasha said in broken common.

Blyss looked down on the bed in thought.

Paasha moved closer with an understanding and loving gaze on the goblin. "He make wonderful clan father, but he no take Nuha and Keefa. He need to make us strong. Choose you as chieftess. He, chief of goblin Blackwood Clan."

"Lady Elara should be chieftess," Blyss said with worried eyes.

"She not goblin," Paasha said matter of fact.

"Asher not goblin," Blyss said.

Paasha touched Blyss's cheek with motherly understanding. "Lord Blackwood is strong. Clan must be strong."

Blyss's large green ear drooped, as her other ear was mashed against the pillow. Her heart swirled with uncertainty, unsure if she was ready to be chieftess.

"You strong. You be great chieftess. Must speak to clan father. Tell him. We support you. We love you."

Blyss turned away from Paasha and stared at nothing. The motherly goblin moved closer, putting her hand over Blyss's stomach. Body heat glowed between the two goblins.

Blyss closed her large, oval eyes, as her heart beat with an edge of worry about their future, and their new clan.

Chapter 6

Passion for a New Day

Dreamy sleep drained away. Asher opened his eyes to a blend of cool air and warm body heat. As he stirred, he quickly noticed arms and legs across his body. He was on his back as he turned his head from side to side, seeing that he was between Elara and Nyn. The pair of elves were close, snuggled to him as they slept soundly.

Asher lifted his head just enough to look at the rest of the bed. Amber and Tianna were nowhere to be seen. When he looked at the mostly closed curtains, shafts of sunlight beamed into the bedchamber.

When Asher's head fell back onto the bed, he let out a cleansing exhale. Memories of the night swam along his waking thoughts. The passion, love, and lust they all felt was primal, needed, and wanted. The young lord lost count to the many orgasms, which he was fine with. It was less about the count, and more about the connection and bonds they all felt.

A dreamy image of Nyn filled his mind's eye, seeing her letting down her inner walls as they spent more than once in intimate embraces. Another image pressed on his mind, seeing the joy in Elara's eyes as they were getting closer, without pretense, or disguised as simple lust. The fantasies fell to the background, as they shared their bodies and their sultry, joyful heated moments.

A flutter beside the young lord drew his gaze. He looked over to Nyn's icy blue gaze as she snuggled close to him.

"Good morning," Asher smiled.

"Good morning," Nyn said with a breathy whisper.

Her hand moved down his chest, along his stomach, and touched his morning wood. Her fingers wrapped around it like it was her favorite toy, and began stroking him. Asher let out a soft exhale, enjoying the morning touch.

"You were a beast," Nyn said coolly.

"I thought I was passionate?" Asher joked as his hand found her full breast and gave it a squeeze.

Milk dripped as the elf gasped. She leaned a little closer, feeling his palm as fingers pressed into her flesh. The tingling grew, as did her desires. She moved her leg over Asher's thigh, enjoying the touch of naked skin on naked skin. Milk dripped into Asher's hand as he fondled her.

Asher turned to her, the pair staring into each other's eyes as hands played with each other.

"If I stay, there will have to be agreements," Nyn whispered.

"Say your terms," Asher whispered back as his other hand touched her wet slit.

Nyn closed her eyes as he easily found her clit, and began to massage it. Swirls of bliss coiled along her nerves as she moved her hips to his touch.

"I require a place to be with my thoughts. A quiet place so I can write. Not a room, or study, but a place of my own, on the estate," the elf said with a sultry whisper.

Asher nodded as she slightly upped the tempo of her stroking.

"I'm nearly finished with my first book, but I want to write more," the elf said before a small gasp escaped her lips. "I must have assurances that I can chronicle our sensual adventures."

Asher listened as he enjoyed her experienced stroking.

"We enjoy plays, but I want private plays, between you and I. I want to explore some deeper fantasies, and I will need you to be open-minded about them."

The couple writhed to each other's touch, bodies betraying each other. They moved closer, their body heat rising.

Asher nodded. "Anything else?"

Nyn's icy blue gaze weakened. He could see she was becoming uncomfortable.

"I," she began and hesitated. "I need to know, if your feelings change for me, that I can leave, without retaliation, or manipulation."

Asher looked at her with serious eyes. "Did someone hurt you?"

Nyn looked sideways to her pillow. "It was a long time ago, but the scars remain. I gave myself to him, and he cared little for me once he had my heart. I promised, I would never let that happen again. Promise me, we'll always communicate, through the good and the difficult."

Asher's gaze softened. "I promise, and give a solemn oath, to always communicate with you, through the good and the difficult, and to your requests."

Nyn's eyes watered as her lips parted and let out a small moan. She let go of Asher's manhood and touched his hip, giving it a gentle pull to her.

"Let us seal our agreement," Nyn said with urgency.

Asher rolled onto her with his own urgent needs. The loving passion stormed as his cock touched her dripping valley entrance. With a small push of his hips, he invaded her tight realm. Inches sank into her inner world and a long moan floated up. Her arms moved under his arms. Fingernails dug into his back as he forced his way deep into her.

Asher let out his own groan as he pushed to the hilt. The pair stayed in the moment, holding onto each other for dear life. Hips moved and writhed as he made short, strong thrusts.

Elara's eyes slowly opened to Asher on Nyn. She watched as they moved with primal desires. Nyn snuggled to Asher's neck and closed her eyes. Asher moved like a caged beast, driving his love into the mature elf. The sight of them was enough for Elara to rub her thighs together. Love filled her eyes, seeing the two of them enjoy each other.

Moans began to grow between them. Nyn shuddered to every thrust. Asher looked down on her like a hungry beast. Hands glided over strong bodies.

Elara moved closer until she was right beside them. The scent of sex and bodies filled her nose as she basked in their heated embrace. Her hand moved to her own elfhood, making slow circles around her clit before rubbing it directly. Asher and Nyn's passion bled into her, igniting her own flame. Hips moved as she rubbed her clit.

"You both make me so happy," Elara said with a dreamy whisper.

Asher could hardly hold back. Love pushed at his loins, wanting to spray it all over Nyn's soul. To his surprise, Nyn's eyes squinted as she bit the side of his neck. Lips sucked on his skin as teeth gnawed on his flesh. The sensations pulled at him, his cock thickening and ready to release his loving affections.

Nyn was first to let out a heated moan against his neck. Her body shuddered and trembled, magical explosions laying waste to her doubts and insecurities. She let go of his neck and threw her head back, moaning deeply as she was lost to a flood of ecstasy. Her eyes fluttered as her body shuddered to Asher's strong thrusts.

Seeing Nyn lost to a flood of bliss was too much. His cock thickened, pressing her inner walls to nearly the breaking point. She moaned louder as his size opened her world. Asher grunted as thick ropes of molten seed filled her tight world. Wet inches appeared and disappeared from their union. A moment later, love leaked from their connection. Bodies slowed down as senses buzzed with feverish joy.

Elara let out her own moan, her body shuddering to her own orgasms. She watched her lovers slow down. A warm hum filled her neck as she moved against her wet, sticky fingers.

Asher huffed as he was over the beautiful elf. His eyes widened as she coiled a hand around the back of his neck, lifted her face to his, and kissed him on the lips. Tongues invaded mouths, sliding over one another. Asher stayed on top of the mature elf, his cock still buried deep within her.

"We are going to have so much fun," Elara smiled as she lazily rubbed her clit.

***

Asher stood up from the edge of the bed and turned around to face it. Elara and Nyn were still in bed, facing each other. They held each other as they talked in a hushed tone. Asher simply stood naked as he looked down on them with a light spirit.

The last hour was nothing more than sharing bodies once again. Asher, nor his inner demons, complained. A strange clarity filled his mind and spirit. There was little discussion during their trysts, but it seemed, since he got up, the two elves wanted to talk more.

Asher would have stayed with him, but half the morning was already gone. He had some plans for the day, but those plans changed after everything Nyn said. His heart swelled for Nyn and Elara, and he wasn't one to simply sit back and accept their affections. Purpose fueled him as he wanted more for them, all of them.

"It makes me so happy you want to stay," Elara said with a tear in her eye.

Nyn wiped away her best friend's tears as she fought back her own. "I couldn't leave, not after everything we've gone through."

The two elves hugged each other and blubbered in unison.

Asher's heart lifted in his chest. Elara and Nyn had many centuries of experience in their long lives, but to see them so honest, and youthful with their emotions, caused his cock to twitch and fill with blood.

Nothing will get done today.

Asher sighed as he stepped around the bed and moved to the window. He pulled back the curtain to a new day, sunlight bathing his body. He looked at the blue sky with the occasional puffy clouds floating by. His gaze fell to the trees on the east side of the farmhouse. When a hint of movement caught his attention, he focused to see Amber by the fence, talking to a taurnar woman on the other side of it.

Asher became still as he looked upon them, through the leafy trees of his property. The taurnar was barely wearing clothes, and she was fanning her neck. She had a voluptuous body. Her head had small horns, dark skin, a small snout, and black eyes. Her small tail whipped around behind her as she leaned against the fence.

Amber was standing, but was animated as her hands moved as she talked. Her back was to him, so he couldn't see her expression, but she moved like she was in good spirits.

Thoughts and memories stabbed into Asher's mind, of how the bull taurnar Jarrag Hornspear took over the property east of his, thanks to Mayor Windswell. The mayor thought it would be healthy competition to have two different milk farms beside each other. While Asher's estate produced potions and milk, the Hornspear estate produced highly prized taurnar milk. It was a delicacy, from what Asher knew, many of the wealthy elite saying it was better than normal cows' milk by many degrees. To Asher, he saw through the smoke to the fire that was Mayor Windswell causing him some kind of torment since he rejected her attempts to join the Opal Society on a united front.

The more the young lord thought about it, the more he felt unprepared for the current situation. Despite having a pair of spies in the mayor's home, he wasn't sure if they would live up to their side of the bargain. It was a calculated risk, one he had to make to give him some kind of edge, but it still wasn't enough.

Asher thought back to his former guild. The faces of friends and colleagues floated through his thoughts. In a true conflict, the young lord knew many from the guild would heed his call for assistance, but Mist Valley was not a dungeon, or kingdoms in conflict. It was a sleepy town on the border of nowhere. There were no monsters to slay, or wars to fight. He was in a small conflict between farming communities. Hardly, a war that required soldiers.

Asher looked to the side as he realized there was a way to ensure greater protection for his growing family, and the estate.

The young man stepped over to his desk, pulled out his chair, and sat down. He pulled out a piece of parchment from a desk drawer, including a small inkwell and quill. He placed them on the desk. After a small preparation, he dipped the feathery quill into the inkwell and began to write on the yellow parchment.

Elara and Nyn stopped talking and looked at Asher. Their gazes lingered on his naked back as he was hunched over, with a quill occasionally moving into view.

"We could try to tempt him back to bed?" Elara said with a wicked smile.

"I doubt he would resist," Nyn said with a rare smile.

Elara looked at her friend and grinned. "We're going to have such wonderful times together."

Nyn gave a small nod.

Asher continued to write, ignoring Elara and Nyn, because if he took a moment to listen, he would be right back in bed with them. His quill continued to move as he put his thoughts down to paper. When he was finished, and the ink dried, he folded the letter and placed it in an envelope. He then stood up and glanced down at the roll of parchments he took from the slythans the other night. It gnawed at him that the mayor was going to hold a banquet for the end of summer, but that was still weeks away.

Asher stood up and walked to his closet and dresser. He pulled out clothes for the day, a loose-fitting shirt, slightly baggy leggings, socks, and boots. He began to get dressed as the two mature elves watched him dress.

"Sigh, he's putting on clothes," Elara lamented.

"Can sex slaves do that?" Nyn said with a rare happy gleam in her deep blue eyes.

The pair giggled as Asher finished getting dressed.

"Ladies, I have a few errands to run, but you both can't stay in bed. We have an estate to run. If you're not up by the time I get back, you both will be thoroughly punished," Asher grinned.

"Ooooo, punish me, Lord Blackwood. Punish me," Elara laughed.

Asher kept his bright gaze on the pair for a moment, before tearing it away and walking toward the desk, snatching the letter, and making for the bedroom door.

The door closed behind him and he let out a frustrated exhale. If he stayed a moment longer, he would have fallen back into the bed with the elvish succubi. Their libidos were just as high as his, and he wasn't sure there was a limit to their trysts. But duty called, and the former ranger reluctantly answered it.

The young lord made his way along the corridor and down the stairs. He emerged into the common room, when a voice, and hooves, followed him. He stopped at the front door and turned to see Blyss and Fern walking to him, side by side. The goblin was wearing a simple shirt and leggings, but her eyes were as bright as her smile. The uni-goat stared at him with inhuman eyes, her golden horn glowing in the morning light.

"Master," Blyss said as her brightness dimmed into slight shyness.

"Hello my lovely Blyss," Asher said enthusiastically.

The goblin looked away as she moved from side to side on her small feet. Asher had never seen her act like this, seeing an almost timid side to her.

"Is anything amiss?" Asher asked.

"No master," the goblin said a little too quickly, and with a nervous smile. "I... I only wanted to tell you that everyone is fed, with extra food waiting for you, Lady Elara, and Lady Nyn."

Asher's stomach growled, but he thought to grab something in town.

Blyss's gaze fell to the letter in his hand. "You can stay and eat, and I will deliver the letter," she offered.

Asher smiled warmly. "It's okay. There are a few errands I have to run in town."

The goblin nodded as she looked at him with nervous eyes. "I can come with you."

Fern stamped a hoof in agreement.

Asher hesitated. He hoped to just go to town, run his errands, and return shortly after. Remembering what Tianna told him last night, the evening was going to be spent continuing the seductive play with Megeth, Lynette, and Tianna.

Blyss caught the hesitation in his eyes. "It's okay, master. I know you're busy. I have chores to do. But can Nuha and I go to your workshop? She wants to see where you work."

Asher's heart melted as he looked at the beautiful goblin. "Sure. And just so we're clear, no place is off-limits, except for the alchemy lab. It's only because of the sensitive nature of our work. You understand?"

Blyss nodded vigorously. "I understand."

Asher stepped closer to her as she looked up at him with wide, warm eyes.

"Blyss, you're very important to me, to all of us. I'm sorry I've been busy, but I promise to make it up to you."

Blyss lifted her arms and hugged Asher around the waist, pressing the side of her face to this stomach.

"I know, clan father," Blyss said with closed eyes.

Asher bent slightly over, and hugged her awkwardly because of their height difference.

The couple held each other as Fern stared at them in silence.

Blyss pulled away first. She sauntered to the black uni-goat, and touched her furry neck. The goblin walked toward the kitchen with Fern in tow.

Asher's heart sagged in his chest. He adored the beautiful goblin, and wanted nothing more than to take her to his bedchamber, but he had to be practical with the rest of his day. It still burned at him to not stay.

Annoyed at his own choice, he opened the door and stepped out into the hot daylight.

Asher stepped off the porch and onto the dry, dirt path. The sun beat down on him as the humid weather pulled down on his muscles. The house had some cool air within, but by early afternoon, the place would be as hot as it was outside.

We need more frost crystals throughout the house or everyone will be spending their entire day in the master bedchamber.

Asher smirked at the thought, and wasn't completely against it. When a figure appeared in the corner of his eye, he turned to face Amber as she walked toward him.

The faun was radiant as she approached him. The leafy tree blocked out part of the bright day, shafts of light touching her short, emerald green dress.

"Asher," Amber said warmly.

"Amber," Asher smiled.

The faun walked up to him and hugged him tight.

"I had so much fun last night," she whispered in his ear.

"As did I," the young lord squeezed her close.

When they parted from their embrace, Amber's gaze fell to the dark welt on Asher's neck.

"Oh! Someone marked you. Was it me? It's hard to remember everything from last night."

Asher rubbed his neck where Nyn bruised him this morning. "Nyn was a little rambunctious this morning."

Amber looked at the Asher with a sly gaze. "I completely understand. It's hard to resist when in the throes of passion."

The faun glanced down at the letter in Asher's hand. "Going into town?"

The young man nodded. "Yes, just to run a few errands."

"I'll take care of the potion brewing this morning. I have so much energy, I feel like I can take care of the entire estate myself. Take your time. We will have everything in order."

The faun moved a little closer and looked up into Asher's eyes with a seductive edge. "I know you must tend to Megeth tonight, but I will do anything to become your next acolyte. If you need me to aid you, I will be happy to be at your side."

Asher looked at the hungry sultry eyes of the faun, and deeply considered it.

"I will let you know," he smiled.

Amber licked her lips. "In the meantime, there is plenty of lich, goblin, elf, and my milk to brew into potions. I will be downstairs for most of the day, if you need me."

"Noted," Asher grinned, before he remembered what he saw from his window a little while ago.

"Amber, were you talking with one of the taurnar from the Hornspear farm?"

The faun nodded. "Yes. Iska is very nice, and we were simply talking about the weather while staying cool in the shade. We didn't discuss anything about each other's farms. I know to keep everything a secret. It was just nice to commiserate about the oppressive heat. It if continues, I might have to spend the rest of the summer in your bedchamber."

Concern slipped into Asher's eyes.

"Please be careful when interacting with anyone on the Hornspear farm. I don't want to give them any excuse to hate, or spy on us, if they are not doing that already."

"I know. This kind of business can bring the worst out in some. I will keep any conversations light, and pleasant. It might be nice to show them that we mean them no harm."

Asher nodded. "Alright. I'll be back in an hour or two."

"Have fun," the faun said as she gave him a big hug.

When Amber pulled away, she sauntered to the front porch of their shared home.

"It's starting to be a good day," Asher whispered to himself as he watched her go inside the home and close the door.

The young lord turned away from the house and walked to the gate. He let himself out and made his way east to Star Fall in the short distance.

The sun was merciless as he walked. For Asher, he knew it was only a matter of time before he started to sweat. He tried to think cool thoughts as he walked along.

When he passed the front gate to the Hornspear estate, he looked over to see small groups of taurnar women clustered under shaded trees. Many of them looked like they were napping, while others simply talked.

On the porch of the new Hornspear house, Jarrag sat in a wide, thick chair. It was made of wood, but it looked like a throne on his porch. His massive, bull-like form fit perfectly within the sturdy chair. A ring hung from nostrils, as thick braids framed his snout and face.

The taurnar looked at Asher, and his brow made a hard, wrinkled V. He let out an agitated huff as he saw the Lord of Blackwood walking by.

Asher thought to wave, but decided against it. The taurnar wasn't pleased to have his farm next to his, the mayor giving him a false pretense about buying land in Mist Valley. The fame of Asher's uncle didn't sit well with the taurnar for some reason, and instantly disliked Asher for taking over the farm.

The former ranger simply looked ahead and kept walking.

He reached the edge of town, seeing that Dina's construction shop was open. He mentally noted to stop by with ideas for future estate projects.

A short time later, he entered Star Fall, and it was abuzz with activity. The townspeople were all out, enjoying the summer day. Some residents waved to the young lord. It still astounded him that the people were still friendly with him, despite word getting out that he had a demon on his estate. Even after he killed demon assassins meant for Katriss, they still treated him normally.

Asher noticed the Drunken Seahorse was open, people going in for an early morning drink.

He walked along Main Street, until he reached the town's only raven tower. There were no ravens perched on the top of it, Asher figuring they were sheltering inside from the sun and heat.

Asher walked into the Raven's Flight entrance at the base of the tower. Inside, cool air washed over him. It was a simple chamber, with a counter desk in front of him. To his right was a shelf with cubby holes, some filled with letters. To his left, a bulletin board with parchments for the Summer's Dusk Banquet pinned to it.

A door opened from behind the counter, and a woman with black and white clothes stepped out. She smiled as she looked at Asher.

"Welcome Lord Blackwood! How can I help you today?" Maggie Raveneye greeted him

Asher approached the counter, and lifted the letter into view. "Thank you. I have a letter that must be sent by raven to Summer Spire. It's addressed to someone in my former guild."

Maggie nodded. "I can send it later today. It's quite a distance, taking about three to four days. Maybe a little longer in the heat. The ravens don't like humid weather.

"But the raven towers in Summer Spire are a well-known route for most ravens across Valoria. It shouldn't be much trouble. Five copper pieces will be the price."

Asher lifted an eyebrow. He reached into his pocket and pulled out a gold coin.

"I wasn't sure how much it would cost," he shrugged.

Maggie smiled. "It's alright. I can give you back change, or hold onto it to pay for future letters until it is used up. You're not the only one in town with a heavy purse," she laughed.

Asher nodded in slight embarrassment. It still took some getting used to his growing wealth and influence.

The young lord handed over the letter and coin. Maggie took it and made sure the letter was sealed.

"Do you want a letter back, saying the letter was delivered? It will only cost another five copper pieces."

"Yes, thank you," Asher smiled.

"I'll get this out right away," Maggie said, turned around and headed into the back.

Asher let himself out of the shop, happy to send the letter, but nervous about the response. He pushed it from his mind as he strolled out onto Main Street.

A door slammed shut in the small distance. Asher turned to see a woman with glasses hastily rushing out from the Book Guild. She charged down to the street, and bolted toward him.

Asher smiled as Nadia ran toward him like her hair was on fire. She had a satchel at her hip and wide eyes. He walked toward her as she ran toward him. Her foot didn't clear the edge of a cobblestone on the cobblestone street. Her eyes widened as she flailed forward. Asher darted to her with his arms out, catching her halfway into her fall.

The book shop owner looked up at him with wide, happy eyes from behind her glasses.

"If you're free, let's have a drink!" the clumsy book shop owner said quickly.

Asher held her as he looked at her with amused eyes.

"Sure," he said with a happy smile.

Chapter 7

A Sultry Proposal

The Drunken Seahorse was strangely busy as Asher and Nadia walked in, side by side. The bar was partially filled with locals enjoying an early afternoon drink. A bard played a soothing tune in the corner. Light spilled in from high windows, and the murmur of conversation filled the local drinking hole with a comfortable white noise.

Cool air touched Asher's features as he stepped in. Glancing to a high shelf on a wall, a frost crystal hovered in a metal stand, similar to the one he crafted with Nyn. Realizing that the bar tavern was cool, and serving cool drinks, it was apparent to the ranger why the place was filled with bodies so early in the day.

Bolla stood behind the oval bar in the middle of the place, pushing a large mug into a local's hand. Her golden blonde braid swung behind her head as she smiled and laughed at a small humorous tale she overheard. The dwarf turned her gaze to the lord and book shop owner as they walked in. Asher caught a glimpse of a knowing smile on the dwarf's lips as she shyly looked away.

"Let's get a booth," Nadia said as she grabbed Asher's hand and pulled him with her.

The young lord stumbled after her, forgetting that the book shop owner was stronger when she was excited.

The pair sat down at a booth as the bard's mandolin continued to play a soothing tune.

Asher looked at Nadia, the shop owner looking around with excited eyes, before her gaze met his. A pink glow touched her pale cheeks as her eyes took a warm gleam. She reached across the worn table, her palm up. Asher lifted his hand and placed it on hers. Fingers curled together as a relaxed sigh fell from her lips.

"It's good to see you again," Nadia began, her voice above a whisper. "I know you're very busy, but when I saw you, I couldn't resist racing out to you."

"It's good to see you too," Asher said warmly. "I wish I had more time to come to your shop. The estate library is sparse, and I wanted to fill it with more books. Not just black books, but I do want a dedicated shelf to those kinds of books."

"I'm sure we can come to some kind of arrangement," Nadia said with a happy glow.

A shadow touched the edges of their gazes. The pair turned to Bolla as she stood at the edge of the booth table.

"Can I help you this fine summer day?" the dwarf asked with interested eyes.

"Two cold ales," Asher said before he caught himself. "If that's something you want to drink, Nadia?"

The book shop owner nodded. "Yes, I would love a cold ale."

Bolla nodded. "Any food? I can have the cook whip something up?"

Asher parted his lips as his stomach growled. He was in such a hurry to deliver the letter this morning, he forgot to get any food. His stomach growled again, angry with his lack of focus.

"Yes, food would be great. What do you suggest?"

Bolla smiled. "We have a fresh catch today. Fished it myself. We also have cut potatoes cooked in oil. It's a new dish, one I like to call fish and chips. Many of the locals seem to really like it."

"MMMmmm," Nadia cooed.

"Two plates then," Asher nodded.

Bolla bowed slightly. "As you will, Lord Blackwood."

The dwarf turned around and marched to the kitchen door in the back of the tavern bar.

"Bolla loves to fish, almost as much as he loves the sea," Nadia mentioned.

"I've met dwarves, but never one that liked the sea. They don't even like deep lakes," Asher smiled.

"Bolla is an enigma. She founded this tavern when she first arrived. She sank every gold coin into it, saying it was where she wanted to be. I think she wishes she could be out on the sea, but being close to it is enough for her. She never talks about her life before arriving at Mist Valley. If anyone questions her, she simply states it was another life, and changes the subject."

Asher felt distant memories crawl along the edges of his mind. "Mist Valley seems like a place for many to escape the rest of the world. Not that I'm complaining. It is starting to feel very much like home."

"You don't know how happy that makes me feel," Nadia grinned.

A comfortable silence filled the space between them.

Nadia looked down. "You may have guessed, I didn't just want to have a drink."

Asher leaned forward a little with amused eyes. "False pretenses? How scandalous."

Nadia let out a sharp, happy laugh. Asher smiled, the book shop owner's mood infectious.

"You are fresh air to my soul," Nadia said honestly as she looked into the young lord's eyes. "I can't stop thinking about that rainy day. It haunts me, how you fought off attacking goblins. How much Blyss, and the others look to you."

Nadia looked away with heat in her cheeks. "How you let me join you to aid new visitors to the farm. I have kept it secret, and will never tell anyone. I understand what it means to lead a secret life."

Asher's interest was piqued. "A secret life? You have my attention," he said playfully.

Nadia became shy once again. The young lord could see her internal battle play out in her eyes. She was struggling with something, and was trying to find a way to say it out loud.

When Nadia parted her lips to speak, two frothy ales were placed on the table between the pair.

"Enjoy," Bolla said as she turned away.

Asher caught the tiny moment of the dwarf glancing at him before she walked back to the bar.

Nadia snatched up her ale and brought it to her lips. She tilted her head back and gulped down a few mouthfuls before pulling it away to inhale. Asher took a long sip, knowing he had an empty stomach and didn't want it to go to his head.

Nadia seemed to gather her courage as she stared at the handsome young lord before her.

"I normally close the shop in the latter half of summer, and reopen in early fall. I tend to take trips to nearby cities or towns, just to appreciate what I have here in Mist Valley. But since you arrived, I think I want to do something different this year."

Asher took another sip as he listened patiently.

Nadia took a deep breath and let out a long exhale.

"I want to stay on your farm, as a special guest," Nadia confessed.

Asher lifted an eyebrow at the word "special guest."

Nadia continued, "As I said, I can't stop thinking about that night. I... opened up in a way I only felt in my fantasies. I've read a lot of books, too many to count. I have my favorites, the ones I read over and over again, but after that night, those same books that made me happy, simply didn't satisfy me."

She looked at Asher with bright, wanting eyes. "When I was younger, I never fit in. I know I'm clumsy, and many have used it as a means to belittle me. I felt different and odd most of my life, but when I was with you, and on that magical farm, I felt normal. I felt like I belonged.

"I want to be a guest on your farm, but not a normal one," Nadia said and then opened the flap to her satchel.

Asher watched as she rummaged through her satchel. She took hold of something and pulled her hand out. In it were two, thin, black books. She placed them on the table, between their mugs of ale, and slid them closer to the young lord.

Asher picked them up and looked them over. They were both black, with gold lettering for the titles. One read, "Silence," while the other one read, "The Mithril Heart."

"Silence is a new book, one I wanted to share with you and some of the ladies on the Blackwood Estate. Nyn told me in passing that she was looking for a new story to read, so this is a gift to you and your farm.

"The Mithril Heart is one I wanted to share with you. It has been around for many years, but it is one of my favorites. It is a tale of a milk farm, but the lord running it, Lord Drex, is a much darker character than many books I've read."

Asher saw the glow of excitement in Nadia's eyes as she continued.

"He tells every woman who comes to his farm that he is their new master. The moment they stepped onto his property, they became his property. He has them sign contracts with lengths of time of their stay. He is honest with telling new guests that his farm is a cult, worshiping the dark side of the Divine Mother. All must pay a tithe of milk and honey. He is their dark lord, and they are his slaves. They must do as he says, or the price of honey is doubled.

Nadia looked away as heat crawled up her neck. "Honey is intimacy, if you understand?"

"I understand," Asher said as he listened with attentive senses.

Nadia nodded. "He doesn't hurt them in sadistic ways, but they are his prisoners. He rewards the eager, and chains up the ones that resist. He calls the guests his pets. If a pet says no, he makes them watch as he takes others in front of them and rewards them. Those who resist are forced to... climax, many times. When they give in, he treats them like they are special, with loving words, and gentle caresses."

Nadia blanked out as pink skin glowed from her cleavage, neck, and cheeks. She then picked up her ale and took another long drink, before putting the mug back down on the table.

"I'm sorry. It's very hot in here."

Asher chuckled. "It's okay. I'm getting a little hot as well."

Nadia looked at him with a sly gaze. "I don't know if anyone else on your farm may be into it, but I would be happy to live that life for a time. I've never truly trusted anyone with such a fantasy, but after that night at your home, you're the only one I can trust with my favored fantasy."

Asher kept his gaze on the beautiful book shop owner with glasses.

"Nadia, just to be clear, the farms are not those stories. I know, the Opal Society puts out those stories to entice women to give milk to create potions. From what Elara, Nyn, and others on the farm have told me, the connection they feel to the Divine Mother, after taking the elixir, is like a sacred and humbling experience. An experience that can change how you feel, and see the world. As much as I enjoy the work, I don't want to set a false expectation."

Nadia smiled warmly. "I know. It's something I have thought about a long time, and now feel ready to explore. I like you, Asher. I like you a lot. I know your heart belongs to many on your farm, and to some in town. I'm not asking you to fulfill just my fantasy. I want to live a life I always felt I belonged to."

Nadia touched her mug, but didn't drink. She looked down on the half-full cup, her eyes taking on an understanding gleam.

"I always felt different from the rest of the world. I relate to the monsters, the outcasts. For a time, I want to let my monster out. I want to surrender it to you. I know I'm asking a lot, but for the first time in my life, I feel like I am actually free. I want to be free with my mind, and my body. I want to live like one of the monsters, giving into my urges."

Nadia blinked and fear filled her eyes. "Oh, I'm sorry. I didn't mean to say so much! I wanted it to ease into it, maybe over wine, or dinner. I must be a fool in your eyes."

Asher reached across the table and took her hand into his. He clasped it tight, holding her panicked attention.

"Nadia, I can be good with secrets too, and I am honored that you told me. As for what you're asking, I'm willing, but the rest of the household must know. We do have sensual plays, where we play parts from shared fantasies. Considering what we've performed so far, your play may be welcomed. Even if it isn't considered, you and I can live this fantasy."

Asher smiled with understanding eyes. "I like you, Nadia. But as you may know, I have deep, and hungry appetites."

Nadia nodded feverishly. "I know. I felt it. It consumes you, and I want to receive your lustful wrath."

Asher felt his manhood begin to harden under the table. His own demons licked their lips as they listened to Nadia. Remembering her touch, and moans, caused blood to drain from his mind.

"I'm wet just thinking about you," Nadia said with a very low, whisper.

The mood took on a rosy hue as the pair looked at each other with lustful eyes. Asher could not deny the attraction between them, turning into another log on the blaze of his demonic urges. A calm acceptance flowed over his soul, further proving this life was the life he truly craved. It clawed at him, wanting to read the books she gave him, and then seeing how their play would act out.

"One night soon, I will come to your estate. I want you to let me in. Prepare a simple contract for thirty days. I will sign it. After that, I am yours to do as you please. I will pay with milk and honey. I will beg, but only for you to treat me like a slave. I won't say no. I will never say no."

"Is there something that will take it too far? I don't want to sour our relationship," Asher asked with the last drop of clarity he had.

"Bruise me, mark me, like the one on your neck, but don't cut me. I want to earn my way to your heart. I want to be your prized pet. I want you to be my monster lover, and master."

Asher rubbed his neck with his other hand, feeling the tender bruise from Nyn's overzealous sucking.

"We have an agreement," Asher said with a low tone.

Nadia smiled brighter, when a pair of plates were put on the table. The sudden movement shocked the pair out of their sultry exchange, and turned their gazes to Bolla as she stood by the booth table.

"Your meals. Enjoy," the dwarf said with a smile.

Asher had to fight off the foggy haze filling his mind. His manhood was rock hard, and he was thankful for the table hiding it. Nadia squirmed in her seat as a flustered heat filled her eyes.

"Let's enjoy our meal and talk a little more," Asher said.

"Yes, let's enjoy our meal," Nadia said with a faraway voice, her mind lingering on their spoken contract and adventure to come.

***

Asher walked down the street, heading for the west side of Star Fall. He walked with a lazy gait. His eyes were half-closed as a calm feeling flowed over him, despite the dreadful sun.

The meal and drinks with Nadia went for over an hour. Despite eating, the drink still went to his head. He was as relaxed as molasses as he parted from the happy book shop owner. Their conversation was enlightening, interesting, and fun. The pair enjoyed it, often laughing very loudly a few times. When they parted, Asher had a new level of respect for Nadia. She overcame her shyness to discuss what she wanted. It was enough for the young lord to entertain her proposal, and their agreement.

In his hand were two black books.

Time moved in unusual waves. Asher blinked and he found himself at the edge of town. His gaze was drawn to Dina's shop. He quickly turned and walked towards it. As he stepped closer, he saw a carriage with a pair of horses in front of the shop. A driver sat in the coach chair, staring at nothing.

Asher walked past them, not bothering to give them a second glance. His heart yearned to see Dina, and maybe speak to her about some new projects for the farm. When he reached the door, his hand nearly missed catching the handle. He took hold and pulled, a bell sounding off.

The young lord walked into the cool shop to see Dina speaking with a man. A slythan woman was not far from the man. Asher's gaze was drawn to her, seeing a maid's uniform dress. It was blue and white, her head covered with a flowery hood.

When she glanced at him, the young man sobered up. It was just a glance, but there was a pain in her slitted eyes before she looked away to a window.

The man speaking to Dina turned his head and smiled at Asher.

"Lord Blackwood! So good to see you on this hot, summer day," the man said with a cheery tone.

Asher gave Lord Roland Windswell a small, polite smile. Memories crashed into him from when he first arrived. How the Lord and Lady Windswell tried to convince him to work together, so he could sponsor them to join the Opal Society. It went as far as Lady Windswell offering her body, and Lord Windswell encouraging her to do it, so they could secure a relationship. Asher declined, which inflamed Lady Windswell's vindictive wrath.

Much to Asher's surprise, he heard and saw little of Lord Windswell. It was apparent from the start, Lady Windswell held the reins of their relationship.

"Greetings Lord Windswell. Greetings Dina," Asher said as he approached.

"Please, please, call me Roland. We may have titles and wealth, but no need for us to be strangers."

Asher caught Dina rolling her eyes from behind Roland as he stood before the tall man.

Roland was six feet, three inches tall. He only had a few inches on Asher, not that he cared. Asher knew, a person's worth was not their title or wealth, but their honor and kindness. Roland acted like any wealthy person Asher encountered on his travels, entitled and blind to anyone deemed beneath them. The young lord didn't want to judge too harshly, not knowing the man very well. He hoped Roland was the nicer side to the Windswell family.

Roland continued as he turned slightly to see Dina as well. "One of our frost crystals faded away, and needed replacing. Despite the cool wind off the ocean, our estate has experienced some this oppressive heat. The sheep and cattle have had a difficult time of it lately.

"I didn't want to leave all the work to the help. I too, enjoy coming into town to see my favorite people," Roland winked at Dina.

The shop owner simply smiled.

Asher held his tongue, never realizing that frost crystals were sold here.

Dina slid a small, wood box across the counter to Roland. "Are you sure you only need one?"

Lord Windswell gave a hearty nod. "Yes, one will do. The crystals we have are much larger, and last for much longer. I think one of them was defective, and wore away much sooner than anticipated. I'm sure my wife will have harsh words with our resident mage. Something I have no desire to get in the middle of."

The lord turned to Asher with knowing eyes. "I know of the ongoing feud between you and my wife. I have no part in it. It's a small town, and everyone already knows how she can be. Take solace in knowing her anger burns out. With time, she will move on from her petty jabs at you, onto something else more interesting."

Asher was slightly stunned at how open Lord Windswell was with discussing his wife's attitude.

"I look forward to that day. I wish no trouble for anyone within Star Fall and Mist Valley."

"As do we all," Roland winked. "I do hope you come to the Summer Dusk Banquet. There will be plenty of food, drinks, and music. Most of the town comes out to enjoy it. It is one of the celebrations I enjoy the most. A fitting farewell to summer, and welcoming autumn, as it were."

Roland picked up the small box and held it in his hand.

"I bid you both a good day. Stay cool," Roland said with a cheery grin.

Asher and Dina watched as the tall man walked over to the slythan servant.

"I'm finished here. Let us take our leave," the tall lord put his arm out.

The slythan curled her arm around his, but she kept her head bowed. Asher spotted her dark green lips, not hidden by the robe. It stunned him, for he didn't know any slythans to have lips before. She didn't look at him again as the pair walked toward the front door, opened it, and stepped out.

Asher and Dina watched as the pair made it to the carriage. The driver was holding open a door, Roland aiding the slythan maid to step into the carriage. He followed, and the driver closed the door behind him.

Asher's gaze fell to the corner of the shop, seeing a metal ring stand with a floating blue crystal within it.

Dina let out a soft exhale. "The man is insufferable."

Asher turned to the beautiful shop owner as she seemed to relax.

"He talks and talks, boasting about stories and experiences. If you didn't come in, he would have been here another hour."

"It's good I stopped by," Asher smiled.

Dina looked as the handsome lord and her own features relaxed. "How can I help the Lord of Blackwood?"

"We've missed you. Or better yet, I've missed you," Asher smiled.

Dina's eyes gleamed with desire. "I've missed you, and everyone else on the farm. I have been so busy with projects, preparing some buildings and homes for the colder seasons. Despite the protective mountains of the valley, sea air and harsh winters affect everyone here. Some have started early, preparing storerooms. When winter strikes, the town will grind to a halt."

"Good to know. I will prepare more firewood, and ensure our stores are filled to the brim," Asher said.

"I've really missed you," Dina said again, with sorrow in her eyes. "I wish I could visit the farm, but I am leaving town tomorrow. It's a business and supply run to the city of Dranmar.

The whole journey will be a little over a week, but I doubt I will have time to simply relax.

"How's the winery and barn?"

"Well. I'm eager to use the winery, but the grape crops won't be ready until autumn. I fear for my first batch of wine, since I am still a novice. Lurking and fighting in dungeons are one thing. Brewing a good wine for others to enjoy, another thing entirely."

Dina nodded as she stepped around the counter and walked toward the shop door. She spoke over her shoulder as she stepped along.

"Strawberries are in season now. I know a farmer in Dranmar, who will be eager to offload some of his crop. On my way back, I could pick up enough strawberries for you to use the smaller vat in the winery? It may help you know what to expect, and prepare for when your grapes are ready to be harvested," Dina said as she reached the door, lifted a hand, and locked it shut.

Asher watched her as she turned around and walked back to him. When she stood before him, she lifted her arms and rested them on his shoulders, the couple gazing into each other's eyes.

"I don't normally do things like this for others, so if I were you, I would enjoy such generosity," the shop owner said with a sultry whisper.

"I do enjoy it, and am grateful. I would of course pay you for such a generous offer," Asher said warmly.

Dina leaned her body closer, pressing her chest and stomach against Asher's chest and stomach. He put his hands around her waist, the couple enjoying each other's touch.

"I also wanted to stop by to discuss the estate a little," Asher said as he leaned in and kissed her neck.

Dina let out a sultry exhale as her pulse quickened. "What does the Lord of Blackwood require of me?"

"The farmhouse is getting crowded. It has fourteen bedrooms, and they are nearly full."

"Your farm has grown popular," Dina said as Asher kissed her neck again. "There is enough room on your estate for another house. I... could draw up some simple plans with my artisans. We could have it finished before winter, if you're interested?"

"I'm interested," Asher said as the mood glowed hotter between them.

Dina curled a leg around Asher's leg, moving her body against him like a snake in heat.

The mood blazed brighter from his talk with Nadia, and now Dina. It overpowered his reason as his manhood struggled to rise to attention in his leggings.

"We can discuss a little more in the back. I can give you my full attention about the future," Dina said with a wicked whisper.

Asher simply nodded, the mood's hooks deep within his spirit. A thought struggled to the surface of his mind as Dina uncurled her leg, took his hand, and walked him toward the door behind her counter.

"Oh, do you have any more of those frost crystals and rune stands?" he asked.

"Yes, we do," Dina said as she gently pulled him into her office.

"I'll take three," Asher whispered.

Dina simply nodded as she lowered to her knees with Asher reaching back and pushing the office door closed.

Chapter 8

A Dark History

Asher stepped out of Dina's shop with two metal stands in one hand, a stand and two black books in the other, a wood box stuffed in the top part of his leggings, and a smile on his face.

The sun beat down on him the moment he was outside, but the good feelings remained as he walked down the dirt path to the main road and headed home. Intimate moments washed on the shores of his mind, Dina more than happy to please him before he pleased her. Moans and naked bodies curled along Asher's thoughts as he walked without a tense muscle on his body.

I'm going to miss her.

Dina was only going to be gone for over a week, but the young lord was already missing her before today. With such a busy schedule, and spending time with all the women he loved, for a brief moment, he wondered if it was all too much.

No. This life is not too much.

Asher chuckled to himself as he walked. Thinking about everyone at home caused blood to pool once again in his member. The urges began to awaken once again, and the former adventurer and ranger kept his brilliant smile.

When he reached the corner fence of the Hornspear Estate, Asher's smile dimmed. Senses drank in his surroundings, and when he glanced over, he saw the larger taurnar stand up from his porch, and make his way down to the dirt path.

Asher slowed his pace as the hulking Jarrag made a beeline for his fence. When the taurnar reached it, he put a large hand on a post and vaulted over. Hooves hit the ground, a small cloud of dust and dirt billowing up. The taurnar folded his large arms and waited with a menacing stare.

Asher approached the taurnar and stood before him. He looked up at his horned head, small snout, and angry eyes, not intimidated by his obvious displeasure about some perceived slight.

"Good afternoon, Jarrag. You don't have to vault over the fence, unless your gate isn't working," Asher said plainly with his hands full.

"The gate is working fine," the taurnar huffed. "I wanted to give you a warning, keep your people from talking to my people."

Asher stood his ground as he looked at Jarrag with cool eyes.

"Even if I told them to stop, they will do as they wish."

Jarrag's eyes narrowed. "You can't keep your women in line? Pathetic."

"Keep them in line? I'm not out here threatening you about your women's behavior. We're neighbors, and I don't see anything wrong with being neighborly."

Jarrag's dark eyes filled with distilled rage. "You Blackwoods are all the same. Think you're higher than everyone else. I see you for what you are, and I will not tolerate it. Keep your women from speaking to mine, or I will personally do something to ensure your face never heals right again."

A raging flame burned within Asher's spirit. But his mind kept it under control, for the moment.

"You seem to have bad blood with us Blackwoods. Since we only met over a month ago, I can assume your ire is for my uncle."

Jarrag gave a single, hard nod. "Your uncle was a man who hid behind a façade. He claimed to be a man of the people, but he worked with others in secret. He was a spy, feeding information to others. His accursed farm was a hub, visitors staying for an experience, but guests who fed him, or others, secret information."

"If he was a spy, I can only assume you're angry because you, or people you knew, were rightfully caught. I doubt you have any proof. Even if you did, I care not to hear it. He's gone, and your colleagues most likely deserved what they got."

Asher's hands tightened around the metal stands in his hands. "And if we are throwing around threats, if you speak ill of my uncle again, I will be sure to not only break your horns, but your taurnar women will become my taurnar women."

The young lord watched as Jarrag's thick arms unfolded and hung at his sides. His large fists shook, not in fear, but in blind rage.

For Asher, he had encountered some Taurnar during his travels. Their horns were displays of strength and power. To break a horn, or both, was the greatest disrespect one could experience. To take their women was an equally devastating insult. Asher had no intention of taking anyone, but the threat was a means to an end, showing the taurnar bull that he was not to be trifled with.

"You step too far," Jarrag growled.

"You step too far. For better or for worse, we are neighbors. I don't know what game you and the mayor are playing, but leave me out of it. I seek a peaceful life, and I will have it, one way, or another."

Asher didn't wait for a response as he stepped around the hulking taurnar and continued to walk home. His pulse quickened as he listened intently, waiting for the taurnar to strike him from behind, but it never came. After a few dozen steps, Asher glanced over his shoulder to see Jarrag already back on his property and walking back to his farmhouse.

A sliver of relief washed over the young lord. Feuds can be deadly, and Asher certainly didn't want any more Mist Valley blood on his hands. His wandering adventures had come to an end, and his new adventures as a lord had just begun.

Still, questions lingered as he approached the front gate to his estate. He pondered about his uncle and secret dealings he may have had. He also wondered if Jarrag was hinting at a deeper history. He knew next to nothing about the taurnar, only that he was invited by the mayor to purchase property next to his farm. During that first encounter, Jarrag appeared displeased with having a neighbor, especially a Blackwood. Now that Jarrag revealed that people he knew were affected by his uncle's dealings, if it were true, only added more questions.

Asher used his pinky to open the gate lock. He stepped in and kicked the gate closed with his boot.

A memory swirled along his mind, of the time he used Megeth's milk to spirit walk and visit his uncle in the spirit realm. He relived the moment of his uncle's death, fighting sea serpents as the guests, crew, and his lovers, made their escape.

The serpents never went after the fleeing boats. They stayed to fight his uncle, and eventually, killed him.

The memory pulled at Asher's spirit. His uncle explained that he did make some enemies. The young lord wondered if Jarrag, and people the taurnar knew, were among those enemies?

The front door opened and Amber stepped out. The faun was drenched, sweat darkening her short, green dress. But her eyes were wide, focused on the metal stands in Asher's hands.

"Thank the Divine Mother!" the faun leapt off the porch, landed, and darted for Asher.

Asher smiled as sweat dripped down from his own temple. The heat of the day, and the exchange with Jarrag, made him so hot, he felt like he was going to melt. Amber took two ring stands from Asher and held them to herself like they were worth their weight in gold.

Elara stepped out of the house and looked at Asher and Amber as they approached. She smiled, as her thin, white dress began to have sweaty dark spots.

"I'm happy you brought new stands. The house is unbearably hot, and many of us were tempted to simply stay in the bedchamber," the mature elf said with a weak smile.

Asher stepped up to the beautiful elf, and gave her a quick kiss on the lips. Just as he pulled away, Amber pushed past them and back into the house.

"Quickly! Activate the frost crystals or I'm going to perish in the heat!" the faun shouted with a crazed tone.

Asher and Elara stepped back into the house. Nyn was on a couch, fanning herself with her hand.

Asher placed a stand down by the fireplace. He placed the two black books on the coffee table, and reached for the wood box at his waist. He pulled it out and opened it. Three dark blue crystals were inside, perfectly arranged. He picked one up and placed it in the center ring of the rune stand. No magical words or incantations needed, as the crystal hovered in the middle of it.

Amber stared at the crystal, pleading with her eyes for cooler air. After a short moment, tendrils of misty, cool air began to bleed from the floating crystal. Amber fell to her knees before it, letting out an exhale of relief as chilly air washed over her.

"I had no idea Dina sold these, or I would have bought them sooner," Asher remarked.

"It will save us the trouble of creating more," Elara said as she stood closer to Asher.

Nyn looked down at the two black books on the table. She picked one up and began to read.

The air in the common room grew cooler with each passing moment. It didn't take long for the temperature to lower. Relief filled eyes and bodies, the oppressive heat finally defeated for a time.

"Dina told me we should put the other two in the corridors. We can find corners for them, but that also means we have to leave all doors open to allow cool air to come in," Asher explained.

"The doors are rarely closed or locked anyway," Elara mentioned as she ran her fingers through Asher's hair. "I love when you look messy."

Asher smiled as the mature elf made sure his hair was unruly, and untamed. He then turned to the three women with curious eyes.

"Where are the goblins?"

"They went into the western woods," Amber said with relief in her eyes. "They said they were helping Nuha find more snakes for her stew."

Asher scratched at his head. "More snakes? How big is this stew she's going to make?"

Amber and Elara shrugged. Nyn continued to read.

"I believe I overheard Blyss and Nuha talking about a proper clan meal. All of them have been rather secretive lately," Elara added.

Asher nodded, not sure what any of it meant. With his entire body cooling off, he gathered his thoughts and addressed everyone in the common room with serious eyes.

"A few things happened in town, and on my way back..." Asher began before telling them what transpired with Nadia, plans with Dina, and his encounter with Jarrag.

The two elves and faun listened intently as Asher explained almost everything. Asher didn't speak about his intimate encounter with Dina, saving that for later. When he finished, Elara and Amber glanced at each other, while Nyn returned to the book.

"This is my fault," Amber sulked. "If I wasn't trying to be nice to the taurnar, Jarrag would have never approached you."

"I doubt that. Jarrag looks like a taurnar searching for any excuse for a confrontation," Elara said.

Asher looked at the beautiful elf in subdued amazement, she clearly reading his mind.

"True, but let's not further antagonize him," Asher said. "Maybe with some time, he will relax a little, and become a better neighbor. For now, let's keep a healthy distance from the taurnar. Are we in agreement?"

Elara, Amber, and Nyn nodded, Nyn still reading the book.

"We have a lot of things to prepare for," Asher began. "The farmhouse is getting crowded, and if we have more guests, we won't have many rooms to house them. That is why, a new guest farmhouse will help us greatly in the future.

"We also need to prepare the barn, and winery for Dina's return. She is going to bring back a wagon load of strawberries. Enough to brew our first batch of wine.

"In the coming week, we will need to purchase sugar, yeast, and a few more ingredients for the first batch. It will give us some experience before we harvest the grapes in the fall."

"I'm looking forward to more wine, and cooler weather," Elara said with dreamy green eyes.

Asher looked at Amber, the faun still by the floating frost crystal. "How are we with potions?"

"Our stores are nearly full. I could use some help with the remainder," the faun said over her shoulder, not moving away from the crystal.

"I'll help you with that, after putting the ring stands and frost crystals in place," Asher said as he mentally planned out his day.

"With a cooler home, perhaps we can continue with our play?" Elara asked with a wicked gleam in her eyes.

Asher approached the beautiful elf with a loving gaze. "I must tend to Megeth, Lynette, and Tianna, tonight. But after that, I don't see why we can't continue with our monastery play."

Elara put her arms on Asher's shoulders as he put his hands on her hips. The couple stared at each other with loving eyes.

Nyn glanced up to see her best friend hug their lover. She kept her cool gaze on them as they briefly brushed lips against each other before fully kissing. Hands held each other close, as if they would be pulled apart if they let go. The romantic kiss caused Nyn's stomach to flutter, as her face remained frozen with bright blue eyes.

The elf lowered her gaze to the book in her hands, drinking in every word.

Not far from the three of them, Amber moaned her relief at the cool air flowing off the frost crystal.

Chapter 9

Blessing the Dead Heart

Elara looked at the large bed with a wry smile. The bedchamber was empty, save for her. The world beyond the windows grew darker as night's cloak flowed over the valley.

The mature elf let her mind wander to the rest of the day, helping Asher place the ring stands and frost crystals in the main corridors of the home. Afterwards, she joined Asher and Amber as they made their way down to the alchemy lab and worked on potions. Happy memories danced in her mind, of when she first arrived. How she and Asher bonded, and worked together to unravel some of the mysteries of the Lac Codex and create elixirs.

To the mature elf, it felt like a lifetime ago. She reached down a little and touched the bed, her mind replaying how she and Asher climbed in and spent hours getting to know each other. Faces touched her thoughts, how their unusual family grew. How a motherly feeling took root as many in the household came to her for advice, or speak their feelings. Her old life was fading away as she embraced this new life in Mist Valley. It wasn't always roses, but the good outweighed the bad.

Elara turned and sat at the foot of the bed. Her thoughts wandered to her capture and imprisonment. How she feared she would never return to the magical farm, and the young lord she confessed her love to. When Asher came to her rescue, never before did she feel a greater love than that moment. He risked everything to save her, and that moment haunted her in a deep and loving way. In the empire, if one could not stand under their own power, mind, will, or strength, they were not worthy to be part of it. Those ideals created a society fearful of emotion and acceptance.

Elara stared at nothing, realizing shortly after arriving in Mist Valley, she was a prisoner in her old life. Laws and rules confined her spirit. When she was given a black book by a friend, it awakened something that always lurked there under her skin. A need to be free, with her mind, body, and soul. Asher was a ranger, free to explore the world. His spirit glowed, calling to her like a moth to a beautiful flame. It was the beginning to a new life, one she would enjoy every moment of, for as long as she could.

The elf sighed happily. She turned her head and glanced at the big empty bed. A short time ago, she saw Asher dressed in a black robe. He kissed her forehead, and told her he wouldn't see her until the morning. As much as she wanted to pull him into bed, she let him go, knowing his heart truly belonged to her. There was no jealousy, only a greater understanding of his urges, and her own. The thought of a confined relationship didn't sit well with her, but the relationship they all had under one roof tantalized her soul in such a way, she never experienced it before. She looked forward to him coming to bed, and her wrapping her limbs around him, or her lips around his impressive manhood. Wetness bloomed as she thought about him. It became involuntary, her needs burning for the young lord, and their found family.

A knock at the door woke the mature elf from her thoughts. "Come in," she said.

The door opened and Blyss peeked in. The goblin remained mostly hidden behind the door, her oval eyes filled with a dark shame.

"I didn't want to disturb you," Blyss said with sad eyes.

"Little heart, you know you can come in here anytime you wish. Come in and sit with me. I could use some company."

Blyss stepped into the cool room and closed the door behind her. She walked closer until she stood before Elara. Instead of sitting on the bed, the goblin knelt and bowed her head.

"Mistress, I'm sorry," Blyss said softly.

Elara touched her shoulder. Blyss lifted her large, oval eyes, and looked up at the beautiful elf.

"Has something happened?" Elara asked with concern.

Blyss's lip trembled. "I... I have been keeping a secret. I'm sorry."

Elara could see the goblin was distraught. She patted a space on the bed beside her.

"Please, sit with me. I'm here to listen," Elara said with a soothing tone.

Blyss stood up, and hopped onto the bed. She was wearing one of Asher's long, black shirts. It barely contained her voluptuous chest as she looked down in defeat.

"Speak your mind. What has you so tied in knots?"

Blyss looked up at Elara again, her eyes wet. "I… I've been keeping a secret. I don't want to hurt your feelings. I needed to tell you."

The goblin took a deep breath and let out a long exhale. She gathered her strength and began talking.

"My clan was destroyed when they tried to take me back. Clans mean safety. Paasha, Nuha, and Keefa had nowhere to go, but when master… I mean, Asher, took them in, it gave them hope. When Asher accepted Paasha as Clan Mother, he became clan father. But clan father and clan mother are different. We start a new clan, the Blackwood Clan."

The goblin looked down and made faces, trying to find the words. Elara listened patiently as Blyss let out an annoyed huff.

"Clan needs a chief… and chieftess. Asher is our clan chief and clan father. Paasha is clan mother, but not chieftess. Master needs a chieftess," Blyss said, some of her broken common coming back.

The goblin turned her wide eyes up and stared into Elara's eyes. "I wanted you to be chieftess, but our clan said no. For our protection and our bond, they want me to be chieftess."

Elara looked at the beautiful goblin with understanding eyes. "Blyss, my little heart, I understand your plight. You fear hurting my feelings. I can assure you, my feelings are not hurt."

Blyss blinked, her anxiety confusing her, unsure she understood what Elara meant.

"I didn't know goblin clans were so complicated," Elara said warmly. "But if you must become clan chieftess, I will not stand in your way."

"You... not mad?" Blyss asked with a timid tone.

"I'm not mad. I understand, your new clan must be strong. You will make a wonderful chieftess."

Blyss looked down with a heavy heart. "Clans survive by having close bonds. Not all bonds are perfect, but they help to survive in the forests. Master is strong and smart. He can protect us, and we can protect him, but a strong clan needs to be close.

"He hasn't claimed Nuha and Keefa. They worry, he doesn't want a clan."

Elara smiled brightly at the sad goblin. She placed her hand on Blyss's hand, giving it a warm squeeze.

"Asher has been busy, but he is also an honorable man. He won't simply claim them, unless their intentions are clear. I think he is giving everyone time to adjust to living here. Your goblin sisters only lived in forests, and simple huts, if I am correct. Living in a home is quite different, yes?"

Blyss nodded. "Living here is wonderful. It is so big. Water tastes so good. Master's cock tastes and feels so good. Mistress tastes so good."

"Thank you," Elara smiled at the compliment. "But Asher will act when the time is right, or when the mood strikes. I wouldn't concern yourself."

Blyss gave the mature elf a small smile. She then looked away and her eyes darkened.

"Is there anything else troubling you?"

Blyss gave her a sheepish look. "I have a secret. Not supposed to tell, but I want to tell you because I love you."

"Can you say part of the secret?" Elara asked with attentive pointed ears.

Blyss tilted her head, unsure what to say. She righted her head and simply spoke.

"Paasha and me have plan. I can't say what it is, but we want to welcome Asher as our clan chieftain. Nuha and Keefa help."

"Can I help?" Elara asked.

Blyss grinned. "Yes. When time right, help bring master to the western woods. When Asher is chief, he can add whoever he wants to our clan. I want you in our clan. We become clan sisters."

"I am honored you would have me as a clan sister. Yes, I will help you with your plan."

Blyss grinned from large green ear to large green ear. "I'm happy."

Elara nodded with a smile. "So am I."

The mature elf glanced at the big, empty bed.

"Blyss, master will be very busy most of the night. Will you stay with me and keep me company?"

"I would be honored," the goblin said with bright eyes.

***

Asher walked along the corridor with a sense of purpose. He wore a black robe as he walked along the quiet home. With the frost crystals cooling the house, it erased the oppressive heat, giving everyone a sense of relief. For Asher, a cool home was a happy home, which meant he could return to his duties as lord of the estate.

When he reached the door to the worship chamber, he saw that it was slightly ajar. Dim light spilled out as a soft moan flowed with it. Asher reached the door and opened it. He stepped in with a neutral gaze as another moan floated up.

The chamber was sparce, with only a few hanging lanterns. Each lantern was shaded, giving off a comfortable light. A wood statue of a robed woman stood on a small pedestal. She had a motherly form, while her hands were cupped before her, a carved sparrow within.

The Divine Mother has always been the deity of fertility and nurturing growth. She is a goddess, integral to all religions and faiths, from the tribal to the most devoted. Her influence could never be denied, the needful urge to mate, and raise offspring.

Asher stared at the statue for a moment in time. The statue was found buried in the place where the winery now stood. It was hidden, by his uncle, for its safety and discovery. Once found, it was cleaned and placed in the simple worship chamber. Asher could not deny the goddess's influence, remembering how the statue seemed to look at him at one point, and then returned to looking at the sparrow in its hands. He could also not deny that the goddess gave him a divine gift. Large sparrow wings unfolded from his back when he went to rescue Elara. They protected him from magic, and gave him the ability to fly. Elara was in his arms as they flew back to the portal and returned home. He had only used the divine gift once, but he could still feel it, blended with his soul.

Asher's gaze lowered to three women on their knees before the holy statue. Venette, with her crimson red hair, had her head bowed to the statue.

Tianna, with her purple hair, and simple cloak, also had her head bowed to the statue.

Between them, a woman with long white and alabaster skin, was on her knees, moaning. Her pale skin had patches of black veins. Small flares of energy puffed up from her at odd intervals. Her skin burned, and quickly healed in a blink. Asher looked at her as she wore a long, silky black dress and purple top. It hugged her chest and midsection, but her shoulders were bare.

Megeth was a lich of great power. The holy energy of the chamber burned her, but she resisted. As she once told Lord Blackwood, she came here to feel, and atone for the darkness within her undead spirit. Taking the elixir, it brought her closer to life than she felt in a very long time. And now, she basked in the pain, and bliss, of life and death.

Asher stepped further into the chamber until he stood behind the kneeling lich. The play they shared, was one where

Asher was a priest for the Divine Mother, and the three women were trying to cleanse their souls of a deep darkness.

"How long have you prayed?" Asher asked with confidence.

"A whole night, and a whole day," Megeth said weakly.

"Has she spoken to you?"

Megeth gave a weak nod. "She has spoken with burning light, chasing away the darkness, for a time."

Asher stood behind her as he put his hands on her shoulders. "You seek a blessing, to wash away your sins."

"I do," Megeth whispered.

Asher mentally rehearsed this moment, taking inspiration from the black book titled: The Monastery.

"I am here to test your faith. Do as you're told, and the Divine Mother may grant you forgiveness. A dead thing like yourself, can feel love again, and know her warm embrace."

"I... will do anything for the Divine Mother's forgiveness," Megeth said weakly.

Asher nodded and let go of her shoulders. "Novice Venette, and Tianna, rise and escort Novice Megeth to the Confessional chamber."

The two women slowly stood up. They reached down and helped the weakened Megeth to her bare feet. They turned around and Asher had to hide his surprise.

Half of Megeth's features were skeletal, while the other half was full and healthy. To Asher, it was almost as if she was burning away slowly, the flesh on one side of her face gone and only bone exposed. Her remaining eye had a fanatical gleam to it, almost like she was enjoying the torment.

"Follow me," Asher said with a bank gaze.

The young man turned and led the way as the three women followed. They all exited out of the prayer room, walked over to another door, and stepped into the library. The room was empty as they walked to a scarcely full bookshelf. Asher touched a secret lever within the shelf case. There was a click, and the shelf came away to reveal a secret door. Asher opened it and walked down a short corridor into a secret chamber.

The chamber had a large bed in the middle. Wood cabinets lined some of the walls, each one filled with sensual, and intimate items. Metal poles stabbed up from the corners of the bed. Happy memories rolled through Asher of time spent here with the women he loved, but now, the chamber was converted to a secret confessional room. One where they could work in peace, and solitude.

Asher glanced up at the metal rings he installed in the low ceiling of the chamber. He then moved to a cabinet, opened it, and pulled out rings of rope.

Small memories crawled over his thoughts, how Megeth and Venette taught him the ancient art of Chibari, a form of rope bondage. It is a skill that can add to intimate moments in a way to bring greater pleasure. The art is not widely known, for those who practice it keep it to small circles. For what was to happen this evening, Megeth wanted Asher to know it to enhance their blessing when the time came.

Asher stepped to Megeth. The lich's face was fully healed. She looked the same as when he met her the first time, but instead of exuding dark power, she appeared humble, and smaller.

"Novices," Asher referring to Lynette and Tianna. "Prepare Novice Megeth by undressing her."

The two women moved to their mistress's sides. Lynette's mouth twitched, trying to hide her crazed smile. Tianna's expression was blank as she lifted her pale hands. Megeth simply stood with a faraway gaze. Their hands worked with expert skill, unbuttoning, and unfastening Megeth's tight, corset top. The dress loosened and slid down. The top came away. In mere moments, the lich stood nude before Asher.

He drank in her beauty. Pale, flawless skin covered her womanly form. Large, heavy breasts fought gravity's pull. Pale pink nipples stood erect. Asher's gaze slid down her body, to a hairless valley, and plump, firm thighs. Much to Asher's delight, her body was a mature femininity he greatly enjoyed and desired.

Without a word, he loosened a ring of rope and stepped closer to the naked lich. Megeth kept her blank gaze as Asher began moving the rope around her. The smooth rope slid over pale skin, circling around her torso, waist, and along her arms. Asher moved with skill, the rope wrapping around thighs, and reaching her ankles.

Tianna and Lynette watched as Asher worked, tying up their mistress. Asher moved behind Megeth, bringing her arms back and securing her wrists. He knew from working with them with the secret art, that despite Megeth's greater strength, even she would not have enough leverage to break her bonds. The ropes were meant to incapacitate and hold, without causing pain. It was a pure form of bondage, where he would have all control, and she would surrender to him.

Ropes neatly bound arms, legs, torso, and waist. Ropes were above, and below her swollen breasts, but not obstructing them. Each rope hugged her flesh, pressing in slightly. When he was finished, he took hold of four rope ends and moved closer to the bound lich.

"The Divine Mother has heard your pleas for forgiveness, but she is not convinced. To earn your title of acolyte, you must confess, and be tested. When you renounce your dark ways, then you can enter her light."

Asher had practiced his speech, but deep down, he knew it was simply part of the play. The Divine Mother may have touched him, and granted him some power, but she never spoke to him like most holy figures who claim to speak to their deities directly. His relationship with the Divine Mother walked a tightrope of faith and questions.

"Master priest, I surrender myself to you and the Divine Mother," Megeth said in a low whisper.

Asher gave a single nod. He then lifted the ropes in hand, putting each one through a metal ring attached to the low ceiling. When every rope was through, he brought them together and curled them around until they became one rope.

He moved to a wall with rope in tow. He put it through a larger ring that was screwed into the wall, sideways. Once it was through, he pulled with strong hands, arms, and shoulders.

Megeth was lifted off her feet with her hands bound behind her. Her weight shifted along the carefully placed ropes, the lich now horizontal to the floor. Her body hovered at Asher's waist. The tight ropes caused the lich to squirm slightly, testing their strength. She discovered quickly that she could not break them.

Heavy breasts hung. A fierce tingling filled her nipples as Megeth felt helpless. Small beads of milk appeared along the tips of her pale, pink nipples. White, milky drops began to fall, and splash on the floor.

Asher tied the rope to the ring. He turned to see Megeth hanging with milk dripping from her engorged breasts.

Lynette licked her lips as Tianna stared with unblinking eyes. They stood close by, seeing their mistress in a compromised state. Megeth's arms were bound behind her. Her waist to upper body was bound tight, but her legs were parted. Ropes were snug along her inner thighs and hips, but her legs were not bound together. They were parted, with nothing standing in the way of her unholy valley entrance.

Asher stepped to Megeth's head, and looked down on her with hard eyes.

"You must truly let go and feel her power," Asher said.

The young man moved to a cabinet and pulled out two medium sized jars. He uncorked them and picked them up. He moved to Megeth's side and knelt to his knees. He watched as milk dripped from her full breasts. She squirmed, but that was all she could do.

Asher picked up a jar with one hand as he gently took hold of a swollen pale breast. He put the open mouth of the jar to her leaking nipple, while squeezing her breast with his other hand.

Megeth's eyes fluttered as life was squeezed from her sensitive breast. A thin stream of milk flowed into the clear jar. Cloudy tendrils of paradise snaked into the lich's broken soul. She gasped and bit her lip, pleasure roaring along her. The more milk she produced, the deeper the velvet touch of ecstasy. Living sensations burned at her undead senses. They collided together as the master priest milked her like some holy cow.

"I... I feel her," Megeth said with a sultry whisper.

Asher was silent, enjoying the touch of her full flesh as milk streamed into the jar. A tingling filled his own senses as his manhood began to harden under his robe.

A low moan dripped from the lich's parted lips. She stared at the floor, but her eyes saw nothing. Sensations curled along all her senses, diving deeper into her body and spirit. The firm touch of Asher's hand, and the life leaking from her, glowed brightly against her senses. It was quickly overwhelming her and she let out a long, deep moan.

"Novices, to me," Asher commanded.

Lynette and Tianna stepped closer, listening to their mistress's deep moans.

"Each of you take a jar and a breast. Milk her until I tell you to stop," Asher commanded.

The two women did as they were told. Lynette knelt beside her mistress, taking hold of the jar in Asher's hand. She touched Megeth's breast and squeezed gently. Tianna did the same on the other side. The pair gently coaxed and squeezed the lich's swollen breasts as milk streamed into jars.

Megeth's eyes rolled into her head. Moans fell from her open mouth, lost to a sea of living sensations. Her mind was washed away to such intense feelings. There was little to no thought, as she was caught in a web of ecstasy. Her body shuddered as it hung. When it shuddered again, a small orgasm exploded along her nerves, warning her of larger ones to come.

"I can smell the sin coming off your soul," Asher said as he stepped over and stood before her hanging head. "Once the darkness along your soul fades enough, only then, can I fill it with the Divine Mother's blessing."

Megeth gave a small, weak nod. Her willpower began to crack, piece by piece. The lack of control burned her in such a way that she surrendered to it.

Asher looked down on her with understanding eyes. He undid his robe, parting it down the front. His member thickened and fought gravity's pull. Lynette looked over with hungry eyes as Asher took hold of his manhood and stroked it. With his other hand, he grabbed the lich's silky white hair and pulled her head up.

Megeth's eyes were still rolled into her head as Asher looked down on her.

"Accept the Divine Mother's blessing," the young man said as he rubbed the head of his cock against the lich's full lips.

Megeth's tongue snaked out, licking at his throbbing head like it was ambrosia. Her eyes continued to flutter as the head pushed past her lips. She moaned as inches sank between her tight lips. Her tongue ran along the underside of his cock, pressing it to the roof of her mouth.

Asher enjoyed the view, seeing the lich taking his veiny cock. There was no protest, or whining. She made her mouth tight as he slid his manhood back and forth. Her teeth grazed his shaft, and that only further inflamed his own pleasure.

"Novices," Asher said to get their attention. "Cork the bottles, put them aside, and drink from her."

The two women did as they were told. Lynette smiled happily as she moved under her bound mistress and closed her lips on Megeth's leaking nipple. Tianna did the same. The pair suckled as Megeth moaned louder. A living heat filled the chamber. It wrapped around Megeth like a thick blanket. She could do nothing, helpless to Asher's control. The more his cock touched the back of her throat, the deeper she surrendered to him. Pleasure grew like a symphony, caressing pieces of her broken soul she never knew she had. Wetness dripped from her slit, creating a tiny puddle on the floor. Her body swung from the hanging ropes. The slight pull of Asher's hand controlled the tempo, as his cock spoke to her spirit. A pit formed in her belly, needing to taste life so the pit would be satisfied.

The wet sounds of suckling, and lips running along his cock, sent Asher to blissful lands. His demons sang in the moment, eager to have their way with the bound lich. Asher watched like a hungry wolf staring at its prey. He enjoyed the metaphor of hunting, and eating. He snared the beautiful lich, and now, he would enjoy the spoils.

"Is this pleasant? You're in your rightful place to receive her blessing. Shall I bless your throat, before I bless your demonic cunt?"

Megeth moaned louder as thick inches filled her mouth.

The vibrations felt good against Asher's cock as a pressure began to build. It nearly blinded him, increasing the tempo by pulling her hair and stabbing her mouth with his rigid member. When the moment approached, he looked down with kind eyes, and a demonic flame dancing within them.

"I bless you, dead thing. Taste the Divine Mother's blessing," Asher said with a harsh whisper.

Megeth moaned loudly as thick ropes of come splashed against the back of her throat. Her eyes stayed rolled in her head, waves of pleasure slamming into her soul. She drank down his holy seed, and was blessed with more. Life slipped down her throat, to the waiting pit. It glowed as it swamped her broken spirit.

Asher grunted as a third volley of seed painted the lich's throat. Tingling warmth filled his own body, like part of his soul was pulled from him and into the lich. A golden light touched him, and then it was quickly gone.

What was that?

Asher grew confused as the lich sucked on his cock, milking it of every drop of come. The feeling he felt before vanished, his hand gently caressing her head. When the last drop was gone, he pulled his cock out of her mouth. Megeth's head flopped forward, bliss cascading over her entire body.

"Novices, clean my member," Asher commanded.

The two women broke away. They moved on all fours to the standing master priest. They rose on their knees and licked at his slick cock. Lynette moaned loudly, eager to please as she licked and gently squeezed Asher's balls. Tianna licked along the shaft like a dutiful disciple.

Asher kept his gaze on Megeth, the lich seemingly defeated as she hung.

The young man stepped away from the two women on their knees. Lynette let out a whine when his cock was pulled from her.

"I will bless you both, after I have fucked the darkness from your mistress," Asher said darkly.

Tianna and Lynette watched as Asher moved to the other side of their mistress. He stepped between her parted legs. His cock was standing and throbbing as he looked at her dripping slit. He put his hand on the small of her back, as he pressed his firm head to her line.

"I bless you, Megeth Faydra," Asher said as his cock slid into her.

Megeth let out a long moan, thick inches spearing and spreading her inner world. Tight walls were pushed to their limit. Asher felt resistance, but soon, a deluge of honey aided with spearing her depths. With a simple push of his hand on the small of her back, the lich swung horizontally. The young man simply stood as Megeth slid back and forth on his granite hard cock. Each invasion, and slight retreat, sent shockwaves of pleasure through the lich. She moaned like a beast in heat, squeezing his girthy member. Toes curled as ropes bound her. Each shockwave brought her closer and closer to the edge of madness.

Asher stayed to task, sliding the lich on his member. Each push felt the edges of ropes around her thighs. Their bodies met when he was hilt deep within her. He felt her powerful squeeze as she slid away, halfway along his cock. Milk dripped from the bound lich.

Tianna and Lynette could not fight their own desires, rubbing thighs and milk leaking into their tops. They squirmed, wanting to be there, feeding off Asher's member.

The strange tingling returned. Asher's eyes widened a hair, but could not break the tempo or intense sensations. The pressure within surged close to the surface. Time flowed as Asher fought tooth and nail not to come, and enjoyed the heavenly touch of the lich's valley.

"You are forgiven," Asher said with an other-worldly tone.

Megeth's eyes widened as they gleamed wet. Asher looked down on her with a loving gaze. Their souls touched and mystical explosions went off like a furious storm.

Asher could not control himself as spurts of molten seed quickly filled her tight, inner world. Megeth let out strange moans as strings of orgasms exploded along her broken soul. The pair moaned loudly as come leaked from their union. Bodies shuddered, but never broke the connection. Asher's hands fell on her hips, driving his cock to the hilt as she squeezed and moaned.

Time lost all meaning as Asher swam in an ocean of euphoric ecstasy. He basked in it, drinking and swimming in it. His soul felt light, as all seemed right with the universe.

A darkness closed in. Asher tried to wake from the moment. He blinked as his world became a stygian black, and he was gone.

The darkness was warm, and inviting. Asher felt like he was floating, but he wasn't sure. It all felt natural, and unnatural at the same time. He couldn't feel beyond the darkness, and it concerned him.

A light appeared, and the young man swam to it. After a moment, the light spread, and he fell into it.

Asher's eyes fluttered as pleasure ran along his cock. He looked down to find himself standing in a doorway, naked. Paasha was on her knees, deep throating his cock as her hands wrapped around the base of it. She moved with an eager hunger, sucking, and stroking him. Her eyes were closed as she sucked on him, inches appearing and disappearing between her lips.

Confusion sunk deeper into the young lord. The last memory he had was coming in Megeth. Now, he stood in Paasha's bedroom doorway, the goblin sucking on his cock.

The motherly goblin moaned as she tasted pre-come, and the honey of others on it. She opened her eyes and looked up.

Asher continued to look down on her, when an overpowering urge took over. A loud grunt filled the air as his cock thickened in her mouth. The goblin sucked and stroked faster, begging with her tongue for her master's seed. Thick, white seed struck her throat and tongue. She moaned louder, sucking it down as more pumped into her mouth.

For a small moment, Asher was lost again to the throes of bliss. He pushed his cock a little deeper into the goblin's eager mouth, pumping the last of his seed into her.

Paasha pulled the thick member from her mouth and licked at it as it hung.

"You taste so good, clan father," Paasha cooed on her knees.

Crystal clarity filled Asher's mind, but it didn't give him any answers.

"Paasha, why am I here?" he asked, the words sounding odd as he spoke them.

The goblin looked up with loving eyes. "Clan father asked to have his cock sucked. I can never refuse you. You were hard for a long time, but I good at sucking cock. You came a lot. My belly warm with your come."

Asher lifted an eyebrow, unsure if that explained anything. When a deluge of memories crashed into his befuddled mind, answers swirled as he tried to make sense of it.

Images played on of Asher untying Megeth. He led the lich to the large bed and helped her onto it. Lynette and Tianna came closer, Asher pulling them both into the bed. A cacophony of moments filled his mind's eye, the four of them caught in lurid embraces. Milk, honey, and come splashed or spilled from bodies. Asher spoke the words, blessing the three women, and elevating them to acolytes in their play, but a muddled confusion sunk in, feelings like he was in his body, and not in his body at the same time.

After a long time, Asher left the secret chamber without a word. He walked through the house, up the stairs, and onto the second floor. He walked toward his bedroom, but stopped at Paasha's open door. He stepped in and she woke to see Asher naked and in her room. She slipped out of bed as Asher stepped back. He spoke to her, but the words were strange. Paasha fell to her knees, took his cock, and began sucking on him, lovingly.

The young lord looked down as memories swirled. Paasha continued to lick the shaft of his cock.

"Umm, thank you Paasha. I think it's late. I think I'm exhausted, and need some rest," Asher said in a state of confusion.

Paasha nodded. "It almost dawn. Clan father should sleep."

Asher stepped away from the goblin's touch and walked toward his room.

The door opened and he stepped in. He looked at the bed in the dark room, seeing Elara and Blyss sleeping close together. Rubbing the side of his head, he made his way over and crawled into bed.

The muddled feelings remained as he stared at the dark ceiling.

What happened to me?

The thought lingered without an answer. Exhaustion and sleep took hold. Asher's eyes slowly closed. He fell into dreamscapes as memories twisted in unusual ways. When slumber pierced his confused mind, he fell into a deep sleep before dawn's light touched the horizon.

Chapter 10

The Dreamy Unknown

Asher slowly opened his eyes to cool air, and bright sunlight. A groan escaped into the air as he turned away from the light pouring into the bedroom. A quick shift of his arm and leg, and he discovered he was alone in his bed. Adjusting to the bright light, he quickly lifted his head and looked around, the entire bedchamber empty.

Small thoughts preyed on his mind. Images played out of the night, but they were disjointed, and slightly confusing. He was there during those moments, and not there. The idea of losing control over himself didn't sit well with him. On his many adventures, there were moments when evil creatures befuddled or charmed him, or his companions, into violence. It was a risk that came with adventure life, but his new life was that of a farmer of an unusual farm. There really wasn't a reason for it.

An image of Megeth filled his mind's eye, and Asher's brow furled.

Did Megeth charm me for the evening? Was it part of the play?

Asher rolled onto his back and stared at the ceiling. The thought didn't sit well with him. Megeth had been honest and honorable her whole time here. It didn't make sense that she would charm him, especially since she didn't need to. He was eager for their time together, and he didn't say no to anything discussed. The more he thought about it, the odder last night truly was.

The young lord sat up. Glancing at the window, the sun was high. He figured it was late morning, and time to get up anyway.

Tossing the blankets aside, Asher swung his legs over the side of the bed and stood up. Scratching his head, he made his way over to his dresser and dug out a few articles of clothing. Leggings slid up his legs before a white shirt was pulled down over his head. He looked in the mirror, making sure his hair was a little messy, because Elara liked it a little messy. With a turn, he made for the bedchamber door.

In the main corridor, the smell of cooked food and light conversation floated to his senses. He followed it, making his way to the stairs, down them, and onto the main floor. When he walked into the common room, a small smile formed.

The common room was crowded with everyone in the house. Most of them were drinking cups of tea. The coffee table was filled with plates of food, and mostly empty plates. Breads, cooked eggs, berries, and cheeses filled the middle. Elara and Nyn held teacups as they looked over at Asher with happy smiles. Blyss and her fellow goblins mostly sat on the floor. Keefa stared at Asher with bright eyes and a happy smile. On the couch, Megeth, Tianna, and Lynette sat next to each other. Each woman bowed their head and smiled at the young lord. Amber sat in a lone chair with a plate of food. She tried to smile, but had food in her mouth. She tried to chew it quicker.

Fern was laying down next to the common room frost crystal, snoring lightly.

"Welcome back from the dream lands," Elara said as she stood up, closed the distance, and gave Asher a morning kiss on the lips.

Asher put his hands on her hips, giving her a loving gaze. "It was a late night."

"We know," Lynette said with a crazed grin.

Megeth took a sip of her tea, before lowering it to her lap. "We were just discussing the play. Last night, you were unchained."

"Isn't that most nights?" Elara winked before turning and standing beside Asher, her arm entwined around his.

Heads nodded in agreement.

Keefa and Nuha looked down.

Asher looked at everyone gathered, the oddness of last night bleeding away, and replaced by a full heart.

"It was fun, but it seems the play is slowly coming to an end," Asher remarked.

Megeth nodded. "True. As fun as our stay has been, myself, and my lovely apprentices, will be taking our leave in a few nights. It is only a matter of time before duties beckon my attention.

"I wish we could stay to enjoy another play. I must say, everyone here has been so delightful and free, it saddens me to think of leaving."

"You all will be missed," Amber said with sad eyes.

156

"No sad goodbyes. We may see each other again," Tianna said with a warm smile.

Elara leaned in a little closer to Asher's ear, "We were just discussing new plays once this one is concluded."

Megeth spoke up, "Lord Blackwood, treasure the farm life you all have created. Many others can have dull imaginations, or very strict rules. But here, part of the charm is the freedom everyone has here. It does lend some ideas to running an effective design, not just in farms, but other places."

"Are you talking about your dungeon, or dungeons?" Asher asked with a warm smile.

Megeth looked at him with strangely happy eyes. "Time will tell. All of you are welcome to visit me. Of course, you all will be treated as royal guests. No need to lurk down in a dungeon. I would be more than happy to portal you into the nicer sections of one of my dungeons. I have special gardens, and even forests underground, where no one would disturb us."

"We will consider it," Asher said to the beautiful lich, not sure how he felt about visiting a dungeon ever again.

"Should we celebrate your last night here?" Amber asked with curious eyes.

Megeth closed her eyes and shook her head. "No need. Our entire visit has been a celebration of life. I will treasure it, until our next visit, if you will have us?" the lich asked while looking at Asher.

"You're more than welcome to come back and visit us, anytime," Asher said honestly.

"Splendid," Megeth said with a warm smile.

Paasha stood up from the floor and walked toward the empty dishes on the coffee table. Asher and Elara uncurled their arms from each other and moved to help the goblin.

"No need, I take care of," the goblin said with a dismissive wave of her hand.

Blyss was still on the floor, staring at Asher, but not getting up. She glanced at Nuha and Keefa. The two goblins looked over to her. Blyss gave them a small nod.

The pair of goblins stood up and walked over to Asher.

"Lord Blackwood," Nuha said with an uncertain tone.

Asher turned and looked down on the four-foot-tall goblins.

"Can you show me how to cut wood in the workshop?" the goblin asked with a timid tone and uncomfortable eyes.

"I want to see," Keefa said with interested eyes.

"Oh, um, sure. The day is kind of free for me, so I would be happy to show you, if that's what you're interested in."

The pair of goblins shook their heads in unison.

"We'll take care of the daily chores," Elara said as she turned to the young lord. "You worked yourself to the bone last night. I'm sure we can manage for the day."

Asher smiled, the innuendo not lost on him.

Keefa took Asher's hand and pulled. Nuha led the way as Asher and Keefa followed. The three made it to the kitchen door, and stepped out into the oppressive heat of the late morning.

Asher kept his cool as he and the two goblins made their way to the workshop. The door opened and they stepped in.

The kitchen door opened again. Blyss slipped out and made her way north of the farm. She walked toward the chicken coop, and the rows of grapevines standing just past it.

Asher looked around as many of his tools were simply placed on worktables. He raised an eyebrow as Nuha quickly rushed to them and tried to pick many of them up.

"I'm sorry, Lord Blackwood! I looked at tools, but not put back. I forget places they go," the tomboy goblin said quickly.

"It's okay. We can put them away together, but didn't you want to see how to cut wood?"

Nuha nodded.

Asher moved to stacks of rough wood in the corner pen. He took out a medium sized piece and walked over to his wood saw. It was a table with a saw in it, a mana crystal powering the simple mechanisms.

"Let's start simple," Asher said.

The two goblins looked at him as he began talking about the finer parts of cutting wood.

***

159

Elara flopped into a comfortable chair in the library. The elf was dressed in leggings and a shirt. Her boots had some grime from watering the grapevine field. The day had shifted from late morning to midafternoon. A relaxed exhale flowed as she enjoyed the cool room, and respite from the work.

Her gaze wandered to a half-full shelf case. She eyed several black books, a thought whispering to her to read for the rest of the day. When she was about to get up to grab a book, the library door swung open again and Nyn looked in.

"Sneaking in some reading time?" Elara smiled at her friend.

Nyn stepped in and closed the door behind her. She had a black book in her hand as she approached the blonde elf. Her often-blank gaze held a gleam of concern, one Elara recognized before. The elf with dark-blue-hair, walked over to her friend and sat down in a chair beside her, book on her lap.

Elara waited patiently as she knew Nyn sometimes needed time to gather her thoughts. The two friends knew each other so well, sometimes words didn't need to be said right away.

"I want to discuss several things," Nyn said.

Elara gave Nyn her full attention.

The dark-haired elf looked down on the book for a moment, before looking over to her friend.

"Asher brought home this book. It's one I haven't read before. I've read it twice," Nyn declared.

"Now, I want to read it," Elara smiled.

Nyn gave a small nod, but her eyes held a shadow's edge. "I know we are free to be as we wish, but I want something private, with Asher."

Elara looked at her friend with understanding eyes. "You feel guilty for wanting him for yourself."

Nyn nodded. "I've never felt this way for anyone before. Now I feel it, for him, you, Amber, and Blyss. I... thought I could distance myself from truly binding my heart from others, but I fear, I've failed.

"The new goblins are slowly joining our family, but my heart yearns for Asher. I enjoy our times together, but this book has changed my perception, and my desires."

"Nynna, you have nothing to fear, from me, or the others. Sharing him is what we all agreed upon. Just as he shares his time with us."

Nyn's heart quickened as she looked down at the book. "I know, but I want something, just between him and I."

"Speak your thoughts. You will have no judgment from me, my friend."

Nyn blinked as she continued to look at the book. "The book is called 'Silence.' It is a story of a milk farm, but the lord of it rarely ever speaks. There is almost no dialogue, everything taking place is purely body language. As you know, our people discuss many things, almost to the point of dismay. But this book opened my mind to simple, intimate, body language."

Pink touched the elf's pale cheeks as she continued. "The lord takes what he desires, as do the guests. The only sounds often heard are grunts and moans. It's a freedom I crave. To simply give a glance, or a touch, and to be taken like I was always his."

Elara looked at her friend with understanding eyes. "I know the feeling you speak of. When he desires me, it is a sense of overwhelming I greatly enjoy. But for you, I understand what you desire, a private play, of sorts?"

Nyn gave a solemn nod. "I don't wish to steal him for myself. If he threw me on the bed with you, or another, I would never fight his desires. But there is a part of me, who wishes to shed manners and social practices. To be like Blyss, a woman of primal desires, who simply lets herself to enjoy carnal acts with reckless abandonment, is something I have dreamed often of."

The elf lifted her gaze and looked at her dear friend. "I have tasted that freedom here, but never to its fullest degree. I love and respect you. I had to speak of it to you, so there is no misunderstanding. Asher has chosen you as his lady, but I want him as a primal lover."

"I thank you for your honesty, but you will not hear a drop of jealousy from me. Blyss has spoken to me as well of her feelings. I fear there is an outside view that I would not approve. Nothing could be further from the truth."

Heat crawled up Elara's neck as she continued, "He makes us all happy, in one way or another. I enjoy seeing him wanting more. I adore his mind, body, and soul. I have exiled myself from my home, because I found what I was always searching for. If our love affair is brief because of his short life, I want our lives to blaze with loving glory for as long as it can.

"Nyn, you can have that too. Despite the long courting process in our homeland, there are elves who take many lovers. Males and females will endure the process to take on new lovers. We can have that here."

"I want that, here," Nyn admitted.

"Then you shall have it. Let us celebrate our desires. If you wish a private play with our lover, do it with all our blessings."

Nyn's eyes watered. "Thank you, my friend."

Elara looked down at the black book. "I wish to read it as well. If it speaks to you, I want to know that feeling as well."

Nyn lifted the book and handed it to her. "Take it, and perhaps, don't wear clothes as you read it," the elf said with a small smile.

The two elves laughed.

Elara put the book on her lap, her interested mind eager to read it.

"I am nearly finished with our black book," Nyn said.

"Oh, yes. From what I've read, it still makes me hot," Elara said with a sly edge.

Nyn's smile stayed for a moment, before it dimmed.

"There is something else I wanted to discuss. Last night, I was missing time."

Elara looked upon her friend with serious eyes.

"I cannot explain it, but I lost time as I was reading. I didn't fall asleep. As I tried to regain my thoughts, memories came back to me of reading and remembering everything I read, but I didn't feel like I was there as it happened."

"That is odd," Elara said with a concerned tone.

"It felt like I had a waking dream…" Nyn said as she continued to talk.

Sunlight glowed from the window of the library.

***

Amber rushed around outside from the field. She moved like she was possessed, trying to outrun the oppressive heat and light. Sweat clung to her as she put the watering cans away.

The morning mists had been sparse. The collection rods barely captured dew from the morning mists, which meant, watering the vines at the hottest time of the day. It was the only way to ensure the vines had plenty to drink, or they risked dying from the heat.

Amber put away the last watering can, her thoughts dreaming of stripping naked in the now cool house. When she closed the outside shed, she turned on her hooves to a peculiar sight.

The chicken coop was clean.

Cleaning the chicken coop was the hardest job on the farm, as far as Amber knew it. No one liked doing it, and she often did it herself when she had time. The chickens themselves were indifferent, but when Amber took too long to clean it, feathers would be everywhere. Now, it stood with happy chickens inside, not a stray feather to be seen.

Amber stepped closer, admiring the thorough work of whoever cleaned it.

A chicken moved to the wire mesh, and looked up with its head cocked to the side.

"It seems you have a fairy chicken mother," Amber smiled.

The faun put her finger close to the mesh wire. The chicken looked at her finger, and then jabbed it with her beak.

Amber pulled back her hand at the flash of tiny pain. She looked at her finger, as a drop of blood bloomed.

"You mean little bitch!" Amber scolded the chicken as it wandered off.

***

"And that's how you get a solid cut of wood," Asher finished as he put down a perfect block of wood with a few others.

Keefa sat on a chair, staring off at nothing, but Nuha was all eyes and ears for the Lord of Blackwood.

The heat in the workshop was stifling. Asher wiped away some sweat from his brow. The two goblins were perfectly normal.

"I wish I could control my body temperature like you do," Asher said to Nuha.

The goblin nodded as she stood before him. "Goblins sweat too, but we control body heat in hard conditions. When hot summer over, we return to normal."

The goblin yawned.

"We get tired sooner. I'm tired," she said with a weary tone.

Asher looked at the open door, seeing that the light had dimmed, signaling the late day. He also felt the sweat that seeped into his clothes.

"You go inside. I clean up," Nuha smiled.

Asher was about to offer to stay and help, but the heat was making him dizzy. He simply nodded and walked toward the open door.

Keefa looked at him go, her oval eyes drinking in his strong form. When the young lord stepped out of the workshop, she turned her gaze to Nuha.

The goblin with short, black hair, moved quickly, picking up different tools. She placed them in a small pack. She then moved to the blocks of wood and picked them up.

"Help me carry wood," the goblin instructed.

Keefa jumped off the chair and moved to Nuha's side. The goblin with long blonde hair, picked up blocks of wood.

The two scurried out of the workshop, Nuha with a pack, and wood in her arms. Keefa followed with some lumber in her hands.

The blonde goblin turned her gaze to see Asher step into the farmhouse. Her heart swelled at the sight of him. A shy smile bloomed as she turned and followed Nuha, who was several yards ahead of her, walking toward the western woods.

***

Asher stepped into the cool house, relief washing over him. Paasha was in the kitchen, cooking a chicken over the metal stove. She stood on a stool by the kitchen table, filling bowls with cut fruit, and berries. The scent of cooking food made Asher's mouth water.

The goblin with long, black hair with a white lock, turned her head to the young lord, and gave him an endearing smile.

"Dinner ready in a while," she spoke in crude common over her shoulder.

Asher nodded as he caught a whiff of his own, sweaty odor.

"I'll be taking a bath. Can you please send someone to get me?"

The motherly goblin gave a single nod. "I will."

Asher was about to turn away, when Paasha spoke up again.

"Clan father, you taste so good. Let me suck cock anytime," the goblin said like it was the most normal thing to ever say.

Asher smiled. He walked over to the goblin with her back to him. He put his arms around her stomach. The goblin leaned against his strong chest and stomach.

"Paasha, you were very good to me. I know I was out of sorts last night, but we can do that anytime we want," Asher said as he hugged her.

Paasha's heart fluttered to his words, and his embrace. One of her hands touched his arm.

"You make us happy. You make Paasha, happy," the goblin said as she snuggled the back of her head to his neck.

Asher nodded before letting go of her. Paasha returned to cutting fruit. She stopped mid cut, and turned to see Asher walk out of the kitchen.

"Blackwood clan will be strong," the goblin whispered before returning to cutting fruit.

Asher climbed the stairs to the second floor. As he walked down the long corridor, his spirit filled with a calm peace. Everything seemed to fall perfectly into place. The farm was prospering. Megeth, Lynette, and Tianna were enjoying their stay. Everyone on the farm seemed to be in a better place.

When the young lord entered the bedchamber, he quickly saw Elara in bed, with a blanket over her, and a book in her hand. The blanket was only to her waist, her upper body visibly naked.

She put down the book like she just woke up from a spell. Her other hand was under the blanket, still moving slightly.

"Did I interrupt?" Asher smiled as he closed the door behind him.

"No, just enjoying an excellent read," the elf said with a sultry tone, before a small moan escaped her lips. "Join me before we go down for dinner."

Asher wanted nothing more than to crawl into bed to snuggle with the voluptuous beautiful elf, but he knew he had an odor.

"I'm a little sweaty. Wait for me after I take a bath?"

Elara put down the book and whipped the blanket off her. She stood up completely naked, and walked to the young lord. Asher was mesmerized by her beauty, a part of him getting harder by the moment.

"I've been a little dirty myself," Elara said with lustful eyes. "We should bathe together," she said as she put her hands on his waist.

Asher put his hands on Elara's waist, the two lovers gazing into each other's eyes.

"Yes, bathing together would seem the thing to do. You can tell me about the book you're reading."

Elara looked at him with adoring eyes.

"My morsel," the mature elf said before leaning in for a deep kiss.

Their lips met as they held each other in a passionate embrace, two hearts beating as one.

***

Stars twinkled along the celestial night. A crescent moon rose into the sky, casting a pale light across Mist Valley. Cool air flowed down from the mountains, breaking the oppressive heat for a time. The song of crickets played like a midnight symphony.

The front door to the Blackwood house opened slightly. A dark shadow slipped out of the unlit common room, and slinked into the inky shadows of the porch. It moved to the side and slipped over the railing of the porch, moving like a silent ghost.

On the Hornspear estate, a side door opened. A taurnar woman stepped out and silently closed the door behind her. She breathed in the cool, night air, enjoying the break from the relentless heat.

A small moment flashed across her mind, of her taurnar sisters telling her she should not go out at night. The valley was not completely safe. Iska ignored them, telling them they cannot live their lives in fear, for there is a much larger world to enjoy. After that, she made her way downstairs. Jarrag's snoring from his room brought a small smile to the taurnar's snout.

Outside, Iska stepped out onto the grass. She looked up at the starry sky and moon, basking in their light. Cool air filled her lungs as she walked further out into a field, to see the night in all her glory.

A gentle peace washed over her senses. She continued to look up with dreamy eyes, pondering on the great unknowns of the universe.

Iska gazed upon the celestial world above her, as a dark shadow slinked across the grassy field.

The taurnar closed her eyes as she enjoyed the simple night air.

The shadow moved like a haunting wraith. The moment Iska's eyes closed, it shot across the grassy field. A hand stabbed out, grabbing the taurnar by the neck and forcing her down onto the ground.

Before Iska could scream, a mouth latched onto her neck. Teeth touched her thick skin, but didn't penetrate. Instead, living energy flowed like water.

Instead of screaming, Iska let out a low moan. The taurnar's eyes fluttered, unable to resist her living life draining away into the shadow over her. The flowing shadow covered most of the taurnar. It suckled at her neck, drinking more lifeforce.

"I... don't... want to... die," Iska said as a tear steaked from her eye.

The shadow didn't listen. It continued to drink from the taurnar until she became still.

The shadow pulled up its head, and stared down at the pale taurnar. It moved off her, and grabbed Iska by the ankle.

The shadow dragged the taurnar across the field to a patch of trees, bordering the Blackwood farm. It pulled Iska to some bushes and let go, her hooved foot striking the ground.

The shadow weaved for a moment, before slipping back onto the Blackwood estate. It moved to the front door, opened it, and slipped in. The door closed without a sound.

Crickets resumed their nightly symphony as the stars and moon glowed in the vast distance.

Chapter 11

The Horror of Rage

Moans floated up from the large bed. Elara was on her stomach as Asher was over her. Their snug connection sent tendrils of bliss through their bodies. The sound of skin on skin, filled the intimate space between them as the morning light penetrated the cool bedchamber.

Elara turned her head, lips parted and eyes half-closed. She moaned louder as she saw Asher's expression was one of demonic wanting. Hips slammed into her ass as his cock filled her thin, inner world. Each thrust and pullback, caused the elf's toes to curl.

For the couple, a night of intimate lovemaking sang to their desires. The pair passed out after each session, and woke a short time later to start again. Their urges bound them in a cycle of love, sex, and dreams. There was little discussion, only a pull to each other's forms.

Elara's fingers curled, bunching up blankets. Despite her soreness, she fought past it so she could enjoy her lover's attention. The pure wicked pleasure was enough to soothe away any pain, as white touched the edge of her gaze.

Asher was numb, his body constantly betraying him. Dreamy moments of the couple in the bathtub before dinner, and then rushing to the bedroom after dinner, filled his mind. Lustful madness consumed them, but in the beginning, after the first few climaxes, the pair laid in each other's arms, talking about everything. It was never just their bodies, for their minds connected like they had known each other their entire lives.

Elara let out a defeated moan as her eyes rolled into her head. Asher grunted his defeat as he joined her. The young lord's cock sank deep as the mature elf shuddered. Honey surged as spurts of milky seed flooded her inner world. Bodies continued to move, milking each other of every drop of blissful pleasure.

Asher let out a sharp grunt, and a long moan. The younger man huffed as Elara squeezed him for more. His wet cock slid out of her, and Asher flopped onto his back. Ragged breathing carried on with a rhythmic inhale and exhale.

Elara remained on her stomach, trying to claw her way back to her senses. With a small movement, she moved closer to Asher. Erect nipples leaked milk. It was too much energy to get any milking jars, so she grabbed her breast and pushed it to Asher's mouth. The young lord didn't hesitate to clamp his lips on her engorged nipple and began to suck. Creamy milk slid down his throat and into his belly. The elf's mystical milk slowly fueled his own mana, returning some of his energy.

"Your lips always feel so good," Elara said and then gasped as Asher's tongue played with her nipple. "Stop teasing or I will want to go again."

Asher didn't stop. The elf squirmed against him as he drank her milk. With energy returning, a playful feeling struck both. Elara took hold of Asher's half-hard cock and began stroking him. Soreness caused Asher to grunt with his mouth full. He applied some pressure with his teeth. Elara gasped, and only jerked him faster.

The two fought back laughter and giggles until they couldn't take it anymore. Asher let go of her swollen breast and she let go of his cock. The two were on their backs, breathing hard and laughing at the same time.

"I... don't think I can ever get tired of this...of what we have," Asher said between breaths.

Elara simply nodded with closed eyes and heavy breath.

Asher turned onto his side and looked at the beautiful elf. He took hold of her swollen breast and gave it a slight squeeze, milk leaking from it.

"My lewd morsel," Elara smiled as her eyes fluttered to his touch.

"Lewd morsel?" Asher said with a raised eyebrow, and a wicked smirk. "I have something more than a morsel you can suck on."

Elara let out a breathy giggle. "Give me a little time, and I'll suck on that cock until you beg me to stop."

Asher's eyes gleamed with a happy shine as the morning was just getting started.

***

Amber entered the kitchen and looked around. The kitchen was empty, much like the rest of the house. The faun listened for anyone else moving around or talking, but the home was eerily silent.

Amber checked in on the guests, looking into bedrooms that were cracked open to allow cool air to flow in. Megeth, Lynette, and Tianna were in the same room, sleeping together. Amber saw that they slept like the dead, not moving, or even stirring. She thought for sure Megeth would have some supernatural senses to alert her, but since the house was so free, Amber figured the lich was comfortable enough to let her guard down a little, much to the faun's approval.

When Amber checked the other rooms, the goblins and Nyn, were nowhere to be seen.

The faun made her way downstairs to the first floor. Fern was sleeping in the common room. The uni-goat was deep asleep, and didn't stir as the faun walked in, looked around, and left.

Standing in the kitchen, she hoped Paasha was making a meal to break their fast. Instead, the stove was cold, and nothing was prepared.

Amber shrugged before moving to the pantry to find something to eat before going down to the alchemy lab. She wanted to get her day started early so she could enjoy a well-earned rest. Seeing the new black books in the library tickled her curiosity, and she couldn't remember the last time she sat and simply read a good book.

The faun picked up a loaf of bread before walking over to a cold chest. She opened the lid and spotted the butter. She reached down for it, ready to settle her growling stomach.

***

The sun shined bright in the partly cloudy sky. A side door opened to the Hornspear farmhouse, several taurnar women stepped out onto the grassy ground. Three of them talked and walked, while one of them looked around with alert eyes.

"Another day in paradise," a taurnar woman said.

"I do love this valley," another one said.

The one with alert eyes shook her head slightly. "Iska didn't come back in from last night. I'm worried."

"You worry too much. She's fallen asleep under the stars before. You know she's a heavy sleeper. She's most likely under a tree, waking up to the warm morning."

"I don't know. This doesn't feel right," the taurnar said with a worried tone.

The other three ignored her as they walked along in the sunlight.

The further they walked, the better they felt. The air was crisp, and not as humid as it had been. The sun was hot, but it was welcomed, warming their muscles. Each one wore a simple dress, light and airy. They all admired the beautiful day.

The worried one glanced over to the fence border of the Hornspear estate, and the Blackwood estate. She visually scanned the fence and trees, looking for any sign of Iska. She knew the taurnar liked to speak with the faun on the Blackwood estate, despite Jarrag's protests. He was in charge, but he didn't fight too hard to keep everyone in line.

The taurnar looked down for a breath, wondering if she was worrying too much. When she lifted her gaze again, she saw a hoof poking out from beside a bush. Her heart leapt into her throat as she charged toward it. Her eyes grew wider and wider, seeing the hoof and leg, not moving.

The taurnar reached the edge of the bush. She looked down on Iska's pale form, and she let out a horrific shriek.

***

Asher and Elara were laughing when a scream pierced the world beyond their window. The pair sat up instantly, with Asher jumping out of the bed next. He rushed to his dresser, opened a drawer, and pulled out a shirt and leggings. He dressed quickly as another scream went off.

Elara slipped out of bed with a small panic in her eyes. Asher slipped on his leggings and stepped over to the closet. He grabbed a belt with a short sword and dagger, hanging on a peg.

"That doesn't sound like anyone we know," Elara said as she grabbed a dress and put it over her head.

"We don't know what is happening. I'm going to go out and investigate while you make sure our people are close by and safe," Asher directed as he rushed over to his boots and slipped a foot into each one.

Asher's mind stayed a deadly calm as he darted out of the bedchamber and down the long corridor. He heard Elara behind him a distance as he rushed down the stairs to the first floor.

The former ranger rushed into the common room just as Amber stepped in as well. A look of fear filled her eyes as she looked at Asher.

"Help Elara check for our people. If anything happens, get everyone to the lab and lock the door!" Asher commanded, knowing the door to the lab was strengthened against brute force and magic.

Amber simply nodded as she darted to the main corridor of the home.

Asher rushed to the front door, opened it, and charged out. Hand on his sheathed short sword, he slowed to a walk as his senses drank in the world around him. Ears flexed as he listened. When he heard a distant commotion to his left, he rushed to the east side of the house.

Moving with liquid, but cautious ease, he heard voices talking with a heightened edge, but couldn't make out what they were saying. He walked over and looked past a tree, and the dividing, two beam fence. He quickly saw several taurnar, two of them consoling a crying taurnar. Another taurnar was looking down at something in the bushes with wide eyes.

A loud bang vibrated in the distance. Asher glanced over as Jarrag launched from the side door of his home, and charged in their direction. The taurnar bull huffed with crazed eyes, moving like a titan across the grassy field.

"Shit," Asher cursed as he eased his hand off the hilt of his sheathed short sword.

The former ranger moved closer to the fence to see what was happening. The taurnar woman by the trees spotted him and backed off, with fear in their eyes. The crying one screamed at the sight of Asher.

"Stay away!" one of the taurnar women shouted.

"I'm here to help," Asher managed before the world spun into chaos.

Jarrag moved quickly, soaking in the situation. He glanced at the retreating taurnar women. His gaze fell to a hoof sticking out from a bush. He turned his gaze to Asher on the other side of the fence. Wide, dark eyes, shifted from fear, to a maddening rage.

The large taurnar huffed angrily as he shifted his run into a charge, beelining for Asher.

"Jarrag! We're not responsible," Asher shouted as he backed off.

Jarrag ignored him as he lowered his center of gravity in his charge. The taurnar bull roared as he closed the distance and slammed his thick shoulder into the two-beam fence, shattering it to kindling.

Asher kept his body loose as the wild taurnar charged him. Feeling the house wall close behind him, he waited until the last moment before diving to the side.

Jarrag's hands stabbed out and slammed his palms against the house, cracking the wall pane. He pushed off as he charged Asher with murderous rage in his eyes. Asher witnessed how fast he was, but didn't draw his blades. A thick, ring covered hand shot out, with Asher spinning away and trying to keep a healthy distance.

"Jarrag! Stop this!" Asher shouted.

Jarrag let out a growling huff as a ring glowed on his finger. In a blink, Jarrag was before Asher, his fist swinging out and slamming into Asher's chest.

A bone cracked as Asher was lifted off his feet and flung ten feet. When he landed, he rolled back to his feet as an ache filled his entire chest. Instinct took over as Asher drew his short sword and dagger, but didn't press an attack.

"Ready to finish what you started? The truth reveals itself, Blackwood!" Jarrag roared as he charged.

Asher stood his ground as the raging taurnar came for him. Ignoring the pain, he waited until Jarrag was to him, when the former ranger swung his short sword, slamming the flat side of the blade against the side of the taurnar's throat. Jarrag grunted as it gave Asher enough time to back-peddle to give him some clearance.

"I don't want to hurt you!" Asher shouted a warning.

"That's funny because I'm going to fucking kill you!" Jarrag shouted back and charged.

Asher glanced at his blades. Not wanting more bloodshed, he re-sheathed them. Hands empty, Jarrag was over him, his shadow casting a cool darkness.

Asher's hand shot up, striking a jab to the taurnar's throat. Jarrag swung his arm as pain flared. The arm connected and lifted Asher off his feet. The young lord hit the ground and rolled onto his feet, but wavered.

A few more hits like that and I'm going to have a few broken bones. Keep moving and avoid his strikes.

"Stop moving so I can smash you into the ground!" Jarrag roared as he charged.

Asher glanced down to Jarrag's knees. When the bull was on him, Asher shifted his body down, and to the side. A leg bent and a heel slammed into the side of his knee. Jarrag lost his balance as he stumbled. Asher bent his legs and launched at the taurnar. Asher's fist slammed into Jarrag's unguarded eye. His horned head shifted away, but a thick arm swung with a wide arc.

Asher grabbed the arm, and swung under it. While still holding, he slammed a heel into the armpit of the taurnar, driving it hard into the tender flesh over his robust ribs.

Jarrag let out a painful shout as Asher let go and landed on the ground. A hoof lifted, and Asher rolled away as it came down on the spot, he was just a second ago.

"Squirming little worm!" Jarrag raged.

He has endurance and strength on his side. I have to end this quickly or I'm a dead man.

Asher kept his body loose as Jarrag charged. Thick fists flashed out, the former ranger ducking them each in turn. When a fist pulled back, Asher aggressively charged and drove his fist into a pressure point where the neck and shoulder met. The strike landed and Jarrag roared in pain. His right arm went numb as Asher capitalized on the moment.

Knowledge filled his mind as he stepped in close. Knowing the pressure points and kill spots of animals glowed in his thoughts. He spotted several areas to strike, picking a place to incapacitate the large bull taurnar. When he saw the neck was unguarded, Asher brought two fingers together on his right hand, and jabbed at the bottom of the throat with such force, he should have penetrated the skin.

The jab hit, but the taurnar's thick hide kept Asher's fingers from penetrating. Pain exploded within Jarrag's throat. One thick hand grabbed at his own throat while his other fist shot out. Asher planted his feet to dive to the side, but the fist came in quicker than he thought. It struck his shoulder and sent him spinning five feet through the air and he hit the ground hard.

Pain crawled along Asher's senses as he struggled to get back up.

Jarrag choked and gasped for air. A ring on his finger glowed blood red. The taurnar stopped gasping and looked at Asher with hard eyes.

"Regeneration," Jarrag said with confidence before he charged the young lord.

Asher leapt to the side, but his footing slipped. He was airborne as a large, open hand, smacked him from the air. Asher hit the ground and rolled onto his back. A shadow was over him as Jarrag leapt up with both fists over his head. A look of victory filled his crazed eyes as he came down.

Asher crossed his arms as energy filled his entire form. Brown, feathered wings flashed out and covered him as thick fists came down, hitting them hard.

Jarrag looked down in stunned astonishment, seeing wings protecting the young lord. He raised his fists again to beat them until they were broken, when a strong wing flashed up and struck him.

The force of the blow was strong enough to send the taurnar flying ten feet through the air and land on his back.

Asher slowly stood up with feathered wings out. Pain still radiated through his body, becoming harder to ignore. The power of his wings fueled him to keep fighting.

Jarrag curled back onto his hooves and let out an annoyed huff.

"Stop this before either of us get hurt," Asher huffed as he stood in a fighting stance.

The taurnar sneered before he charged. Asher readied his wings as the taurnar pulled back a large fist. A ring glowed as he threw a punch.

Asher leapt up and used his wings to block the punch. The moment the fist connected with a feathery wing, a pulse blasted out, knocking the young lord from the air.

Asher tumbled through the air as his wings rippled, and faded away. Hands out, he hit the ground and rolled to his feet again. Weakness bled into his muscles as he tried to summon his wings again. But his wings didn't re-appear.

Jarrag approached with a menacing and amused stare. One of his several rings glowing with a pale white light.

"You're not the only adventurer who decided to settle down," he said as he lifted his hand to show his arcane rings. "A dispel magic ring is enough to keep this a fair fight, which is more respect than you deserve."

Jarrag lowered his center of gravity and charged.

Asher backed up. Pain radiated along several parts of his body. It stripped away his focus a layer at a time. He watched as the bull taurnar came at him like a battering ram, ready to pummel him into the ground. Asher's hand rested on his dagger, ready to use it if he needed too.

From the front of the house. Amber and Elara rushed out, potions bottles in hands. They looked in fear as Jarrag was nearly on Asher. Elara lifted a hand, reciting an incantation, when she gasped as the taurnar slammed into Asher and sent him spiraling to the ground.

The young lord mentally cursed himself as he didn't move fast enough. Gathering his wits, he tried to move when a thick hand clamped on his throat. Asher fought for air as the taurnar was over him with mad eyes.

"You killed one of my people, one of my lovers. I will squeeze the fucking life out of you for what you did!" Jarrag said with a burning rage in his eyes.

Asher couldn't catch his breath as he felt the strong hand squeeze a little more. In a flash of survival instinct, Asher lifted his leg and clamped them around the taurnar's thick arm. His ankles crisscrossed and slammed into the side of Jarrag's neck. The taurnar lifted Asher up while holding his throat, swinging his arm to shake his legs off him. Asher had a firm grip with his hands, arms, and legs. With a straightening of his spine, and using every muscle in his body, he pushed with his legs into Jarrag's neck, and twisted his whole body. There was a snap, and a loud grunt. Jarrag roared in pain as his arm was dislocated from the shoulder. His arm and hand spasmed, falling to his side with Asher still holding him. The hand let go and Asher took a deep breath.

Knowing he had to be quick, Asher was upside-down, clinging to the useless arm. He grabbed the finger with the regeneration ring, twisted it so hard that bone snapped. The former ranger slipped the ring off and flung it back onto Jarrag's property. Only after that, did Asher let go and crumble to the ground.

Dust billowed up as Asher heaved for air. He glanced at the taurnar as he stumbled to the side and sat down. He held his useless arm to him, huffing and breathing heavy. The pair looked at each other, trying to catch their breath.

"I can still fight!" Jarrag growled as he tried to get back up, but his body refused to work.

Asher rolled onto his stomach and pushed up onto his hands and knees. He twisted and sat down, looking at Jarrag who was fifteen feet away. Bruises glowed against his senses as the taste of blood filled his mouth. Asher wiped away a drop of blood from the corner of his mouth, and stared with annoyed eyes.

"Jarrag, stop being a fool. If I wanted anyone dead, I wouldn't have sheathed my weapons, or tried to speak to you. There must be an explanation for what happened."

The taurnar shook his head as rage continued to taunt him.

Elara was at Asher's side, healing potion in hand. She lifted it to his lips, but it was Asher who shook his head.

"Give it to Jarrag," Asher said with heavy breath.

Elara's eyes widened as she tried again.

Asher brushed her hand away. "He needs to see that we are not a threat. Leave a potion, but give one to him."

"He'll attack you again," Elara said with concerned eyes.

Asher stared hard as the taurnar. "No, he won't," Asher said loud enough for Jarrag to hear it.

Elara left a potion beside Asher. She stood up and walked over to the taurnar. He glared at her as she approached. When she lifted the potion to him, he spit on the ground.

"Keep your poison," the taurnar growled.

Elara's eyes narrowed. Arcane words spilled from her lips as she lifted her other hand. Lightning arced and swirled around her hand. Jarrag struggled to get up as she pointed her hand at him. A storm filled her oval eyes as energy arced around her fingers.

"Witch," Jarrag said as he looked at her with defiant eyes.

Elara shifted her hand away, and a thick bolt of lightning blasted out and struck the ground a few feet from the wounded taurnar. Grass, dirt, and pebbles exploded upwards, some of it striking the taurnar. Jarrag grunted before looking up at the mature elf with cautious eyes.

Asher watched with knowing eyes and a small smirk.

Elara bent at the hips slightly as she looked down on the taurnar. "I would have killed you for hurting my beloved. The only reason you're still alive is because of my love and respect for Lord Blackwood. You will do well to remember that, for if you lay a finger on him again, I will raze your home to the ground, and make your estate unlivable with salt and your bones."

Jarrag's glare softened, and he looked down.

Elara put the potion close to his snout. "You still have one good arm. Take the potion and drink it."

Jarrag did as he was told. He let go of his useless arm and took the potion. He popped the cork with his thumb, lifted it up to his small snout, and began to drink.

Asher was drinking his potion, one hand still resting on his dagger if the taurnar's rage had not abated.

Not far from the trio, Amber rushed into the bushes of the Hornspear property. She rushed to the pale body of Iska. She sat down beside her, resting a hand on her chest. The faun focused, trying to find any hint of life. When she felt a pulse, her heart lifted in her chest as she uncorked a potion. She lifted it to Iska's lips and poured the red liquid into it.

188

Amber watched with unblinking eyes. Iska's head moved slightly. Color began to return to her features. She blinked as strength returned to her. When she saw Amber, a sigh of relief escaped her parted lips.

Jarrag grunted as healing energy filled his body. Flesh and muscles pulled, snapping the arm back into the socket. Relief washed over the taurnar, until he looked over to Amber beside Iska.

"Stay away from..." the taurnar stopped as his eyes widened.

Iska sat up with color in her features once again. Amber gave the taurnar another potion, ignoring Jarrag as she tried to help Iska.

A shadow touched Jarrag. He turned his horned head and looked up to Asher, the young man with his hand out.

Jarrag brushed Asher's hand away, and slowly stood up under his own power. He towered over Asher and Elara, a serious look in his eyes. He let out a huff, before turning and walking over to Iska and Amber.

"Thank you," Iska said as Amber helped her up onto her hooves.

Jarrag approached and looked at Iska. "What happened?"

The taurnar weaved a little as Amber helped steady her. She looked up to Jarrag, before she flung her arms around his thick neck.

Jarrag held Iska to him, her sobs breaking down his rage, piece by piece.

"I was just enjoying the night and stars, when something attacked me," Iska sobbed.

Jarrag held her close. "Tell me anything you know. I will make them pay."

"I don't... know. They had a cloak, and madness filled eyes. I think it was a woman. She was wearing a one piece, and a hood. She drained my energy. I thought I was going to die."

Asher and Elara glanced at each other, before looking back at the two taurnar.

Amber slowly moved away from the couple. She stepped to Asher and Elara's side, the three of them listening in.

Jarrag lifted his head and looked over to Asher, while still holding Iska close.

"I've seen strange folk on your farm, Blackwood. Because you're honorable, I will not take any further action today. But tomorrow, if I see a hint of anyone in your home meeting that description, they are dead.

"If you are truly honorable like you claim to be, you will get your home in order, or I will do it for you," Jarrag snorted.

The bull taurnar curled his arms under Iska and lifted her up to his broad chest. He started walking toward the farmhouse.

One of the other female taurnars picked up a ring from the grass. The small group of taurnar women looked over with angry eyes. They quickly followed Jarrag and Iska back to the farmhouse.

When the taurnar were far enough away, Asher, Amber, and Elara turned to each other.

"Let's get inside. I think a discussion needs to be had," Asher said as his heart sank in his chest.

Chapter 12

A Shadowy Hunger

Asher, Elara, and Amber marched into the house. They made their way to the stairs and climbed them, Asher leading the way.

On the second floor, they walked directly to a trio of rooms that were side by side. The young lord reached a door, lifted his fist to knock, when he stopped. The door opened to Megeth's serious eyes. The lich stepped aside to allow the trio in.

Asher shifted his gaze from the lich to Venette and Tianna on the bed. Venette had her pale hand on Tianna's shoulder. Tianna herself was looking down with blank eyes. The mood was a dark one, the three entering the room, and Megeth closing the door behind them.

The beautiful lich stepped past Asher, and sat down on the other side of Tianna.

"We heard the commotion outside," Venette said without her signature mad smile and crazy eyes.

Asher shifted his gaze to Tianna and Megeth. "Do you know what happened? Did any of you have a hand in it?"

Tianna lowered her head another inch.

"Tell them what you told me," Megeth said with a calm tone.

Tianna lifted her gaze to meet Asher's eyes. "I... thought it was a dream."

The lich apprentice shifted uncomfortably as she continued, "I didn't know anything happened until afterwards. I saw that my bare feet were covered in dirt, but I didn't step outside. I pondered on it as I was already in bed. A short time later, memories came flooding back.

"Moments flashed of gnawing hunger. I needed energy, but I was still full from our night together. I shouldn't have been so hungry, but I was."

Megeth nodded. "Sometimes, the arcane energies seeping into an apprentice's soul, can cause unusual hungers. Sometimes it is for blood, or meat. Other times, it's for souls, or living energy. It is a side-effect from the process, but I didn't sense such hungers in Tianna, or Venette. They have had more than enough energy from our sessions," the lich explained.

Tianna continued, "I... I remember leaving the farmhouse, because there was a part of me that didn't want to feed on anyone here. It had to be a stranger, someone I didn't know. I crept out of the house, and I sensed... her."

Tianna looked away. "I... wasn't in control. I attacked her, pulled most of her life essence from her. And when I had my fill, I looked down in horror at what I had done. I pulled her away, and left her hidden in the bushes. I came back into the house and went to bed. It was a short time later when I woke up, not sure what had happened."

The lich apprentice looked up at Asher with resigned eyes. "I never felt horror, or regret, when I have taken lives before. I

193

never had that part of a soul. There is no embarrassment, or fear, but this time, I felt all those emotions. I was afraid, and I didn't know why. They continue to linger, like a curse."

Megeth looked up at Asher with blank eyes. "Something took possession of her, which should not have happened. To become a lich, there are dozens of elixirs to take over time periods. They break you down, harden many aspects of a soul and body, preparing them for the final ritual.

"Tianna is far along in the process. She is immune to mind control, or charm spells. This should not have happened, but it has. I do not have my books, or artifacts, to ferry out the truth of what happened."

Asher looked at the three women, before focusing on Tianna. His recent missing time swirled along his thoughts as he hardened his resolve.

"The same thing happened to me," Asher said.

Everyone looked at him with surprised eyes.

Asher continued, "I lost time during our session in the secret chamber. The next thing I knew, I was standing in front of Paasha's room entrance. She was on her knees, pleasuring me, because I asked her.

"I didn't remember anything, until a short time later. Memories came flooding back, showing me that we continued with our session, but I wanted more. I left the chamber and came upstairs looking for more.

"Tianna, what happened to you was not an isolated experience."

"Nyn said the same thing happened to her," Elara said with a gleam of worry in her eyes. "She didn't remember how she moved around the house, before memories came flooding back."

Megeth stood up and looked at Asher with knowing eyes. "Lord Blackwood, you have an anomaly on your farm. It has infected one of my people. I have concerns it will affect Venette, or myself. It may take control of Tianna again. I cannot allow such a risk to continue."

The lich moved closer to Asher, keeping her unblinking gaze on Asher's eyes. "Control is the greatest tool of a lich. If I cannot control myself, the consequences will be dire for not only this farm, but the entire valley. With regret, we must leave at once."

Asher suddenly felt a piece of their connection pull away.

"We can discover the cause of this anomaly," Asher said.

Megeth's lips smoothed into a small smile. She lifted her hand and touched his cheek.

"You are a treasure, my handsome Lord Blackwood. But we must be prudent. The risk is too great. We have enjoyed our stay immensely, but it is drawing to a close. For a time, we must ensure safety above all else."

The lich put her hands to Asher's strong chest, as her eyes gleamed with a sultry edge.

"Our time here was memorable. So memorable in fact, I feel an emptiness at having to leave. Should you discover the anomaly, and neutralize it, we can schedule another visit and stay. For now, we must part, or your neighbor may turn the valley into a battlefield."

The lich leaned in and kissed Asher on the lips. The kiss between them lingered, before Megeth pulled away.

"We will have to leave under the cover of night, to see you to the wild gate," Asher said.

"No need," Megeth said before an arcane word escaped her lips.

Dark energy rose around everyone in the room like a black flame. It engulfed everyone present, before there was a muted, dark flash.

Darkness washed away, Asher quickly seeing that they were at the edge of a clearing. He looked over to see the three, short standing stones. He then turned to Megeth, Tianna, and Venette. Elara and Amber were beside him, glancing around in subdued shock, but the shock quickly melted away from their demeanors.

Venette and Tianna moved away from the group. One stood before a standing stone, while the other stood before another one. Megeth moved to the standing stone closest to the small group.

The lich turned around in her cloak, and bent witch hat. She looked at Asher, Elara, and Amber with warm eyes.

"The time spent here was lovely, Lord Blackwood. You may not be your uncle, but I can sense you will surpass him in many ways. I look forward to seeing each other again."

Megeth looked down on the standing stone. "The wild gates are marvelous feats of stable magic, but their secrets were lost many eons ago. Good for you, I discovered a small secret, and I am willing to share it.

"The wild gates follow patterns to different gates, depending on the season, time of day, and lunar cycles, but they are designed to transport more than one or two individuals to specific locations."

Venette touched the stone she stood before. Tianna did the same thing.

Megeth reached down and touched the stone next to her.

Faint runes glowed along the weathered stones. Each rune shifted its place, moving across the hard surface. When they rearranged in a new order, the gate hummed with power. The very air vibrated as energy appeared and widened.

Megeth stood up, and turned slightly to look at the portal, but spoke to the young lord.

"It takes three to focus on a specific destination. It ensures it cannot be manipulated by one. With three, you can use the portal to go anywhere there is another wild gate. Take that knowledge as a gift, for your loving hospitality."

The beautiful lich turned her gaze to Asher, a small smile blooming. "I look forward to our next meeting."

"As do I," Asher smiled, but his eyes shined with a sliver of sorrow.

Megeth gave a single nod to the young lord, before turning her attention to Elara, and Amber.

"Take care of each other. Let our next meeting dive a little deeper into sensual possibilities."

Elara and Amber smiled and nodded.

Megeth turned to the portal. She walked toward it until she stepped in. In a blink, she was gone.

Venette looked at Asher with her crazy smile. "I will dream of our time together. I look forward to sucking your cock again."

Asher chuckled as the mad apprentice stepped into the portal and vanished.

Tianna hesitated as she looked over to the Asher. Her lip trembled, before a blankness fell over her features. She stepped closer to the portal, but her gaze lingered on the young lord.

"I'm sorry for any trouble I have caused. When I return, take what you will, for I will never deny you. Farewell."

Asher watched as Tianna stepped into the portal and vanished.

The oval tear in reality collapsed onto itself, and faded away.

Elara moved to one side of Asher, while Amber moved to the other side. A gloom descended on the trio, as minds worked.

"Could what happened be some kind of mystical attack from Lady Windswell?" Amber asked.

A faint memory drifted into Asher's mind. It was small, but spoke volumes the more he thought about it.

"Let's start walking back home. I think what happened might be something of our own doing," Asher said as an image of a few goblins remained in his mind's eye.

***

The secret chamber was silent as a tomb. Nyn laid on the bed, black book in hands. Her eyes moved from left to write, re-reading the book a second time this morning. The chamber was sound and light proof, only a lone lantern glowing on the nightstand next to the large bed.

The page turned. Nyn squirmed as she read on. The written words created such intense mental images, she didn't fight the tingling below, and along her nipples. Despite milking herself a few hours before, the black book stoked a fire she had not experienced before. It licked at her mind, as she read on.

Thighs moving, the elf held the book with one hand, while her other hand moved to her long dress. Slits ran up to her hips, leaving her legs partially exposed. The mood deepened into a silky hue, as her hand moved to a slit along her blue dress. Her hand moved like a snake hunting. When fingers touched her valley, she let out a soft sigh.

Continuing her reading, fingers moved with practiced skill, running along her engorged clit. The sensitivity only grew as she massaged herself with slow circles. Pink touched her cheeks as she devoured each sentence. The tempo grew a step at a time, rubbing herself to primal urges.

Full lips parted as lurid passages flowed. An image of Asher touched her fantasy, and her hips moved to her own touch. The

199

symphony grew as she rubbed herself faster, fingers making deep swirls.

A moan touched the air. Nyn tried to concentrate on the book, but the mood took full control. She put her hand down with the book in it. Her eyes closed as the tingling grew and she bit her lip. The vivid fantasy played on as she could not hold back any longer. The tension reached its crescendo, before her world flashed with blissful fire.

Nyn cried out as wetness surged. Her body shuddered as heavenly spirals cascaded along her senses. The tingling along her nipples stormed on, before wet spots appeared on her top. Body writhing, she milked her own orgasm as magical explosions ran through her.

When the heated moment faded a little, the elf relaxed into a living puddle. She stared at the ceiling, breathing heavily. Images of Asher floated along her addled mind. A warmth crawled along her body and soul, as deeper needs cried out for more.

The elf's eyes half-closed, an internal decision made. Legs moved slightly, enjoying the private moment.

Her hand never strayed from her private touch. Instead, fingers moved in slow, steady circles, ready to re-live the fantasy, as a deeper part of her mind planned for an intimate discussion with the Lord of Blackwood.

Chapter 13

Goblin Visions

Three figures emerged from the forest. Asher led the way as his gaze caught sight of the farmhouse in the short distance. A relaxed feeling eased the tension in his shoulders. The tension wasn't from traveling through the forest and back home. It was because there was going to be a serious discussion with the goblins, one he wasn't looking forward to.

Asher, Elara, and Amber walked over lush grass as they made their way toward the road and front gate of the estate. The silence between them was heavy. Elara looked at Asher, her heart filled with concern as recent events put all of them in harm's way.

Amber looked down as she walked. The faun felt the mood, coupled with the fight with Jarrag, set her mind to work. A small plan formed as she kept to herself.

Asher slowed down when the three of them reached the road. He turned to the elf and faun with serious eyes.

"A discussion must be had with the goblins, but I don't want anyone to think they are in trouble. Something has happened here, and we simply must know what it is, and try to prevent it from happening again," Asher said.

"What if it's something beyond our control? Are we to send one, or more of the goblins away? They have no place to go," Elara said with a sad tone.

Asher rubbed his jar. "We're not sending anyone away, but we will have to discover how to not allow this to happen again. Megeth, Tianna, and Venette returned home, but when we have any unusual future guests, we shouldn't chance a similar event.

"Jarrag was ready to kill me over a perceived slight, or history about my uncle. As nice as many are here in Mist Valley, my concern is more of that bleeding over. Things can get ugly very quick."

Elara and Amber nodded.

"I just wanted to make potions and perform in sensual plays," Amber sighed.

Man, and elf looked at the deflated faun. Then they both smiled.

"Is that all you think about?" Asher laughed.

"Yes," Amber said while she nodded.

The trio laughed in the middle of the dirt road, bathed in sunlight.

Elara turned her attention to Asher. "I do enjoy our plays, but now that Megeth and her apprentices are gone, do we continue our monastery play? I haven't had much time to partake, and I wanted to convince the master priest I was worthy of his blessing."

Asher grinned as he looked at the two beautiful women in the sunlight. "We haven't had a proper ending to our play. I think we should continue until we finish it. I have some ideas for the next one, but we will also have to welcome Nadia for her stay on the farm. She was very specific on what she desires, and I haven't read the book she wanted me to read yet."

The mood shifted as Asher thought about the farm and their growing family.

"I know we must handle a few things, but I don't want what we have to stop. We have all grown so close, or better, I have grown so close to everyone here, I don't want our happiness threatened."

Asher held out a hand to Elara and Amber. The elf took one hand, as the faun took the other. They held each other's hand, the three of them forming a triangle.

"I don't know what the future holds, but I want all of us who live here to have an unbreakable bond. Guests may come and go, but we will always be there for each other."

"This is our home, and we will do everything to protect it, and each other," Elara said with confidence.

"My only desire to be with the people I love," Amber smiled.

"As long as we are honest, and close, our bonds will never break," Asher said warmly.

The trio squeezed each other's hands. When they all let go, they turned and walked toward the front gate.

A short time later, they walked in through the front door of the home. The common room was deserted and quiet. Asher listened for any noise, but none came. As far as they knew, the goblins had not returned.

"Should we go searching for them?" Amber asked.

Asher shook his head. "They may return as we look for them. We will give them to sunset. If they are not back, I will go out and track them. Tracking at night isn't easy, but we have to give them the benefit of the doubt that they will be back for supper."

Asher thought about their recent disappearances and shrugged.

"They seem to be up to something, but I didn't want to press," Asher mentioned.

Elara's eyes widened a hair, but she kept quiet.

"I have to work in the lab for a little bit. If there is going to be a conversation with the goblins, I want my work finished beforehand," Amber said.

Elara looked down at her white dress, dirt and stains covering the hem. "I'm going to have to change. I may have to start wearing leggings more often."

Asher looked at the beautiful elf, and smiled. "But then, I will have to work harder to get you undressed."

The elf laughed as she looked at the young lord with adoring eyes. "Then maybe I shouldn't wear anything at all? Or maybe, just a collar?" she said with a sultry edge.

"I'm not against it," Asher said as his inner demons licked their lips.

"I better go, or I will drag both of you upstairs," Amber said as she walked toward the stairs and basement door.

Asher and Elara watched her go. When the faun disappeared down the stairs, the couple turned to each other.

Elara stepped closer to Asher. The pair looked into each other's eyes as their private song played across their souls.

"I was so scared for you," Elara said as her emotions crashed into her.

Asher watched as her playful demeanor fell apart. Her eyes gleamed as she held back tears. The worry she felt was plain as day, filling her expression with untold sorrows.

The young lord put his hand around the small of her back. He pulled her close and embraced her. Elara returned the embrace, fighting every urge to sob.

Asher never saw her like this. The well of emotion was overflowing, not just for the beautiful elf, but for himself. They started this journey together, and now, it was much bigger than either of them ever imagined.

"I was going to kill Jarrag," Elara whispered.

"I know," Asher said as he held her close.

"I'm not a killer, but I would have been today. I want you. I need you. You are so special to me, and I cannot imagine a life without you," Elara confessed.

Asher lifted a hand and touched a finger under her chin. He lifted her face up to his, tears streaming down her smooth cheeks. She looked up at her strong lover, drinking in his features like a fine wine.

Asher kept his confident, loving gaze on Elara's eyes.

"Always know, there is no enemy or situation, great or small, that will prevent me from loving you. I have hunted for the other half of my soul, and I found you. We share this journey together. Let the storms come, for we will defeat them, as one heart."

The mature elf's eyes trembled as she stared into Asher's soul.

"Divine Mother, he makes me so wet," Elara said with a harsh whisper.

The couple laughed as they held each other. A moment later, lips touched as tongues danced in mouths. Body heat grew, despite the cool air of the living room frost crystal.

When they parted from their loving kiss and embrace, it was Elara who let out a breathy sigh.

"I need to change. We can continue this discussion, after we finish with this mystery. I fear I may need a master priest so I may unburden my soul, and seek many blessings."

"I am sure something can be arranged," Asher smirked.

The elf turned and walked up the stairs. Asher watched her go, fighting the urge to follow her.

With the room empty, Asher wondered where Nyn was. Amber and Elara most likely searched the house for others, but didn't come back with the quiet elf. A thought stabbed into his mind, and the young lord made his way to the main corridor of the first floor.

After a twist and turn, Asher arrived at the library. He entered and looked over to the shelf hiding a secret door. He stepped to it, lifted a hand, and touched the hidden lever. The shelf came away from the wall, and Asher slipped inside.

He walked the very short corridor to the secret chamber. The inner door was ajar. He stepped into dim light, and found Nyn sitting on the edge of the bed, a black book beside her on the bed.

Sapphire eyes rose and looked at Asher.

"I was just getting up to find you," Nyn said.

Asher nodded as he stepped in and stood before her. "I assume you were in here for a while?"

Nyn nodded. "I wanted some private time to read this morning. This chamber is perfect for it. Did something happen?"

Asher nodded and told her what happened with Jarrag, and Megeth leaving. The more he explained, and told her about the oddness they all felt recently, the more Nyn realized that she was affected as well.

"This is troubling, but you think the goblins have a part in this?"

Asher nodded. "Not all of them, just one. We need to speak with Keefa to understand what happened, but I don't want to just single her out. All the goblins need to be present when we talk about it."

Nyn nodded. "That would be prudent."

The elf put her hand on the black book as she looked up at Asher. "If we have a moment, I wish to discuss something with you. Please, sit with me."

Asher sat down on the bed, the black book between him and Nyn.

The elf continued, "This book, the one Nadia gave you, has become special to me. I read it three times, and I think you should read it too.

"Not to give too much away, but it speaks on a subject I hadn't seen written before. The book is called Silence, and the plot revolves around a farm where everyone chooses not to speak, but let their desires speak for themselves.

"There are plenty of descriptions, but little to no dialogue. It has intrigued me enough that I wish this to be our private play."

Asher listened as she continued.

"In elven society, there are great discussions about everything, from politics, to food, to private intimacy. For as far back as I can remember, I endured such discussions. Elves think that only primal creatures grunt, moan, or growl. Words are the poetry of the soul, but I prefer written words over spoken ones. It has created a paradox for me as one of elven society."

The dark-blue-haired elf looked down with a longing in her eyes.

"I want our private play to be one of silence, and desire. I want you and I to speak the language of touch. Let our hands and bodies say what our urges want. It could be a playful glide of fingers on skin, or it could be forceful, taking each other without a single word spoken."

Nyn lifted her blue eyes to Asher. "The others would know, when these moments happen, they must be silent as well."

Asher nodded. "Can we grunt, moan, or growl?"

Nyn gave a rare, small smile. "Yes, for the throes of passion will never truly silence our hearts."

Asher smiled. "If this is what you wish, then I am willing. But as you know, it may happen often, especially if we are enjoying ourselves."

A warmth filled Nyn's eyes as pink colored her pale cheeks. "I know, and look forward to it."

"When do you wish to begin?"

"When we are ready. We will know the moment, when it strikes us," Nyn said softly.

The pull of their souls was undeniable. Asher lifted a hand and touched hers. Nyn looked at Asher with a gleam of happiness in her often-serious eyes.

"I have nearly finished my book. When it is finished, I will bring it to you to read," Nyn said before pulling her hand away.

Asher watched as she stood up, leaving the black book on the bed. She exited the secret chamber, with a small sway to her hips.

The young lord watched her go. When he was alone, he looked down on the book for a moment before picking it up.

"Better get started," Asher whispered to no one as he opened the book and began to read.

***

The sun hovered over the mountains, its radiant glow shifting from yellow, into a burnt orange. The air was still hot, but the humidity abated a little. As the sun sank lower, its light touching the tip of mountains, four goblins emerged from the western woods.

Blyss led the way, dirt on her face, hands, and bare feet. She glanced down at a small satchel at her hip. She opened it and looked down with wonderous pride on the collection of white mushrooms with tan brown-tops inside. She closed the flap and smiled as Paasha, Nuha, and Keefa followed. All the goblins had patches of dirt on them as they walked single file back to the fence of the Blackwood estate.

One by one, they slipped between the wide, two beam horizontal fence. Blyss led them with a happy spirit.

They made their way past the new barn and winery. They slowly approached the house, when Blyss noticed the kitchen door opening. Her smile faded slightly as Asher walked out, followed by Elara, Amber, and Nyn. The four of them walked toward them as the goblins walked in their direction.

"Do not speak of it," Paasha warned Blyss.

The goblin's eyes shifted to the side, a feeling of regret overcoming her.

When the two groups met, the goblins looked up to Asher and Elara's curious eyes.

"We should speak," Asher said to Blyss, seeing the patches of dirt on her clothes and emerald green skin.

Blyss slightly nodded, a feeling of dread filling her oval eyes.

"It's a little cooler now that the sun is going down. Maybe we should talk on the patio?" Elara asked.

"Yes, let's relax outside for a moment," Asher said with a small smile before leading the way.

Everyone moved as one group. They reached the covered patio beside the sitting pond. A few dragonflies hovered over the still pond, catching flying insects. Their wings vibrated as they darted around. Fireflies began to appear, their light glowing in and out of the growing shadows.

Everyone grabbed a seat under the patio roof. Asher purposely sat next to Blyss. The goblin glanced at him with nervous eyes. She sat on the chair, clasped her hands between her legs, and tilted her gaze downward.

A rough semi-circle formed as eight bodies sat, the goblins sitting beside each other.

Asher looked at Blyss, seeing the look of fear in her often brave and understanding eyes.

"We must have a talk, but fear not, we are only seeking information," Asher began before detailing what happened earlier in the day.

The goblins listened as Asher told them of the weird moments the last few nights, and the altercation with Jarrag from the Hornspear estate. Blyss's eyes widened as she heard about the harrowing fight. She mentally cursed herself for not being there to defend her lord and clan father.

When Asher finished, he shifted his gaze to Keefa. The goblin with long blonde hair looked at him with knowing, sad eyes.

"I remembered when you arrived, Paasha mentioned you have visions. I've been on enough adventures to know there are gifted people across Valoria. I've had to stop, or restrain those who could not control themselves.

"Keefa, because of recent events, I have to ask, did you have a hand in our missing time, and unusual actions?"

Blyss and Paasha jumped to their feet and stood before the blonde goblin, with their arms out.

"Master! She can't control it sometimes!" Blyss shouted.

"She try hard to control gift!" Paasha added in broken common.

Asher's neutral gaze softened. "Blyss, Paasha, this is not an attack. Keefa is not in danger, or in trouble."

Keefa sat up from her chair and put her hands on Blyss, and Paasha's shoulders.

"You no have to defend me. I will leave, and be taken away by wolves," the goblin said with a sad tone.

Everyone's eyes widened a little.

"Keefa, no one is telling you to leave," Asher said.

The goblin looked away.

"Master! Keefa is good goblin!" Paasha pleaded.

The young lord smiled. "I know she is. I know all of you are. The bigger concern is, if Keefa is affecting us, we need to find a way to stop it. Her gift took over a powerful lich's apprentice. Tianna attacked one of our neighbors, and nearly killed her. If it happens again, one of us may do something terrible."

"I no want anything bad to happen," Keefa said with mature eyes.

"I think we should be asking, how Keefa is able to take over our minds?" Nyn asked.

Paasha and Blyss lowered their arms. They turned and looked at the blonde goblin.

"Tell them," Blyss said with an edge of defeat.

Keefa gave a weak nod. The four-foot-tall goblin lifted her head and looked at Asher with shame painting her gaze.

"I... I leave my body. I take over minds, when I'm... hungry," the goblin admitted.

Asher lifted an eyebrow. "When you're hungry? There is plenty of food."

Keefa lowered her gaze, and shifted on her green feet.

"Hungry... not for food," the goblin said with a low tone.

Asher looked at her, unsure what she meant. A tiny moment later, it hit him like a boulder to the head.

The realization washed over everyone who was not a goblin. Amber hid her mouth with her hand, trying to not show her smile. Nyn's blank expression took a warm hue. Elara let out a relieved exhale, followed by a wicked smile.

Blyss walked up to Asher and looked him in the eyes. "Keefa is good, but always hungry. She need attention, but not from us. She needs attention from the clan father, or her dreams, her gift, will allow her to leave her body. She will hunt to satisfy her hunger."

Asher scratched at the back of his head, wondering how on Valoria these things happened.

Nyn looked over to Asher. "You have been remiss in your duties, Lord Blackwood," the elf said with deadpan clarity.

Laughter erupted from Asher, Elara, and Amber. The laughter carried on as the four goblins looked at them with confused eyes. Soon, they began a half-hearted laugh, unsure what was happening.

Asher wiped away a tear from the corner of his eye. He looked at the four goblins, a sense of relief and understanding filled his expression.

The young lord slid off the chair and was on his knees, before the four goblins. They looked at him with scared eyes, unsure what he was doing.

"You're telling me, Keefa has a gift of visions and mind control, and the only way to control it is to satisfy her hunger?"

The goblins nodded in unison.

"I think we can ensure Keefa, and all of you here, are well-fed," Asher winked.

"You no get rid of Keefa?" Paasha asked.

"What kind of clan father would I be if I kicked anyone out of the clan? A bad one. No, I think we can ensure this doesn't happen again, if you are sure that is the root of the problem?"

Keefa nodded, hope filling her eyes again.

Blyss stepped to Asher and threw her arms around his neck. She hugged him as he hugged her.

"I was scared. I thought you would be mad," Blyss whispered with trembling eyes.

"Never. You're important to me, to our family. If this is part of our family, then I embrace it, goblin traditions and all," Asher smiled.

The man and goblin pulled away from each other, love, and relief in their eyes.

Paasha stepped closer and looked at Asher as he stood up.

"We need you, clan father. We need you tomorrow evening. Come with us, after we have snake soup," Paasha said.

Asher looked at her with curious eyes. "Need me tomorrow? I thought tonight we would help with Keefa's hunger?"

Paasha shook her head. "Can't tell you everything now. Tomorrow, you come with us, at sunset. We tell you why, tomorrow."

Asher's eyes took on a confused look.

Elara looked at the young lord with a knowing smile. "I'm sure we can manage everything tomorrow evening. The goblins need you, and as clan father, you must listen."

Asher looked at the mature elf, seeing that she knew more than what she was saying. For Asher, he would interrogate her at another time, but for now, he would play the little game they all created.

"Okay, tomorrow," Asher smiled before looking at all the dirty goblins. "But before dinner tonight, baths for everyone."

Nuha eyes widened. "I'm not dirty!" she shouted as dirt clearly covered her face, arms, clothes, and feet.

Asher's eyes narrowed. "Everyone," he said with amused sternness.

"Run!" Blyss shouted.

The goblins scattered in different directions, laughing in the dying light of the day.

"Everyone, capture a goblin!" Asher shouted before he darted for Blyss.

Elara, Amber, and Nyn, chased after the fleeing goblins. Laughter filled the evening air, as fireflies hovered, lighting the growing shadows with their simple, natural magic.

Chapter 14

Soup and Primal Bonds

The dreamscape fell away as Asher slowly opened his eyes. A smile bloomed as he saw Elara on her side, looking at him with adoring eyes. Sunlight glowed from behind her, the curtains pulled back from the window.

"Good morning," the elf said with love in her eyes.

Asher reached over with his arm, touched her waist, and pulled her closer. She moved closer, snuggling close to him again.

The two were silent, enjoying the touch of their naked bodies. Small memories played on in their minds, the previous evening spent chasing and capturing goblins. Laughter echoed as the goblins couldn't stop their own laughing, even when they were caught. For most, the captured goblins marched back to the house. For Blyss, she was carried over Asher's shoulder, not putting up much of a fight.

Once inside, baths were prepared. Goblins stripped and climbed in. Elara, Asher, and Nyn proceeded to scrub them down, while Amber prepared supper. Elara gasped when Nuha playfully bit the elf's arm in protest, but she didn't penetrate skin. The beautiful elf growled as she splashed the goblin in the face with bath water. Nuha looked like a drowned cat as Elara held her in the water to scrub behind her ears.

Blyss nearly clung to Asher's arm as he scrubbed her down. She often kissed his arm as he washed her. For the young lord, he knew the goblins could bathe themselves, but this activity brought them all closer. Elara agreed as she helped scrub them down. Only Nyn seemed to not show any emotion as she scrubbed Keefa.

After everyone was cleaned, and clothes were changed, everyone marched down to a small feast. Amber was all smiles as she prepared the dining room with large plates of food. It didn't take long for everyone to dive in, and eat so much, at the end, they all slumped in their chairs, fat and happy.

Nyn was first to retire, the elf leaving the dining room without a word. Paasha stood up and moved about the table, cleaning up dishes. Blyss looked at Nuha and Keefa. The three of them nodded to each other, before Blyss led them away. Asher thought it was suspicious, but Elara distracted him by feeding him a morsel of food.

Amber yawned and left, heading to her room. Not long after, Elara took Asher's hand and led him upstairs.

Despite Asher and Elara's own appetites, the meal had a much more powerful effect. When the couple was naked, they fell into bed, and passed out with the lanterns still on.

This morning, the couple held each other in serene silence.

Asher was first to break the silence.

"You know what the goblins are up to," he said flatly.

"I don't know what you mean," Elara said as she snuggled closer.

219

"I didn't know you were a partner in their hidden scheme. You're not going to tell me?"

Elara smiled with her eyes closed, drinking in her lover's warmth.

"I promised," she whispered.

Asher looked down on her as she snuggled to his neck.

"Should I be worried?"

"No," the mature elf whispered.

The couple was silent for a moment. Asher's mind worked as he held the beautiful elf to him. A stirring had awakened, his manhood hard and throbbing against the elf's thigh.

Elara pulled back and lifted her upper body a little. She looked down on Asher with lustful morning eyes, her fingers running along his veiny cock.

"I have more questions," Asher grinned.

Elara let out a tired sigh. "If I fuck you, will it stop your questioning?"

"Perhaps," Asher said as his gaze fell to her large, full breasts. They began to leak milk, but the elf seemed unbothered by it.

"Trust the goblins. Afterwards, I want to hear all about it," Elara said as she moved over him and straddled his waist.

Asher reached up and cupped her firm ass cheek as the mature elf took his hard member and slowly impaled herself.

She slowly slid down to the hilt before their bodies began to move of their own accord.

For a moment, Asher wondered what tonight would bring. The moment slipped away as it was replaced by loving pleasure.

***

The day carried on with a touch of mystery. Asher and Amber worked in the lab, preparing batches of potions. Elara, Nyn, and Blyss, tended to the grape crops by watering and cutting away dead vines.

In the kitchen, Nuha toiled over a large pot on the stove. The goblin stirred the contents as Paasha and Keefa cut up more ingredients. The two goblins often walked over with hands full of ingredients, and dumped them in the soup. Nuha smiled as she looked down at the soup, a full feeling filling her heart.

The day wore on. Elara, Nyn, and Blyss came back into the farmhouse mid-afternoon. The elves were exhausted as they made their way upstairs to wash the layer of dirt off them from tending to the field.

Blyss stayed with the other goblins in the kitchen, as they cooked the special soup. After a few quick words, she made her way upstairs, to join the pair of elves as they bathed in the master washroom.

When the sun was low in the sky, Asher and Amber emerged from the basement lab. They were greeted by Blyss, the goblin fresh-faced and all smiles. She told them to get cleaned up for supper.

An hour later, everyone came down, clean and relaxed. They made their way to the dining room, and when they entered, they looked around in amazement.

The long dining table had a fresh tablecloth. Large bowls lined the table, each one filled with a dark, chunky soup. Nuha finished pouring soup into the final bowl and looked at everyone at the doorway with pride. Large plates of breads, fruits, and cheeses lined the middle of the table. Silverware lined the table beside each full bowl.

"Impressive," Asher smiled.

Blyss walked over to Asher and took his hand. She led him to the head of the table, where he sat down. Blyss glanced at Elara. The mature elf gave her an approving nod. The goblin smiled and sat in the chair to the right of the young lord.

Nyn, Elara, and Amber, sat at the other end of the table. Paasha sat on the left side of Asher. Keefa sat next to Blyss, as Nuha sat next to Paasha.

Asher looked at the seating arrangements, before looking down at the soup.

"This looks delicious," he said, remembering when he had snake soup before on his travels.

All four goblins smiled.

"Before we begin," Blyss said with a happy glow in her yellow eyes, "I must speak about goblin tradition."

Everyone listened as the goblin continued.

"When there is a change within a clan, or at the beginning of a new clan, a special soup is made to honor such a change. It is a celebration, and a bonding experience," the goblin said in perfect common.

Blyss turned her attention to the goblin with short hair. "Nuha Snakeeater is the keeper of our tradition. She cooks the soup as the rest of the clan aids her. We thank you, Nuha, for cooking our traditional soup," Blyss bowed.

The goblins bowed to the Nuha. Everyone else followed, mirroring the goblins.

Heads up, Blyss turned her attention to Asher.

"Master, you saved our lives. You fought for us, and took us as your own. For that, we create a new clan, in your honor. The Blackwood Clan is our new clan. You are our clan father, as Paasha is our clan mother, but all clans need a chief, and chieftess."

Asher listened as it all came together.

They're making it official, but who will be the clan chieftess?

Blyss's green cheeks turned a dim shade of pink. "Tradition demands we consume the soup, and follow the forest spirits. They will lead us to a special place, where you must decide who will be your clan chieftess.

"This decision can only be made when the time is right. We will all see the signs, as the forest spirits speak to us."

Nyn looked down at her soup with a questioning rise of her thin eyebrow.

"Please, everyone partake, but only goblins may lead," Blyss said cryptically.

Asher hesitated. He had snake soup before, but not goblin snake soup. From what Blyss said, he wondered if there was more than pieces of snake meat and broth. When he looked at the happy goblin to his right, he couldn't deny her bright happiness. She looked like she was in a trance, like something was happening that she may have only dreamed about.

Despite his hesitation, Asher remembered Elara's words from this morning. Seeing Blyss so happy, and knowing her heart, she would never hurt him. Taking hold of his spoon, he dipped it into the soup, and lifted a chunk of cooked snake meat and cloudy broth.

"We honor our tradition," Asher said with a bow of his head to the goblins.

Everyone took hold of their spoons. They dipped it into the soup, and lifted them up.

Asher was first to put the end of the spoon in his mouth. After a sliver of time, an explosion of delightful flavor struck his tongue.

Asher's eyes widened with how good the soup was. He quickly dipped his spoon into the broth and lifted it to his mouth. The taste of meat and broth stunned him, as he felt he couldn't get enough.

Across the entire table, everyone took their first taste. Eyes widened as they quickly scooped up some more.

Nuha watched with proud eyes as she too had her soup. Spoons dived into bowls, and came up with dripping broth and chunks of cooked snake. Nyn took small spoonfuls, but even she could not resist the divine taste of the odd soup.

Hands soon lifted and picked up other items from the center of the table. Bread was dipped into the broth and consumed. Pitchers of water were poured into cups. Warmth filled bellies in the cool dining room.

A warmth wrapped around Asher like a cozy blanket. When his bowl was finished, he turned his gaze to Blyss, and a weakness pulled at every muscle in his body.

The goblin was radiant to the young lord. An aura surrounded her as her beauty seemed magnified in his eyes. A drunk feeling cascaded over the young man's senses as he couldn't look away from her.

A voice from deep within whispered to Asher. He looked down at the empty bowl. The edges of the bowl began to move, and ripple. The voice in the back of his mind continued to whisper, experience from years ago came clawing to the surface of his mind. He tried to talk, but his lips moved without sound. When he tore his gaze from Blyss, and looked across the table, he noticed the wide eyes and odd movements of everyone at the table.

The dining room began to waver and blend together. Elara smiled brightly as she relaxed in her chair. Amber stared at nothing, lost to some inner thoughts. Nyn smiled as she picked up her bowl of soup and drank the last of it down.

Asher turned his head to the goblin with short hair. "Nuha... is there a special kind of mushroom in this soup?"

The goblin nodded, her head leaving a trail of movement after each nod.

"Many sacred ingredients," the goblin said with a toothy smile.

Asher nodded, his head feeling heavy. A memory caressed his addled thoughts, a time where he was in the forest with his father identifying mushrooms, those that were edible, and those that could poison, or create odd effects. To be a proper ranger, some of the mushrooms had to be ingested to know the effects. The memory opened further, remembering how one mushroom in particular caused an unusual, but harmless effect.

Paasha stood up and took Asher's hand. She pulled it as she looked at him with loving eyes.

Asher didn't think as he stood up.

Blyss, Nuha, and Keefa stood up from their seats, and crowded around the young lord. Asher looked at the others. Elara and Nyn looked around lost, but Amber looked back at him with calm, happy eyes.

"Don't worry, Lord Blackwood. I've experienced this before. I will ensure Elara and Nyn are safe, and enjoying the experience," the faun reassured him.

"This is delightful," Nyn said as she looked at her hand.

Elara looked across the table to Asher.

"Have a grand time," she giggled before blowing him a kiss.

Asher smiled with half-closed eyes, before he blinked. A hand tugged his, and he started walking without looking.

The young lord finally turned his head as he walked, surrounded by four goblins. He walked with careful steps, as reality pulsed and shifted around him. Paasha had a firm grip on his hand, leading him out of the dining room, along the corridor, through the kitchen, to the side door.

The door opened and they all stepped out into the evening light.

Asher's breath was taken away as he saw the glorious sky. A pinkish glow filled the heavens, and the symphony of crickets played in the background. Lowering his gaze, he saw the gentle flashing of fireflies as he walked like one of the dead. A happy feeling poured over his senses, letting go of any tension in his body. As far as he knew, he belonged to the goblins, nature, and the coming night.

The young lord looked down at Keefa. The blonde goblin's blonde hair glowed like a golden river. She glanced up at him with shy eyes, but the longer Asher looked at her, laughing demons filled the centers of her eyes. When he looked away to Nuha, the goblin glanced at him, her eyes slitted like snake eyes.

"Where are we going?" Asher asked with a faraway voice.

"To our destiny," Paasha said in perfect common.

Asher chuckled, unsure if he should be afraid, or excited. His spirit glowed, as a near child-like wonderment filled his eyes. The air was perfect as shadows grew longer across the grassy ground. Fireflies lit the way as the five of them reached the west fence, before the western forest.

Goblins climbed between the two horizontal beams. Asher stepped to the fence and climbed over. He lost his footing and crashed onto the soft ground. A scent of dirt touched his nose, and he wanted to dig until nature hugged him.

Laughter filled his ears as he lifted his head, the four goblins taking hold of him and helping him to stand up. On his feet, Asher was led by his hands into the forest.

Time made wonky jumps as Asher walked through the endless forest. He would occasionally look down with confused eyes, the goblins taking turns holding his hands. Paasha let go of his hand, and she darted into the darkening forest.

"Paasha, wait!" Asher shouted.

"She will be okay," Blyss said as she pressed Asher's hand to her cheek.

Asher fought through the effects of the goblin soup. He tried to regain his wits, but everything he tried was thwarted by distractions. He turned his head to see a wood spirit walking along a low branch. It had leaves along its tiny arms and legs, its body made up of pieces of bark. It waved at him, and Asher waved back. A weight was on his arm. Asher looked down to Blyss hanging on it as he waved. The goblin laughed as he put his arm down.

"The forest spirits are with us. They are here to witness, and bless our bonding," Keefa said with knowing eyes.

"I've seen forest spirits before, but they were never this cute," Asher grinned as he walked.

The trees swayed to a light breeze. Movement moved along branches, and along the sides of the thin path. Shiny eyes looked up at the man and goblins. Many waved as Asher's gaze darted from one forest spirit to another.

"We're surrounded," Asher laughed. "I think we're in danger."

The goblins laughed as they led him along.

"They are here to protect us," Blyss grinned.

Asher looked down on the beautiful goblin, and smiled.

"I believe you. I trust you."

Blyss giggled as forest spirits did cartwheels or waved at them.

A light touched the edge of Asher's gaze. He lifted his head to see a glow among the trees in the forest. It called to him, like moths to a flame. He, and the goblins, walked with purpose as they approached it.

The sun vanished behind the horizon. Darkness swallowed up the forest, except for a small part. Asher and the goblins stepped into a tiny clearing, his unblinking eyes drinking it all in.

A small, rough platform was in the middle of the small clearing. Lanterns hung from tree branches, illuminating the area. Small bowls filled with herbs lined the area at the base of the trees, small plumes of smoke rising from them. The scent was one of lavender, and a few other herbs. Asher knew the scents, a repellant of insects, but together, they seemed more powerful.

On the small, raised platform, thick blankets, and large pillows filled it. They were arranged in a way to look like a bird nest.

"This is what you've been working on?" Asher asked in a subdued tone.

The goblins nodded all at once.

From behind a tree, Paasha stepped into the warm light. The motherly goblin was naked, white runic markings painted along her body. Her emerald green skin glowed in the lantern light, as she held a small bowl with what appeared a white paste.

Asher was mesmerized as he stared at the beautiful goblin. When something shifted in the dark forest behind her, he lifted his gaze. Glowing eyes of different sizes hovered in the inky darkness. Some were animal eyes, while others were alien. They didn't blink, staring into Asher's soul as he stared back at them.

"I see you," Asher whispered, not afraid of the unusual forest spirits.

When he pulled his gaze away, he saw that Blyss, Nuha, and Keefa were undressing.

"Tonight, we bond as a clan," Paasha said as she stepped to Keefa.

Asher watched with subdued eyes as the motherly goblin dipped her fingers into the white paste. Keefa's clothes fell away as she stood naked. Small breasts defied gravity as her silky-smooth green skin absorbed the light. Yellow eyes held a primal understanding, as Paasha ran her fingers along parts of her nude body. Asher's gaze was drawn to her sensual thighs, and tuft of blonde hair above her goblinhood.

When Paasha was finished, she stepped over to Nuha. The slender goblin stood with brave eyes. Her body was thin, having small, but noticeable curves. Her goblinhood lacked hair. Her limbs were a little longer than her sister goblins. Short hair flopped to one side as she stood, Paasha marking her body.

Asher turned his gaze to Blyss. The voluptuous short goblin stood without a drop of shyness or fear in her eyes. Swollen breasts fought gravity's pull as she stood on thick legs. Her eyes were locked on Asher, a rising hunger filling them.

Paasha made her way over to Blyss. Her fingers dipped in the thin paste mixture and began marking her body. Time sped up and slowed down as Asher watched. The forest was alive with spirits, many of them witnessing the primal ritual.

When Paasha was finished, she moved to the edge of the clearing and put the small bowl down. She then turned around and addressed everyone present.

"Clan father, the time come for you to become our clan chief. We bond to be one clan, under your protection, and love. Clan Blackwood must have chief, and chieftess. You choose which of us to be chieftess.

"Chief and chieftess will be grand tree of clan, strong, and sturdy. All clan obey you. As clan mother, I make sure clan is tended too, but I no can be chieftess. You must pick another, from clan.

"When chieftess is chosen, we bond as clan. We become one. Choose."

Asher didn't hesitate. He turned his attention to Blyss, and bowed slightly at the hip.

"I choose you, Blyss," Asher said with a loving tone.

Blyss's eyes trembled as her heart leapt in her chest. She stepped forward to him, and knelt before him, her head down.

"I accept," the goblin said loud enough for all to hear.

Paasha nodded. "Clan chief, take her. Make her yours."

Asher knelt to the beautiful goblin. She lifted her head, looking up to him with watery eyes.

Paasha moved behind Asher. She took hold of his shirt. Asher lifted his arms, the shirt coming up. The moment he was shirtless, Blyss coiled her legs under her and sprang up like a snake. She pressed her lips to his as she threw her arms around his neck.

Asher took hold of the goblin's thin waist and stood up with her. Her legs dangled as she held on, not wanting to break the kiss. For a better hold, Asher cupped her ass with both his hands, as other goblins' hands grabbed at his belt and leggings. Tongues danced as leggings came down. Asher stepped out of them until he too was fully naked.

The warm air, and hot goblin body pressed to him, sent a surge of blood to his manhood. It stood up instantly between Blyss's thick thighs. Hands and cock held her up as they continued to kiss.

"We witness," Paasha said.

Asher barely heard her as he stepped back. His calf muscle touched the edge of the raised round platform. Sitting down on it, comfortable soft blankets and pillows greeted his naked rump. Blyss's feet came around and landed on the platform. She pushed with her whole body, Asher falling back into the middle of the nest.

The forest and night sky above swirled into a halo of light and trees. Every one of Asher's senses was magnified as he looked up in wonderment. When Blyss's face came into view, she looked down on him with happy eyes.

"My strong chief," the goblin said as she rubbed her dripping slit against Ashers's standing cock.

"My beautiful chieftess," Asher said as pleasure glowed from skin to skin contact.

The forest bent inward to them, as glowing eyes watched with muted fascination. Blyss slid her body down against Asher's body. His cock bent until it reached between her breasts. The goblin moved so her master's cock was against his stomach. Her tongue slid out, Asher's member between her warm mountains. She licked the shaft and head, while moving her body against his.

Asher lifted his head slightly, and looked at the goblin. She moved like a primal creature in heat. Low moans dripped as she licked his cock like it was an ancient god. Paasha, Nuha, and Keefa, sat around the nest. They watched with warm eyes as their new chieftess licked their clan father's cock.

Keefa couldn't contain herself as she watched. Her hand slipped between her thighs, touching, and rubbing herself as she watched the lovers enjoy each other. A small moan floated up, joining the sounds of the magical forest night.

The young lord watched as Blyss closed her dark green lips around his cock. When she began to suck and bob her head, a small groan fell from his lips. Sensations glowed brighter, hotter, each stroke like touching a goddess on the edge of realms. The loving bob of her head caused his manhood to throb. Memories of their intimate times together crashed into him, seeing, and feeling their connection.

Asher's eyes softened as he saw the truth. The moment he saved her from the wolves, she gave everything to him. She wanted him for all time, and he knew he wanted the same.

The clan chief reached over and touched her chin as she sucked his cock. She opened her eyes and looked up, still sucking on his member.

"Sit on your throne, so I may admire your beauty," Asher said with a commanding whisper.

Blyss let her lover's cock slip from her mouth. She crawled up closer to him. When she was on his lap, she lifted her hips up as his cock head touched her dripping valley. With a long moan, the goblin impaled herself on him, thick inches spearing her inner world. When she reached the hilt, the goblin let out heated gasps, the yawning abyss in her soul now filled.

Asher sat up, his strong arms embracing her. The goblin snuggled to him, as her hips bounced slightly. The wet sounds of their union joined the songs of the forest. Blyss clutched at her master, feeling his love stretch her inner world to the limit. She squeezed him with each bounce, wanting this moment to last forever,

The young lord looked down on Blyss with loving eyes. Their scents rose from their union. Wetness touched his chest, feeling goblin milk running down his skin. Animalistic moans vibrated against his chest, the goblin increasing the tempo.

Keefa moaned as she sat back, one arm holding her up while her other hand rubbed her dripping slit. The blonde goblin whined as she watched the couple with hungry eyes.

Nuha stared, watching how Blyss humped their master. She studied it, committing it to memory, eager to please him as well.

Paasha touched her swollen breast. She gave it a squeeze, feeling the tingling sensation along her nipples. Soon, a bead of milk appeared. The connection to the Divine Mother struck her, and soon, rivulets of milk began to spill. The motherly goblin let out a loving moan, seeing Blyss happy.

Time slowed to a crawl as the couple held each other close. Blyss kissed Asher's shoulder a few times, before she bared her teeth.

Asher stared at her as she bit down on his shoulder. There was a sharp flash of pain, but it quickly diminished. The goblin continued to move her hips, as her tongue lapped at some blood. Her grunts grew as she sucked on the small wound. Asher continued to hold her close, letting her drink from him.

Nuha gasped as she caught the scent of blood. Seeing how calm and relaxed Asher was, her own hips began to move. She fell forward on her hands, unable to control her own body. She watched with wide eyes as her entire body tingled.

The tender, intimate moment glowed between man and goblin. Asher's cock was rock hard, the goblin moving on it, punishing herself on him. Dark green nipples leaked milk as she licked at his small wound.

A demonic hunger took hold of the young man. Asher's eyes hardened as his urges whipped into a frenzy. A growl filled his throat. Blyss humped his cock faster, getting close to her own orgasms. When she was nearly to the zenith, she was turned while still clutching to him. Her back slammed down in the middle of the comfortable nest. Asher was over her, driving his rigid member between her parted, thick thighs.

Blyss cried out in ecstasy as Asher grabbed her engorged breast and squeezed it. Milk spurted slightly before he clamped his mouth over it. He sucked from her and she moaned so loud, the forest sang with her. Teeth held her nipple like a vice, milk spilling into his mouth, the young man drinking it down.

Asher didn't care that goblin milk caused a temporary madness. He drank her soul as he pinned her down. His manhood stabbed her over and over, the goblin crying for more.

When the goblin milk touched his stomach, no madness came. Instead, power and confidence grew like a bonfire. It fueled his already mad mind, driving his soul into the goblin.

Blyss's clawed fingers raked down her master's back. Lines of blood bloomed as she reached the edge of ecstasy. When Asher pulled his head up from her breast, and looked down at her with a deep, primal hunger, white touched her gaze as a swarm of explosions shattered her soul. Eyes slowly rolled into her head as each thrust caused many orgasms to glow brighter. Her soul was blasted to glass as she let out unusual moans.

Asher's eyes gleamed with demonic light. He bared his teeth, the forest spirits invading his spirit. He clamped his teeth on her shoulder, biting so hard, blood bloomed. The feral lover licked Blyss's blood as her legs trembled. She moaned louder, magical explosions carrying on like they would go forever. Whimpers and seductive moans matched curled toes. The power in Asher's thrusts caused her body to bounce. Milk surged from her nipples as her soul left her body.

The taste of blood fueled the young lord. He savored her taste as it tingled along his spirit. When the moment struck, Asher thrust deep into his goblin lover. Thick ropes of seed flooded her already flooded inner world. Honey and come dripped from their connection, the young lord unable to stop himself. Blyss clung to him, her eyes still firmly in her head. Weakness flowed into her muscles, and she let go. She fell a very short distance to comfortable blankets and pillows. There she stayed as her lover pushed every drop of his love into her.

Asher lifted his head like a wild animal on a hunt. He turned and glared as the goblins surrounding them, each one caught in the throes of sultry desire.

"To me, my clan," Asher said like a feral monster.

The goblins instantly where to their feet. Asher licked at Blyss's cheek before pulling out. Come leaked from the goblin's abused valley as Asher sat down. He glowered as two goblins were to him. He stared at nothing as Nuha licked his shaft, while Keefa sucked on the wet, come-covered tip of his cock. The goblins snuggled closer, eager to please their clan father and chief.

Paasha moved until she was between Blyss's parted thighs. The motherly goblin looked down to Blyss's slit, seed and honey dripping from it. She lowered her mouth until lips touched tender flesh. Her tongue snaked out, licking the thick come into her mouth, and swallowing it. Eyes trembled as she tasted the soul bond. It inflamed her own desires, licking more and letting the tip of her tongue caress Blyss's clit.

Blyss let out soft moans as her eyes fluttered.

Asher watched with amused and loving eyes, Keefa and Nuha trying to take all of his cock. The hunger within him grew as his manhood stayed fully hard. The lustful needs clawed at him. Keefa moaned until hands took hold of her. The goblin let out a whine as his cock was pulled from her mouth. Her body was turned around and forced on all fours. A strong hand held her in place as something touched her dripping slit.

"Mine," Asher growled as his hips pushed.

Keefa's eyes widened as her mouth made a perfect oval. Her entire world was forced open as her clan father's cock slowly invaded her. Inch after inch caused deep gasps as she adjusted to his size. She looked over her shoulder to see Asher looking down at their connection with inhuman eyes.

"Yours," the blonde goblin said as she surrendered to him.

Nuha whined as she moved behind Asher and Keefa. She stood up and watched as their clan chief punished Keefa from behind. She arched her back so deep, it allowed their lord to plunge her depths with ease. Raised veins slid against pink lips, their connection snug.

Nuha looked at Asher's back, seeing the lines of wet blood. She lowered her head and licked at his small wounds, savoring the taste of his soul.

Asher punished the goblin's green ass with hard thrusts. Keefa's eyes rolled into her head, feeling deep waves of bliss as they crashed on her spirit. Her body shuddered with each impact of his hips, driving her closer and closer to the edge of the abyss. All the moments of wanting, needing, the young lord vanished. She basked in his attention, moaning for more as her nails shredded a blanket in her grip.

The forest leaned closer, witnessing the primal bonding. Eyes watched with a haunted glow, the new clan leader taking his clan, one by one.

Lustful passion stormed the blonde goblin. When she reached the edge of the cliff, she willingly jumped to Asher's soul. When his cock thickened, she fell into his embrace. Inner explosions set her world on fire. Odd moans fell from parted lips. Sultry pleadings continued as her thighs trembled from his unyielding power.

Asher let out a hard grunt, spurts of thick come flooding her inner world. The fire of passion grew as Keefa let out exhausted moans. Arms and legs trembled as her body shuddered again and again. A tsunami of pleasure crashed down on her, and she was swept from the tide.

Asher grunted as the blonde goblin collapsed. His cock slipped from her and spurted on her lower back. Keefa gasped for air as every nerve vibrated from ecstasy's embrace.

The new clan chief felt Nuha behind him, licking his wounds. A hand reached around and grabbed her arm. The goblin was pulled around to the front of him.

Nuha stood with wide, hungry eyes. Asher looked at her like a predator admiring his prey. When his gaze fell to her thin thighs, he noticed a drop of honey sliding down her inner thigh.

"I serve, clan chief," Nuha whispered.

"Yes, you do," Asher said as he grabbed her arm again and pulled her close.

Nuha let out a happy sigh as he took hold of her. She spread her legs as he pulled her down on his still standing, wet cock. She sat down on his cock, Asher's hands on her thin waist. Wetness bloomed as she was slowly impaled on him.

"You want me?" Nuha gasped as her master's cock parted her tight world.

Asher grunted as he pushed her down, taking every inch.

"No one wants Nuha," the goblin said as pleasure caused her body to tremble.

"I want you. I want all of my clan," Asher said as he roughly helped her to bounce on his throbbing manhood.

Nuha let out a deep moan as her body surrendered to their new clan chief. The thin goblin grabbed Asher's wrist. She pulled his hand away from her hip and put it to her throat. Asher looked at her as reality wavered.

"Please, if you care for Nuha, you choke Nuha," the goblin begged.

Asher stared at her as she looked at him with pleading eyes. His heart glowed for the goblin, unsure what trauma she had endured, but the desire was there like a flaming forest.

Asher's hand tightened around the goblin's throat.

"Yes," Nuha said with a straining voice.

"You are mine, to do as I please," Asher said with a threatening tone.

Nuha's eyes rolled into her head, his strong hand having tight control of her. She bounced on his member like a dutiful goblin. She struggled for air, blooms of ecstasy filling her. Ragged moans rose up as Asher stabbed her thin valley with his girthy member.

The goblin fell into a deep, relaxed state. She held his wrist with both hands, not trying to push his hand away, but keeping it to her throat. She moved her hips, trying to coax his seed from him, to secure her place in the clan.

Asher felt he could read her thoughts. They pressed on him like they were sharing the same mind. He squeezed a little more, and Nuha let out a long, ragged sigh.

Wetness surged into a squirt. Asher stared at the goblin as her body trembled, wetness soaking both. Their connection was still snug, inches appearing and disappearing. Body heat glowed as wet sounds blended with ragged breathing.

The thin goblin's head lolled to the side. Asher let go just as his cock thickened. Spurts of molten come filled the thin goblin. Her hips continued to move as her mind was lost to seas of paradise. Weakness flowed into her as she wilted. Asher took hold of the goblin and gently laid her on the pillows, her body spasming from the string of powerful orgasms.

When Nuha was down, Asher turned to see Paasha's head buried between Blyss's thighs. Blyss moaned as the older goblin licked at her. With Paasha's ass in the air, Asher moved with liquid ease to her. Wetness and come dripped off his cock as he took it and pushed it into her unguarded valley entrance.

The motherly goblin didn't break away from licking Blyss, as their clan father pushed into her. She pushed her ass to him, making sure he was inside, and squeezed him.

"Make her come, and I will make you come," Asher commanded as his inner demons sang.

Paasha stayed to task, licking Blyss's clit as she was punished from behind.

Asher's body moved like a beast. The world around him took on a dreamy haze. Spiritual chains connected to his heart, and spread out to other hearts close by. As he fucked Paasha, Blyss's eyes fluttered open. She looked past her leaking breasts to her lord before her. He was on his knees, but he looked as powerful as the first day she met him. The feeling of love overwhelmed her, and in a flash, orgasms stormed past her gates of control. Her thick legs trembled as Paasha licked her clit just the right way.

The young lord watched with warm eyes, seeing her enjoy her orgasm. It was enough for him to pull out his cock and spurt ropes of seed all over Paasha's back. The touch of hot come caused the motherly goblin to moan her delight, her body betraying her. Wetness dripped from her slit, several orgasms causing heat to glow from her body.

Paasha moved aside as she tried to collect her wits. Asher gently fell on Blyss, kissing and licking at her skin. The goblin held onto him, keeping him close as he nuzzled her.

"We... are... a... true... clan," Blyss whispered.

"Yes, we are," Asher smiled as his cock bounced.

The former ranger felt bodies getting closer. He and Blyss turned their heads to see Keefa, Nuha, and Paasha moving closer. The three goblins moved with primal hunger as the forest waved to their union.

"To me, my clan," Asher smiled.

The goblins launched and crashed into him. Asher was knocked off of Blyss and onto his back. Bodies crowded around, kissing, and licking at him. Blyss joined the rest of the clan as they crowded around him.

Asher continued to laugh and smile, as the forest spirits, the Divine Mother, and the starry sky, gleamed with dreamy blessings.

Chapter 15

Living a Dream

Asher opened his eyes to the bright morning. A low groan floated up from his lips, his body bruised and sore. Stiffness filled every limb as he attempted to move one. His body didn't respond, as a weight pushed at him in several directions. Lifting his head slightly, he saw and felt goblins piled on, and against him. They were sound asleep, breathing gently in the morning light.

The young lord blinked as he resigned himself to his fate of being trapped in the woods. The scent of morning air and goblins filled his nose. The lanterns hanging on trees had long gone cold. The temperature was cool, but he could only tell by the air touching his face. The rest of him was warm, with naked goblins all over him.

A headache reared its ugly head, Asher wincing in pain. Flashes of last night crawled into his waking thoughts. The obscene and lurid moments were burned into his mind, reliving a private orgy of clan chief, chieftess, and clan members.

Asher looked at the goblins on him again. Blyss was sleeping on him, as Paasha was to his right, against his arm. He could feel Keefa snuggled to his left. Between his parted legs, he could feel Nuha there, snuggled to his manhood.

"Damn," Asher whispered as a sore tingling filled his manhood. It began to rise, despite the pain.

The young lord simply laid there, trying to ignore it. The night had been a fever dream of coiling bodies and intimate moans. It carried on, Asher not sure where he began, and each goblin ended. The effect of the soup had worn off, but the spiritual experience stayed with him. His demons slept, fat and exhausted. Never in a million years would he have guessed that he reached his limit, but he had. There was not a drop of tension in his body. He stared at the blue sky, lost in ancient understanding of everything, and nothing.

Nuha was first to stir. Something thick and warm pressed against her cheek. She opened her eyes to her clan chief's cock. Sultry eyes stared for a moment before she took hold and closed her lips over it.

Asher let out a long exhale. Despite the deep soreness, his body refused to simply relax.

Blyss was next to stir. She opened her sleepy eyes and looked at Asher. She grinned with half-closed eyes, as she remained on top of him.

"We... should get back to the house," Asher said with a hoarse whisper.

Blyss made a weak nod, lifting her head up. She looked over her shoulder to between her own parted legs. Nuha's head bobbed with the clan father's cock in her mouth.

Blyss looked back at Asher and yawned.

"Should Nuha finish with you first?" the goblin said with a small stretch of her arms.

"Maybe... later?" Asher said through clenched teeth.

Blyss nodded and tapped her foot on Nuha's shoulder.

"Later," she shouted.

Nuha took a long drag of her lips before letting go, disappointment in her eyes.

Paasha and Keefa stirred. The blonde goblin hugged Asher's arm tighter, not wanting to let go.

"We should get back," Asher said as he tried to get up.

Goblins fell to either side of him as he sat up. The morning air felt good on his skin as he looked around to the plain forest.

"Now that we are formally a clan, what happens next?" Asher asked as he scratched at his disheveled hair.

"We live our lives," Blyss yawned again. "We make sure we are protected and happy."

"We want you happy," Nuha said as she licked her lips.

Asher smiled, despite a dark thought at the back of his mind. After such a boisterous night, his body will recover, and will want more.

The young lord yawned. Thoughts of Elara, Amber, and Nyn touched his mind.

"Let's get home. We have to check on the rest of our clan," Asher said.

The goblins nodded as they stood up. Everyone rushed to their clothes as Asher stared at the forest for another moment.

"What a night," he said to no one as birdsong filled the morning air.

***

Bodies shambled out of the western woods. Asher led the way, eyes vacant and his clothes disheveled. The haunted darkness under his eyes told the story of the entire night, and he wondered how he was going to get through the day.

Most of the goblins marched behind the clan father and chief. Their spirits were high, as their bodies moved with a little extra energy. Only Blyss, the clan chieftess, walked along Asher's side, her chin held high.

Asher glanced at the beautiful goblin, his heart swelling with love. Blyss had a look like she was ready to take on the world.

The small clan reached the fence of the estate, and climbed over it. They continued to make their way toward the house. After a few long moments, Asher stepped into the kitchen with concerned eyes.

The kitchen table was filled with bowls, and half-eaten breads and cheeses. To the young lord and former ranger, it looked like the aftermath of some kind of feeding frenzy. Half full bottles of wine were strewn about, with one tipped over and a puddle of dried wine on the floor.

"We weren't the only ones to celebrate," Asher mentioned as he made for the main corridor, and the stairs.

The goblins followed, eager to know the details from the two elves and faun.

The group made their way upstairs, following crumbs and pieces of food left behind. On the second floor, the trail of food and crumbs led to the master bedchamber. Asher walked with purpose, moving along the length of the corridor until they reached the bed chamber. He put his hand on the half-opened door and gave it a small push. The young lord stepped into the bedchamber, celebratory carnage greeting his tired eyes.

The chamber was a mess. Clothes, empty wine bottles, and half eaten food everywhere. On the bed, Amber and Nyn were snuggled to Elara. All three were half-naked, or completely naked, limbs all over each other. Small snores floated up as the trio didn't stir at all from the lord and goblins.

"At least they're okay," Asher said with amused eyes.

Blyss turned to the other goblins. "We gave them the soup, so we must clean the house."

The three goblins nodded to their new chieftess.

Asher glanced over his shoulder to the goblins separating in different directions, and began to pick up items and clean.

Asher returned his gaze to the women he loved on the bed. Amber was first to stir as she slowly opened her eyes. The faun saw Asher as the foot of the bed and a happy smile bloomed.

"Welcome home, Lord Blackwood," the faun said with a cheeky grin.

"It's good to be home. Did everyone have a good night?"

The faun slowly sat up and yawned. She scratched under her naked breast as she tried to ignore the sour taste in her mouth.

"It was a marvelous night. We talked for most of the night. We opened our souls to each other, before a hunger took us all. I had experienced something like last night before, but Elara and Nyn never had. It was an eye-opening experience for them, spilling their souls between the three of us.

"After eating and talking for hours, we made our way up here. I dared not leave them alone. There was such a closeness, we kept each other company in bed. Despite a night of many orgasms, you, and the goblins, were missed."

Asher nodded and yawned.

"I'm glad to hear it. I was worried, but happy that we all made it through unscathed," Asher said with tired eyes.

Blyss moved to Asher's side and looked up at him with a cheery smile.

"You sleep. We will take care of the farm and chores."

The young lord was about to protest, when the soreness along his body pulsed like needles under his skin. He simply nodded at the goblin before he fell face first onto the bed.

Amber crawled over to Lord Blackwood. She picked up his head, and his body shifted. She looked down with loving eyes as she pressed a nipple to his mouth. The young lord took hold with his lips, and began to suck and drink her healing milk.

Elara stirred from her slumber. She lifted her head, disheveled blonde hair clinging to the side of her face. She saw Asher drinking from the faun. She then looked at the goblins cleaning everything up.

"You're all safe," she said with a tired whisper.

Heads nodded as smiles bloomed.

Elara looked at Amber with half-closed eyes. "When you're finished, bring him to me."

"Yes, mistress," Amber said with a loving tone.

Elara fell back into bed, her heart full as their family was all together again.

***

Days spun on as life returned to normal on the Blackwood Estate. Asher's spirit felt light and airy as he, and everyone else on the farm, carried on with their chores and duties.

The young lord quickly noticed the goblins were energized since their night in the woods. They worked harder, ensuring everything was taken care of around the farm. Blyss was a natural leader, and her fellow goblins followed her like she had led them their entire lives.

The days blended together, and Asher found himself smiling more. When wagons arrived at the front gate of the estate, the young lord smiled from ear to ear at Dina arriving with two wagons filled with burlap sacks. When he went to greet her, she opened one of the sacks to reveal vibrant red strawberries.

Asher's heart began to thud in his chest. Dina said she would bring him a shipment of fruit to make into wine, and the young lord was eager to create his first batch of wine.

Everyone in the house came out as the wagons were wheeled onto the property. All hands rushed to pick up sacks and place them within the winery. Sacks were clustered together on the stone floor. When they finished unloading the shipment, Dina flung her arms around the young lord, giving him a deep kiss. Afterwards, Asher paid her for the shipment in coin, and invited her to stay the night and join them for dinner. Dina accepted, and later at dinner, told everyone about her small adventures outside of Mist Valley.

The very next day, Asher, Blyss, and Elara, made their way into town. Asher had a list of items to purchase, needed for cultivating wine. Since the first batch was experimental, he wanted to make sure he had it right for when the autumn harvest was ready.

At the General Good shop, Asher purchased sacks of yeast, sugar, and a few more vials to aid in wine production. The owner, Stukard, was happy to aid with finding items, and giving his advice on creating wine. He had made his own from time to time, as a hobby, and enjoyed speaking on the finer aspects with Asher and Elara.

Not long after, the group found themselves back on the estate, and within the winery walls. The goblins, Nyn, and Amber, had started the process of cleaning and cutting up the strawberries. Buckets were filled with cleaned and sliced strawberries. Asher, Elara, and Blyss joined them, sitting down on the stone floor and aided in cleaning and cutting the rest of them. By late afternoon, empty sacks laid to one side, and dozens of buckets were filled with fresh cut strawberries.

Asher led the charge as he grabbed a full bucket, took the small stairs up to the raised platform. A small wood pit with a screen on the bottom was before him. He dumped the strawberries within with a smile.

Everyone picked up buckets, and handed them up to Asher. The young lord dumped bucket after bucket of strawberries until the entire batch was within the crush pit. When Asher came down the small set of stairs, everyone else was washing their feet with buckets of water. The young lord joined them, taking off his boots and washing his feet. The floor was wet with water, most of it flowing down a separate drain in the middle of the winery floor.

One by one, everyone marched up to the platform. Asher took the first step into the crush pit. Strawberries were mashed under his feet as he stepped further in. Soon, others stepped in to join him. The crush pit was not big enough for everyone. At first, only Asher, Elara, and Blyss were in the crush pit. The moment that had been discussed had finally come, and everyone was eager to partake.

Asher, Elara, and Blyss, began stomping their feet down, smashing the red berries. Elara stomped her dainty feet as she watched Asher stomp around like a giant attacking a small village. Blyss stomped in circles, each footfall hard enough to turn berries into mush. Red juice covered their feet, and most of their ankles and shins.

The young lord enjoyed the process, knowing that their stomping would squeeze out the juice. It would flow down, past the fine screen meant to stop larger chunks from mixing with the juice. The more they stomped, the more juice it would create. It would flow down the pipe, and into the smaller, covered metal vat.

After a time, Asher, Elara, and Blyss sat down on the edges of the crush pit, their feet still inside. Amber, Nyn, and Paasha were next. The trio stomped their feet and hooves into the mushy strawberries. Much to everyone's surprise, Amber's hooves were well made for the job of crushing berries. She playfully stomped around, making the mushy pulp into a liquid sludge. Juice filtered down into the small metal vat, but the faun was in her element, crushing strawberries like they were being punished for murder.

Nuha and Keefa joined in, the goblins enjoying their time of jumping and stomping berries. Everyone involved took turns crushing and resting. The process took a few hours, red strawberries crushed to a paste as juice continued to flow down the special pipe and into the covered vat.

With red stained feet, Asher made his way down the small set of stairs and to the glass porthole of the vat. He peered in, seeing red berry juice rippling to more juice trickling in. They had crushed as many strawberries as they could.

The small vat was only half full, Asher making a mental note to ensure the next batches would have to be doubled, or even tripled for the small, and larger vat. Despite the vat being half full, it was still a good start.

The young lord moved to a sack of sugar, and a small sack of yeast, on the floor. He picked up the small sack of yeast and stepped to the porthole. He unlocked it and opened it. He poured some of the yeast powder into the vat. When he was finished, he put the small sack down and picked up a full sack of sugar. With a heave, he put the open end to the porthole and dumped all the sugar into it. When it was empty, he put the sack down and picked up a long, wood rod. Slipping the rod into the porthole, he began to stir the mixture.

Content purpose filled the former adventurer as his strong arms and shoulders used the oar-like rod to continue to stir the mixture. In a small sense, it reminded him of working in the lab, creating potions. It further calmed him as he continued to stir their first batch.

Bodies with red stained feet walked down from the elevated crush pit. They all watched Asher's intense calm as he stirred. Many of them sat down and began to scrub their feet with hanging cloths on the edges of buckets of clean water. Elara walked over to Asher's side and looked into the porthole as he stirred. The mature elf turned her proud gaze to Asher, seeing him fully embrace their new life.

After a time, the sun touched the western horizon. Asher pulled the stirring rod from the vat and put it down. He closed the port hole, and locked it shut. He turned to everyone gathered with proud eyes.

"It's getting late. It will smell, but we will clean the crush pit in the morning," Asher said with tired, but satisfied eyes.

Heads nodded in agreement. A short time later, everyone was leaving the winery and making their way back to the house, barefoot.

The evening air carried the scent of trees and approaching evening. Asher took a deep breath, savoring it. Another step was made in their new lives, and it sang to his spirit.

When they reached their home, everyone made their way upstairs to the bathing rooms. Only Asher and Elara made their way to their private washroom. Once inside, man and elf disrobed as hot water filled the metal tub. Not long after, the couple slipped into the hot water and eased down, the mature elf laying her back against Asher's strong chest.

The pair lingered for a time, enjoying the warmth of their bodies and the water. When Asher picked up a cloth and soap, the two took their time scrubbing each other, while taking moments to steal intimate kisses.

When they emerged from the tub, the pair towel-dried each other before slipping clothes back on.

The rest of the evening fell into a loving routine. Supper was made, and everyone sat down for a hearty meal. When everyone finished, food and exhaustion set in from the day. Paasha remained to clean up, but one by one, members of their found family peeled off from dinner, and made their way to their rooms to crash and pass out. At the end, it was only Asher and Elara at the dinner table.

The mature elf eyed the young lord with loving, yet, predatory eyes.

Asher simply glanced at her with knowing eyes, their bond growing stronger with each small passage of time.

"Should I fear for my life?" the young man smirked.

Elara let out a haughty laugh as she placed her hand over his.

"Fear for your life? No. Fear for a part of you belonging to me, yes."

"For the night?" Asher said with an amused tone.

Elara was silent as a grave as she stood up, her fingers curling into his hand. She gave him a gentle tug, and the younger man stood up. They made their way down the main corridor and to the stairs. They climbed each step, the heat between them growing.

Asher squeezed Elara's hand as he now led the way. The elf looked at him with a shy smile, being led by the man she had fallen deeply in love with.

Night had fallen beyond the windows of their home. When the couple stepped into the master bedchamber, they couldn't keep their hands off each other. The pair embraced as they kissed, and their tongues danced. They made their way to the edge of the bed, before their legs hit it. The couple fell into bed together, enjoying warm touches and deep kisses.

A small, sharp sound clicked against the bedchamber window.

Asher and Elara stopped their advances, the pair lifting their heads. They listened as the farm house was as quiet as a cemetery in the dead of winter.

The former ranger kept his steady gaze on the bedchamber window, when something small bounced off the clear glass.

Asher's dark gaze looked down into Elara's oval eyes. He pulled away from her and stood up.

"Is it the slythans?" the mature elf asked as she sat up.

Asher nodded. "They may have some news if they are trying to get my attention."

The young lord moved to the closet and pulled his belt with a sheathed dagger from a peg. He put it around his waist before closing the closet door.

"I don't expect trouble, but listen for me. If you hear any shouting or fighting, alert everyone else," Asher instructed as he made his way to the bedchamber door.

Elara simply nodded as she looked at him with worried eyes.

The house was quiet as Asher made his way to the stairs. He carefully made his way down, trying to not make any noise. On the first floor, he made his way to the front door and opened it.

Silence greeted him. There were no songs of crickets. The air was still warm from the summer day. Stars gleamed high in the night sky.

Asher made his way across the porch and down the stairs. He walked with his hand on his sheathed dagger, expecting anything to happen. When he reached the front gate, and peered into woods across the dirt road, only the gentle winking of firefly lights greeted him.

Asher remained where he was, eyeing the darkness and fireflies. A bush moved, and two cloaked figures stood up.

Even with hoods over their heads, Asher could make out the gleam of reptilian eyes staring back at him. Small snouts were not covered by the shadows of their hoods. The pair stepped out from their hiding spot, crossed the road, and stood on the other side of the fence.

"I was wondering when I would get a visit," Asher said in a low tone.

The two slythans glanced at each other. The female nodded to the male. He turned and looked at Lord Blackwood with a heavy gaze.

"We are keeping to our bargain," the slythan hissed.

"As am I," Asher said.

The slythans nodded in unison.

"Lady Windswell is putting a plan into place to buy the property on the west side of your farm. Many of us have glimpsed her plan in her study, along with notes and letters to others not of Mist Valley," the male slythan said.

"She is scheming to have her allies surround your farm," the female slythan said, and continued, "She has been speaking with members of the town council to convince them to allow her to purchase the land. Since she is mayor, she cannot buy it outright, and needs the council's approval."

"We don't know how much she has convinced the town council, but at the Summer Dusk Banquet, she plans to entice enough members of the council to swing a vote to her."

"How many members are there on the town council?" Asher asked.

"Five. Dina Hammer, Nadia Tome, Bolla Brewblade, Stukard Goodfeather, and Maggie Raveneye. She has been spending extra time with each member, trying to shift their vote in her favor."

Asher rubbed his jaw as the information settled in his mind. He wished he was surprised, but considering how quiet the mayor has been of late, it was easy to make the connection that she was working against him.

"Thank you for telling me. When you next arrive, I will have your payment, and a little extra, for the information," Asher said with grim eyes.

The slythans glanced at each other again. This time, the female spoke up.

"Lord Blackwood, we have something else to tell you, and seek your aid."

Asher's eyes narrowed, not liking the sound of that.

The female slythan continued, "One of our own... is in danger. She has voiced on several occasions she has feared for her life."

The female slythan reached into her cloak, and pulled out a rolled-up scroll, sealed in red wax emblem of House Windswell. The slythan held it out to the young lord.

Asher was hesitant to take it, unsure how deep this request would take him. Reluctantly, he took the scroll and stuffed it in his belt.

"Please read it at your earliest convenience."

"I will read it, but I must know more. What kind of danger? Why ask me for help?"

The slythans lowered their hooded heads.

"Because the one in danger is an ally to you, and to us," the male said with a low tone.

Asher didn't let the shock bleed into his features, knowing they were talking about his mysterious ally who warned him before about Lady Windswell's lies, and her plot to help her become mayor of Star Fall.

"We cannot speak on it any more, but we will continue to honor the bargain between us," the male said.

"Lord Blackwood, you have many allies in Mist Valley," the female slythan added.

Asher was silent as the two slythans turned, and walked across the dirt road. In a matter of moments, the pair melted away into the late, dark evening.

Asher remained by the front gate, hand on the scroll in his belt, and staring at nothing. A plot against him and his estate was unfurling, and it seemed he was going to fight harder to keep everyone he loved safe.

The young lord turned and walked back to the house with long shadows under his eyes.

Chapter 16

Wine, History, and Secrets

The door opened to an empty common room. Asher stepped in and closed the door behind him. A heaviness weighed on his spirit, the petty dispute between himself and the mayor was growing with each passing day. The conflict was turning into its own monster, for the simple fact that the mayor didn't get what she wanted, more power and influence.

Asher made his way to the couch and sat down. Several lanterns were lit, giving the large room a relaxed gloom. Mist flowed off the frost crystal, keeping the room cool. Inky darkness filled the cold fireplace across from the young lord.

Asher's gaze lowered in thought, but he quickly saw the rolled-up scroll stuffed between his belt and him. Taking hold, he pulled it out and lifted it up to his eyes. He visually inspected it, seeing the Windswell crest imprinted on the red wax seal.

For a moment, Asher wondered if the scroll was a magical trap. He had seen it happen a few times during his adventures, a guild member opening an unknown scroll and receiving a magical blast to the face. But the thought drifted away, knowing Mist Valley was not some forgotten dungeon in the middle of nowhere.

Breaking the seal, Asher quickly unfolded it and began to read.

Lord Blackwood,

Plans are unfurling as I write this, and I fear for not only you and your farm, but Mist Valley as a whole.

Lady W is attempting to win a vote with the town council to buy the land west of your estate. She seeks to squeeze you out of Mist Valley. She sees you, and your estate, as a threat to her plans. She wishes to grow Mist Valley, turning it from a town, into a city. She has designs to use every piece of land to build, and grow her influence.

But this letter is not simply about Mist Valley, and ruining your farm. I fear for my life, and the lives of people working for Lord and Lady W. There has been discussion of leaving their employment, but there have been instances in the past where a servant has left, and they are never seen again. Many of us are fearful of the lord and lady's reprisals.

You have opened the door of hope for us. A few of us know about the bargain struck between you and two of our people. We encourage it, and will relay more information when it is deemed safe, and important.

The only thing I ask, when the last straw is broken, and we cannot endure this any longer, will you help us by guiding us to the portal? We don't know how it works, and fear that we will appear in strange lands instead of our ancestral home. I know it is a grand request, but if we leave by the main road out of town, many, if not all of us, may not make it back to our homes.

We don't expect an answer right away. We only seek a peaceful and free life.

I fear my life is forfeit, but that will not stop me from helping others.

Please burn this letter when you finish reading it. Our shared conspirators will remain in contact with you.

Thank you for listening to those without a voice.

~A friend

Asher read the letter three times before putting it down on his lap. His heart ached, but his mind stung with experiences of feigned hope, and dark betrayal. There was no way to know if the letter was real, or an elaborate ruse. The only request made by the mysterious author of the letters was to guide them to the portal should they wish to leave. Asher wasn't sure if the mayor knew about the portal, or its location. Thoughts clashed in the young man's mind, turning everything into a muddled mess.

Elara stepped into the common room, her gaze on the young lord with an open scroll on his lap. She made her way over to him, eyes filled with loving concern.

Asher glanced up at the beautiful elf and gave her a weak smile.

"We can talk, if it will help?" the mature elf offered.

Asher gave a single nod.

Elara sat down on the couch, her legs folded under her as she sat sideways, facing him. A dark tan dress hugged her top, while the rest flowed from her waist. The fabric was between her legs as she made herself comfortable.

Asher parted his lips and began explaining everything that happened outside with the two slythans, and the contents of the letter. Elara gave him her full attention as she drank it in. When he was finished, Asher simply looked down.

"I spent many years helping and saving as many people as I could. Sometimes it was thankless. Other times, there were tears of joy in their eyes after aiding and defending them against bandits and monsters.

"Here, on the farm, I sometimes feel I put in my time from my previous life. I did right for many years, but now, I simply want to live our life here, in our home."

Elara watched him with serious eyes. She reached over and put her hand over his, giving it a squeeze.

"You fear, the more you help, the more will be expected of you. That if you deny anyone's request for help, you will not be living the life you lived a long time."

Asher nodded, his heart heavy in his chest.

"You have nothing to fear, my love," Elara said with a loving tone. "We both know, if anyone asks for help, you will help them. We will help them.

"As for what is happening here in Mist Valley, Lady Windswell will never let you rest until she has taken everything away from you. We both know, she cannot attack you directly, so she will manipulate everything around you, probing for weakness. Little does she know, you have the support of many who love and adore you."

Asher looked away. "There is something else you should know about me. Something I have spoken little about, to anyone."

"Is this a wine conversation?" the elf asked with a small smile.

Asher nodded.

Elara stood up. "I'll get us some wine and glasses."

Asher watched the beautiful elf walk toward the kitchen.

A short time later, she came back with an open wine bottle and two glasses. She placed them on the coffee table before lifting the wine bottle again and pouring into each glass. Wine bottle down, she picked up both glasses and handed one to Asher.

The young lord took a deep sip, enjoying the velvet taste of red wine. The moment it touched his stomach, he began to relax a little. Elara sipped her drink, her legs folded under her once again. She waited patiently as Asher gathered his thoughts.

"You know some of my adventurer life before I came here, but I haven't spoken much about some of my dark missions for the guild."

Elara was silent as she looked at the young lord she loved.

Asher continued, "Before I became a full member of the Rook Guild, I had to help in a mission by proving my worth. I knew what was expected, my father telling me how it was for him when he first joined the guild."

The former ranger's eyes took a faraway gaze as he remembered the experience.

"It was supposed to be a simple mission. Find out who had been stealing livestock from a local town. It was believed to be the work of wolves, or a lone monster. It should have been easy for us. We had several experienced members to our fellowship. We believed we could find the culprits if we staged a trap.

"Little did we know how dangerous the situation truly was. I won't bore you with the finer details, but what we were looking for was not wolves, or a lone monster. A small army of kobolds were in the area, and taking livestock was only part of their plan. They targeted the family and their farm, who we set up the trap and were protecting.

"The kobold forces overran our positions. They killed some of the family we were protecting, and snatched some of the younger members. They took them to an ancient, abandoned fortress.

"We tracked them down, made our way in, and walked into a trap. We fought for our lives to protect the last remaining member of the slaughtered family. I..." Asher trailed off.

Elara watched as Asher relived the moments. A haunted look filled his eyes as he stared at nothing.

"We lost two of our members. Two people I was just beginning to know, but already admired and respected. They fought to the very end, as the rest of us escaped."

Asher blinked the haunted look away as he took a breath.

"We returned the last member of the family back to town. The kobolds spilled barrels of oil to burn away any sign of them. Their fortress was an empty, burn out shell, but what happened there followed me for some time during my days as a member of the guild.

"The kobolds worshiped some demonic force, or elder primal spirits. They were part of some cult that worshiped these beings simply known as Pale Eyes. They would consume the flesh of others, and could change their appearance to mimic people. It only worked with people who were already known, and they could not change their shape into someone new.

"The cults were discovered many times during my adventures. There were more than a few times I walked into hidden chambers with half-eaten corpses. But that is not the root of the problem I feel at this moment.

"The Pale Eyes seemed to connect with those of dragon descent. Kobolds, slythans, dragonkin, and a few others, were often part of these cults. There were other races involved, but those of dragon descent were often the most numerous.

"After years of hunting, and fighting these cultists, I grew paranoid. The Pale Eyes gave them the gift to shape change, only after they consumed flesh. I lost many friends to these fiends over the years. Because of them, I have a deep mistrust for those of dragon descent."

Elara looked down at her drink as her heart ached for her lover. "You fear, the slythans who serve the Windswells, may have ties to these beings, or connections to the cultists in some way."

Asher gave a grave nod. "I don't trust dragon and lizard folk. Especially after what they did to my friends and colleagues. I've tried to forget it, but their faces come back to haunt me at times.

"Coming here, to my uncle's farm, was a blessing in many ways. Meeting you, and the rest of our family, while improving the farm, distracted me from many things in my past I wish I could forget forever. But now, those experiences I pushed away, have started to return. Part of me distrusts my mysterious contact, and the slythans working for the Windswells. But there is another part of me that can't ignore their requests for help."

Elara's eyes gleamed with warmth. "You have a noble spirit. You should be proud."

Asher's eyes darkened. "A noble spirit didn't save many of my friends."

"But it did, in a way. I must admit, I don't know every detail, but I know you. I know you saved many more lives than those taken away from you."

The mature elf looked down, her spirit taking on some of Asher's emotional burdens.

"I want to help heal you, but I also know, some wounds can only be healed by ourselves. I've seen it many times before, elves leaving the academy, yearning for adventure and knowledge, only for some to return, a shell of what they were.

"Valoria can be as dangerous as it is beautiful. Adventurers help keep the people safe, and bring back important knowledge, or artifacts, from our distant past. While lords and ladies fight wars with different factions, it is adventurers who truly embody the best of us, with hope, and bravery."

Asher looked at the beautiful mature elf, seeing the small movements in her expression, feeling her spirit take on some of his darkness that stained his soul.

"The only adventure I want is for us to live our lives together. When this business is concluded with the Windswells, I want us all to simply love and take care of each other," Asher said with a serious tone.

"It is what we want as well," Elara said with loving warmth. "And we are all here to support you, no matter what you decide.

A silence flowed over the couple. They sipped their wine, their minds digesting everything that was said.

Elara looked upon the man she loved.

Asher returned her gaze, his heart beating for the woman he had fallen for.

The mature elf downed her glass of wine and placed it on the short table. Asher did the same. When he put his glass down, Elara stood up and stepped over to him. She reached down and took his hand. She gently pulled at him, and he stood up.

The wine bottle and empty glasses remained as Elara led the way, her hand still holding Asher's hand. They made their way to the stairs, climbed them to the second floor, and made their way down the long corridor. When they reached the master bedchamber, they stepped in, and closed the door behind them.

Elara turned to Asher, stepping close enough for their bodies to touch. She looked at him, feeling his body heat, and the weight of his soul. She lifted her hands and took hold of his shirt. With a gentle pull, she pulled up his shirt over his head and let it fall to the floor. She took hold of his belt and undid it. Belt with dagger, and his leggings, fell to the floor, the young man stepping out of them.

The beautiful elf didn't look at his strong, virile body, but looked into his eyes, his soul. She saw his pain, and she didn't blink.

Asher lifted his hands and took hold of the fabric along her shoulders. He pulled them aside, and down her arms. The one-piece dress flowed down, freeing her large breasts and erect nipples. The dress flowed down, past her hips and puddled on the floor. His hand lingered on her hip, but his eyes drank in Elara's soul.

The couple moved to the bed and crawled in. They made it to the center and laid down, inches apart.

"I just want to hold you," Elara whispered.

Asher nodded as he moved closer.

Elara embraced him, touching her body to his. One arm curled under his head, while her other arm was around his shoulders. The couple snuggled together, Asher's face against Elara's smooth neck.

Bodies entwined, the pair simply laid together. Heat bloomed from their close bodies, but it was a comforting, loving heat. Elara glided her fingers along his strong back, while Asher's hand gripped the side of her waist, as if afraid to let go.

"Your watch is over for tonight, my handsome ranger. You may rest, for it is I who look after you. Be strong tomorrow, for tonight, I will be strong for both of us."

Asher's entire body relaxed. Every muscle bled away a tension he didn't know he had. Eyelids grew heavy as dreamy warmth floated along his body and soul.

"That's my loving morsel. Let the dreams come. I will be by your side as we explore them together," Elara whispered.

Asher's mind began to drift, as if the weight of his soul was suddenly lighter. He sank deeper and deeper into dreamy tendrils. The last thing he remembered was Elara's dream-self, holding his hand as they explored the dreamscape together.

Chapter 17

Master's Blessing

Darkness parted. Asher eyes slowly opened and closed, adjusting to the morning light. He lay on his side, the world blurry as he tried to wake up. Dreams lingered as his mind tried to wake. They slipped away, and were replaced with new, waking energy.

Something moved alongside the bed, just out of focus.

Asher blinked, the world falling into focus. He stared at Amber, the faun on the floor beside the bed, wearing a black top. The young lord stirred, lifting his head and upper body up as he looked at the smiling faun.

Amber was on her knees, beside the left side of the bed. She was wearing a short, black dress, the top hugging her firm breasts. A hypnotic grin filled Amber's face as she looked at Asher with wide, excited eyes.

"Master Priest, you have awakened," Amber said with an electric smile.

Asher partially sat up, a blanket up to his midsection. Bare-chested, he lifted a hand and rubbed the back of his head, as if to help stimulate his waking mind. When a muffled sound came from behind him, he turned his head to see Elara and Nyn, their wrists and ankles bound in fuzzy-lined, metal cuffs. Their mouths were gagged with tight fabric. The two busty elves were naked, aside from cuffs and gags. Each of them looked at him, not in panic, but with sultry, half-closed eyes.

Asher turned his head to the happy faun on her knees. The mood, and play, struck the refreshed young man. With a light spirit, he fell into his role, eager to see what the three of them planned.

"What is the meaning of this?" Asher asked with hard eyes.

Amber bowed her head. "I thought you would be pleased? I brought two lost souls to you. They could not control their lustful desires. I knew you would want them brought to you, to wash away their dirty desires and only know your blessings."

Asher swung his legs over the side of the bed, before the kneeling faun. The blanket shifted, uncovering his legs, but barely covering his thickening manhood.

Amber glanced down at the outline of her master's cock, and fought the urge to lick her lips.

"Explain what happened," Asher said with a tired voice.

Amber nodded. "While you were away, tending to the goblins, these two could not control their desires. I listened to them, speaking of how much they wanted to seduce you, and break your will. They planned to prey on you as you slept, and do unspeakable things to you.

"I knew I could not let this stand. I endured their discussion, eager to bring it to you when the time was right."

The faun lowered her head in shame. "They forced me to come, and enjoy myself. I endured it, only for I knew, I would bring them to you for your judgment. When they slept, I captured them, and put them in your bed.

"I beg for your forgiveness. I was unclean, but I know my lord will forgive me for bringing two lost souls to your attention."

Asher eyed the faun, deep in her part. Pink touched her cheeks with an eagerness in her eyes. She played the part of willing disciple to the hilt. But for the young lord, he felt better than he had in a long time.

Glancing over his shoulder, he saw Elara's loving gaze. The voluptuous mature elf turned on her side, showing her bound, naked body. Erect nipples leaked pale milk, as a moan filled her throat.

Nyn was still on her stomach, looking at Asher with blank eyes. When he shifted his gaze to her naked bottom, her hips moved like they were no longer under her control.

The entire bedchamber filled with a growing mood, the young lord ready to play.

Asher returned his gaze to Amber, a stern look in his eyes.

"You did well, my novice. Well enough that you may become an acolyte at my side."

Amber's eyes trembled in excitement. "Yes, master priest. I live only to serve you, and the faith."

Asher gave a stern nod. "Faith must always be tested. Are you ready to be tested?"

Amber nodded quickly. "Yes, master priest. I am ready."

"Good. Come closer," Asher commanded.

The faun leaned forward and crawled on all fours to her master priest. As she moved closer, she could see the blanket shift as his member stiffened. When she was between his legs, she looked upon his covered member with a fire in her eyes.

Asher gave the eager faun a knowing smirk. "Take hold of my scepter. Stroke it as you tell me of their lustful sins."

The faun reached up and snaked her hand under the blanket. She took hold of his hard and veiny member. With gentle, slow strokes, she looked up at her priest and let out a small whimper.

"It was terrible, master priest. They spoke of taking turns, sucking on your cock. They wanted to make you weak, sucking on you and drinking your seed. When you begged them to stop, one said they would sit on your mouth to quiet you. The other would sit on your cock."

"Nefarious," Asher said in a low tone, enjoying Amber's stroking.

The faun nodded. "When you didn't return, they turned their lustful desires on me. They tried to break me, but my soul only belongs to you."

"What did they do to you?"

Amber's eyes half-closed as relived the night of the snake soup.

"They touched me in ways I shouldn't be touched. One of them parted my legs, and licked at me, while the other watched. I tried to fight, but they were like succubi. The one with dark blue hair, she licked at my clit, making me come, but I thought of your love in that moment, not giving in to their temptation."

Asher nodded before he spit on his cock with Amber's hand wrapped around it. The faun didn't blink, stroking her master's manhood as she continued.

"I knew they needed to be taught by you. They whispered that only a true blessing would heal their demonic desires. Once healed, they would serve the faith, and you."

The young master priest nodded as his cock grew hard as stone.

"You did well," Asher said with a fatherly whisper. "Now, we must save them from themselves. This will require both of us. If you accept my blessing, you will be at my side for all time."

"I am ready," Amber smiled.

"Good. First, you must suck on my scepter, so I may bless your throat. After that, keep sucking on me until I'm hard again. This will show me your true faith. Can you do this for us?"

"I can," Amber said with a sultry whisper.

Before Asher could say another word, the faun grabbed the base of his manhood, stood it up, and lowered her head. Warm lips wrapped around the head of his cock, sliding down a few inches. A muffled moan filled her throat as her head gently bobbed, sucking on his throbbing head while licking at it.

Bliss crawled down Asher's cock and into his body. He put a hand on her head, helping her find the proper rhythm, which didn't take long. A long exhale fell from his parted lips as he enjoyed Amber's lips around his shaft, sucking on him like her life depended on it.

"It feels good in your mouth, like it always belonged there," Asher whispered.

A muffed moan drifted up from his lap, the faun increasing the tempo.

"Such a good disciple. I will enjoy you on your knees, proving your faith to me, time and time again."

Asher turned his head and looked over his shoulder to the two bound elves. They could only see Amber's shoulder as her head bobbed. Sultry moans filled their throats, the clinking of metal links keeping them prisoner.

Asher returned his gaze to the faun, her mouth dragging along his sensitive thick shaft. The muffled moans continued as she tasted some of his come, savoring his taste.

The master priest leaned back on one hand, keeping his other hand on her head. He watched his cock shaft appear and disappear between them. Pleasure curled along his spirit as meaty flesh filled her mouth. The tip of his cock touched the back of her throat, and it made him hard as granite.

"When I come, you will be my new acolyte. Drink my seed like holy water, like the good soul you are."

Amber let out a muffled cry. Between her legs, wetness dripped on the floor. Her black dress grew wet along her chest, hugging her firm breasts. Sensitive nipples leaked milk, spreading further into the dress top. The faun's entire body betrayed her, drops of wetness running down her inner thighs.

Asher leaned his head back, his sensitive nose taking in the faun's scent. It was like distilled love, curling along his senses. Basking in it, he remained in the moment for a short time, before his urges welled up. They struck at him, like a hammer. His cock thickened, and that caused the faun to suck and bob faster.

"Accept the blessing, my beautiful acolyte," Asher said.

Amber's lips ran down the length of her master priest's manhood. The meaty cock twitched, before ropes of come splashed against the back of her throat. Amber's eyes widened as she drank it. Then her eyes half-closed, as more seed spurted into her throat and on her tongue. She rocked her body, back and forth, drawing every last drop of her master's faith.

The faun didn't let go as her head bobbed again. She remained to task, sucking on his half-hard member, feeling it fill with life once again.

"Good, very good. You understand, my acolyte. Keep sucking. Make it hard again, and then our work may continue."

Elara listened with pointed ears. Wetness had long bloomed between her thighs, enjoying everything she heard. Thighs rubbing together, she could barely keep her own desires under control.

When Asher was fully hard again, only then did Amber let go with her mouth, and kissed the side of the veiny shaft. She took heavy breaths, her own desires whipped into a storm.

"You... taste so pure," Amber huffed as wetness dripped from between her thighs, and from her swollen breasts.

"Stand up and undress, my acolyte. Let me see all of your beauty."

Amber stood up. The faun took hold of her black dress and lifted it over her head. When the fabric cleared her horned head, and was thrown aside, Asher lifted a hand and touched her furry hip.

The master priest admired the faun's beautiful body. Swollen breasts leaked milk, but his gaze was drawn to the hairless space between her hips. Her naked womanhood was shaved bare. The fur between her hips was shaved down to pale skin. Pink lips glistened and dripped with wetness as the faun displayed herself proudly.

"I did it for you," the faun said, indicating the missing fur between hips and thighs.

"I do love it," Asher said as his finger touched her budding line, exposing her clit, and rubbing it.

Amber's thighs trembled as she fought the urge to move to his fingers. Her lips parted as a small moan dripped.

"I love your divine touch. Please, keep touching me. It makes me so wet," Amber begged.

Asher continued to massage her clit, as his member bounced, wanting more. He turned his head again, looking down on the two, bound elves. His inner demons licked their lips. New energy filled him, wanting nothing more than to defile them as he saw fit.

He turned back to the moaning faun as she moved her hips to his touch.

"My acolyte, I have need of you."

"Anything, master priest," Amber moaned.

"Lick the blue-haired one until I tell you to stop," Asher said as he rubbed her clit and turned his eager gaze to Elara. "I will fuck the darkness from the blonde's soul, and bless her with my seed."

"Yes, my master priest," Amber said with shaky legs.

Before Asher pulled his fingers away, a loud moan filled the chamber. Amber let out animalistic moans as explosions tore her soul to pieces. Wetness surged and dripped from her hairless slit, as her hips moved of their own accord. She fought to stay in her body, as waves of exploding pleasure crashed against her spirit.

Asher quickly stood up and scooped the faun into his arms. Amber's head lolled back as her body twitched. He could see she was overwhelmed as he turned around. Placing the twitching faun on the bed, beside Nyn, he kissed her forehead and stood up.

Nyn watched as Amber was close to her, letting out weak moans and her eyes fluttering. The elf moaned through her gag, the mood sinking its teeth further into her spirit.

Naked, Asher walked around the bed to Elara's side. She moved her head, trying to keep him, and his wet cock in sight. When he was at her side, he climbed onto the bed, and was over the bound elf.

"It is my turn to watch over, and bless you," Asher said with hungry eyes.

Strong hands took hold of the elf. Elara was turned onto her side, facing Nyn and Amber. Her hands were bound at the wrists, as were her ankles. A longer chain connected between her ankle cuffs, giving them a longer berth. As she remained on her side, powerless against the master priest, she felt his strong hands on her.

Bliss ran along every nerve as Asher grabbed at Elara like he owned her. A muffled moan floated up from the gag as the young lord's hand grabbed at her naked breast, and his other hand grabbed at her ass. Fingers pressed hard against soft flesh, the elf moaning louder. Asher lowered his head closer to hers, while manhandling her. A tongue slid out and licked at her pointed ear. Goosebumps raised along the elf's skin. A muffle gasp floated up as fingers touched her dripping slit, playing with her.

"Bad elves are punished before they can be blessed," Asher said darkly as he continued to molest her.

Elara could say nothing as her body writhed to his touch. The more he played with her, the wetter she became. When fingers rubbed her clit, her body shuddered hard, unable to pretend she wasn't turned on.

Amber slowly fell back into her body. Blissful clouds floated along her soul as she turned to see Nyn staring at her with blank eyes. The faun glanced up to the master priest, playing with Elara. She saw his strong hands all over her, squeezing her flesh as she moaned with a gag in her mouth.

The faun returned her gaze to Nyn, and moved closer. The elf stared at nothing as Amber gently kissed at her naked flesh. The faun licked and kissed at the elf's smooth skin, as her hands glided along. When her fingers snaked between Nyn's thighs, the elf was silent until a touch sent a thrilling chill through her. Nyn's thighs parted slightly as Amber rubbed her clit. Fingers dipped into her dripping slit, before coming back up to massage her.

Amber used her other hand to push the elf onto her back. Nipples leaked milk as Nyn was also powerless to the faun. Chains clinked as legs were parted as far as they could go. Ankles strained as pleasure sank deeper into her, the intimate song growing between them.

Asher allowed himself to look over as the faun and elf. Amber followed his commands, making Nyn writhe to her touch. A greedy perversion filled the faun's eyes, eager to please her master priest. When the horned faun lowered her mouth over Nyn's standing wet nipple, she closed her lips on it. Amber pulled a little with her mouth, while suckling on Nyn's swollen breast. She watched Nyn let out muffled moans and whines, unable to stop her from taking her milk.

Asher turned his gaze back to Elara. He enjoyed the view of her bound and leaking milk. She writhed like caught prey, and he wanted nothing more than to free her to his whims.

The young lord's cock bounced. He pulled back his wet fingers from her and licked her honey from them. He then grabbed his member and put the throbbing head to her elfhood.

Elara was on her side as she glanced up at the master priest. He was looking down on her as something pushed at her now thinner valley entrance. She squirmed, knowing he was big already, but now, there would be a little more resistance. His strong hips pushed as he stroked his cock. Wetness surged in self-defense as the master priest pushed his hard manhood into her.

Inner walls parted to his slow invasion. Elara's breathing increased, as did her pulse. The elf let out heavy muffled moans as the master priest forced her to take every inch. She dared not protest. Instead, she squirmed to help his slow invasion.

When the master priest's cock was halfway in, she moved to it, squeezing, and trying to coax it in deeper.

Asher watched with amused eyes as the bound elf wriggled. When he grabbed her breast, a thin stream of milk squirted and Elara's eyes fluttered. Hips pushed harder, thick inches sinking deeper into her tender slit.

Elara's soul flashed with dripping fire. Muffled moans continued to sing as Asher's hips moved with slow, deliberate power. Each push in caused her to shudder. Each pull back, caused her to whimper. After a time, the tempo increased, and the sound of skin on skin filled the room.

Elara's body shuddered with each loving impact of her lover. She looked over with dreamy eyes as Nyn's eyes were closed. Muffled moans rose up as Amber was between the elf's thighs. Her face was snuggled between trembling thighs as she licked and nuzzled at her elfhood. Chains clinked louder, Nyn caught in a storm of ecstasy.

For the master priest, everything had become a holy experience. He looked down at Elara with tender eyes, his hips pushing his scepter to the hilt. He squeezed her breast as he licked at her pointed ear.

Elara's eyes rolled into her head as the dam of willpower cracked. Heat glowed along her body as she felt the moment of climax approaching, but it was much bigger than she expected. Feeling Asher take complete control over her awakened her own demons. It burned with a raging fire, the control beginning to slip. There was a moment when panic lit every nerve. When she reached the edge of the cliff, her body betrayed her. Power bloomed as the world turned a ghostly white.

The mature elf let out a muffled scream as she was launched off the cliff. She fell into paradise waters, waves of dreamy bliss crashing into her. She tumbled through the warm storm, electrical arcs running along every sensitive nerve. All control was lost as her soul cried out.

Asher continued to drive his urges into the bound elf. There was a surge of wetness, followed by a stream. It splashed against the master priest as he didn't slow down his invasion. He looked down at her, eyes closed and body shuddering so hard, he feared for a moment the chains to the cuffs would break. Never the less, he continued to fuck her through the waves of orgasmic bliss of one climax after the other. He sometimes could keep count by her reactions, but he quickly lost count as she seemed lost to an endless river of exploding stars.

Asher pulled out his member, slick with Elara's honey. He stroked himself to her blissful twitches. It fueled his ardor as she swam in heavenly waters. A grunt filled the air before thick ropes of seed splashed on her arm, and ran down to her hip. A few more strokes, and more seed painted the mature elf as she continued to shudder.

"You are blessed, my sinful elf," Asher said as he continued to stroke his cock, the last drops of come splashing on her hip.

The master priest watched as seed ran down her naked flesh as wetness dripped from her slit. He then turned his attention to Nyn and Amber. Nyn had her cuffed hands over her head, grabbing at pillows under her head. She looked down with weak eyes as Amber licked her further into submission.

Asher crawled over to the dark blue-haired elf. She whimpered as her legs were over Amber's slender shoulders. The tender, but deliberate licking from the faun sent tendrils of pleasure along every nerve. Hips moved to her tongue, milking every drop of pleasure. A finger slid into the gag along her cheek. Nyn looked up at Asher with helpless eyes. He was on his knees, his wet cock dangling close to her face.

"I'm going to remove the gag. Be a good girl, and maybe I will let you drink my seed," Asher said with confidence.

Nyn remained silent. Asher pulled at the gag and pushed it down past her chin. It was wet, and laying against her neck. She bit her lip, but didn't make so much as a whimper, trying to be good for the powerful priest.

Asher grabbed his member by the hilt. He put the head of his cock to her cheek, and moved it so it brushed the corner of her lips. Nyn let out a whimper, her hips moving deeper to Amber's invading tongue.

"Good girls know what they have to do," Asher said with a wicked gleam in his eyes.

Nyn moaned as she closed her lips over the tip of his throbbing cock. Inches pushed past lips as she tasted her best friend on Asher's cock. She closed her eyes, sucking on Asher's member as Amber licked her further into submission.

Asher remained on his knees beside Nyn's head. He watched with loving fascination as she sucked on him hard enough to ignite his urges again. Veins raised along the shaft as her lips hungered for more of him. Rivulets of milk spilled from her engorged breasts, the tension in her entire body growing. A fever took hold, the elf sucking and grazing her teeth along the sensitive flesh of his shaft.

Asher couldn't hold back his own groan. The elf was ravenous, sucking on him like her life depended on it. His hips moved slightly, as Nyn's head lifted to take another inch.

Reality fell into tiny, intimate moments. Asher stared at the elf as she moaned with her mouth full. When Nyn opened her eyes, she looked up at him with such a monstrous hunger, the young lord could not look away. She pulled him with her lips, begging for him to force his cock deep enough for her to choke on. When her teeth gently gripped the shaft, she made her intention's clear.

Asher was on his hands and knees, his body sideways over Nyn's head. Hips moved with power as his cock stabbed deep into the elf's throat. Grunts dripped from his mouth as he forced her to take more.

Nyn sucked on Asher's member as he fucked her mouth and throat. She remained calm as she followed her purpose in the moment. Veiny inches pushed past full lips. Throaty moans vibrated against the thick cock in her throat. Pleasure curled around her like a warm blanket. Her body glowed with a growing heat. Tingling nipples pushed her further to the edge.

The world grew quiet before the chains of tension snapped all at once.

Tight nerves exploded to dripping passion. The elf shuddered as inches moved back and forth between her tight lips. Her tongue pressed under the shaft, pinning his cock to the roof of her mouth. The tightness caused Asher to slow down, enjoying the sensations as she shuddered multiple times.

Amber didn't flinch as a flood of honey burst onto her tongue and open mouth. The faun licked away like it was just another day, enjoying the taste of the mature elf. She kicked her legs back and forth as she continued to abuse the elf's clit with her tongue.

Asher could feel control slipping away. He thought she had enough, but through her orgasms, she sucked on him, refusing to let go. His soul was being pulled into her, and he could not stop it if he wanted too.

The moment of truth slammed into him as his cock sank deeper into her throat. The veiny shaft thickened as Nyn continued to suck on him. A loud grunt filled the air.

Nyn's heart hammered in her chest as thick spurts of come painted her throat. She quickly swallowed, and was rewarded by more. Another barrage of orgasms struck her as she tried to pull Asher's very soul through his cock.

Asher's wide eyes stared at nothing, his cock firmly in control of Nyn's mouth. Hips bucked as she milked every drop of seed from his lions. Time stood still, before dreadful sensitivity cascaded along his manhood. His willpower laid in tatters, unable to pull his cock from her hungry mouth.

Nyn slowly opened her eyes. When the last drop of come had vanished down her throat, then and only then, did she let go.

Asher pulled back and nearly fell back. One hand shot down to the bed to steady himself. He looked down at Nyn as she licked her lips, staring at him with primal eyes.

"We... have much more work ahead of us," Asher said in lurid astonishment.

Nyn simply moaned as the faun continued to lick at her clit.

***

Asher was laying on his back. Elara was against his right side, Asher's arm curled around her. Nyn was to his left, his arm curled around her. Between his parted thighs, Amber was on her stomach, lazily sucking on his abused manhood.

292

A warm, tender mood enveloped the four of them. Asher, Nyn, and Elara watched with loving eyes as Amber sucked on Asher's cock.

"This was a lot of fun," Elara sighed as she writhed against Asher.

"Yes, it was," Asher said as pleasure ran up and down his member.

Nyn ran her hand along Asher's chest. "Was this a successful conclusion to the monastery play?"

"I think so," Asher said, despite being distracted.

Nyn nodded as she touched his nipple. "If it is, I look forward to our next one. Our plays have been wonderful, but I may wish to orchestrate our next one."

Asher and Elara looked over to the beautiful elf with curious eyes.

Nyn continued, "We've enjoyed ourselves by following similar plots to black books. I propose we create our own. The book I'm writing has opened my eyes, and inspired me to want to try a different path."

"Do you have a play in mind?" Elara asked.

Nyn nodded. "I am writing notes on one. When I am finished planning it out, I will bring it to you both."

Asher squeezed Nyn close to him, and smiled. "I'm sure it will be incredible."

Elara ran a finger along Asher's strong chest. "Was this morning a fun surprise?"

The young lord turned his attention to the beautiful elf. "It was. When did you have time to plan it?"

"The night you were becoming chief of the clan," Elara said with a seductive whisper. "The three of us talked and planned a proper end to the play. We thought, what better than your eager cleric to bring two lost souls to you."

"Amber made it clear she wanted to be the hero of the play, saving our souls and being in your good graces."

Asher let out a warm chuckle. "It certainly worked," he said as he glanced at the faun still sucking on his member.

Amber moaned as her head continued to bob.

The chamber filled with a dreamy heat. The four lovers enjoyed the closeness and freedom that filled their minds, bodies, and hearts. Elara licked at Asher's chest like a primal beast. Nyn snuggled to Asher's neck, her leg coiled around his, and her elfhood rubbing on his hip.

Asher was relaxed, enjoying the closeness of the women he loved.

Elara moved her lips to his ear. "I like when you come in her mouth. Make her drink every drop," the elf said with a seductive whisper.

A flame burned brighter within the young lord. As if by a mystical command, his cock thickened. Amber upped the tempo. A tension bloomed, and Asher's hips pushed up of their own accord. Amber ran her lips down his cock until white seed spurted from the tip. Amber continued to suck and bob her head, enjoying her lord's taste before drinking it down.

Asher relaxed and his head fell back onto the pillow.

"I'm very hungry now," he said, followed by a defeated sigh.

Elara giggled. Nyn continued to writhe against him. Amber's lips let go of Asher's cock. She licked the length of the shaft as she fingered her own slit.

Mid-morning sun glowed beyond the bedchamber windows. Birdsong flowed into the day. A peace filled Asher's soul.

The young lord curled up from the grasp of two elves. He moved to the edge of the bed, and put his bare feet on the floor.

Elara, Nyn, and Amber stayed in the bed. The trio watched Asher as he stretched his arms into the air.

The young lord made his way to the window, refreshed and ready to take on the new day.

When he looked past the trees, to the dirt road leading to the farm, he spotted two figures walking side by side. Narrowing his gaze, he quickly saw that it was Dina and Nadia. The pair talked to each other, walking further up the road, and closer to his estate.

"We better get dressed. I see Dina and Nadia on the road," Asher said, wondering if this had anything to do with Lady Windswell's plot to destroy him.

Chapter 18

Guarding the Future

Blyss was upside down on the couch. Her head was hanging off the seat, as her legs kicked in the air. The goblin stared at nothing as her mind wandered. A memory of Amber coming to her, telling her that she, Elara, and Nyn, would want time with Asher this morning. The goblin nodded, knowing it was important for the clan to be happy and free with each other.

Thoughts shifted to Asher, and a flutter filled her chest. The goblin could never put it into words, how happy she was. The traditions of her people were met, and now, she had a say on how their clan would proceed, under Asher's leadership.

Blyss kicked her legs more, when a hard knock at the door woke her from her thoughts.

The goblin turned around in one, smooth move, planting her bare green feet on the floor. She stood up and walked toward the door.

"Yes?" the goblin called out.

"It's Dina and Nadia," Dina said through the door.

The goblin opened the door and looked up at the two women with a bright smile.

Dina smiled at the beautiful goblin. She wore her overalls, and white shirt underneath. Workers boots finished the look.

Nadia wore a thin, black robe. She also smiled at the goblin, while pushing her glasses up on her nose.

"Please, come in," Blyss said as she stepped aside.

The two women walked into the common room, cool air greeting them. Blyss closed the door just as several people stepped into the common room from the stairs.

Asher walked in with a welcoming smile. He was flanked by Elara, Nyn, and Amber. Everyone was dressed in simple attire, except Asher, the elves, and faun, were barefoot.

"Welcome," Asher said as he walked toward the two women. "What brings you by?"

The two women smiled as they shot each other a quick look.

"We should sit down and have a talk," Dina said with a disarming smile.

Asher knew instantly what this was about. He gestured to the couch. The two women sat down, side by side. Asher sat in a chair across from them, the cold fireplace to his left, and little further back.

"Is this something we should be here for?" Amber asked with curious eyes.

Nadia nodded. "It affects everyone, so yes, you should stay to hear it."

"I'll get us some drinks," Blyss smiled before she turned and walked toward the kitchen.

Elara, Nyn, and Amber, sat down in comfy chairs scattered around the common room. All eyes were turned to the two women as they sat with concern coloring their eyes.

Dina cleared her throat and spoke first. "This isn't pleasant news. The mayor is trying to buy the land west of your estate.

"Nadia and I received letters from the mayor, detailing her plans for the property, saying it will add to the value of the valley as a whole. If she can purchase it, she will increase farmland in the valley, and increase the size of the town."

"We sit on the town council, as does Maggie, Stukard, and Bolla. Since Lady Windswell is an elected mayor, she cannot simply buy the land outright. She needs three votes to allow her to purchase it," Nadia added.

"Nadia and I have had a few discussions about it. We both came to the agreement of voting against her plan. But we believe Maggie and Stukard may vote for her plan. Stukard is friends with everyone in town, but he gets a large part of his business from the Windswells. Lady Windswell also helped invest in the raven tower. We're sure Maggie may feel indebted to her," Dina said.

"That leaves only Bolla," Nadia said and looked down in defeat. "We tried to find out which way she would sway on such a vote, but she had been tight-lipped about it. She tells us, she doesn't speak about her vote to anyone."

Dina looked at Asher, "The vote isn't until the day after the Summer Dusk Banquet. We believe she will use the dinner to convince us to see her side of things."

Asher nodded grimly, already knowing the mayor's plot. He didn't let it on as he rubbed his jaw in contemplation.

"We thought you should know," Nadia said in a small voice.

"Thank you for telling me," Asher said warmly. "As for this vote for purchasing land, wouldn't the rest of the town be against it?"

"The town generally fears the mayor. She has grown bloodthirsty, making snide remarks that Mist Valley needs to grow to survive. She uses your estate as an example of what could go wrong. After your uncle closed it down and left, the town was struggling. Many thought to leave, but since you arrived, most of the townsfolk feel better.

"But they know anything can happen. As much as many townsfolk love the town as it is, they know, if changes aren't made, many of us could be right back where we started," Dina said.

"The Hornspear farm is bringing in extra gold. The mayor uses it as an excuse to aid in bringing prosperity to Star Fall and Mist Valley," Nadia said.

"We support you, Lord Blackwood," Dina said with a gleam in her eyes.

Nadia nodded.

"I thank you for that support, but as I see it, there is little I can do."

"Not true," Nadia spoke up. "Connect with Bolla, before, or during the banquet. She may sway to our side."

"Speak to Stukard and Maggie during the banquet. If you wish for this town to truly welcome you, invest in them as you have invested in us," Dina said.

Nadia nodded. "Your constant visits have improved sales at the Book Guild. The projects for your farm have helped Dina's business as well. The more you invest in the town, the more it will truly welcome you."

Inner thoughts churned through the young lord. Never having a sizable income, it was harder to think beyond his needs for a day or two. Now that he had gold coins coming in, sitting on it would do nothing for him.

If Mist Valley is truly to become my home, I must be a good neighbor, and help it remain a beautiful place. I doubt the mayor will make my life easier if she boxes my estate in. Something must be done, and I have to be the one to do it.

"It sounds like we have a plan," Asher smiled.

Dina returned his smile. Nadia looked away with sad eyes.

"I fear my stay at the farm will have to be postponed," the book shop owner said in a small voice. "The mayor will use anything against us. If I stay, even for a month, she will use it to sway others to her side."

Asher's brow wrinkled. "This cannot stand."

Nadia turned her wide gaze to Asher.

The young lord leaned forward, elbows on knees. He looked into Nadia's bespectacled eyes like a demon king on a throne.

"I won't allow the mayor to control any of our lives. When the time comes, we will show her we are a united front," Asher said with firm confidence.

Everyone in the common room nodded in unison.

Nadia's eyes gleamed and trembled as she looked at Asher. Pink touched her cheeks as a small smile bloomed.

Blyss came out with Nuha and Paasha. Each of the goblins held several wood mugs, and bottles of wine. They were placed on the small table in the middle, each goblin pouring into each mug.

"I thought we were being served tea, or water?" Dina said with an amused tone.

"Discussions need wine," Blyss said as she continued to pour.

Amber hid her smile. Small chuckles and giggles filled the common room.

Cups were given to each person sitting. Asher raised his cup, and everyone did the same.

"We are coming together to guard our lives, and our future. To us! May we defend against those with black hearts and dark intentions!" Asher toasted.

Everyone nodded in agreement, before taking deep sips of red wine.

Dina held her cup as she looked at Asher and the elves sitting on either side of him.

"Have you given any further thought to building a new house on the property?"

"We are greatly considering it," Asher smiled.

"We could…" Dina was cut off as a loud ringing can be heard from outside.

Everyone turned and looked at the door. Asher stood up and made his way to the door. When he opened it, he could hardly believe what he was seeing.

A carriage stood before the main gate. The coachman was standing by the gate, his hand on the rope to the bell.

A covered wagon was behind it, Samuel Throne, the consignment agent for the Opal Society, was seated in the driver's seat. The unpleasant man, with a permanent scowl, gave Asher a small wave.

Another, larger wagon was behind Samuel's wagon. It had six horses, and the wagon had a thick, wide frame. Stepping down off the wagon was a giant woman. Her long red hair was tied into a thick braid. Wisps of hair hung from the sides of her head as she stood on two powerful legs. She had a womanly form with a blend of strength, power, and feminine beauty.

 The tall, strong woman turned her gaze to Asher, as she lifted two broadswords. She sheathed them over each shoulder in a crisscross, the thick pommels protruding from behind each shoulder. A leather harness was wrapped around her shoulders and midsection. She had a cloth top that hugged her rather impressive chest. A simple belt was around her waist, with a long loin cloth draped down, leaving the sides of her legs uncovered.

Asher stared at the woman. He knew a giant when he saw one. He guessed her height to be about nine, or ten feet tall. The way she stood he could see she was an experienced warrior. But the longer he looked at her, her eyes shifted, and she looked away.

"Greetings, Lord Blackwood," came a familiar voice.

Asher shifted his gaze back to the gate, Claudia Frost stepping out of the carriage with a warm smile. She stepped onto the dirt road and made her way toward the front gate. The coachman opened the gate with a slight bow.

Claudia looked over to Samuel, still sitting in his covered wagon. "Go about the usual pick up, as Lord Blackwood and I have a little chat."

Samuel nodded and dismounted from his wagon seat.

Asher stood on his porch, seeing the regal agent of the Opal Society approach. When she reached the stairs, she bowed slightly to him.

"It's good to see you, Lady Frost," Asher smiled.

"The feeling is mutual, and please, Claudia is fine," she said as she straightened up and made her way onto the porch.

The pair made their way inside.

Claudia kept her smile as she walked into the common room, filled with beautiful women.

"Greetings," Claudia said without batting an eyelash.

Everyone bowed to her, returning her greetings.

"I hope I'm not interrupting?" Lady Frost asked as she turned to Asher.

"We were simply discussing the future," Asher smiled.

Claudia nodded.

"Then I arrived at an opportune time. I don't wish to take you away from your day too much. Is there some place private we can speak?"

"We can talk in the library," Asher said and pointed his hand in the direction of the main corridor.

The pair walked side by side out of the common room, the rest of the household watching them go. When they were gone, everyone turned to each other.

Elara looked at Nadia and Dina, her mind filling with an idea.

"Dina, and Nadia, Asher has a deep love and respect for both of you. That is why, we should discuss the future," the elf said with a wicked gleam in her eyes.

Chapter 19

A Society's Pact

The door to the library opened. Sunlight poured into the chamber as Asher and Claudia stepped in. The young lord closed the door behind him as Claudia made her way to a comfortable chair. She turned and sat down. Asher approached the pair of chairs, and sat down in one across from the beautiful woman with raven black hair.

"I see the farm is prospering well," Claudia said with a sly smile.

Asher nodded, not wishing to boast.

"I do not wish to fill our time with idle conversation, so I will get to the point. The society has had some concerns with your farm, and location. Word has traveled about Mist Valley, and your new mayor is at the crux of it."

Asher leaned back in his chair. "I know. She's had a vendetta against me and my farm since I refused to aid her with joining the Opal Society."

Claudia nodded with serious eyes. "We at the society thank you for it. The Windswells have attempted on many occasions to join the society, but were denied because their ambition is too great. They have a history of backstabbing partners, and not completing their ends of bargains and contracts. Because of this, they cannot be considered for membership."

Claudia put one leg over the other as she looked at the lone window to the library.

"Lady Windswell has made some recent dealings with several nefarious organizations. She is probing, trying to find a weakness in our network. This of course cannot be allowed. I have talked to others within the society, and your farm is the weakest point.

"This has nothing to do with your ability to defend your farm, but more to do with forces aligning against it. You are still a probationary member, and there is still plenty of time to consider membership, but before a decision is made, we must ensure your farm, and its secrets, are well guarded."

"Before you continue, I am happy to say, I wish to become a full member of the Opal Society."

Claudia eyed the young lord with curious, yet satisfied eyes. "When we first met, you didn't seem so eager to join. If you don't mind me asking, what changed?"

Asher looked at Lady Frost with knowing and understanding eyes. He felt the tugs along his heartstrings, images of the women he has grown to love, and the legacy his uncle left behind. Where once it was only a possibility, now, it had become his destiny.

"I... accepted this new and different life. I know it has only been a few months since I arrived, but I am finding, my heart belongs here, in Mist Valley.

"The work is coming along well. There have been some improvements to the farm, with more to follow."

Asher hesitated before he continued, a deeper understanding swamping his mind and heart.

"The Divine Mother has touched me, in a way. I think it foolhardy to step away when so much progress has been made. We Blackwoods, usually are the first to battle. If we survive, we are last to leave."

Claudia gave Asher a sad smile. "Your uncle was the same. It took years for him to give this all up, but he did it for the right reasons. He found true love, with several women. He was an honorable and true ally to the valley, and the society. As you know, he was a larger-than-life soul. His final wish was to travel Valoria and see it all before he would settle down in his autumn years.

"It crushed many of us about his passing. That is why, I do have some information to give you that may help with some closure."

Asher's eyes widened a hair. He leaned forward, eager to hear what she had to say.

Claudia continued to speak while looking out the library window, "Asher, your uncle had many friends, but he made his share of enemies. One such enemy is a group by the name of the Ivory Crow Clan. They have been around for centuries. They began as a small collective of murderers and thieves, and over the years, turned into a group that hunts down magical items, weapons, and artifacts. They often sell to the highest bidder, and have no qualms with acquiring items in less than honorable ways.

"Lady Windswell has had recent contact with the clan. Our sources went through great lengths to get this information to our society. After combing through it, we discovered, your neighbor is an Ivory Crow member."

Asher lifted an eyebrow. "Jarrag?"

Claudia turned her attention to Asher and nodded. "We believe he is here to collect your Lac Codex, but he hasn't been activated yet. Jarrag may not be aware of his true purpose here, but once his superiors send the command, he must fulfill it. The Ivory Crows do have some legitimate operations across Valoria, but they are all fronts to their true dealings.

"The society believes the Ivory Crows, and maybe one other organization, had a hand in your uncle's assassination."

Asher's hands tightened on the armrests of his chair. His pulse quickened as rage curled around his soul. A fire filled his eyes, the very thought of his neighbor poisoning his mind with cruel intentions.

"We do not have any solid proof, and we are still gathering information. But this leads us back to earlier in our discussion. If you truly have decided to become a member of the society, it is important that you, and your farm are protected. The Opal Society protects its own, as we have for many centuries.

"You noticed the giant outside?"

Asher nodded, trying to quell his furious anger.

"Her name is Brynda. She has been a member of the society for the last few years. She knows all about what we do, and why we do it. She has seen her fair share of conflicts and battles. She has shared with several society members that she wishes to aid in a location for an extended period of time. I thought your farm would be perfect for her."

"Thank you, but I can defend my farm," Asher said plainly.

Claudia nodded. "I know you can, but that is not how we do things in the society. The reason the Opal Society has endured for centuries is our ability to protect ourselves, and each other. You are an experienced ranger and adventurer, but even you cannot stop a large enough force if they come for you.

"As a member, you will be privy to greater knowledge and secrets, but we all have to protect those secrets. Brynda's size, and skills, will be an effective deterrent for many who believe they can take what they want. She is a lovely woman, ready to help and fight to the death. I believe you both will make a great team."

"I don't really have a choice about this, do I?"

Claudia shook her head. "No. Not when it comes to having an enemy clan residing next to you, and a mayor who wishes to dismantle everything your uncle, and you, have built. I wish there was another way, but for now, this is the only option."

"She might be too tall for this house. We had a demon that was seven-foot-tall, and could barely fit in one of the larger rooms."

Claudia smiled. "Asher, we both know giants tend to sleep outside. I saw your new barn, and she can reside there for the winter."

Asher looked at Claudia with grim eyes. Putting himself in danger to protect others was already part of his code of honor. To have a bodyguard didn't sit well with him. It felt like something was taken away from his spirit.

I shouldn't be difficult about this. I decided to join the society, and much like my former guild, everyone who is part of it, must work, defend, and fight together. I have to give her a chance. At best, she will become bored and ask to move to another location. Her stay will be temporary.

"Okay, we will manage," Asher said with blank eyes.

"Excellent," Claudia said as she stood up.

Asher stood up with her.

"Before I leave, I want you to know that your farm has had steady production since your arrival. Because of that, Samuel will be handing over a bonus after he collects this shipment. I'm sure it will help ease the transition."

Claudia's eyes softened as she continued, "I will let my superiors know about your acceptance to join the society. We will prepare the contract and bring it to you. There is no secret ceremony or such. Sign on the line, and you will be one of us.

"It does come with some perks. Aside from the extra gold, you will be invited to gatherings in the future. We tend to speak and connect with others across Valoria. Most find it beneficial, and rewarding, for the work we do.

"I'll return in a few weeks. The summer is almost over, and I have a few places to visit before making my way back to Mist Valley."

"We'll keep the light on for your return," Asher said with a small smile.

Claudia eyed the young lord for a moment. "Asher, I know the burden of justice weighs heavy on you. It did for your uncle as well. Have clarity of mind that revenge never eases the pain. Until Jarrag Hornspear does something to provoke you, do not go searching for an excuse to end his life. We don't know if he had any direct involvement with your uncle's death. But if Jarrag is killed, the Ivory Crows will want their pound of flesh. They are fiercely protective of their agents, and Mist Valley should not be turned into a battleground."

Asher gave a slow nod, and his lip wrinkled in dismay.

The raven-haired woman gave Asher a small, understanding nod.

"I will take my leave, and oversee the shipment pick up. I look forward to when we meet again. Keep up the great work."

Lady Frost turned and began walking toward the door. Asher followed. When they reached the door, Claudia stopped, and turned to Asher.

"I almost forgot," she said as her hand slipped into her robe.

Asher watched as she pulled out a sealed letter. The lower corner of the letter bulged, like there was an item within it. Claudia handed it over, and Asher took it.

"It's a letter from one of your uncle's old friends. He is part of the society. He and your uncle had regular correspondence. He wanted me to give this to you personally. Read it at your leisure."

Asher nodded, holding the letter in his hand.

Claudia opened the library door and stepped out, with Asher following. They returned to the common room. Everyone was still sitting there, except for Amber and the goblins.

"It is a pleasure to see you all again. I will return in a few short weeks," Claudia smiled, before she made her way to the door

Asher saw her to the front door.

Elara looked at Asher, seeing a sliver of shadow under his eyes. His demeanor had changed, and her heart twisted in her chest with concern.

When Asher stepped outside with Claudia, he looked out to the wagon on the estate. Amber, and several goblins, were carrying small crates of potions to Sameul's wagon. The agent leaned against the side of the wagon, not lifting a finger to help. Not far from them, the giant woman stood. She observed with a blank expression, like it was simply another day.

A part of Asher's spirit wilted. A small fear bloomed, his simple life in Mist Valley becoming more complicated than he expected. Despite his concern, he knew the inner anger would drain away, and life would continue.

Asher made his way across the grassy field. Amber was carrying a crate as she looked at Asher with warm eyes. She watched as the young lord walked past her and approached the giant woman.

Brynda turned her gaze to the approaching lord. She lowered her gaze to him as he looked up at her. The height difference was about three feet, and she was slightly wider than him.

"It's a pleasure to meet you, Brynda," Asher said and bowed to her.

The giant woman looked down at him and blinked. She then bowed to him.

"It is a pleasure to meet you, Lord Blackwood," Brynda said with an almost shy tone.

The pair stood at their full height, looking into each other's eyes from a slant.

"Welcome to Blackwood," Asher said with a small smile. "We do not have any accommodations for you, but we can convert part of the barn for your stay."

"Thank you. I may only use it if it snows. I tend to sleep outside, in nature's beauty."

Asher's heart melted a little as he saw the genuine gleam in her eyes. She was truly a giant, a creature of the forests and mountains. Memories floated along his mind, of his encounters with giants, good and bad. Some simply wanted to be left alone, while others hunted and killed all those who encroached on their territories. To know a giant that has embraced society's ways was a rarity, but Brynda appeared to the ranger, as a soul caught between worlds.

"I will not be in your way, Lord Blackwood," Brynda said with a small voice.

Asher nodded and smiled. "We'll see how it all works. And please, call me Asher."

The giant woman gave a small nod.

The young lord felt the letter in his hand. He turned and made his way back to the house. He glanced over to Claudia, the lady speaking with Samuel. The man in black looked down as she spoke to him. A moment later, he walked over to Blyss, and picked up the crate from her hands. The goblin looked at him bewildered. Samuel walked the crate back to the wagon, giving Asher an annoyed smile.

There seems to be many small benefits to joining the society.

Asher nodded to the man in black before making his way inside.

When Asher stepped in, he was greeted by everyone. Elara looked at him with concerned eyes. Nyn, Nadia, Dina, had curious eyes.

"I need to go upstairs for a moment. I'll be back down and explain a little more about the changes here," he said.

Elara touched his hand, and Asher squeezed it. He looked into her green oval eyes with a drop of happy sorrow.

"We will talk more. I simply need a moment," Asher whispered before letting go and making his way to the stairs.

Elara's heart sagged in her chest, seeing the love of her life so troubled as he walked away.

Conflicted emotions stormed along Asher's spirit. He climbed the stairs and made his way back to his bedchamber. The knowledge that his neighbor may be part of a faction that directly, or indirectly caused his uncle's death, curled around his soul.

Memories pressed on him of his spirit walk. He saw and met his uncle, seeing his last moments before his life was taken. Aric's spirit told Asher not to seek vengeance, but the pain of his loss whispered otherwise. It brewed with darkness and shadow, snuffing out his hope for a better life.

Asher woke from his thoughts, seeing that he was in his bedroom, letter in hand. Mentally, he pushed away the dark thoughts as he lifted the letter. He was about to open it, when a short figure stepped into his doorway, rubbing an eye.

"Clan father?" Keefa said like she had just woken up.

Asher turned to her, putting the letter on the desk. The blonde goblin was in a simple sleeping shirt. It was long enough to be a dress. Her blonde curls lay in haphazard ways as she put her hand down and looked up at him.

"You're just waking up?" Asher asked with a small smile.

Keefa nodded. "Terrible dreams. I could not sleep well. I saw you, with a dagger in your side. Blood dripped. It woke me. I fall back asleep. I saw it over and over again. I was worried."

Asher put a hand on her shoulder. "I'm okay."

Keefa grabbed his wrist and looked up with haunted eyes.

"I see pain, and hope. We will protect you, as one clan," the goblin said as her fingers held his wrist tight.

"That's good to hear, just as I will protect all of you," Asher said with an endearing smile.

The goblin moved her hands and took his hand into hers. Fingers laced as she looked up at him.

Asher smiled as he squeezed her hand.

"Let's get downstairs. We have a lot of company, and have to get the day started."

Keefa gave an enthusiastic nod.

Man, and goblin left the bedchamber and made their way toward the stairs. The sealed envelope remained on his desk, morning light pouring into the still room.

Chapter 20

Silence

Days slipped by as the summer drew closer to the end. The oppressive heat abated. The mornings grew misty once again. The rains brought further relief, and the Blackwood farm continued to change.

Days were busy for Asher and all who dwelled on the estate. The young lord spent part of his time checking in on the fermentation process of the small batch. As far as he could tell, it was coming along nicely.

While at the winery, he kept a leatherbound book as a log, filling it with details and time frames of the process. By his calculations, the experimental batch would be ready by the first week of autumn. Asher was eager to try it, hoping it would come out like fruit wines he had with his mother on occasions.

After Claudia's visit and the shipment pick up, Asher was astounded at the payment and bonus. Two small chests were handed over, with not only gold coins within each one, but various gems mixed in. Their work paid well, but for the young lord, he was not like a dragon, hoarding every coin. He and Amber sat down in the alchemy lab, writing down amounts in a book-keeping tome. They worked out that everyone who lived there would receive stipends of coins, per month. It was more than enough for everyone, and even after that, there was still plenty of coin left over. For Asher, almost too much.

Dina visited the farm almost daily. She met with Asher, the pair sitting at the kitchen table to discuss further changes and upgrades to the farm, and estate. Plans were sketched and refined. Asher asked for a small cottage to be built on the north side of the estate. It would be Nyn's cottage, past the grape field, and far enough to provide the elf with her much needed solitude to write.

Next, the pair worked on the new farmhouse. Asher wanted it to not only be well-made, but strong. Dina often nodded, knowing she could complete the project before winter. The young lord was meticulous, wanting it to accommodate all manner of visitors to the farm.

The current farmhouse was simply to be known as "Farmhouse East." While the new one would be a small distance from the main house, and built to the west of it, not far from the fence and main road. It was to be known simply as "Farmhouse West."

There were brief discussions of Asher extending his property west, but with the mayor being difficult, Asher knew he would have to wait for the proper time to consider such an expansion.

When their meetings were finished, Dina often stayed for dinner, joining the household. Lively discussions took place, everyone excited for the additions and changes to the estate.

Asher found himself smiling more. He tried to push away the small revelations from Claudia. It was easier with each passing day. The busier he was, the more he didn't waste any time on dark thoughts. Focus fell on the farm and the women he loved. There was little time to waste on revenge.

Despite the growing harmony across the farm, there was one note of discord Asher had difficulty with.

The young lord often found himself looking out the windows of the west side of the house, late at night. He saw Brynda, sleeping on the grass. She truly had no difficulties with sleeping outside in the night air. The giant woman remained to herself for the most part. When she wasn't patrolling the grounds, she spent her time staring at the forests or sky. The giant barely spoke to anyone.

Elara often brought large plates of food to the giant for lunch and dinner. Brynda was gracious, taking each plate with a thank you and a nod. She then used her large hand to pick up food and stuff it into her mouth. To Asher, that didn't bother him. What bothered him was his reluctance to fully embrace the farm's new bodyguard.

In small moments, Asher felt tendrils of losing control. Joining the society seemed the right course of action, but in the process, he had the same feeling as when he was part of his guild for a time. Despite the freedom of going on adventures, he still reported back to the guild, handing over everything they worked for, only for a much smaller amount coming back to him. Working with the Opal Society wasn't exactly the same as working for the guild, but there was a sliver of concern it could become that again.

When Asher would check the farm's coffers, he often chuckled to himself, knowing he was being absurd. He had much more freedom, and coin, to do as he wished, with little oversight. With time, bigger changes would come, much to everyone's benefit.

Days and nights floated along, the last days of summer coming to an end. A nagging thought often touched Asher in those last days, knowing he had to go to the Summer Dusk Banquet at the Windswell's estate. He had never been there before, and considered not bothering to go, but Dina and Nadia's words stayed with him. The mayor was trying to buy the land west of his estate, and he had to go to convince others in the town's small council to deter her from boxing his estate in. The young lord knew he couldn't let the mayor bully him. He had to go and see if he, or his gold, would change the possible outcome.

The thought of the banquet often caused the young lord's mood to become withdrawn. It was a mood Elara was happy to pull him from. Most nights, she pulled him into bed to help keep away those thoughts. And some nights, she pulled him into bed with several goblins as well. The goblins and elf were eager to ease his tensions, the clan only growing closer.

When the days fell into normalcy, Asher found himself having a constant assistant. Nuha was often at his side when a repair was needed. The goblin had an affinity with tools, building, and repairs. When there was a leaky roof from the sudden downpours of rain, Asher was on the roof with Nuha at his side. She was focused as she watched him repair a roof slat. When another one needed repair, she was quick to ask if she could repair it. Asher smiled, seeing the goblin work. She was very good at it, making sure to follow his directions and advice.

When the summer drew to a close, tension once again began to build in Asher's shoulders, and spirit. Dreadful thoughts haunted him about the banquet, and he found himself unable to escape them. The Summer Dusk Banquet was tomorrow, and he found it difficult to relax.

Night had fallen on the second to last day of the summer. Asher was in the library, looking at small collections of books. Two shelves were now full of books, from wine making to history books. One shelf had two inner shelves filled with black books. The young lord had spent many hours reading them, some of them several times. His fingers touched one of them, and he lingered on it, remembering it was Nyn's new favorite.

Inner thoughts shifted to the often-silent elf. Asher saw her around the house. Her eyes were often caught with a distant gaze. She would go about her daily chores, but would often retire to her room early. Elara would tell Asher that Nyn was still writing her book, but for Asher, the quiet elf was distant.

When Asher pulled the black book titled "Silence," from the shelf, he opened it and re-read passages from it.

Night touched the valley beyond the library windows. The young lord looked over some of his favorite passages from the book, how the main character and his love interest fell into primal moments, saying nothing to each other and allowing their hands, and bodies, to speak an intimate language between them. Other than the first chapter, there was no dialogue. The book was short, but the descriptions were very detailed. He saw the appeal to such a relationship. The tension in his shoulders lessened as he looked over a page, reading it once again.

A mood tapped his spirit. An image of Nyn filled his thoughts. The mature elf seemed to invade his thoughts many times, but he never saw a signal from her to play their intimate game. He wondered if she changed her mind, but when he was re-reading a page, he saw that the main character didn't wait. He simply took what he wanted, just as his love interest did the same.

Memories of previous fiery encounters and trysts colored his thoughts. Life as an adventurer was filled with similar moments. He remembered being in taverns. If his gaze met a woman's gaze, little to nothing was said as they went back to his room, or theirs. But here, on the farm, different relationships had taken root. Where he once didn't give a tryst a second thought in the morning, all he could now was think about the women who won his heart. His thoughts were further refined, thinking about Nyn and her desires.

Asher closed the book and slid it back onto the shelf. A hunger grew, but not for food. He left the library and stepped into the main corridor. He glanced to one side, and then to another. His eyes took on a predatory gleam, seeing the elf in question walking toward him, a book in her hands.

Nyn walked with her gaze on Asher. In the dim lantern light, she could see a hungry look in his eyes. She didn't slow down, walking toward the library to put a book back.

Asher turned and walked toward her. The two met in the middle. Nyn simply looked at the young lord, before attempting to step past him. Before she could slip past, Asher's arm stabbed out and planted his open palm against the corridor wall.

Nyn stopped in her tracks. She turned her gaze to him. Asher turned his body to her as his arm continued to block her way.

Nyn shifted, pressing her back to the wall. The mature elf looked up into Asher's hungry gaze. She clutched the book tighter in her one hand. She barely blinked, making not a sound, or a movement. She simply kept her back to the wall, looking up at Asher with a blank gaze.

Asher lifted his hand and touched her chin. Fingers glided along her jaw, until he reached her pointed ear. Nyn let out a small exhale, the young lord's fingers gently running along and touching her sensitive ear. It sent a thrill and a vibration along her entire body. She had forgotten his alluring touch, and now that he was focused on her, her muscles wanted to melt. She stayed standing, not allowing herself to show the sudden shift in mood.

The young lord looked at Nyn, seeing pink radiating along her cheeks. It was more than enough to see that the mood had struck her as well. When he let go of her ear, he leaned forward, his lips close to hers.

Nyn readied for his kiss, but it didn't come as expected. Asher moved his head and pressed his lips to her alabaster colored neck. Heat bloomed along her sensitive flesh. She bit her lip so as to not let out a heated gasp. A swirl filled her stomach, and a tingling began to grow. The moment had come, and it caused her heart to flutter in her chest.

Asher kissed and licked the elf's smooth neck. He brought his body close, ensuring she could not escape. Nyn's breathing changed, but Asher ignored it. Nyn's flesh was tantalizing to his senses. Her scent filled his nose. It hinted at creamy milk, and divine flowers. He always enjoyed Elara and Nyn's scents, but this evening, Nyn's scent stoked his inner fire. There was an edge to it, something he couldn't put his finger on, but one he wanted more of.

When Asher's strong hand touched Nyn's waist, she fought off a shudder. His lips remained on her neck. His hand traveled up the side of her form. When a thumb and finger touched under her heavy breast, Asher's teeth pressed against her neck.

Nyn's body reacted, pushing her hips to his. A small moan dripped from her parted lips as the Lord of Blackwood sucked on her neck. Heat bloomed further as she writhed against him, unable to hide her desires and urges any longer.

Asher pushed his hips against Nyn's hips, pinning her to the wall. He closed his hand against her breast, squeezing it and feeling a drop of wetness against the fabric. He didn't stop for a moment. He ran his thumb over her covered nipple, more wetness greeting him.

Nyn kept her lips closed, trapped by the man she grew very fond of. Something thickened in his leggings. It was pressed against her and she writhed to further entice him. A thrill filled her form, knowing in this moment he could do anything to her, and she would not stop him. It fueled the mood further, heat filling her as a drop of honey ran down her inner thigh.

Asher pulled his head back and looked at the elf with near demonic eyes. Nyn tried to control her breathing, when the young man grabbed her arm and pulled her with him. Nyn stumbled, but was kept up by Asher's strong hand and arm.

The pair stepped into the library. Asher walked with determination in his eyes. They reached a bookshelf. Asher's hand slipped into the shelf and pulled the secret lever. The hidden door opened. Nyn quickly put the book in her hand on a shelf. Man and elf stepped into the small corridor, the door closing behind them. They emerged in the secret chamber, dim lights glowing to life.

Asher brought Nyn around to face him. He took hold of both of her arms, walking her backwards until her legs touched the edge of the bed. With a strong push, Nyn fell onto the bed. The elf bounced on the soft bed as she looked up at the young lord.

Asher stood with strong, hungry eyes. Nothing was said as he grabbed his shirt and pulled it over his head.

When Nyn saw what was happening, it curled along her spirit. Despite knowing Asher would never harm her, his silent, wanting presence caused the swirl in her stomach to grow. A wet tingling grew between her legs as she eyed him. He undid his belt and pushed down his leggings. When they reached his ankles, he stepped out of them and kicked them away.

Nyn eyed him, her gaze falling to his now standing manhood. It throbbed with thick veins. He took hold of it, like a favored weapon. He stroked it to her, the lord watching her like he was contemplating what he was going to do to her.

The mature elf let out a small gasp. Her long, blue dress covered her parted legs. She made no move, watching the young man stroke his member to her.

Asher's hand shot out and grabbed her naked ankle. Nyn's eyes widened as she was pulled by his strong arm to her. When she was by the edge of the bed, he let go and reached for the hem of her dress. With a strong pull, he brought it up to see her naked thighs and elfhood. Even in the dim light, Asher could see the gleam of wetness from her pink slit. When he glanced up, he could see wet spots growing along her top. She took deep breaths as he eyed her like a new prize.

Asher's left hand slid down her leg to her inner thigh. Fingers slid in, touching her wet slit, and seeing the mature elf shudder. When his finger grazed her clit, Nyn's fingers grabbed and bunched up the top blanket of the bed.

A sense of uncertainty swamped the elf, unsure exactly what he was going to do to her. But another side of her knew she would not stop him. Primal desire filled his eyes and she let out a soft exhale. The room was soundproof, and she was trapped with him. She was his, to do as he pleased.

For Asher, the elf was his play thing. He pressed the head of his cock to her thin opening. He rubbed the throbbing head against it, as if readying to plunge it into her.

Nyn's thighs trembled. She thought he would sink down and lick her into submission first, but the strong lord had other ideas. She attempted to crawl away, as if to flee. For Asher, it only charged the mood. His hand clamped on her hip and held her in place. Nyn struggled to pull from him, when his thick manhood slowly speared her elfhood.

Pleasure bloomed as a small moan escaped her lips. She tried to pull away, but her attempts grew weaker as inches parted her inner world. When he was half in her, her hips betrayed her, moving to his rigid manhood.

Asher kept a tight grip on her waist, keeping her in place. He slowly invaded her wet valley until he reached the hilt. Only then, did his right-hand flash forward and grab her top. With a hard tug, he pulled down her top, exposing one full breast. Milk leaked from the erect nipple, sliding down her engorged breast. Asher's hips worked slow and deliberate, pushing deep and pulling back. His hand grabbed at her breast, fingers pressing into soft flesh as milk continued to leak.

The tension within the elf drained away as pleasure filled her. A powerless feeling merged with blissful ecstasy. A fantasy she often had, bloomed into reality. Wetness surged as his thick member slid back and forth. She squeezed him, yet he seemed not to care. His gaze was filled with greedy strength.

The tempo increased with Asher's hips slapping against inner thighs. He squeezed and fondled the mature elf, doing as he pleased. She bit her lip and watched him with sultry eyes. His power was cresting and falling over her spirit. Nothing was said for it didn't need to be said. She moved her hips to his invasion, which made him thrust harder. Her body and breasts bounced. When she tried to sit up, Asher pushed her down, keeping her on her back. Nyn writhed as she remained in his power, unable to break his will, or his desire.

Milk leaked and spilled. Her one covered breast was wet from her creamy milk. The other breast was free, milk sliding down her side and seeping into the blanket. The messy bonding only enhanced the moment.

Nyn's breathing grew deeper and quicker. Memories of an organized and orderly life began to crack and fall away. The thrill grew deeper with each deep thrust. Control was dwindling as she was his, to do as he pleased. A loud moan escaped her lips, the moment growing deeper. Nyn's eyes closed as she did something she never truly imagined she'd ever do, she fully surrendered to the young lord.

The moment of surrender, her willpower cracked. The need to climax struck her like an arrow to her soul. The rougher Asher grew, the more every nerve curled tight. Strong hands took hold of her dress and pulled it over her head. Now naked, her body bounced as he took her. His movements were like a rutting demon. The very thought of anyone else taking her like this, was alien to the mature elf. She allowed herself to be Asher and Elara's third, but this was different. There was no one else. She was not part of a shared moment with others. This time it was only she, and him.

The truth ignited her own passionate urges. Her eyes rolled into her head, as her head laid on the bed. Darkness, heat, and lust curled along her entire body. The moment flashed, and Nyn was swept away by a flood of pure bliss. Her body shuddered beyond her control. A series of mystical explosions blasted her nerves to glass. Heat filled her twitching body as the young lord continued to rail her further into loving submission.

Asher watched with a wry smirk. His hips continued to thrust as Nyn's eyes fluttered and her body trembled. The mature elf let out ragged moans, caught in a swell of blissful explosions. Her soul dripped as she bounced to the lord's strong hips.

Asher leaned over her, his rigid cock continuing its repeated invasion. He clamped his mouth over her leaking nipple, and sucked. Sensitive nerves along the nipple and areola flared to his lips and suction. Nyn's arms instantly wrapped around his head, keeping him to her naked breast as sultry moans filled their ears.

Nyn's moans grew louder. She writhed like a snake under Asher, losing her mind to flaring senses. The tingling grew deeper as the lord drank her creamy milk. She pushed her breast into his face, wanting him to suck the very life from her. Legs came up and curled around his lower back, giving the young lord full access to her dripping slit. She gave him a loving squeeze, but it was lost to the heated moment.

Asher let go of her nipple and shoved her arm down from his head. He lifted his upper body as he pounded the elf into further submission. She huffed as orgasms continued to assault her. Strange moans floated up as Nyn could barely remain coherent.

The urge of release slammed into the young lord. Seeing, and feeling the elf lose control set his own spirit ablaze. His cock thickened, which only made Nyn moan louder. Her inner walls were pushed to the near the breaking point, when Asher pulled his cock out and stroked it. He was standing as thick ropes of molten come splashed on her breasts, and trailed down her stomach.

A loud grunt filled the chamber as Asher stroked and milked his own cock onto the writhing elf. Seeing his come on her skin, caused him to groan, another spurt of come landing on her stomach, knowing she was truly his.

Nyn fought through the waves of pleasure. The elf sat up as come slid down her smooth skin. She pushed at Asher hard enough for him to stumble back a step. She slid off the bed and landed on her knees. She looked at his hanging, wet cock. A drop of come dripped from the tip, before her lips closed around it.

Asher was frozen as the elf sucked on his hanging member. Her hands were on his hips as she lifted herself up on her knees. With cock firmly between her lips, she sucked on him, breathing new life into it.

The young lord grunted, his soreness slowly drained away. Demonic urges continued to sing, his member rising to the occasion. When his cock was rigid once again, Nyn looked up with primal eyes.

The couple was locked in the moment. Asher was powerless to break free, not that he wanted to. Nyn changed the power dynamic to herself, knowing she rendered him powerless in the moment. Her teeth grazed his shaft, which only made him harder.

Asher grabbed her by the hair, trying to shift the power and control back to him. Nyn's teeth sank a little deeper into his flesh, but not breaking skin. Asher let go, and her head began to bob with urgent need.

Seed dripped down her skin, as milk leaked from her full breasts. She upped the tempo and looked up with hungry eyes.

The couple locked gazes, but it was Asher lost to Nyn's primal urges. She sucked on him like she needed his cock just to survive. Dreamy bliss ran along his shaft, while the elf's hand ran down her smooth stomach and reached her dripping slit. Fingers massaged her engorged clit as honey and seed dripped from her. Bliss stirred and spiked as her head moved with urgency. The tingling in her lower abdomen grew deeper as

Asher's cock filled her mouth and throat. She pressed her tongue along the underside of the shaft, making her whole mouth tight as she tried to pull his soul though it.

Asher continued to watch the often-reserved elf turn into a primal creature. Muffled moans filled her throat. The scents and sounds of their bonding wrapped around senses. The chamber became their secret place, able to truly be themselves without judgment.

When Nyn slowed the tempo, she looked up with loving eyes. She slowly dragged her lips along his cock, while her tongue ran along the shaft with arcane movements.

Asher looked down with a loving gaze, as he surrendered. His cock thickened before spurts painted the back of her throat. Bliss flowed up from his cock, invading every point of his mind, body, and soul. He let out a grunt as the mature elf milked his member with her lips.

Nyn basked in the moment. She felt Asher's surrender. When his seed touched her tongue, it tasted better than ever before. An inner knowing swirled, seeing, and feeling him give his soul to her. Where there was a small distance between them since she arrived, that distance was now gone. The trysts between them were wonderful, but this moment proved, they were meant for more.

The elf lazily sucked on her lover's cock. She reached up and gave his balls a gentle squeeze, signaling he belonged to her now.

The scent of sex filled their noses. The couple were lost to it, not speaking a word, but experiencing the same thing. Asher touched her pointed ear, and the elf shuddered in pleasure. She rubbed her clit as his touch urged her hunger for more.

Asher reached down and took a handful of hair. He pulled gently, Nyn rising. Asher's cock slipped from her mouth as Nyn stood to her full height. Asher let go of her hair, grabbed her shoulders, and turned her around.

With a push, Nyn was on the bed. She rose up as milk leaked from her. She looked back to Asher grabbing her hips and pulling them up. She was on her knees as he took hold of her hip with one hand.

Asher's cock didn't weaken as he pushed the head to her abused slit. The mature elf lowered her hips to give him easier access. She remained on all fours, when Asher's member penetrated her inner world again. He kept her thin waist in his tight grip, pushing his urges into her like she didn't have a say.

Nyn moaned her approval, the young man controlling her. She leaned her ass to his invasion, the pair meeting in the middle. A warm, relaxed feeling filled the pair, enjoying the simple, primal act of copulation, like two animals in a dark forest.

Bodies moved in loving need as they carried on with their quiet tryst.

***

Asher was on his back as Nyn was draped on him. The secret chamber glowed with dim light as the couple snuggled and enjoyed a moment of respite.

The young lord looked down with loving eyes as Nyn rested her head on his chest. Her breathing was relaxed and even. Body warmth glowed between them, the pair holding onto each other as if fearful of letting go.

"It was amazing," Asher said softly, breaking the silence.

Nyn gave a lazy nod. "It was," she whispered back.

Silence filled the space around again, enjoying the touch of their bodies.

Nyn opened her eyes and stared at nothing. Something changed within, and she could not deny it any longer. She gently lifted her upper body, and looked at Asher with warm eyes.

"Elara told me she never wants to leave here. She has fallen deeply in love with you. I see it with Amber, Blyss, and the other goblins. I have tried to keep a small distance, knowing one day, I would return to my old life."

Nyn's eyes trembled before she continued, "But now, I cannot see myself returning to my old life."

Asher looked at her with loving eyes. "Nor would I want you to leave. If you told me you would be returning, I would have to chain you to his chamber until you changed your mind."

Nyn let out a warm laugh, the kind she never let out before. Her body felt loose, and relaxed. She looked at Asher as her lips grew into a smile.

"Lord Blackwood, if you continue to take on lovers, you will be greatly out-numbered."

"I think we can manage," Asher smirked before he thought about the situation. "But, does it bother you that I take on lovers?"

Nyn let a sultry smirk form. "Should it? I'm not blind to what is happening here. But if we are being honest, I did warn Elara about loving you. Elven lives are much longer than most other peoples on Valoria. I feared for my friend, that once you were gone, she would dwell in misery and loss. I didn't want that for her. I wanted to see, with time, if this was a simple lewd tryst, or something more?"

Nyn rested her chin on Asher's chest while looking at him with warm eyes.

"I can admit, I was wrong. I spent my entire life living a certain way, more so than Elara. Where she focused on her duties, and yearning for a new life, I spent my days knowing my life, in a way.

"The best way to describe it is, I thought I would serve the empire to the end of my days. My life and destiny were planned out in meticulous detail. I allowed myself to dwell in fantasies, but my world was in my province, writing about many other lives, and not my own.

"But when I came here, everything changed. I not only noticed the change in my dear friend, I felt my own change. It has shifted my destiny in a new direction, and I am eager to follow it, if you would have me?"

"I would. I do," Asher said warmly.

Nyn snuggled closer, letting out a relaxed sigh. She stared at the bedside lantern, the glowing flame within swaying slightly from side to side.

"I will write about our intimate adventures. They will make us immortal, giving inspiration to others for a very long time."

The elf shifted her gaze back to Asher's gaze. "But first, I need you again. I need what we have."

The young lord held her close. He kissed her forehead before looking into her oval, sapphire-colored eyes.

"I need you too. And when the time comes, I want us to write a book together," Asher said, wanting nothing more than to do something special and important, bringing their bond ever closer.

Nyn's heart fluttered as she looked at the handsome, young lord.

Man and elf kissed as they held each other. Soon, bodies bonded as they embraced, tongues playing an intimate dance.

The swaying lantern flame glowed as two souls, and bodies, became one.

Chapter 21

The Banquet

Asher stood before the mirror in his bedchamber. He drank in his white, billowy shirt. It was laced along the top center, revealing some of his strong chest. Cuffs cinched along his wrists, and part of his forearms. The open collar brought attention to his defined neck and jaw.

The young lord's leggings were tight, and black. A square, silver belt buckle graced the front. Leather, shin-high boots completed the outfit.

Despite his relaxed appearance, a small apprehension tugged at his spirit. The Summer Dusk Banquet was to begin in just over an hour, and the young man was having second thoughts on attending the town holiday ritual.

Letting out a small sigh, he pushed the concern from his mind. Internally, he told himself it would only improve townspeople relations if he showed up, and became part of the celebrations. It still weighed on him, no matter how much he tried to tell himself otherwise.

Turning away from the mirror, Asher's gaze fell on the beautiful elf standing in front of another standing mirror. His breath was taken away as Elara turned slowly from side to side, examining herself in her dress. For Asher, what a dress it was.

The beautiful elf moved easily in a thin, dark red dress. It adhered to her feminine form perfectly. It had a plunging neckline, and slits ran to just below her hips, giving her freedom of movement without showing extra skin. Her arms were bare, allowing her to stay cool as the last day of summer was still very warm. Her blonde hair was pinned up into a stylish bun, keeping it off her neck. The swirls of pinned hair took on almost symbolic edges as they merged into the stylish bun. When she turned and looked at the handsome young man, Asher could see nothing but distilled, ethereal beauty.

"You look incredibly beautiful," Asher said without hesitation.

Elara smiled as heat touched her cheeks. "Thank you, Lord Blackwood. And I might say, you look incredibly dashing, like a prince from a fairy tale."

Asher smiled as he couldn't take his gaze off her.

A heat filled the bedchamber as the two lovers looked at each other.

"We should get downstairs, or we will be very late from tearing our clothes off each other," Elara giggled.

"How can you read my mind so easily?" Asher said with relaxed humor.

"Because we share the same thoughts, my lovely morsel," the mature elf winked.

Elara held out her hand. Asher stepped to her and took it.

"They are not happy to stay," Elara mentioned.

Asher nodded. "I know, but Blyss volunteered to stay behind. I think she is uncomfortable at events. Paasha is pleased to stay behind, but Nuha, and Keefa, not so much."

Elara touched his collar and fixed it a little. "What about the farm bodyguard?"

"I think, no matter what I say, she's going to do as she wishes," Asher admitted.

"Nevertheless, it should be a fascinating evening. One, I do hope we get through unscathed. I look forward to spending the last night of summer in each other's arms."

"Me too," Asher said as he took in her milky cinnamon scent.

"Let's start our journey, and pray to the Divine Mother my dress stays as nice as it is for the entire banquet."

Asher nodded and put his hand out. "After you, my love."

Elara blushed as she took his hand and led him to the bedchamber door.

The couple left the bedroom, walked the long corridor, and made for the stairs. They reached the first floor and walked toward the noisy common room. When they stepped into it, they were greeted with beauty, and chaos.

Fern clopped and jumped around with small, excited screams. The uni-goat's golden horn shined in the late afternoon light as she swung her head around and jumped. Nyn stood in a long, flowing dark blue dress. It covered her a little more, not displaying a plunging neckline like Elara's dress. The beautiful elf was surrounded by three goblins. Nuha was lifting the hem as she looked at the dress with inquisitive eyes. Keefa sat on a couch, staring at the beautiful elf with stars in her eyes. Blyss stood on the couch, next to Keefa, slowly brushing Nyn's long, dark blue hair. Nyn herself was a beautiful statue in the eye of the storm. She only shifted her gaze and smiled, as she saw the couple as they entered the common room.

Not far from the chaos, Amber stood in a long, forest green dress. She was dressed modestly, but it didn't hide her beauty. She glued a few small jewels to her horns, giving them a dazzling gleam, and nearly fae like glow. She had a leather strap over her shoulder, cutting across the front of her body, as a small satchel lay against a covered hip.

"So pretty!" Keefa said as she looked at each woman in turn.

"Never forget, you're beautiful as well," Nyn said with a comforting voice.

The blonde goblin grinned, before looking away with shy eyes.

Blyss continued to run the brush through Nyn's long, lustrous hair. The goblin did glance at Asher, before returning her gaze to combing hair.

Asher let go of Elara's hand and walked over to the goblin and elf. Blyss looked up at him again, her brushing slowing down.

"I wish you would come with us," the young lord said to the beautiful goblin.

Blyss looked at Nyn's hair as she brushed it. "As chieftess, it is my duty to guard our home. The demon mayor may try steal from us. We stay and protect."

Asher grinned.

Nuha lifted Nyn's dress higher and poked her head under it.

"Too much dress! And you not wear small clothes," the goblin laughed.

"There is no law that I must wear them," Nyn said with deadpan delivery.

Small laughter filled the common room.

Asher smiled as he turned at Amber approaching him. The faun was beautiful, looking up at him with warm eyes.

"We should leave soon. It will take us a little time to get into town, and then walk to the beach," the faun said with subdued excitement.

Asher put his hands on her hips, visually drinking in her beauty.

"You are gorgeous," he said to her.

Amber's eyes widened a hair as pink flooded her pale cheeks.

"Where's the cake?" Elara asked.

"I have it," Nyn spoke up. "It's in a dimensional pocket. I will bring it forth when we arrive at the banquet."

"Then, we are ready to leave?" Asher said as he took his hands off Amber's hips and faced everyone.

Paasha stepped into the common room, from the kitchen. She was covered in patches of powder, and a streak of chocolate on her green cheek.

"Tell me if you like. I like making cake," the motherly goblin grinned from pointed ear to pointed ear.

"If it was anything like the batter, everyone is going to love it," Amber said with a cheery smile.

Nuha pulled her head from under Nyn's dress. "I want more batter, and cake!"

"Me too!" Keefa nearly shouted.

"Smaller cake and bowl on the table," Paasha said proudly.

"Have fun!" Nuha shouted before darting to the kitchen.

Keefa was off the couch and following, but she stopped short at Asher's side. The blonde goblin looked up at her clan father, her smile dimming a little.

"Have fun, and beware of dagger," the goblin said in a small voice.

Asher's eyebrow went up. Before he could ask what she meant, she ran off toward the kitchen, almost like she didn't say anything at all.

Blyss hopped down from the couch, and looked up at everyone still in the common room.

"We will be okay. Have fun," the goblin said before she turned and marched toward the kitchen.

Asher's hand twitched, and lifted, reaching for the goblin. Elara intercepted his hand with her own, curling her fingers into his. The young lord turned his attention to her, and blinked.

"She will be fine. The decision was hers to make. We will honor it. When we come back, she will be treated like the beautiful chieftess she is," Elara said with understanding eyes.

Asher nodded, knowing she was right. The longer they were all together, the tighter the heartstrings and bonds grew. He didn't want to leave any of them behind, but with everything that had happened since they arrived in this valley, they needed to be extra careful, and not be blind to possible plots.

"Alright, let's go," Asher said.

Everyone remaining in the common room nodded, before they made for the front door.

Fern watched them go, and shifted on her hooves in uncomfortable silence.

Asher, Elara, Nyn, and Amber, stepped out onto the porch. They made their way down the small steps and onto the dirt path. They all looked ahead to see a giant woman standing by the front gate.

Brynda looked at the four of them with half-closed eyes. She wore the same clothes she always wore, a knee-length dress, with slits up to her hips. Her stomach was bare, but her voluptuous top was covered with cloth and leather straps. A

343

broadsword pommel stabbed out past each shoulder. Her red hair was in a thick braid. As the group approached, she opened the front gate.

Asher stepped forward and smiled at the nine-foot-tall, giant woman.

"Thank you," he said.

"I'm coming with you," the giantess stated.

"Brynda, I doubt we will run into any trouble at the banquet celebration. Besides, I thought you were here to protect the farm?"

Brynda's gaze took on a steely sheen.

"I protect the farm, but I also protect you, Lord Blackwood."

Asher let out a small sigh.

"I doubt I can change your mind."

Brynda shook her head.

Asher looked to the west, seeing the sun hovering over the western valley mountains.

"Then let's not keep the celebration waiting," Asher said as he reached up his smaller hand, to her larger one.

Brynda looked down on the lord with confusion in her eyes. When he took hold of her hand, and led her through the gate, the giantess's eyes widened a hair.

Elara, Nyn, and Amber watched, as the Lord of Blackwood led the giant woman to the road. They walked, side by side.

"His charm is lethal," Elara said softly.

"And honest," Nyn added.

"And why we adore him," Amber finished.

The three women looked at each other, their hearts aglow. They soon followed the man and giantess, making their way east to town, and the evening's festivities.

The walk to town was fairly quick. When they entered, little to no activity greeted them. It was like the inhabitants had vanished into thin air. Every shop was closed, and no people were in sight. The further they walked in, they quickly noticed that even the Drunken Seahorse, which was never closed, was sealed shut, and curtains pulled behind windows.

When they reached the center of town, they all turned and looked south.

A cobblestone street stretched on. It passed well past the Drunken Seahorse, which was to their right. Two tall, sheer mountains stood. A wide street ventured on, carved out between two of the many mountains that surround the valley. The scent of the sea flowed from between the mountains, as blue waters gleamed in the far distance.

Asher had been living in Mist Valley for months, but never took the time to venture to the beach. When he reached the center of town, there was also an ocean breeze coming this way, sometimes weak, and sometimes strong. It never abated as the air was channeled between them.

The group walked toward the stony gap, ready to see and explore beyond the mountains.

Asher looked around in subdued excitement. The sheer walls were weathered, and cut a long time ago. Moss grew on the rocky walls in large patches. The scent of the sea grew as they made their way further south. Asher glanced up to see sunlight painting the higher peaks. The mountains were tall, but only half as tall as some of the mountains he explored in his past adventures.

A thought did cross the young lord's mind, wondering why the valley was surrounded by such odd, sheer mountains. Was the area volcanic? Did some ancient event take place, carving out the entire valley? Was this a home to some legendary beast from eons ago? He could not say, but speculation ran rampant as he wondered what deeper story the valley held from an age long ago.

Everyone in the group looked around in stunned awe, except for Elara. The elf looked at Asher with dreamy eyes, seeing him lead, yet still take in the wonders of the world around them. A deeper part of her heart glowed, as she walked with a lightness in her step.

When the group emerged from between two mountains, they all stared out at grass, trees, sand, and ocean waves in the distance.

Much to Asher's chagrin, he thought the south road simply led to the beach. Instead grass and trees spread out on either side of the road. Yellowish white sand could be seen further away, but lush greenery surrounded them. The trees swayed to the ocean breeze. Birds sang in trees, or flew from one to the next. Some looked down on the five newcomers. A few cocked their heads to the side, while others sang to their presence.

The group continued to walk the cobblestone path. Asher led the way, drinking it all in with a happy gleam in his eyes. He mentally cursed himself for not exploring this side of Mist Valley sooner.

Once they passed the trees, green grassy fields stretched out to a sandy beach. The sight of grazing cattle and sheep appeared. Dozens and dozens of animals moved freely, chewing on green and yellow grass. Some looked over with indifferent eyes as the group walked along the cobblestone street. The sky was a majestic blue, the sun getting lower to the west, over the sea.

"I didn't know they simply let livestock roam freely," Nyn mentioned.

"On my trips into town, I heard it mentioned many times about townsfolk running into the Windswell's livestock when making for the beach," Amber added.

"Shouldn't they be penned in, to ensure they don't wander off?" Nyn said.

"There is no need," Asher spoke up and pointed east and westward in turn. "There is nowhere to go. They won't swim away, and the valley mountains do stretch out in places, enclosing the whole area.

The giantess closed her eyes and took a deep inhale.

"I love the smell of the sea," Brynda said softly with her exhale.

"It is magical," Asher smiled at the giantess.

"This is all the Windswell's land?" Elara asked as she looked around.

Amber nodded. "Mostly, but there is an agreement that anyone from town can visit the beach without permission. It was one of the few stipulations for buying the land."

Asher looked at the faun with an inquisitive eye.

"I've listened to the town gossip on more than one occasion," the faun grinned.

Asher couldn't hide his smile as he went back to looking around.

"But where is their home?" Elara asked.

"It's over there to the west, past the trees," Brynda said and pointed in that direction.

Everyone turned and looked at what the giant was pointing to. Past the trees was a tall, gray wall with several towers.

Asher glanced at the cobblestone road ahead of them, seeing that it veered west, toward the sun hanging low in the sky.

"Let's follow the road," Asher said and led the way.

The wind and muffled sounds of crashing waves eased the group as they walked together. Gulls floated on thermals. The air tasted of sea salt, and the trees began to part the further they walked along.

Asher wasn't sure what to expect, but he certainly didn't expect what was revealed as they approached.

The cobblestone path stabbed on and curved to a high wall and arched entrance. The modern stone walls stretched on and connected with the mountain, blending into it. Past the walls, the top of a structure could be seen.

Windswell Castle was a fortress built into the very side of a mountain. Thick walls curved around the castle itself. Thin towers broke up the protective wall. Blue flags with white wisps flapped in the wind. The size and power of the castle and walls was impressive, but much of the castle itself was obscured. A small, hardy stone structure stood beside the castle wall, Asher assuming it was some kind of stable for the animals during hard weather.

The group made their way closer, reaching the main gate. Music greeted them as they walked under an archway so high, there was plenty of room between Brynda's head and the top of the entrance.

A large courtyard spread out before the newcomers. It was filled with long tables, hanging banners, and mingling bodies. Past them, Castle Windswell stood in all its glory. The castle was several stories tall, with towers of its own. Stained glass windows dotted the structure. Colored slats covered the roof and towers. For Asher, it was the most artistic castle he had seen in his many travels.

Garden areas broke up the courtyard with symmetry and style. The mountain behind it rose high into the air, painted in sunlight.

"Welcome to our home, Lord Blackwood!" came a familiar voice from the many mingling bodies in the courtyard.

Heads turned and many smiles bloomed for a moment. When many of the guests caught sight of the nine-foot-tall giant woman, a few gazes grew nervous.

Lady and Lord Windswell walked toward Asher and his companions without hesitation. The regal couple approached Lord Blackwood. They wore loose-fitting, flowy white and blue outfits. They were stylish, and relaxed. Lady Windswell's dress was cut down sideways, revealing one leg more than the other. Her top adhered to her perfectly. Her hair was out, and down, like a flowing dark river.

Lord Windswell wore a shirt similar to Asher's shirt, except with blue accents, and embroidered cuffs. Asher quickly noticed, the Lord of Windswell was fit. On previous occasions, the lord was often covered up with a regal robe. Only his height could not be hidden from any who looked upon him. Relaxed, and almost carefree, the taller man smiled like it was the happiest day in his life.

"Thank you for inviting us," Asher said with a polite bow.

Everyone bowed to each other. When they stood up, the Windswells continued to not give the giant behind Asher's group a second glance.

"Whatever may happen beyond these walls, have no bearing on this wonderful celebration. Please know, we are here to enjoy our time, and see the last sunset of the summer season, together," Lady Windswell said with a perfect smile.

Asher kept his face neutral.

She's being extra kind to ensure there is no drama during the banquet. I can't help but agree with her. Despite the contention between us, I must remain kind, and polite. No need for a spectacle in front of the whole town. And judging from how many attendees are here, the entire town came to celebrate.

Past the Windswell's shoulders, Asher could see many people looking over with drinks in hands, and curious eyes.

Lady Windswell turned her attention to Elara, Nyn, and Amber. She looked at them with wide eyes, and an even wider smile.

"All of you look absolutely stunning," she said as she approached the trio. Her gaze fell on Elara's dark red dress and visually drank it in. "This was made in the Thallmar Province? They have some of the best fabrics in the elven empire. The dress looks incredible, but you make it flawless!"

Elara gave the lady a warm smile. "Thank you, Lady Windswell. You are too kind. And I might add, your dress is equally stunning. Is that Nukarr spider-silk? From the Night Islands?"

Lady Windswell gave an approving nod and warm smile. "It was specially made, during my travels. As you know, the shadow elves of the Night Islands don't take many visitors, but I was fortunate to accompany a diplomatic quest to the islands, about five years ago. They are not as mistrusting as many speak of, and welcomed us with open arms."

The lady ran her hands down her silky dress. "They made this for me, saying I was a breath of fresh air in their society. It's one of a kind, for they never use white or blue colors with their fabrics. You have an incredible eye for detail. We should sit down for drinks at some point."

"We should," Elara smiled.

The lady smiled and turned her attention back to Asher. "I could go on and on about adventures and stories, but we have a banquet to enjoy."

She turned to the courtyard with a wave of her hand, "Everyone is enjoying drinks for now, before we bring out the courses. Please, feel free to mingle and relax. The servants will tend to whatever needs or wants. There will be announcements as the evening continues. Enjoy yourselves!"

Lady Windswell turned to her husband, and put her hand on his shoulder. "Come, my handsome husband. Let us ensure all is well for our honored guests."

Lord Windswell took her hand and held it. "Of course, my dear."

The Lady and Lord of Windswell winked at Asher and his group, before walking back to the party.

Asher glanced around, seeing slythans tending to the guests. Each one wore a regal servant's robe, all of them embroidered with the Windswell family crest on the front, and back of their chests. There were no hoods, their reptilian heads bare. They all had kind expressions. To Asher, it almost looked believable that they wanted to be there.

Elara moved closer to Asher and curled her arm under his. The elf leaned in a little to his ear, while still smiling.

"Did that encounter make your skin crawl like mine?"

Asher simply nodded.

Elara turned to face Asher's ear. "Knowing the shadow elves, they made a dress of discarded botched fabrics. It's true, they don't use blue and white, they tend to use black, purple, and red, but they made that for her because someone failed to dye them correctly, and they sat somewhere until she arrived," the elf said and finished by licking Asher's ear.

"Scandalous," Asher said with a genuine grin.

The couple chuckled privately.

"I require a drink," Amber said and walked past the couple.

"I too require a drink," Nyn said and followed the faun.

Asher and Elara turned to Brynda, the giant standing with her arms crossed along her stomach.

"Are you okay?" Asher asked.

The giant nodded. "I'll be fine. This isn't the first time I was ignored. It won't be the last."

Just then, two slythan servants approached the giant woman. The pair bowed to her as one spoke.

"Please forgive us, but no weapons are allowed at the banquet. We must take, and hold them. They will be returned when you depart."

Brynda looked at the two slythan males with hard eyes.

"Brynda, we are their guests," Asher said simply, understanding that a warrior and their weapons should not be parted.

The giant glanced at Asher, and her gaze weakened a hair. She unfolded her arms, reached up, and took hold of each broadsword. She drew the swords together, and held each one out to each slythan.

Asher enjoyed seeing the giant woman use two-handed swords like one-handed weapons. They looked light in her hands. When the slythans took hold, they grunted at the weight. Brynda folded her arms again as the slythans walked away with the heavy melee weapons.

He turned his attention back to Elara, "Shall we?"

"We shall," she said with an endearing smile.

The couple moved toward the scattered crowds.

The mood of relaxed conversation floated like a blissful cloud. Asher drank it in, a small feeling of discomfort needling him. Spending time in dungeons, and wild forests were his true places of comfort. Regal gatherings, no matter how tame, put him at edge. A few memories caressed his thoughts, of times he, and others from his guild, had to meet with royal figures to discuss problems facing kingdoms, or people. Asher was often withdrawn, allowing others with silver, or gold tongues, to do all the talking. He was happy with hunting, and tracking, but social engagements were a step, or two, beyond his sensibilities.

A slythan walked over with a tray filled with glasses of sparkling wine. She bowed, and presented it to the man and elf. Asher and Elara each took a glass, and thanked the servant. The slythan bowed her head a little deeper, before standing up and walking to another group of guests.

Asher was about to say something to Elara, when a blonde dwarf walked up to them with a smile.

"Greetings, Lord Blackwood," Bolla said with a slight accent. "I thought I saw the Bane of Windswell approach with his small army of beautiful women."

Asher and Elara smiled wide at the dwarf.

"Bane of Windswell? Is that my new title? Should I get it engraved, and hung over my fireplace?" the young lord smiled, instantly relaxed with the dwarf.

"Only if you're having a gathering, and I'm invited. I would love to see the look on her majesty's face when she sees it. It would be a story to tell for years to come," Bolla laughed before taking a long sip of her beer.

"Of course, you'd be invited," Asher laughed.

Bolla nodded as her gaze grew a little darker. "I'm not one to mince too many words. I know at some point, you'll want to discuss with me about a certain mayor wanting to buy the land west of your estate."

"Oh?" Asher feigned ignorance. "I thought we were here to simply enjoy the last day of summer?"

The dwarf eyed them with a knowing gaze. "Everyone across Mist Valley thinks the rumors don't fly at the Seahorse. I should bill myself as proprietor, and spymaster.

"But, to get to the point, we all know what's happening between you and her. She's managed to convince Maggie and Stukard to vote her way. The whole town knows Dina, and

Nadia, will vote your way. I know I'm the deciding vote. What I have to say is, don't think ill will of Maggie and Stukard. Her ladyship has aided them with loans, and business. They are good people, and have nothing against you."

"I know the whole valley is filled with good people," Asher stated.

Bolla nodded. "Aye, they are. Even she has some goodness lurking under that fake smile, and fancy dress. I won't bend your ear with small town politics, nor do I want any tension for the evening. Your uncle was an amazing man, and I know his nephew is cut from the same cloth, that is why, when we hold the vote tomorrow, I will vote your way."

A sense of relief washed over Asher, easing a tension he didn't know he was enduring.

"All I can say is, can I buy you a drink?" Asher winked.

Bolla's eyes widened a little, and then she let out a roar of a laugh. It was so loud, many of the banquet guests turned, looked over, and smiled.

When her laughter died down, she kept a happy grin.

"There it is, that Blackwood charm. How I missed it. Buying me a drink at a function with free drinks is legendary. It's good to have you become part of our town."

Asher looked upon the beautiful, down to Valoria, dwarf. Instantly, he knew they would be fast friends. She displayed something he loved about the dwarven people, they never held back, spoke their minds, and even if there was a disagreement

357

with fists thrown, they could still be friends, laughing about it over drinks.

Bolla turned her attention to Elara, and kept her smile. "We haven't met, officially."

The mature elf kept her genuine smile. "Elara Moonwhisper, of the Thallmar Province."

The dwarf bowed to her, "Bolla Brewblade, of the Harkkon Mountain Clan."

Bolla stood up with a warm smile. "But I consider myself part of the Mist Valley Clan. It's the second family name of all who live and dwell here. You'll understand, the longer you're here."

"I believe I already understand," Elara said warmly.

"I look forward to all our future stories together. But my cup is already drained, and I need to take advantage of others serving me for as long as I can. Enjoy the banquet. I can already tell it will be a very cool autumn, and a frosty cold winter approaching. The valley mountains tend to trap the cold and the snow. There won't be enough salty sea air coming through to melt it. I recommend a good whiskey, or wine, to warm the bones."

And with that, the dwarf turned and marched toward a bar set up on the side of a garden patch.

"That is certainly a relief," Asher said when Bolla was out of earshot, pertaining to the vote.

Elara nodded. "It certainly is. It might be safe to assume that the lady doesn't know how the vote will go. I think we should let her bask in her imagined victory. It may keep her off our backs for a time."

Asher looked at the beautiful elf with loving eyes. "Maybe, things will calm down, so we can focus on ourselves a little more."

Elara giggled, and held Asher's arm a little tighter. "If we focus anymore on us, I fear I will lose use of my legs, and the will to leave our bed."

"It will be a long, cold winter," Asher smirked.

"We will have to keep each other warm," Elara added before her gaze took a sultry gleam. "You can always be warm, between my thighs."

Asher nodded with feigned seriousness. "That would be the best place to put a log to fire."

Lips twitched, the couple fighting back their laughter as it threatened to spill out of them. The mood bloomed further into relaxed closeness, the pair caught in each other's gravity.

For a small span of time, Asher was happy again, truly happy. Despite some trials, for the most part, everything had turned much better than he had ever hoped. When he first arrived at the farm, the dread of losing his uncle weighed on him with chains that would never break. Despite his uncle's passing, he left behind a legacy of mystery, good friends, and adventure. The echoes of his life carried on like a favorite star in the sky.

The young lord eyed the beautiful elf at his side. Her smile was infectious, and loving. She was happy, not because of wealth, or titles, but because they had found each other. In the madness of the world, a daring exploration led to a bond that the very gods would bless with happy smiles. Their lives had become waking dreams, and neither of them wanted to ever wake from.

"Lord Blackwood," a voice came from the side.

Asher and Elara woke from their happy trance. They turned their attention to a woman greeting them. For a moment, the couple weren't sure what they were seeing. A fraction of a moment slipped by, and subtle understanding flowed into their spirits.

A woman with green skin, and short, bob-like, light green hair stood before them, hands clasped before her. Even though her hands were together, Asher could make out three fingers, and a thumb. Scales can along the back of her hands. Her eyes were jade green. Her skin was smooth, but at the edge of her features, were tiny scales. Her ears were small, and slightly pointed. She wore a white and blue outfit, similar to a maid's uniform, but had some differences. Asher guessed it was a higher-ranking servant, from the shoulder, Windswell crest. Her dress was down to her ankles.

The oddness Asher felt before was that he remembered her green lips. Seeing her, without the hood over her head, brought the memory back clearer. The woman was Roland Windswell's companion when Asher ran into him at Dina's shop. The strangeness lingered, because she had some slythan features, but was clearly not slythan. Most of the lizard folk didn't have hair, but this woman did. Where most Slythans had a small snout, she did not. For all Asher knew, she was a half-race, or, much like himself, shared a distant relation to a race from further up her bloodline.

"Please forgive my intrusion," the slythan said as she continued to bow her head. "I'm here to inform you, and Lady Moonwhisper, you both have been invited to dine at the lord and lady's table this evening.

"Your companions will be seated at a table closer to the front table, but I fear to say, the giant will have to sit at a table by herself, for we have no accommodations for her."

"Oh, thank you for telling us," Asher said, any further words vanishing for he didn't know the servant's name.

As if reading his mind, she parted her green lips. "House Stewardess, Reeta Smooth-Tail. I handle all the lord and lady's, domestic affairs, and duties.

"It is a pleasure to meet the new Lord of Blackwood. If everything is in order, will you need anything else from me?"

"Yes, except, Brynda will still need to be seated closer to us. I do not wish for her to be excluded, simply because of her size," Asher said honestly.

362

"An understandable request, Lord Blackwood. I will ensure to fulfill your request before the dining portion of the banquet begins."

The slythan woman looked into Asher's eyes with such a piercing gaze, it cut at his senses. A blink later, the Stewardess turned and walked over to several other slythans by the bar.

"Very odd," Elara whispered. "In most cultures and kingdoms, the steward, or stewardess, never says how pleased they are to meet someone. It is assumed they are always pleased, and never have to say the words."

Asher kept his gaze on the stewardess as she spoke with the servants.

"I think, we just met our secret contact within the Windswell Estate," Asher whispered.

"Are you sure? She is taking a risk, especially in this setting," Elara remarked.

Asher's heart sank in his chest, as he understood the meaning behind it. He had seen it on many adventures, when one, or more people, were being suppressed by others, or by monsters that could manipulate the mind and will of people.

"She took the risk because something is happening, she simply cannot say it. She's afraid," Asher whispered.

Elara looked at Asher with concerned eyes, when a large shadow began to approach them.

The couple turned their attention to the large Taurnar, and a smaller, lady taurnar, at his side.

Jarrag approached with a grim look in his dark eyes. The bull-like taurnar huffed as he towered over Asher and Elara, Iska holding onto his thick, meaty arm.

"Lord Blackwood," Jarrag growled as bards continued to play in the background.

Chapter 22

A Dark Song

"Lord Hornspear," Asher said with full, unwavering confidence.

The man and taurnar stared at each other. Bard music continued to play in the background, neither one of them saying another word.

Iska looked up at Jarrag, and squeezed his arm. The large taurnar continued to look down on Asher with dark eyes.

A small breeze flowed over the two couples. A moment later, Iska lightly smacked Jarrag's large chest.

The taurnar lowered his gaze, and then looked away.

Iska let go of Jarrag's arm, and looked at Elara.

"Lady Elara, care to join me for a drink while they talk," the taurnar said with a sweet smile.

Elara glanced at Asher. The young lord looked back at her, and smiled. The mature elf smiled back, before letting go of his arm. Taurnar and elf, walked toward the bar, Iska instantly talking up a storm as she waved to the slythan bartenders for drinks.

A silence fell between the two males once again. Everyone else stayed a healthy distance away from them, but Brynda stood at the ready a few paces away, her unwavering gaze on the bull taurnar.

Jarrag let out another huff, before he looked Asher in the eyes.

"I apologize."

Asher remained silent, but kept his stance relaxed.

Jarrag closed his eyes as he continued, "I'm sure you understand my concern, and my anger. Iska is important to me, and when I thought she was dead, I thought a part of me died as well.

"I know your kinds of farms take on all kinds of guests. Some stay for a time. Others stay for longer. It was wrong for me to assume you had tried to get her killed."

"Jarrag," Asher interrupted. "You are correct. I found out after our altercation, that one of my guests did try to hurt Iska, but they had no intention of killing her. I cannot go much more into the specifics, but as you asked when we saw each other last, I dealt with the situation, and put my house in order. The guest is no longer there, and such a thing should never happen again. But, since the attacker came from my farm, I must apologize as well. It was never meant to happen in the first place, and for that, I am sorry."

A burning sensation blazed against the young lord's spirit, wanting to question, and demand, what business Jarrag, and his Ivory Crows, had to do with his uncle and his death. It seethed under his skin, the young man ready to pull the very truth from the taurnar, but a prevailing inner wind shifted.

There was a time, and place, for such discussions. The banquet was not one of them. It was something he would have to address sometime in the future, but not now, and not yet.

Asher swallowed his inner poison, remembering his uncle telling him in the spirit realm, revenge is a song best not played. The young lord stored his emotions away in an iron chest, but didn't put it away completely.

"Let it be water under the bridge. We are neighbors. If we look out for each other, We can heal whatever scars may linger from the past."

Jarrag gave a deep nod.

"It is good to come to an understanding. Iska told me this would be beneficial, and I see the truth in her words."

Jarrag's eyes narrowed a little. "But, and I only say this because you should know, your uncle, directly, or indirectly hurt my family in many ways. One of my brothers continues to rot in a cell because of him. I know there is no way to truly speak to your uncle anymore, but if you could, I would ask him, why he turned on people he called friends?"

Asher's heart quickened as he eyed the taurnar.

"I don't know the whole story, and I may never know, but he's gone. I am starting a new life. I have ties by blood to my uncle, but I was not privy to his dealings, or friendships."

The large taurnar dipped his head again.

"You may not, but your Opal Society will have some answers," Jarrag said and glanced at Brynda. "I've seen Opal

Society muscle before. Be careful, Lord Blackwood. Their blades cut both ways."

The bull taurnar turned, and walked away.

"Enjoy the celebration, Lord Blackwood," Jarrag said over his thick shoulder as he walked to Iska and Elara.

Asher ruminated on the taurnar's words. They bit deeper than he expected. Even with his old guild, there were always secrets, and plots. Over the years, the ranger knew when any group grew large enough, there would be those who would manipulate from behind the scenes. The only solace he took was the hands-off approach from the Opal Society. But now that he was truly joining them, there was a chance he could uncover more about what happened with his uncle that made him reviled by some, such as the Ivory Crows.

"There you are," a voice cut through Asher's inner thoughts.

The young lord turned his attention to Nadia and Dina approaching him. The two women were all smiles, with drinks in hand.

"Greetings, Ladies of Mist Valley," Asher smiled as they approached him.

Dina was wearing a simple, flowing yellow dress. A flower was pinned to her hair, making her expression that much lighter. For Asher, it was a different sight to see her in such a relaxed state, not that he minded at all.

Nadia was wearing a black dress. The top adhered to her, but was loose enough to give enough breathing room. Her pale cleavage was on full display, which was different since she tended to cover up. A new confidence filled her eyes behind her spectacles. Her hair was tied back, showing her neck. A single curl lay against her temple, enhancing her beauty.

"We wanted to get to you before anyone else swarmed you," Dina said.

Nadia stepped closer to the lord, took a sip of her drink, and eyed him like she wanted to devour his soul.

Asher readied himself, knowing the book shop owner was often clumsy around him. But thankfully, she kept her balance.

"We believe the town council will vote your way, keeping the mayor from buying the land west of your property," Nadia whispered with a happy grin.

Asher nodded. "It's good to know," he said, already knowing the verdict.

Nadia's eyes half-closed. "Yes. Once this ordeal is over, we can reschedule my time at your farm," the shop owner said, and licked her lips.

Dina laughed. "So, you are going to stay at the estate for a time?"

Nadia nodded, talking to Dina while still looking at Asher. "I need a holiday, and the Lord of Blackwood agreed to let me relax on his farm."

The shop owner lifted a finger and touched Asher's collarbone, running her finger down an inch.

"We have an agreement, one I am more than ready to fulfill," she said with a sultry edge.

Dina eyed Nadia, before turning her attention back to Asher with the same wicked gleam in her eyes.

"I will be working on the Blackwood Estate during the autumn, but winter is the slowest time of the year for me. Maybe I should book my time on the farm as well?"

Asher smiled. "By all means, but I hope I can keep up with the demand for attention. The estate grows crowded with each passing month."

"We know you can keep up with the demand. We've felt every inch of it," Nadia said with such a sultry flair, she leaned closer, and fell forward.

Asher's hand shot up and caught her arm. He helped steady her before anyone else could notice. Nadia giggled as she stood like nothing happened.

"It's not the drink. That's her first one," Dina laughed.

The three of them laughed together.

Asher glanced to the side, seeing Elara looking at him with happy eyes. Jarrag and Iska had moved on to speak to another couple.

"Ladies, I always enjoy our time together. When things quiet down, we should get together again, for drinks, and anything else that may come up," Asher winked.

Dina's cheeks glowed. Nadia swayed.

Asher turned and made his way toward the voluptuous blonde elf waiting by the bar.

The two women eyed them. When Asher reached Elara, she put her hand on his arm, and began talking to him.

"We shouldn't fall in love with him," Dina said softly, her eyes still holding a gleam of fascination.

"We both know that option is no longer possible," Nadia said with an edge of genuine truth.

The two women looked on as music continued to play.

A short time later, the mayor clinked a glass with a fork, and the music stopped.

"Everyone! Everyone! May I have your attention," Lady Windswell said loud enough for everyone to hear.

Everyone gathered, stopped talking, and turned their attention to the mayor.

"Once again, welcome to the Summer Dusk Banquet! We will begin with the first course! Please, find your assigned seating.

"Let us enjoy the last day of summer in traditional Mist Valley fashion!"

"Here Here!" The crowd shouted and lifted their drinks into the air.

***

The sun glowed, half hidden by the horizon. An orange-yellow sky loomed overhead with a few wispy clouds.

The sounds of laughter and music played on in the regal courtyard. Large plates of food were half-empty in the middle of tables. Individual plates were filled with bones, and leftover pieces and crumbs of food. Wine and spirits poured into empty glasses or mugs. The mood was light, welcoming the end to the long summer.

Asher eyed the celebration, spirits making his senses a little fuzzy. The celebratory mood was infectious, filling the air with lively conversation, and bouts of laughter. Everyone was having a good time, the evening air a perfect temperature.

The young lord looked over to his elven companion. Elara sipped her wine, her other hand under the table and touching his thigh. Sitting at the head table, the mayor was surprisingly gracious, and talkative. She and Elara spoke often about places within the elven empire. And for a moment, despite all the hidden plots, and back and forth Asher had to contend with the Windswells, the dinner and evening was pleasantly normal. He wondered, if they could have more of this, if life would indeed be perfect in Mist Valley.

Asher turned his attention several times to Nyn and Amber. The elf and faun spoke to each other most of the time. Sometimes the locals would strike up a conversation with the pair. Dina was engrossed with a small group of townsfolk. Nadia sat by herself and drank, but her eyes always wandered to the young lord.

Lord Windswell laughed loudest during the dinner. He often made the rounds, speaking to others with robust flair. His face was red from his many drinks, but it didn't slow him down as he told story after story of his adventures across Valoria.

Asher's mind began to drift, the tension all but gone from his shoulders. He looked forward to going home, and perhaps asking everyone to sleep in the same bed tonight. The thought tantalized him, when a small voice touched his ear.

"You're drink, my lord," said a slythan woman, placing it down on the table, beside his hand.

Asher blinked, knowing he didn't ask for a drink. When he looked down at it, a small piece of paper was pinned under it.

The young lord quickly put his hand to the side of the cup, took the note, and glanced at it.

Second floor Study.

That was all that was written on the small note. He stuffed it in a pocket.

When the young lord stood up, he swayed a little. He didn't hear any loud boasts, but he did hear the white-noise of the people talking. Large lanterns were being lit, as the sun sank lower, a sliver of light left.

Elara let go of Asher's thigh and looked up at him. He looked down on her, his eyes saying more than words could say.

Something was amiss, and she nodded to him.

The elf turned her full attention back to the mayor, striking up a new conversation. The mayor was enjoying her drink, and fell right into it, talking about her times on the border towns of the empire.

Asher slipped away, and made his way to the open front doors of the castle home. Slythan servants made no move to stop him, simply glancing at him as he walked past them and made his way inside.

***

Fear colored green eyes. A slythan woman stood in her master's study. Her back was to the cluttered desk, her gaze locked on the partially opened door. Her heart raced as she was surrounded by high shelves filled with many tomes. A lantern glowed, giving the room a velvet light.

Reeta uncurled her tight hands, flexing her scaled fingers. Panic grew by degrees as she waited. The tension was trying to break the slythan, but she held fast, knowing if she didn't take a chance, there was no telling what would happen to her.

A shadow darkened on the other side of the half-open door.

Reeta's heart leapt into her throat, a chance of hope glowing brighter than any sunrise.

The door opened, and all hope was dashed on the rocks of her soul.

"Reeta, why are you up here?" Lord Windswell said with a slight slur to his words.

"Lord Windswell, I was taking a moment to tidy up," she lied with nervous eyes.

The tall man chuckled. "You know that can wait. You should be downstairs," he said and blinked as a notion struck him. "Did you come up here for a secret drink with me?"

Reeta's eyes widened. "Oh, no, my lord. I only needed a respite from the celebration. It will never happen again, I swear."

Roland stepped in further with a drunken smile.

"Have you finally come around to my charms? You don't have to play coy with me. It's only us."

"No, my lord. I was simply taking a break," she said quickly.

Roland approached and towered over her.

"The castle is often filled with activity. You thought to come here, because you knew this chamber would be empty?

"While true, I was enjoying spinning my tales of adventure, I wouldn't have come here except for that glance you gave me before you left."

Reeta's heart pounded in her chest. In a moment of watching where he was, she accidently alerted him to her. The hope of distractions and drink was not enough to sway his eye like she planned. Everything was crashing down because a thin ray of hope blinded her.

"Please, forgive me. It was a moment's respite, nothing more," the slythan said with a bowed head.

Roland's eyes narrowed. "You continue to play this game with my heart. You have run from every advance. I have given you everything, from affection to extra gold. I have protected you from my wife's wrath on more than one occasion, and yet you continue to rebuff my advances.

"My dear Reeta, you are beautiful. I only wish to show you how much you mean to me."

"Please, my lord, you've had too much to drink," Reeta trembled.

Roland didn't hear her words as he looked at her with a growing intention.

"I can lock the door. Will that make you happy? It will be quick, and no one needs to know, not that my wife would care. Do you know, she encourages me to simply take you because you belong to us? Maybe I should heed that shrew's words."

A flame of anger filled Lord Windswell's eyes.

"She may be mayor, but this is my home, my castle. She barks like a chimera with a bone, but it is my wealth that pays for everything. Why must I endure such dissatisfaction? How easy it is to please me.

"Lift up your dress, and bend over the desk. Once that hairless pussy tastes my cock, you will want to polish it many times. The other slythan's like it. I only want you to like it."

Fear shifted in Reeta's wide eyes. A deep rage bubbled to the surface, filling her gaze with fierce rage.

"They do not like it," she said loudly to his face. "And I don't want it, or you!"

Heat filled Roland's eyes as his hand shot forward and grabbed her arm. He roughly turned her around, planted his other hand on her back, and slammed her down on the cluttered desk. Reeta let out a sharp exhale, the wind forced out of her lungs.

Roland reached down and grabbed at her dress. He pulled it up as a seething madness filled his eyes.

"You belong to me," Lord Windswell growled.

"No!" Reeta hissed with wide eyes.

Roland fumbled to get her dress up, when hard knuckles slammed into his back, where his kidneys were. The pain was so stark and sudden, the tall man stumbled to the side, letting go of the prone slythan stewardess.

Reeta turned her head enough for one eye to see Asher stepping to the stunned lord, fists tight at his sides.

"Lord Blackwood," Lord Windswell said with a drunken smile, before Asher's fist slammed into his cheek.

The lord stumbled again to the side, crashing into a shelf.

"No titles here," Asher growled as he grabbed the dazed lord by the collar with one hand, and lifted a fist up.

Roland blinked before Asher rammed his knuckles into the man's eye.

Asher drew back his fist, ready to break the man's skull, when a hand shot up and struck under his raised arm. The pain was sudden and powerful. Asher stepped back as a pressure point screamed in torment.

"Do not think me some whelp of a man!" Roland roared as he threw a barrage of fists.

Knuckles struck Asher, but only once. He fought to keep his balance, while blocking the agile taller man.

"You're not the only one who had an adventurer's life!" Roland roared as he threw a storm of fists.

Asher blocked as he lifted his heel and brought it down at the man's knee. But the lord was quicker. Sobering up, he shifted his knee, Asher's heel missing it. Since he leaned in, Roland slammed his elbow into the side of Asher's neck. The shock of the hit caused Asher to stumble back a pace, but he continued to stand with raised fists.

"You forget my hospitality so quickly!" Roland said as he charged the ranger.

Asher ignored the pain as the mad lord was on him. Despite his height and reach, Asher kept his center of gravity low. A fist missed his cheek by a hair, but the young lord was quick, grabbing the man's extended arm as he turned.

Reeta backed up as Lord Blackwood flipped the taller man over his shoulder, and slammed him down beside the expensive study desk. Roland grunted as he turned and pushed off the floor, but it was too late. Asher's boot slammed into his face when he was halfway up, and the tall lord crashed into the side of his desk.

Lord Windswell clung to the side of this desk, breathing hard. He glared at the young lord as he approached with cautious, yet furious eyes.

"I yield!" Roland shouted.

"You yield? In all journeys, bullies never truly yield until they are beaten to an inch of their life. I'm not finished inflicting the amount of untold harm you have tortured others with!" Asher spat as he approached.

"Lord Blackwood! He has..." Reeta didn't finish as she darted for the desk.

Time slowed down as Roland's hand moved under some parchment papers. Vile contempt filled the tall man's eyes as he drew a dagger with runic symbols along the edge.

Reeta's clawed hand flashed, raking down the side of Roland's features. The lord grunted as he shifted the dagger toward the slythan woman.

Asher appeared between them, the young lord planting his hand on Reeta's chest and pushing her away, the dagger missing her neck. The young lord used his other fist to strike Roland, when the dagger spun in Roland's hand, and blurred down in an arc.

There was no pain, but there was a sense of loss, and the scent of blood.

Asher slammed his fist into Roland's face, before mystical wings flashed. A brown and black wing slammed into the lord, sending him into the air and crashing so hard into a shelf, it shattered wood, and caused a river of books to fall.

Asher heaved as he touched his side, feeling his own life leaking between his fingers.

"Lady Reeta, get me a binding," Asher asked, knowing the wound was more serious that it appeared.

Roland launched up from the floor with crazed eyes, and dagger in hand. He roared bloody murder as he was nearly on the winged lord. Asher's wing moved up to block him, when the dagger struck it. Mystical energies flared as the dagger penetrated the magical wing, missing Asher's arm by inches.

The young lord was calm as he lifted his heel, and brought it down on the lord's now exposed knee. Bone cracked, and the taller man yelped as he fell. When he hit the floor, the wings vanished, and Asher slammed his heel on the wrist holding the dagger. Delicate bones shattered, and the dagger slipped from the taller lord's palm. Asher kicked it away as a weakness began to fill his muscles.

Lord Windswell held his broken wrist to him as he sobbed in pain,

Reeta stared at Asher with wide, unbelieving eyes.

"Lady Reeta, I will still need that binding," Asher said with kind charm, and paling features.

The slythan grabbed at an expensive cloth on a shelf. She moved to Asher's side, pressing it to his side, as blood stained his shirt.

Asher's legs began to tremble. The wound was deep. If he didn't have this tended soon, he wouldn't make it back to the courtyard.

Reeta rushed to a small chest on another shelf. She opened it and her hand dove in. Pulling it out, she had a single potion of healing in her hand. She rushed to Asher's side, uncorked it, and brought it to his lips.

"He keeps all manner of items in his study, keepsakes from his old days. This healing potion was a gift from the Southern Kingdoms," The slythan said quickly as Asher drank from it.

Reeta turned her angry gaze to her fallen master. "It pleases me to know, you are drinking one of his treasured keepsakes."

Heat, and power swirled within the young lord. Healing energy poured into the wound, but it wasn't a normal healing. It surged so quickly, Asher was feeling better already. Glancing down, he saw and felt the wound pucker and close. Blood dried as the energy tingled from within. A moment later, the wound was no more.

Weakness still filled Asher's muscles. Reeta took hold, helping him to stay on his feet.

The sound of boots rushed in their direction from the corridor.

"Expecting anyone else?" Asher grunted.

"Only family," Reeta smiled.

Half a dozen slythans reached the study's entrance. They looked in horror at the half-destroyed study, Lord Windswell on the floor whimpering, and Lord Blackwood being supported by Reeta.

"The lady will have us executed!" a slythan servant said with a fearful tone.

"No one will be executed," Asher said with confidence, before turning his attention to the slythan at his side.

"Please, forgive this mess we brought you into," Reeta said softly. "We could not endure being under their rule any longer. Considering how much the lady abhorred you, we knew you could be an ally to us."

She turned her gaze to the whimpering lord on the floor. "They have tortured and abused us for far too long. I sent you those letters, and encouraged others here to befriend you as best they could. It was the only thing keeping our sanity."

Asher nodded as strength returned to him, and he stood under his own power. He then looked at the scared slythans before him, his soul heavy with regret for not discovering these horrors sooner.

"Everyone, gather your things. We're all leaving here, together," Asher said before turning a stern gaze to the whimpering lord.

"And we will ensure all know what has happened here," the young lord said with a deadly gaze at the fallen Lord Windswell.

Chapter 23

Punishment & Hope

Music played on as cool evening air floated down on the joyous banquet. Stars began to appear across the night sky. Lanterns glowed, adding a warmth to the occasion. The sounds of the waves soothed addled senses as drinks and conversations spun on.

Elara looked around with nervous eyes. She didn't dare let it on to the hostess as she droned on about another tale of adventure. Instead, she gave quick glances to Nyn and Amber, the pair keeping her in their sights.

Most of the gathering was up, some dancing, and others standing by tables, talking about the evening, and season to come. It all bubbled like a warm soup to soothe the soul.

Elara turned her head again to the main entrance of the castle. She looked for any sign of her lover. When a group of shadows emerged from the entrance, her heart swelled, before it was shattered with surprise.

A bard looked over to the castle entrance. His eyes widened before he made a hand signal. The other musicians stopped. Heads in the crowd turned. Eyes widened and small gasps touched the air.

Lady Windswell saw many people's gazes, even Elara's, shift. She turned her head to follow them. When she looked at the entrance, her face paled.

Asher emerged, pushing a bloody, whimpering Lord Windswell. The lord was clutching his broken wrist to his chest. Just to the side of Asher was Reeta. After that, many of the slythan servants within the castle followed them out. Each had packs, items, and hard stares.

The other servants of the banquet saw them, and stopped serving. They put down their trays. They tore off jackets with the Windswell crest on them, and tossed them aside. They moved to the sides, joining the crowd behind Asher, Reeta, and Lord Windswell.

Brynda was to her feet, her eyes filled with hard rage.

Asher raised a hand, signaling her not to do anything.

"WHAT IS THE MEANING OF THIS!" Lady Windswell shouted as she was instantly to her feet.

"Be silent!" Asher shouted back.

Lady Windswell's eyes widened in burning madness.

"I will not be silen..." the lady attempted to say when a hand smacked her so hard, she crumbled to the ground.

The lady clutched at the side of her face, glaring up at Elara as she stood over her.

"He said, be silent," the elf said with confident eyes.

The lady's lips moved, but no sound came out.

Asher pushed Lord Windswell to the head table. The lord blubbered as he clutched his wrist. The young lord grabbed him by the back of neck, and held him in place, facing the whole, wide-eyed crowd.

"Lady Reeta, please tell the people of Mist Valley what you told me," Asher said darkly.

The slythan woman stepped forward. She moved around the head table and looked out to the silent crowd.

"I know many of you know me from my visits into town on occasion. For what I have to say, is the truth about the darkness in this very town. Myself, and many of my fellow slythans, were afraid to come forward, for fear of reprisals from our employer, or I should say, our slaver."

"Reeta! Don't say another word," Lady Windswell said, but stopped short when Elara's hand raised a few inches, and the elf continued to give her a hard stare.

The slythan stewardess continued, "The mayor, and her husband, have treated us like we were possessions, to be toyed with, and controlled. Despite whatever appearance she may have shown to all of you here, she was cruel to us, in her own home."

Sorrow filled the slythan's eyes. "She lured many of us to work here, with promises of better pay, and a better life. But once we arrived, it wasn't long before she, and her husband's cruelty, would be known. We were beaten if we made mistakes. We were locked away if we spoke out. Some of us were murdered if we tried to escape, or speak out.

"I could not let this continue. I sent secret messages to Lord Blackwood, in hopes he would listen."

The slythan looked over to Asher, and the young lord gave her an approving nod.

"He answered them, in a way. When we were to speak, Lord Windswell reached me first. He attempted to push himself on me, against my will. If Lord Blackwood didn't answer my request to speak, I doubt I would have lived beyond the week. Lord Blackwood defended me, and took a dagger to the side to stop Lord Windswell from stabbing me in the neck."

A murmur filled the crowd as many of them stared daggers at the defeated lord.

Reeta continued, "When the demons came to Star Fall, it was Lady Windswell who summoned them here. She wanted the blame to fall on Lord Blackwood, and make her more appealing to win the mayoral election. Her scheme worked, but I couldn't stand by, and let her cruelty win again.

"I only wished for Lord Blackwood's aid to help sneak out myself, and others here, from the cruelty of mistress and master. I regret I did not come to anyone else here. I feared word would get back to our mistress, and her punishments would be bloody. We knew Lord Blackwood was her enemy, giving us a better chance of success. We just didn't expect it so soon."

"Lies!" Lady Windswell shouted. "Don't listen to ungrateful servants! They had the best life. I gave that to them! They lie..." Lady Windswell stopped her rant when there was a flash of light.

The lady looked down to the floor beside her head, a burnt mark on the stone. Elara pointed her hand, energy arcing along her fingers.

"Say another word, and the next bolt won't be a warning shot," the mature elf hissed.

Reeta turned her back to the crowd, and looked at the slythans behind her.

"We are all leaving here tonight. We will never have to suffer their torment again."

The slythans nodded with relief in their eyes.

A blonde dwarf climbed onto a nearby table. Bolla addressed the crowd as eyes and heads turned to her.

"Due to this new information, I say we hold a vote to impeach Mayor Sandra Windswell," the dwarf said loudly.

Heads nodded in agreement.

Lady Windswell was to her feet and stepped back, out of reach of Elara. She looked around in a panic as every single soul present looked at her in judgment.

"Lord Blackwood orchestrated this! He brought the demons, and a demon queen, to our precious valley! He killed the previous mayor, and now he is coming after me, and my family! You cannot allow his scheme to succeed. I am here to protect you!"

Lady Windswell stopped short when she hit something. She turned and looked up at a nine-foot giant woman with crossed arms.

"All those in favor of impeaching Mayor Sandra Windswell, say aye!" Bolla shouted.

"AYE!" everyone said in unison, save for the lord and lady of the estate.

Bolla turned her gaze to the shocked face of the now former mayor.

"Sandra Windswell, you are no longer mayor of Star Fall, and Mist Valley," Bolla bellowed with a satisfied nod.

The lady blinked, before she started cackling. She laughed loud and hard, while pointing at everyone like a witch casting a spell.

"You pieces of trash! You have impeached me, but there are no laws against how I treat my servants! Without proof, all you have is the word of a pathetic servant. We have no jail, nor will any nearby kingdom come for me. Even if they did, I have more than enough wealth to change their minds!

"All you have done is destroy what little this town had! Without us, Star Fall would be a ghost town!"

"It will not be a ghost town, for I won't let it," Asher said with confidence.

Bolla crossed her arms as she looked down on the scared Windswell.

"We've had an idea of your cruelty. Tonight was proof enough that you were never a fit for our town. Enjoy living in your empty castle. Maybe you and your husband will use the silence to understand how depraved you both truly are."

The dwarf stepped down and into the crowd.

Asher leaned closer to Roland, still holding him by the back of the neck.

"Learn from this moment. But I will be keeping your magic dagger. Consider it part of your penance, and punishment," Asher said with the dagger sheathed in his belt behind him.

Asher let go of Roland's neck. The tall man crumbled into a sobbing mess. Sandra rushed to her husband's side, sinking down, and holding him in her arms.

Asher turned to Reeta and the slythans. "I know where there is a wild gate. I can guide you all to it, if you have a home to go to?"

Reeta nodded. "We do."

"We will all escort you," Elara said as she walked up to Asher's side.

Nyn, Amber, and Brynda also moved closer.

"As will we!" Dina said, everyone present nodding in agreement.

"Thank you," Reeta said, a tear streaking her green cheek.

The townspeople, slythans, Asher, and many others, began to walk away as one large group. The courtyard emptied out as a column of people left through the front gate of the Windswell courtyard. Slythans carried many of their possessions with them, holding their scaled heads high.

After a few moments, the Windswell castle, and courtyard were empty, save for two people. The sounds of waves, and the sights of twinkling stars, did not sway the taste of defeat for the lord and lady.

Lady Windswell stared at nothing as she held her husband to her bosom. Her heart cracked further, and deeper along her soul, losing everything, as her husband sobbed in her arms.

***

Asher, Elara, and Reeta led the large crowd. The moon began to rise, casting a faint glow over the entire valley. It illuminated the path as a small army of slythans, and townspeople, followed the man, elf, and slythan.

Elara held Asher's hand, looking over at him with loving eyes. Her heart beat with a dreamy pulse, knowing he was a man of few words at times, but his stoic honor, and quiet strength, flared her love for him to greater heights.

Asher walked, not with head held high, but slightly tilted forward. Shadows covered his eyes as he thought over the entire situation. While helping the slythans was the right thing to do, he considered the consequences of such actions.

"You did the right thing," Elara whispered to her lover.

"It may have been right, but it could put all of us in further harm. I want no harm to anyone here, especially us."

Asher lifted his head and continued to speak as they walked. "People in my guild had insulted others, or made many enemies, but they always knew, the guild looked out for their own. No matter the conflict, we were brothers and sisters in arms.

"Out here, and with what I'm sure will be a blood feud, the Windswells will try harder to make us suffer."

"Then, we will protect each other, like a true guild," Elara said with a loving edge.

Asher looked at the beautiful elf, his heart growing warmer the more he basked in her divine beauty.

"How did we get here?" Asher asked.

"Perversion, and love," the mature elf said, knowing what he meant.

"I never want to go back," the young lord smirked.

"Neither do I," the elf said with dreamy eyes.

The couple squeezed each other's hands again, lost to each other's affections.

The large group moved with ease, further out of town, and toward the Blackwood Estate.

The air was crisp, with an edge of the day's heat. It made it comfortable enough, for when the large group reached Asher's home, he turned, and led them into the forest, away from it. The people followed, wishing to ensure all the slythans were returned home.

Nyn and Elara lifted their hands and uttered arcane words. Balls of light glowed and floated above them, lighting the way as everyone walked.

After many long moments through the dark forest, the edges of light touched a trio of standing, knee-high stones. Many townsfolk craned their heads, eager to see the actual wild gate many of them heard about from Asher's uncle over the years. The slythans were close together, following the lord and Reeta.

Asher took the lead, letting go of Elara's hand. He looked at Reeta, and she nodded. They walked together until they reached one of the weathered, arcane stones.

"This is a wild gate. It cycles through to places one can go. But if three beings, each one touching a stone, think of a location, the gate will open to that location. Is there a place you, and your people wish to go?"

Reeta nodded. "Our lands are to the east. We know them well."

Asher nodded and looked at the slythan with dark eyes. "I wish I had known sooner. We all could have done something sooner."

Reeta looked away with sorrow in her eyes. "We do as well. Some of us had tried to flee, and were never heard from again. We were afraid, but are thankful it finally has happened. Many of us can start new lives."

"Will coin be an issue?" Asher asked, ready to aid them with charity.

Reeta gave the young lord a happy, knowing smile. "Knowing what was to come, all of us prepared. We saved what we could, and I'm sure a little more was taken as we prepared to leave the Windswell estate. My people will be fine."

Asher smirked as he internally laughed.

Several slythans moved to Reeta and Asher's side. Reeta quickly explained how the wild gate worked. Three of the slythans nodded, and each walked over to a standing stone. They each knelt to a stone, and put a scaled hand on it.

It didn't take long for a rune-covered stone to glow. An arcane light glowed in the clearing. Many eyes widened as they witnessed a dark patch form with strands of purple light. It hovered over the center patch of ground between the stones. A glimpse of a fertile, green land, bordering a swamp, gleamed to life.

Elara and Nyn's glowing lights moved and hovered in the clearing. The air vibrated with magic as the slythans marched toward the floating portal. The townspeople watched in stunned amazement, a wonderment filling their eyes and hearts.

By threes, slythans stepped into the portal and vanished from sight.

The townspeople waved farewell, some with tears in their eyes. One of the townsfolk stepped to a slythan, telling them that they didn't need to leave. They could stay, and live in town. The slythan smiled and embraced them, whispering that they may come back, after the dread of everything they endured had abated. They let go of each other, the slythan walking toward

393

the portal, and vanishing. The townsperson looked on with tears in their eyes.

When nearly all the slythans finished entering the portal, a few remained, clustered around Reeta.

"It's time to go," one said with sorrow painting their eyes.

Reeta lowered her gaze. "Go home and heal. I must stay behind."

The last three slythans looked at Reeta in shock.

"You made this all possible. Come home with us," a slythan pleaded.

Reeta shook her head. "I must stay, and be a sentinel for our people. I must watch, and ensure there is no reprisal from the Windswells.

"I will stay a year. If all is well, and it is safe to return, then I will. Until then, take comfort in knowing I am guarding our people from any further cruelty, or revenge."

Asher and Elara watched with heartfelt eyes, seeing the look of pain in the last slythans.

The three gave reluctant nods. They turned and stepped to the portal. With sad goodbyes, they stepped through, and were gone.

The gate glowed a moment longer, before it began to shrink. The mystical energies faded away, and the gate was gone.

Tears welled up in Reeta's eyes. The slythan fought back her pain and sadness.

Elara moved to Reeta's side and embraced her. Reeta let out sobs as she hugged the elf back.

Asher watched with dark eyes, and a heavy heart.

The clearing continued to glow with mystical light as a happy sadness filled the crowd, the Windswell's nightmare for the slythans, now over.

Chapter 24

The Coming Autumn

Days slipped by as life slowly returned to normal across the valley. The weather began its shift to cooler days and nights.

The town of Star Fall fell back into routine, despite the truth coming out about the Windswells. Three days after the Summer Dusk Banquet, several horse-drawn carriages came through town, and made their way through the pass, to the beach. A day later, those same carriages left from the beach, riding through town, and left Star Fall, and Mist Valley, without a word to the local inhabitants. Gossip quickly spread, everyone in town agreeing that the Windswells had packed up and left their home. To the few who ventured out to investigate the rumors, they saw that the livestock were free to roam, but the castle was locked up tight, all Windswell banners and flags taken down. A man stayed behind at the stables, but they said nothing to anyone in town, watching over the animals wandering the vast land.

Some parchments were posted, a new election for Mayor of Starfall was going to take place, but it was weeks away. There seemed to be no urgency to electing a new mayor, most of the townsfolk basking in the new freedom of Lady and Lord Windswell's secret tyranny.

On the Blackwood estate, life had returned to normalcy. Work had begun on the new cottage and farmhouse. Dina arrived everyday with her artisans. They brought supplies, and began construction projects. The basic skeleton of the farmhouse had begun. The cottage was nearly completed in a few days, the final touches added in the cooling weather.

The Lord of Blackwood woke every morning with reinvigorated energy, and happy moods. With the looming threat of Windswells over, an immense weight had lifted off his shoulders. It was enough to consider his own new projects on the farm. Despite his encounter with Roland Windswell, he did like the man's study. The young lord had much, but not a private place to spend with his thoughts. There was an extra room on the right side of the library. It had the common room wall connected to it, and it could only be accessed by the first-floor corridor. Asher liked the idea of changing it, and making some new arrangements with the house supplies. With some shelves, a desk, and some attention, it would make a fine study for him.

While he talked about the plan with Elara and Blyss, Nuha chimed in, eager to help build it. Asher smiled as he could not say no to her.

Keefa had fit in well with the clan, often assisting Paasha with her daily duties. The blonde goblin was happier than she had ever been before.

Nyn continued to write, but spent part of her time teaching Paasha, Keefa, and Nuha, the arts of reading and writing. Their lessons started off slow, but the often-emotionless elf told Asher they showed great promise.

Brynda often wandered the estate. Sometimes she simply sat and took in nature. One day, to her surprise, Asher and Elara led the entire household out to the covered patio with trays of food and cake. They threw her a celebration, welcoming her to the family. The giant was so taken aback, she thought it was a cruel prank. But when she tried Paasha's delicious cake, she shouted in pure joy so loudly, birds flew from the trees for miles around, and the sounds echoed off the mountains surrounding the valley.

Amber worked diligently in the lab, her thoughts often drifting to their growing family. The faun would stop working at times, and stare at nothing, wondering how the young lord, and so many beautiful souls got under her guarded skin. She enjoyed her time with Asher, but there was a small distance she kept. Now, that distance had shrunk, and she found herself falling for him, deeper than before.

Elara often walked the field, inspecting the vines. The crop was nearly ready, the grapes thick and juicy. Never had she thought she would live on a farm, but the longer she was here, the more natural it felt. Where once, she had difficulty with the simple watering of crops, she now moved with precision and speed. She studied the books they had on farming, absorbing every word. When not tending to the farm, she spent time with her lover, and their lovers. The passion they all felt only grew with each passing day. The thought of returning to her elven home quickly became a distant memory, for she knew she was already home.

When Asher woke, and dressed to prepare for the day, he noticed the envelope Claudia had given him a few weeks ago. He forgot all about it, quickly remembering it was from one of his uncle's distant friends. Reaching over, he picked up the letter, broke the seal, and opened it.

A black ring with a silver line fell out of the envelope, and into Asher's palm. He eyed it for a moment, before moving his gaze to the letter.

Greetings Asher Blackwood.

My name is Lork Witch-Star. I was an old associate, colleague, and friend, to your uncle, Aric Blackwood. It grieved me to hear of his passing. He was an amazing friend, the two of us enjoying many discussions over spirits. Despite seeing little of each other, we often wrote to one another, detailing our lives. He told me a great deal of you, and how could he not? The Blackwoods have a long history of keeping the monstrous wilds at bay so society may function. But I am going on a tangent, when I meant this letter to be brief, and offer my condolences.

Aric, as you know, was an amazing soul. If you are anything like him, which I'm sure you are, he left the farm in good hands.

Enclosed in the envelope is a gift, a ring of mystical power of my own design. I crafted this ring so you may further enjoy the fruits of the work we provide to Valoria. I only made one, but should we continue our correspondence, as I did with your uncle, I would like to know how the ring fares for you, and those who stay at your farm.

I call it a Shadow Ring. It has the power to create another version of you, a copy, as it were. Your shadow, or shade, will be a mystical manifestation of another you. It may seem like a separate entity, but it is more of a projection of who you are, in mind and body. You, and your shade, will share a mystical bond, feeling, and experiencing everything, at the same time.

The shade can be summoned, and dispelled, at will. It will not go rogue, or try to separate, for it is simply you, times two. You will understand what it means when you try, if you wish to try it.

There is no demand to use it. Think of it as an added power to enjoy time with those who wish to spend time with you.

The ring works off your thoughts, so you are in full control. I care not if you never use it, or use it all the time, it is a gift, and an option.

I fear this letter is already long enough. On the back are instructions on how to send letters to me. I do hope you join our little society, and look forward to meeting in the future at our social gatherings.

With that, I will take my leave. Welcome to your new life, if you accept it.

Lork Witch-Star

Asher smiled, but it quickly vanished as he looked at the ring. It was peculiar to give such a gift, but considering everything he had witnessed and experienced, it wasn't so strange to not intrigue him.

The young lord placed the ring in his pocket, folded the letter, and placed it on the desk with his other papers. With that, he left his bedchamber with a lightness in his step, but a curiosity in his mind.

The day proceeded with dreamy satisfaction. Artisans worked on the new farmhouse. The smell of cooked food filled their house. Asher and Nuha worked together to clear out the storage room, prepping it to become the new study. Items there were placed in another, smaller room on the other side of the dining room.

When the sun sank low in the afternoon sky, Asher walked into the common room to see Elara sitting on the couch, curled up with a book. The young lord walked to her, the elf putting the book down and looking up at him with warm eyes.

"You're all dusty," she said as she eyed his shirt, and strong neck.

Asher nodded as dust, and smudges, ran along his shirt. Some dust was in his hair.

"I may need assistance in the bath," he winked.

Elara let out a happy sigh as she smiled at him. Her gaze held a wicked gleam.

"Just the two of us?"

Asher nodded. "It's going to be a cold autumn and winter. I can sense it on the air. We should take advantage of our time, before we're buried in bodies, trying to keep warm."

"Why do you make, what sounds like a negative, into a positive," the mature elf said and let out a happy laugh.

"They are both positive," the young lord grinned.

Elara licked her lips. "Once we harvest the crop, and press it to wine, there won't be much else to do around here. Maybe we should sit everyone down and come up with a list of plays, to pass the time. It would be therapeutic for everyone to get a chance to explore something about themselves, and each other?"

Asher nodded as he kept his smile. "We will also have Nadia staying with us for a month. I already wrote up a contract. She is eager to begin, and should be here in a few days."

"I like her. She reminds me of a young me, if I were human," Elara laughed.

Asher smiled brightly as the mature elf giggled to herself. He could not take his gaze off her, drinking in every drop of beauty and curve. For the first time in his life, he was looking forward to a long winter, close to her, close to all the women who resided under their roof.

A knock broke the spell. Elara looked over to the door, as Asher walked to it.

For a thin moment, Asher figured someone locked the door, and one of the artisans needed to use the water closet. When he reached the door, he took hold of the knob, turned, and opened the door.

Eyes widened as shock filled them. His heart beat like a drum, a sense of surprise and joy coloring all his senses.

A woman in black leather, and a black cloak with the hood down, stood on the porch, beyond the threshold. She had short, white-ish blonde hair. Her eyes were two deep pools of sapphire blue. An arcane bow was across her chest, one end hanging on her shoulder, while the lower half was against her hip. The bow was nestled between her leather covered breasts. A sinister, warm smile stabbed into her cheeks, as she looked at Asher with deep, knowing eyes.

"Arrow and Blade," the woman said with a brightness to her eyes.

"Arrow and Blade," Asher returned.

The former ranger could not contain himself. He reached for the woman, and embraced her. The two held each other for a time, feelings, and emotions crashing into them like waves on the rocks. When they separated, Asher turned around and guided her in.

Elara was standing with a curious smile, and eyes.

"Asher, please introduce me to your friend," Elara said, keeping her smile.

The young lord nodded quickly as he stayed close to the woman's side.

"Elara Moonwhisper, please meet Lisbeth Shroud. She is one of my guildmates, and best friend.

"I sent a letter to the guild, asking Lisbeth to send me back one of the weapons I had acquired on our adventures."

He then turned his attention to Lisbeth, "But I never expected you to bring it here yourself."

"And miss a chance to see the legendary farm? Not likely!" she said before turning and bowing to Elara. "It's a pleasure to meet you," she said with a knowing smile.

Elara bowed, seeing the instant connection between the woman, and her Asher.

"Let's break out the best spirits! We have much to discuss," Asher said as joy filled his beating heart.

~Fin~

Blackwood Milk Farm Book 4 is part of the Blackwood Series.

You may find Book 1 here!

Book 2

Book 3

Blackwood Side Stories

Arrow & Blade: Pale Fortress

Witch-Star Milk Farm

Enjoy the stories!

Dedications

A special thank you to those who helped make this book possible and a big thank you to everyone who supported me! You all hold a special place in my heart!

Adam Friedman

2Tall12

Aaron Henley

Aerys Aeryn Aurelius

Charles V

Chioke Nelson

Chris Lee

Dave Thompson

David

Jerry Jones

John Baker

Robert Hillman

Terrence Mills

Tjin Tur

Travis Btmb

Acknowledgements and Friends

Below is a list of incredible authors who I have had the pleasure to know and wish to share them with you. Please explore their magnificent works. Tell them Eden sent you.

Daniel Schinhofen
Dawn Chapman
Scottie Futch
Blaise Corvin
Harmon Cooper
James Hunter
Randi Darren
Stuart Grosse
Prax Venter
Angel Ramon
Michael Dalton
Michael Chatfield
Lavelle Jackson
Cebelius
Jamie Hawke
Chase Danger
Zachariah Dracoulis
Apollos Throne
Charles Dean
George Fisher
Paul Bellow
Mike Truk
M Damon Baker
Bonnie Price
Austin Beck
Marcus Sloss

D. Levesque
Bruce Sentar
Jack Porter
Neil Bimbeau

A royal thanks to my ARC Knights. May your armor never dent and your swords remain as sharp as your minds and sturdy as your hearts.

Brandon Patrick Moore
Akryn
Chris Pacheco
Richard G Stahl
Sir Daskarn
Darian Lawnsea
PwrQuad
Angus Hutto
Bob Milne
Ken Thompson
Knight Morgan Fellwyn
James Draven
Patrick Powers
Jon Johnson
Kell EverCross
Bruno Stolte
Greg Heckman
Mike Matthews
Jurjen van Dijk
Steven Sharp
Mr. Stud Muffin
Nigel Tufnel
Rashly the Flirt
Scully
Malaclypse The Third
Tanner Likins
Justin Turner
Michael Crowell
Josh Robinson
TJ Mueller
Roger Robinson-Turner

Daniel Danielson
Jess Wisto
R. Alexander Spoerer
Michael Miller
Daniel Godinez
James Sivers
Stuart Haynes

If you enjoy sexy monsters, fantasy, magic and erotic adventures, join my newsletter and receive three free e-books for signing up!

http://eepurl.com/bhuQdb

A Note from Eden Redd

I wanted to take this moment to thank you for reading!

I hope you enjoyed the story. If you have a moment, please leave a review. If leaving a review is not your cup of tea, then please e-mail me. I try to answer all e-mails as fast as I can and I would love to hear your feedback.

Join my mailing list and receive updates on new titles!

Visit my Website at https://edenredd.com/

Join Eden's Lewd Discord

edenreddx@gmail.com

I am also on twitter! I tend to put sexy monster pics and quirky thoughts/ideas.

Like me on Facebook!

I also run a sexy Facebook group, Eden's Lewd Fantasy and Sci-Fi Garden (NSFW).

Please check out my author page and some of my other works you may like.

Eden Redd Author page

Check out my non-erotic titles under Eden Blue!

Join my Eden Blue FB Page.

The FB groups below are filled with amazing authors, readers and fun! Join up!

Gamelit Society
Dukes of Harem
Lit RPG Fun and Gamelit
LitRPG Forum
Harem Lit
LitRPG Books
LitRPG Rebels
Soundbooth Theater Live
The Lusty Realms of Fantasy
Harem Gamelit
Dungeon Corps
Eden's Lewd Fantasy and Sci-fi Garden
Western Cultivation Stories
Gamelit All Girls
Monster Girl Fiction
LGBTQ+ LitRPG Group

Made in the USA
Monee, IL
05 January 2024